Love or Baseball?

Love or Baseball?

A Novel

Jesse A. Murray

Off the Field Publishing
2018

Off the Field
Publishing

Off the Field Publishing
Saskatoon, Saskatchewan, Canada

Off the Field
Publishing

Book design by Jesse A. Murray
Cover image: © Jesse A. Murray

This book is a work of fiction. Any reference to historical events, real companies, real people, or real places are used to make this completely made up story, a more believable experience for the reader. Other names, characters, places, and events are products of the author's imagination, and any resemblance to actual events or places or persons, living or dead, is entirely coincidental.

For Uncle G. You were the first person I showed my writings to and ever since then, you always said, "Keep writing."

Love or Baseball?

Prologue

Throughout history you will find that greatness came out of times of significant tragedy. What is it about pain, suffering, and loss that motivates someone to do great things? I think people who are lost want to experience, and want the world to experience, happiness. They may also want to make up for all the time they lost when they were down and out. The story of my life is a testament to both of these ideas. —Ozzie Shaw

Chapter 1

It was not long after my accident, that I found myself sitting in the living room of my childhood home in Columbia, Missouri, with my father. We were sharing our first beer together. We sat there in silence for a long time. I do not remember what was playing on the TV that day, but I do remember it was not sports related, and it definitely had nothing to do with baseball. I was back in the home that I spent my childhood learning all that I could about the game I loved. The batting cage in the backyard and the one in the basement were still up—even though they would probably never be used again. All the memories I had were these never ending practices that I had with my father. Those were the memories I could bring to the surface and now they felt like they didn't belong to me. Somewhere else deep in my mind were the memories of the rest of my life. I knew I wasn't ready to bring those memories up quite yet. But once I found them, they would almost lead to my destruction. My father broke the silence.

"Oz, when you were a kid, still in diapers, you used to walk around carrying a bat and ball everywhere you went. And I mean everywhere. Some kids have a favorite stuffed animal, toy, or blanket that they can't be separated from. But for you, it was that bat and ball. When we went to visit anybody, or took you anywhere, there you were with your bat and ball. Sometimes you would go up to strangers and hand them the ball, and then you would get in a little batting stance. More often than not your hands would be backwards, but you did what was comfortable." He paused, took a swig of his beer, and continued.

"One time your mother, you, and me were in the grocery store. We were headed down one of the aisles pushing the grocery cart and you were following along with your bat and ball. You walked right up to this tall man that was grabbing something off of a shelf and you tried to give him the ball. I remember you reaching up with all your might trying to hand him the ball, and the man had this embarrassed look on his face like 'should I take it?'

" 'I think he wants you to pitch to him' your mother said with a smile. So the man took the ball and like always, you got into your little stance. This time your hands were the right way. He threw a pitch underhand and you swung, and the ball jumped right off your bat and knocked off a can of Campbell's tomato soup from the shelf. The sound of the can hitting the floor must have startled you and you dropped your bat and you started to cry. The tall man, your mother, and me all started to laugh. Your mother picked you up and tried to calm you down.

"The stranger said, 'Your boy sure can hit.' 'That he can,' I replied. The man picked up the bat and grabbed the ball and handed it to you and you stopped crying instantly. You were the happiest when you had that bat and ball in your hands. People used to think it was the cutest thing in the world, and some would say, 'That boy is destine to be a ball player.' And they were right."

My father never spoke like this before. He rarely shared memories from when I was a kid. It was always about how I could get better, and what we needed to do to get me to the major leagues.

"I remember that bat and ball. I think I still have it in my closet," I said. It felt good to hear stories like this, and it brought a smile to my face. But that smile did not last. I was destined to be a ball player, but there I was back at home.

LOVE OR BASEBALL?

"What am I destine for now?" I asked.
My father took another sip of his beer.
And so did I.
Then we sat there in silence for a long time.

Chapter 2

In baseball, you can be the best player around, but in a way you are only as good as the rest of your team. Sadly, a lot of times, this is also true with your family. If you have a great family and you are raised well, you have a good chance of having a favorable life. However, if you have a lousy family situation and have many painful experiences, then there is a good chance your life may continue to be a struggle. Thankfully, there are exceptions.

Looking back on my life, it is no surprise that my life did not turn out the way I wanted. It is no surprise, that I made a lot of mistakes. I was a product of my childhood, but I didn't know any better. When you are a kid, and you grow up in a certain environment, and you are raised a certain way, that is all you know. This is a good thing because kids are able to survive horrible experiences in their childhood. But this also can be a bad thing because they often don't realize how screwed up they are until much later in life. Or worse yet, they may never realize it at all.

There are a few memories from my childhood that I cherish and try to always hold on to. There are also the bad memories that I remember, and unfortunately, they define my life just as much, or even more, than the good ones. I wish I only remembered the good ones.

But as a recovering alcoholic, I have been forced to look back and study my past more than the next man. I have looked at the good, the bad, and looked at how what I thought was good, could have been the bad as well. When you look back through the lens of an alcoholic—or anyone in recovery for that matter—you start to see the impact that many things have on your life. You will see by the end of this story, that my childhood had an impact on the way I turned out and the choices that I made.

In order to understand who I am, let's take a look at my family history. My father's father, George Shaw, was a big man who loved the St. Louis Cardinals. He was in the army during World War II, but he never talked much about it. When he got home from the war he played some baseball on a few travelling teams, but settled just outside of Mexico, Missouri. My grandfather became some kind of legend around Missouri for the monster forty-six ounce bat he used. Pitchers feared him and that bat. My father said when he was a kid he couldn't wait to be strong enough to pick that bat up and swing it. He claims it was that bat that helped him develop his strength at a young age. As you will see later, I also developed my strength with the use of a variety of weighted bats.

Anyway, my grandfather was a strict man of few words. Everything was always to the point. He could also yell. One time when I was visiting his old house just outside of Mexico, MO, I went down to the basement and opened a big wooden box that caught my eye. It turned out to be my grandfather's footlocker from the war. It had an old military uniform, boots, medals, and a big knife. That's as far as I got before my grandfather's big booming voice yelled, "Close that lid right now." I was so into my new discovery that I didn't even hear him come up behind me. I let the lid drop, and it slammed shut right on my right thumb. I don't know what scared me more: the voice, or the pain in my thumb. From that day on, I was always scared of him, and never felt comfortable in his presence. The association of his loud voice and the physical pain in my thumb probably

5

had something to do with it. Either way, he was a big, strong man that believed in hard work and discipline; something my father also came to believe in.

There are a few good things I do remember about my grandfather. For one, he made some of the best barbeque ribs that I have ever had—the meat used to fall off the bone. He also took me out back and taught me how to throw a curveball, which he had learned from a friend during the war. He said his friend had "The best damn hook he ever saw." I made the mistake of asking what happened to this friend; my grandfather went on to tell me how his friend was blown up by a grenade right in front of my grandfather, "There were pieces of him everywhere...including on me," he said. This was not the best thing to tell a seven year old, but he added, "A hell of a ball player we lost. The way he could pitch, he would have been untouchable in the majors."

Since then, every time my grandfather saw me, he would ask me if I was practicing my curveball, and I would always reply, "Yes sir" and he would make me show him. "Not bad, not bad at all...keep practicing," he would say. But whenever I saw my grandfather I thought of his words, *There were pieces of him everywhere...including on me.* This made me even more afraid of him. Thankfully we didn't visit much and he rarely came to our house to visit. But I do remember him coming a few times to watch me play ball when I was younger. He wouldn't sit with my parents—he would stand along the fence on the first base side all by himself and take the game in on his own.

When we did happen to visit my grandfather, I remember he used to listen to Cardinals games on the radio, and he would call the pitches and get mad when he heard a pitcher didn't throw the right pitch. He understood the game so well that he didn't even have to watch the game. My father was the same way, but he always watched the games on TV. Later I would find out, that a similar extensive understanding of baseball was a gift that was also passed down to me.

For the most part my grandfather was a lonely man that mostly kept to himself. No one ever knew what went on in that mind of his, especially since he was so quiet all the time.

My father's mother got sick and passed away when my father was younger, so I don't know anything about her. My father never talked about her. I'm not sure if he remembered much about her or not. Consequently, my father was alone at a young age. Like me, we both grew up without a mother, but we will get to that a little bit later.

My father did have an older brother named Frank that was ten years older than my father. With the age gap they were never that close, and my uncle Frank left and joined the army when he was eighteen. I remember my uncle Frank coming to visit a couple times, but he lived somewhere in Indiana, which we never went to visit. My uncle Frank looked like a younger version of my grandfather—with a tall military posture and strict way about him. His booming voice carried, but I remember it being a lot friendlier than my grandfather's. My father would show my uncle Frank how good I was at baseball, and I remember enjoying the feeling of showing others the way I could play. From an early age, impressing others was always one of the things I loved the most about baseball.

When I was younger, I was closer to my grandparents on my mother's side. They came to visit quite often, and I remember going over to visit—especially on the holidays. My grandma Mildred, or Grandma Millie as we called her, was an amazing cook. She would bake cakes, pies, and cookies, but her homemade donuts rolled in sugar were my favorite. My grandma always gave the greatest hugs. It felt like she would swallow you up in her arms. But the best part was that she always smelt like her baking. I still believe that was the best smelling house in the world.

My mother's father, Roy Williamson, or Grandpa Roy to me,

was a hard working man. I remember my grandpa was always working around the house, in the yard, or in his garage. He always seemed to be fixing something. I remember helping him do little jobs and he made me feel like I was the biggest help. I used to love that. He always had to be doing something, and he was always full of energy. But at night, after he was done all his tasks for the day, he used to tell me stories. I would sit on his knee and he would read me books, and sometimes he would even make up his own. He could be very silly at times, and could always make me laugh. He wasn't much of a baseball man, but he still enjoyed watching me play and he always cheered me on. Being the only grandchild in the family at that time, I was always spoiled. When I was younger, my grandparents on my mother's side were very special to me, and I still think about them from time to time.

My mother also had a younger sister named Amy. She was very pretty and always dressed in the fanciest clothes. She must have been in her early twenties when I was just a young kid. She looked a lot like my mother. She used to spoil me and I remember her teasing me and chasing me around when I would go to visit. She was one of the first ones that would call me "Wizard." But I guess when I was around two years old and potty training, I peed my pants and she decided to call me "Wizzy." Even though I hated when she teased me and called me "Wizzy," I knew it was all in good fun. She also had a boyfriend named James that would play with me and we would play baseball together. I remember the first time he pitched to me when I was around four years old. He threw it underhand like I was a little kid holding a bat for the first time. I swung and ended up hitting him right in the chest with the ball. My aunt Amy and my mother were watching, and I remember them laughing away and my aunt asking James if he was okay. I caught him off guard, that's for sure. After that, he wasn't afraid to throw it much harder and he knew he had to be ready after the pitch. Those were some of the best memories that I have with my relatives on my mother's side.

When my mother left us and had her new family, I never got to visit my grandparents or my aunt Amy as often. They would make the odd phone call, and would send me small gifts like clothes and baseball cards for my birthday and Christmas. They would still come watch me play ball in the summer time when they could. But that all faded away as the years went by. I am not sure if my father simply pushed them away like he pushed everyone else away. That's what I assume anyway. After awhile, it became just him and I and that was it.

I wish I would have had the opportunity to spend more time with my relatives when I was younger. I remember thinking how it wasn't fair that I never got to see them as often as I would have liked. But like my father would say, they couldn't go where I was headed.

Sometimes I would wonder if my grandparents and aunt were closer to my mother's other kids than they were with me. When my mother left, I would never be close with my mother or my relatives from my mother's side again. When I think about this, it is no surprise that I had issues with being alone when I was older. I wasn't allowed to be close to anyone, and those that I was close with, I had to push them away. Even though I had to do it time and time again, I never did get used to it.

As you can see I don't remember too much of my extended family, simply because they were not in my life long enough. However, they still supplied me with memories that I will always cherish, and a part of my life that I have always longed for—family.

Chapter 3

I grew up in Columbia, Missouri which is half way between Kansas City and St. Louis. My father and mother grew up closer to St. Louis just outside a small city named Mexico, Missouri. That's right, my parents are from Mexico and eventually moved to Columbia. Sounds exotic and interesting, doesn't it? But the only exotic thing about these two small cities in Missouri are their names. Nonetheless, the location of where my father grew up made him a St. Louis Cardinals fan.

For many families, their favorite sports teams are passed down to future generations. Ours was no different. My father's father was a Cardinals fan, my father was, and so was I—I basically had to be, since I was named after my father's favorite player. Even though my father played in the outfield, pitched, and was a big man, his favorite player was Ozzie Smith—the small defensive shortstop. He did talk of Roger Hornsby and Stan "The Man" Musial, but these were mostly from stories from his early childhood that were passed down from his own father.

Ozzie Smith was eight years older than my father, and my father said that if he had better luck, he should have been a teammate of the "Wizard." From what I know, he sure as hell could have been, but he never was. Either way, that's why my father called me Ozzie. My father used to tell me, "Son, if you can field like The Wizard and hit like Stan the Man, you will be one of the greatest there ever was." Talk about pressure. He chose two of the greatest Cardinals of all time and told me to be a mixture of both. But that was my goal. That's what I lived for.

I never knew what my mother thought of my name, but I felt she didn't really have a say in it. Baseball was my father's life, therefore, his firstborn son's name was destined to be related to baseball in some way. I don't know if it was because of my name or what, but as far back as I could remember, my favorite position was always shortstop.

The house I grew up in wasn't very big. It was a small but long, ranch style house that was actually bigger on the inside, than it looked on the outside. It was a house that was meant to provide the necessities, and it didn't have much character. On the main floor there was the kitchen, bathroom, two bedrooms, a living room, and a few closets. The basement had a furnace room and it housed the washer and dryer, but it was unfinished, which was perfect. It was perfect because in the cold winter months it was converted into my own batting cage, and I spent a lot of time down there hitting off of a tee, and taking soft toss from my father.

My father spent most of his time in the living room watching baseball. Near the kitchen and living room was an old china cabinet which was a prized possession. Ever since T-Ball, my father started to put my trophies, medals, pictures, and newspaper clippings from all of my accomplishments in our newly converted trophy case. In our house, those things were more important than having fancy china.

Growing up, I didn't mind that my house was smaller than some of my friends—mostly because a lot of times the smaller the house, the bigger the yard. We were on a corner lot so we had a lot of space on three sides. No one had a backyard like mine. The backyard was long and wide with a large maple tree in the back corner. That tree was the best. When I was younger I used to pretend that it was the "Green Monster" at Fenway Park and I would try and hit home runs over it. It didn't take me long to hit it over that tree. Beyond our back yard there was a small park that contained mostly trees and small shrubbery. When I would hit my tennis balls out of the yard, I would have to climb over the fence and try and look for it. More often than not I wouldn't find it, but I always tried. Sometimes I would find older balls that I hit over some previous time, instead of the brand new one I was using that day. Luckily my parents supplied me with all the tennis balls I needed, therefore, I didn't have to worry about losing them. Eventually my mother had my father put in a gate in the back yard, so that I could easily get out and look for my ball, and I wouldn't have to risk hurting myself hopping over.

As I grew older, hitting tennis balls over the fence and the "Green Monster" was not as fun anymore. We needed to do something to keep balls in, rather than try to hit them out. That's when my father started to build a long tunnel-like batting cage. In that cage I would be able to use real baseballs rather than tennis balls. Also, my father wanted me to see pitches from a mound so he built a raised, portable, plank style mound. As I got older, we would slowly move it back until I was old enough to see pitches from its final resting place at major league length of sixty feet and six inches exactly. He even bought an official home plate with batters mats, so I wouldn't make big holes after our long daily sessions of batting practice (BP). My father, even though he didn't play ball anymore, would go throw off that mound into a net used as a backstop, to blow off steam. Not many kids had their own pitching mound, or batting cage, but I did. When I was older and stronger my father got an L-Screen so he wouldn't have to worry about defending himself on comebackers. This was a good thing considering he usually had a few beer before and during our practices.

We didn't have much, but my father would buy me the best baseball equipment, because to him, it was an investment; an investment in my future and his.

LOVE OR BASEBALL?

Our backyard was where the majority of my training took place. Much of what happened back there, would shape my future.

Chapter 4

Early on I had a great childhood. It was a loving home, and we had what we needed. The only problem is that my childhood did not last long. My mother moved out when I was nine years old, and that's when my family life fell apart. Living with just my father, I was forced to grow up quicker than most. Some of his favorite sayings were: "Walk it off"; "There is no crying in baseball"; "Quick hands-Quick hands"; and, "Boy, why the fuck did you swing at that?" The latter came a little later, but I heard that more than I would have liked to. In the end, I guess I shouldn't have swung.

Nonetheless, there are a few positive moments that define my childhood. The first is when my father would tell the story of when my mother and father first met. I heard this story a few dozen times, but it always brought a smile to my face. It stills does. There were moments when my father would look at my mother with love in his eyes, he would get caught up in the moment, and would tell the story of how they met, to whoever was there listening. It didn't matter if they had heard it or not. But the story was always the same and it would go something like this:

"When I first met your mother, I'm telling you, Oz, she was the most beautiful girl in the entire town. She was wearing this sunshine colored dress. Her blonde hair was glistening in the sun, and her tan skin was glowing. I stopped right in my tracks. I thought she was an angel. I thought I was witnessing something divine—something straight from heaven. Now, I know there has been movies, books, and stories that mention this type of love at first sight. But I knew I was living it right then and there. There is no doubt about that. In that moment, I fell head over heels for your mother. I knew I was going to do whatever it took to make her mine. Except, in that moment, I was frozen. I did not move or say a word as she walked on by and out of my life. But thankfully, she was not gone for long. I headed off to school and guess who was there? That's right, your mother. I could not have been luckier. Not only was she at my school, she was in my class. I was scared to say anything to her, but for some reason there was something inside of me that propelled me forward. I walked up to her and said, 'I just want you to know that you are the most beautiful person I have ever seen in my life,' and I turned and walked away. I didn't talk to her for the rest of the day. After school I was at my locker, and as soon as I closed it shut, she was standing on the other side of the door. It startled me, but then your mother said, 'Did you mean what you said to me earlier?' All I could say, and all I needed to say was, 'I sure did.' The rest is history. Six years later she was pregnant with you and we got married a few months before you were born. I am the luckiest man in the world."

He always said the last part while looking my mother right in the eye. Hearing my father tell this story every chance he got, was one of the greatest memories of my childhood. My father's eyes used to light up and my mom would just sit there with a coy little smile on her face—while she heard him speak about her like he had so many times before. I know she heard this story a lot more than anyone, but she never did seem to mind. I remember hoping that I would have a story like this of my own some day.

Early on, their love seemed to take over whatever we were doing. For instance, I remember all three of us were playing a game of baseball in the backyard. I must have been around five or six years old. It was my mother and I against my father. I was standing on the on-deck circle—which was an imaginary circle we created for this game—while my mother was up to bat, because like my father said, "Ladies first." On the first pitch my mom hit the ball over my father's head. She was so excited and was running around the old car mats we used as bases. My father went and stopped her in between first and second without the ball. He wouldn't let her by him and he wrapped his arms around her and lifted her up. She squealed and was giggling.

She started yelling, "Runner interference! Runner interference!"

"Hey, that's not fair, dad!" I yelled. "You're cheating!"

He looked at my mother, and said, "If you had someone as beautiful as this...you would never want to let them go," and then he kissed her.

He loved my mother so much. That's the type of family I had early on. My father loved my mother, and everything was perfect.

Another one of my favorite memories of my childhood, was when we would sit together as a family, my mother, father, and I in the living room and go through my father's box that had a bunch of things from his playing days. He had old jerseys, newspaper clippings, photos, and my favorite thing, his old Rawlings glove. I would put that big old glove on my hand, and we would sit there and he would tell us stories from the stuff in the box; like the time he made the greatest diving catch in the bottom of the ninth to end the game in high school; or when he went 4-4 with a home run, two doubles, and a single against one of the top pitchers when he was in College. "I was much better at my job that day, than he was at his," my father would say as if it was no big deal. That same pitcher named, Jeff Giles, went on to win a Cy Young award in the major leagues a few years later.

Then my mother would read us the newspaper article about my father when he was eighteen years old. It had a picture of him as a handsome, young man in a white uniform, a black ball cap, and a bat resting on his right shoulder. It read:

Joe Shaw, an 18-year-old baseball player coming out of Mexico High School, is said to be the number one prospect in the state of Missouri. The six foot four and 225 pound outfielder and pitcher has broken nearly every school record in hitting, fielding, and pitching. Scouts have been looking at him since he was a freshman, but he gained national attention when at the age of 16, he was clocked hitting 95 miles per hour for the first time. Despite his already major league caliber velocity and dominance as a pitcher, Shaw is an elite outfielder, and the way he can swing the bat is too impressive to ignore. The left handed hitter was the district's leader in home runs and RBIs four years in a row.

Everyone wants to know if this young prospect will choose to go to college, or will he make the jump to professional baseball? Shaw is expected to go in the first round of the 1980 June draft. Most MLB teams are interested in this young prospect, both as a fielder and a pitcher. But we will find out where he is headed in the draft in two weeks time. Some have gone as far as to say that he could be the next Stan Musial. Or if he is drafted as a pitcher, he could be the next Bob Forsch. Many have said that Shaw has the natural ability, the work ethic, and the mindset to be one of the best players to come out of Missouri.

As you can see, my father was one of the top baseball prospects in the United States out of high school. He was tall, muscular, and fast. He had the perfect athletic body, and all the right tools for the game of baseball. Another article said that he was good enough to make the jump from high school to the major leagues; with little to no time in the minors. But my mother had other plans.

It was a rare thing for someone in a small city in Missouri to receive all this attention, and my father didn't have much guidance about what he should do. My grandfather Shaw was

17

uneducated, and didn't say much, so the decision was left up to my father. Naturally my father was influenced by my mother and her family. Not only was she beautiful, my mother was very smart. She was at the top of her class as a student in high school and she had the opportunity to be the first person from her family to get a university degree. My grandpa Roy stressed the importance of education, and he encouraged his daughter to go to university after her senior year.

In the beginning, my father and mother were a team. My father would tell me how my mother used to come to almost every game. He would toss her a ball to hold after he played catch to warm up between innings, and she would toss it back when he headed out to the field. "You hold on to this for luck," he told her, and she always did. He made her a part of the game by doing that. He was always thinking about her and never forgot that she was there. They would do everything together. Their story was always about love; just as much as it was about baseball.

Chapter 5

In the 1980 Major League Baseball draft, my father was selected as the 18th pick, of the first round, by the Montreal Expos. My father was disappointed he did not go higher. Being a kid from a small city in Missouri—that had never been anywhere else in the world—I don't think he understood how difficult it was to make it into the major leagues, let alone be higher than the 18th pick overall.

Even though he was drafted in the first round at 18 years old, my father decided not to sign a contract with Montreal. I never knew how much they offered my father, and I don't think he liked to talk about it. I know it would not have been as much as we would see today, but I'm sure it would have been far more than most people would make at that age.

My father knew he would have had to work his way up from the minors, and he would most likely spend the next few years in the United States, but he was not willing to eventually move to Canada. As a young and naive 18-year-old from Mexico, MO, he did not know much about Canada, and he didn't want to move that far away. He heard that the main language there was French and that also made him uncomfortable. The move to Montreal would have been completely out of his comfort zone. I also know that he was hoping the Cardinals would pick him. It was his team and his father's team, and there was no other team that he wanted to play for. He was stubborn like that.

But most of all, I know that my mother had a strong

influence on his decision. My mother wanted to go to university and get an education, which would be difficult with my father moving around in the minors. With the influence of my mother, my father decided to go to university. They loved each other so much. My father didn't sign a contract with the Expos, instead he signed a full athletic scholarship to the University of Miami— which was known as having one of the top baseball programs in the nation.

My father became a notable Miami Hurricane, shattering a number of records in his first season, and leading them to a College World Series appearance. But that year they came up short.

As far as I understand, my mother and father were happy in Miami. My father had baseball and my mother; and my mother had my father and her education. Everything was perfect. But life threw my mother and father a curveball. Just before their second year in Miami, my mother got pregnant. That changed everything. My father could no longer go to school and play baseball. They packed up their life in Miami and moved back closer to home and settled in Columbia, Missouri. On April 23rd, 1982, I was born. The plan was for them to go to school in Columbia, and still be close to my mother's and father's families.

When they moved back, my mother and father got married, they had me, and they never went back to school. Regardless that my father was one of the top players on the team the season before, the Miami Hurricanes won the National title that year without him. Three of the senior players on the Hurricanes that year got drafted. My father probably could have still been drafted by a major league team, but with a child on the way, he needed to get a job. I guess he didn't want to live the unpredictable life in the minor leagues with a new wife, and a newborn baby. My father would never play another game of baseball.

My father took a job at Big O Tires to support his family. It was not the most glamorous job in the world, but it paid the bills, it was with a good company, it had benefits, and it was a stable job. We were never rich, but we didn't need much. I'm sure times were tough for us early on, but all we needed was your basic ball equipment, food, and my father needed his beer.

My mother and father were both a team, and loved each other so much, but something changed when they had me. Baseball was gone from their lives, and slowly their love for each other faded away. But most of all, my father was no longer passionate about anything—until he tried to get some of his passion back by pushing me to play the game he loved.

Eventually life at home started to change, and my family fell apart. It's hard to explain what happened, but I assume my father had something building inside of him that he couldn't keep in anymore. The arguments began, and my father's drinking increased. Life was much simpler before everything got so complicated. I wished for a long time that I could go back to when I was surrounded with love, and all I did was live and breathe baseball. But my father made it clear that love and baseball did not mix.

Chapter 6

On my tenth birthday, my father handed me my first real leather baseball glove and said, "Try it on, Son. With this, you will be able to catch whatever life throws your way." I was only ten years old, and that was the most sincere piece of advice he had ever given me. He taught me a lot about baseball, but that was the only piece of advice that could help me outside of the game. The smell of any leather glove still brings me back to that day. This would typically be a great father and son moment, but that was also the day after my mom packed up her things and left us. My father, mother, and I, were no longer a team.

I was too young at the time to understand why my mother left us, but I do remember one specific argument when I was nine years old.

The evening started like any other. I was in the backyard hitting off the tee, while my father was busy working on a project in the garage. After I had been hitting for awhile, my father came out from the garage with, what looked like to me, a large stuffed creature that was attached to a metal pole. I was intrigued.

"Dad, what is that?"

"What does it look like?" he said.

Still holding my bat, I moved closer to get a better look. With its white pants and old baseball jersey, stuffed with, I didn't know what, I was not quite sure what it was that my father was holding.

"Umm, a scarecrow, wearing a baseball uniform?"

"Close. It's your new first baseman."

He stood my new first baseman upright and while holding the metal pole in his big hands, he pushed it into the ground almost a foot deep. *That thing is not going anywhere*, I thought.

Then he started to count his steps until he got closer to where I was standing. I moved out of the way so he could continue on his path.

"What are you doing now?" I asked.

"I'm pacing out the length of where shortstop should be. Now when I hit you groundballs, you can throw to first."

I immediately realized there was a problem.

"How is he going to catch the ball if he doesn't have a glove?...Or arms?" I asked.

My father looked at me and then at my new, stuffed, and armless first baseman, and then back at me. He had a solution. "Just hit him in the chest, Son. If he doesn't catch it, that's his problem."

That was my father. He would teach me that as long as I did my job, whatever someone else did, was not my problem.

I was excited to try out my new first baseman. I even gave him a name. I called him "Crow"—short for Scarecrow. My father hit me ground ball after ground ball. I would scoop up the ball, plant my feet, and try and hit Crow in the chest. And if I missed my father would yell, "God damn it! Make the fucking throw!"

It didn't matter how many times I hit my new first baseman in the chest, if I missed, I would get yelled at. After what felt like a million ground balls, my mother called us in for dinner.

Nothing seemed out of the ordinary; other than my new first basemen joined the team. My father, like always, was pushing me hard, but he must have been harder on me than usual. If he was, I didn't notice.

When we sat down for dinner, my mother spoke up, "Joe, I

wish you wouldn't push him so hard."

"We are not talking about this right now," my father replied sternly.

"Okay," was all that my mother said, and we continued to eat our dinner in silence.

Later that night, my mother must have brought it up again. I was in bed when I heard them arguing from their bedroom.

"For fuck sakes, Mary, I'm not going to let you keep him from the majors just like you kept me from the majors. You ruined my life and I won't let you ruin his," my father yelled.

My body jumped in my bed at the sound of the bedroom door slamming. I got out of bed and cracked open my door to see what was going on. The house was quiet, but I heard my mother sobbing and saying, "I'm sorry...I'm so sorry" over and over to herself. I wanted to go see her, but when I heard my father open a can of beer in the living room, I decided to go back to my bed. *Why were my parents fighting?*, I wondered. *And did my mom really keep my father from playing in the major leagues, like he said she did?* I was so young and I didn't understand these things at the time. And just like a lot of kids often do, I started to think that maybe it was my fault. Sadly, it was in a way.

From that night on, things were never the same in our house. The affection that I witnessed so many times before, was gone. My parents would still talk to each other but without that spark—without any love in their voices.

Then I started to notice my father would raise his voice to her more often, and he would also insult her and call her names. This was something he had never done before. He would yell and swear more often as well. Looking back, I'm guessing his drinking must have increased, even though I didn't really pay attention to it at the time. Their love no longer took over whatever we were doing. They were no longer a team. We were no longer a team.

The day before my tenth birthday, my mother must have

had enough, and she packed up her things and left. She said she was leaving and I didn't understand. *Was she going on a vacation?*, I wondered.

But it wasn't a vacation. She went to live with my aunt Amy. One of the last things my mother said before she left was, "Ozzie, make sure you listen to your father. Stay strong my little champion. I love you." She kissed me on the forehead as tears fell from my face and just like that, she was gone. That was the last time my mother was in our house.

I visited my mother a few times at Aunt Amy's and I talked to her on the phone once in awhile. But eventually I lost all contact with my mother. In our early conversations together, she said she knew life at home would be hard on me, but she told me that this was the way it had to be. She said I would understand better when I was older. I hated that. *Why couldn't I understand now?*, I thought. I've looked back on this part of my life so many times, and still it's hard to fully understand why she left. Or why she ended all contact. I guess she thought it would be best for my father, and for me. She loved us both, but my father blamed her for everything that got in the way of his dream. She didn't want to hold either of us back anymore. I still wish we would have kept in touch. A boy needs his mother.

I remember one time I told my father that I missed my mother. All he said was, "I know you do, Son. But remember, in a few years she won't be able to go where you are headed. You just said goodbye to her a few years earlier than you had to." This may have been true, but around eight years earlier than I had to? I think that was a little extreme for his logic. But that is the way he was. He always had the same answer for all relationships. He was a simple man that way. What he said made sense to him, he told it like it was, and he didn't sugar coat anything—just like his father. In the next few years I would often be told, "Remember, Son, they can't come where you are going," or, "No one can go where you're headed." Those were his words of encouragement. I was told this by my father, and later I told this to myself over and over—mostly trying to convince myself that his words were true.

When I was a bit older, I would sometimes go through the box of stuff my father kept that had all the articles and memorabilia from his baseball career. There was something significant to me about looking at his old jerseys, his old glove, and everything else from his playing days, but I am not sure what it was. I think it made me proud of my father. On another level, knowing that he was so close to making it, and how hard it must have been for him to give it up, motivated me to work even harder. I wanted to make it to the big leagues, for him. I guess in a way, I did feel guilty that I was born. In a sense, I ruined his life. So I had to do what I could to make up for that. I felt I owed him.

I remember one night when my father and I sat down to watch a Cardinals game. It ended up being delayed in the third inning, and my father and I sat there quietly waiting, and hoping it would start up again. I asked my father why he never went to a Cardinals game.

"I will never sit in the stands in a place where I should have been on the field," he said.

"Will you come watch me play when I make it there?"

"We'll see when the time comes, Son," he replied. "Either way, I will always be watching."

I could tell he was still hurt from not pursuing his dream. He lived with that regret every day of his life. On that night, while we waited for the Cardinals game to resume, I decided I would do whatever it took to find out if he would come and watch me play at Busch stadium or not.

Eventually I did.

Chapter 7

A few months after my mother left, my grandfather Shaw passed away in his house peacefully and all alone. That was the first funeral that I had ever been to. I remember not really feeling that sad when my father told me that my grandfather died. But at the funeral, my mother, my grandma Millie and grandpa Roy were there. I cried as soon as I saw my mother. My mother came over and wrapped her arms around me. "It's okay, Ozzie. Your grandfather is in a better place," she said. I didn't dare tell her that I wasn't crying because my grandfather passed away, I was crying because I missed my mother.

After the funeral, everyone went their separate ways, and I was back at home with my father.

The next day, my father and I drove to Mexico to pack up my grandfather's things. My uncle Frank was there, and him and my father drank beer and worked away at sorting my grandfather's possessions. I also had to help, but mostly, I was trying to find something cool, that maybe, my father would let me keep. I went down to the basement and there it was—my grandfather's footlocker from the war was sitting in the same spot it was the last time I had seen it. I slowly walked over to it, and I was still a little weary of opening it up and having my grandfather yell at me. It was eerie that I was still scared—knowing my grandfather was no longer around. I managed to work up my courage and I was able to look through it freely. But I could still feel his presence there, and I kept looking over my shoulder at every little sound.

I searched through the footlocker in its entirety, and I remember everything seemed so cool. It was like discovering something from the past—almost like a treasure chest. I took out two big black boots that were in the way, so I would have more room to search the contents of the box. As I was digging through the locker, I accidentally knocked over one of the boots, and I heard something roll, and hit another box a few feet way. It turned out to be an old baseball. My mind was racing, and I wondered why my grandpa kept a baseball in his army boot. Then I thought, *Maybe it belonged to his friend from the war?*. I imagined my grandfather and this young soldier playing catch in their army uniforms while there were bullets flying by. Then I thought about him saying, "There were pieces of him everywhere—including on me," and I wondered if there was any blood on the baseball. I examined it closely. Thankfully, for all I could tell, there was nothing but dirt on it. I walked back to the box to see if there was anything else worth keeping. There was an old harmonica that I grabbed. *I'll wash it when I get home,* I thought. After I was done exploring the foot locker, I ran upstairs to go ask my father if I could keep my new findings.

"Keep whatever you want," he said.

I was delighted. But I never found anything else interesting that day. I tried to find his legendary forty-six ounce bat, but I couldn't. I asked my father where it would be, and he said it must have broke and got thrown out a long time ago.

For the next few days, my father and I would drive to Mexico to continue helping my uncle Frank pack up all of my grandfather's things. When we were all finished, I was surprised by all the stuff we had to throw out, all the stuff that my uncle Frank loaded into the back of his truck and took back to Indiana with him, and all the boxes we took home to store in our garage. I was only a kid, but I realized that there was a lot of work that takes place when someone dies, and there are a lot of things that go to waste.

Eventually they put my grandfather's house up for sale, and it sold a few months later. There was no reason to ever go back to Mexico, Missouri, again.

I never did use that harmonica, and it stayed in a box in my closet for a long time. But I did keep that baseball. I would pick it up from time to time and think about my grandfather, my grandfather's friend, and the "best damn hook" my grandfather ever saw. Oddly enough, that baseball gave me a stronger connection with my grandfather, than I ever had with him when he was alive.

Chapter 8

My father pushed me so hard that he pushed my mother away in the process. All things come at a price, I guess. It may be sad, but my father's coaching and pushing me to learn baseball so early, made me further ahead of others my age. I was often the youngest person on my teams when I first started out. They matched me by skill level, rather than age. For example, some kids start to play T-ball at four years old, but more commonly they start at the age of five. Since my father was teaching me how to hit and throw when I was two years old—when I could only say a few words—he had me start T-ball with the 4 and 5-year-olds, when I was only 3 years old. I was smaller than everyone on my team, but I could throw, catch, and hit better than all of them. The funny thing is that my baseball skills were better than my speaking skills at this age. You don't need to speak much in baseball anyway.

In my first year of T-ball, we would practice for fifteen minutes and then play a short two inning game, which would allow everyone to bat and play the field. T-Ball was all about the basics, but I think my father put me in T-Ball early, so that I could see what it was like to play the actual game in a team setting and have coaches. Those were things he couldn't teach me at home. It was a formal intro to the game that would consume much of my life.

Since I was so young, I did not remember much from my first year in T-ball. But I do remember that I hit the ball so far that they ended up putting some of the parents in the field, so the kids didn't have to run for miles when the ball flew over their heads. I also remember hitting a line drive over shortstop and it flew over the left fielder's head, but a dad that was standing a few feet behind the shallow left fielder had caught it in his bare hand. It was probably out of reaction more than anything, but I was upset. I didn't understand how this was fair. Why did the other team get extra fielders? And why were these extra fielders adults? When I complained to my father, he told me not to worry about it. He told me to try and hit it over the adult's head next time. I had a new challenge, and I forgot why I was even upset in the first place. That was something I would end up doing for the rest of my baseball career—no matter what I was put up against, I always wanted to overcome the challenge. If I hit a ball hard and far, I would try and hit it harder and further the next time. I was always trying to one-up myself. I was always trying to be the greatest player that I could be. That is how I practiced and that is how I played. But let me tell you, too many people forget that there is a lot of training and a lot of practice that goes behind what takes place on game day. As you will see, I trained and practiced a lot more than I played.

My father pushed me hard, that is no secret, but a lot of people don't understand how much work really goes into becoming an elite athlete—or an elite anything. They do not see all the hours of ongoing training that is involved. They don't see the sacrifices, the setbacks, the hardships, and the failures that elite athletes all go through. People will watch a baseball game for example, and think that everything just came naturally to everyone out there and that these athletes are gods that deserve these massive paychecks. They think athletes are the luckiest people on earth. They think some athletes are super-human. They are not super-human.

One of the reasons my mother left us is because my father pushed me too hard. My mother did not like some of the things my father made me do. So what type of things did he make me do? Let me tell you.

Most of the time my dad was a hard-ass, and the fact that he drank a lot did not help. The combination of these two things led him to making me do things, that most fathers would not even think of doing. First off, he would take me outside and make me throw to him until I couldn't lift my arm anymore. To add to that, I would not be using an ordinary, brand new baseball. My Father made sure to soak these "heavy balls" in water in order to add a little more weight to them, so that they would strengthen my arm. The next day he would make me hit and hit and hit until I could not hold my bat anymore.

When he pitched to me, he was not throwing like other kids my age could throw. His fastball was hard, and he would throw nasty curveballs, changeups, sliders, knuckleballs, and anything else you can think of. I remember backing out of the box too early on one of his nasty curves. He scolded me for that and forced me to stand in the box while he hit me five times with a fastball. He said, "Just turn your shoulder in, and take it like a man." I wasn't a man yet, but I did what I was told. I stood there while he threw it right at me, I turned my shoulder in, and it hit me right in the lower back. I felt the pain and tried to hold in the tears. He made me stand there again, while he threw the next pitch. This time it hit me square on the side of my left leg. I got a Charley Horse and fell to the ground. My father yelled for me to get up. I wiped the tears from my eyes and tried to stand up. I picked up my bat and got to my feet. He threw the next one and I turned and it hit me right in the middle of my back. It did not feel good, but I was still feeling the pain in my leg. He threw another, and I took it right in the left shoulder blade, right on the bone. I dropped again. My tears fell quicker and my father noticed and yelled for me to get up again. He yelled, "I do not have to tell you, there is no crying in baseball!"

I picked up my bat and slowly got to my feet. He threw one

more and I took it right in the left butt-cheek. I was relieved that the last one hit me where it hurt the least. Even after a number of beer, I knew that my father could throw the ball anywhere he wanted. Him hitting me in the left ass-cheek on the last pitch, let me know that he did care about my wellbeing. What a sweet man he was. My father then told me to, "Walk it off" as he went inside to get himself another beer. I was left hurt and angry. I walked it off by picking up all the baseballs and putting them back in the bucket, and gathering the rest of the things to put in the garage—just like I did every night.

Most people would believe this was child abuse. To my father, this was my training to make me great. The truth is, it worked. I was never afraid to get hit by a pitch ever again. That instinct to move out of the way, was gone. What kind of lesson could be learned from this? Well, maybe when you're about to take a hit in life, just turn your shoulder in, and take it. It may not seem like it at the time, but it will make you one base closer to scoring a run. In other words, taking a hit in life, even though it hurts, may put you on the right path to success.

The training my father put me through was making me well ahead of my time. As tough as it was, it was all I knew, and it did make me a competitor. I was always the top player on my team, and most likely one of the best players in the state for my age. But as you can see, this came at a price. It was a lot of hard work and it was painful, but I survived.

Sacrifices are important in baseball as they are in life. My father taught me that nothing was more important than baseball—not family, friends, school, or love. I always looked up to my father, but the older I became, the more I questioned what he was teaching me.

Chapter 9

I was never concerned with my father's drinking. I didn't know any different, so I could not compare him with other fathers. But there was one specific incident when I was younger that I realized my father's drinking was not normal. I was around eleven years old and my father came onto the bench in the middle of a game.

"Hey, Mr. Shaw," a few of my teammates greeted him.

"Hey, fellas," he said.

He came in and told another player to move over, and sat down beside me. He put his arm around me, and in a calm but stern voice, he said, "Why did you swing at that second pitch?"

"Dad, I hit a double in that at bat."

"Answer my question."

"I don't know. It fooled me, I guess."

"You guess? Damn rights it fooled you. You got lucky hitting a double in that at bat. You will never go anywhere by being lucky."

He stood up and left. That wasn't the first time he had done something like that. But this time it was different. I heard a few of my teammates snickering and saying my father smelt like beer. *So what?*, I thought. *He always smelt like beer.*

Then a few days later at a team practice, a couple of those same teammates were saying my father was an alcoholic. "No he isn't! Shut up!" I said. But they didn't stop. It really bothered me—even though I wasn't quite sure why. I knew that wasn't how I should be treated by my teammates.

That night when I went home, my father went to the fridge, grabbed a beer, cracked it open, and picked up his glove off of the counter.

"Alright, let's go get some swings in," he said.

I finally asked him a question that I was thinking about all day.

"Are you an alcoholic?"

He came to a stop half way through the door and was holding it open with his elbow. He turned and looked at me, and was visibly taken back. "Who told you that?"

"Well some guys on my team were giving me a hard time today and said that you smelt like beer when you came on the bench last game, and they were bugging me today saying you were an alcoholic."

"Who specifically?"

"Some teammates."

"Who?" he asked, this time demanding.

"David and Ryan," I replied.

"There you go. The two worst players on your team. Don't listen to them, Son. They only say those things to try and get under your skin. They are just jealous of your talent. As for your question, no I am not an alcoholic. I drink a few beer here and there. And so do most people my age. Alright? Next time they say something like that just remain silent and focus on your game. Continue to prove yourself on the field and they will keep their mouth shut. Now let's go."

He pushed the door fully open and held it there for me with his beer and glove in hand.

After this incident, I became more aware of his drinking. There were times I did feel ashamed, especially when he would come back on the bench and I knew others would smell beer on his breath. I actually dreaded every time he did. I had to limit those times as much as possible by not giving him a reason to—

in other words, by screwing up as little as possible. But at the same time, I never doubted his knowledge of the game, and I was still proud of my father. I listened to him, and I pretty much always would.

My coaches didn't like when he would come on the bench to coach me during the game either, but they wouldn't say anything to my father. One time when I forgot my glove on the bench, I came back to get it, and I heard my head coach and assistant coach talking about my father. "I hate when he comes and coaches Oz on the bench. It undermines our authority. Why can't he just wait until after the game?" my assistant coach said.

"I agree, but there isn't much we can do about it. I mean, did you know he was drafted when he was younger? He was one of the top prospects in the state. We just have to let him do his thing," my head coach replied.

At first I was embarrassed that they were talking about my father, but what my head coach said, made me even more proud of my father. They knew my father was more qualified than they were, so they were going to let him coach me the way he always did. It felt good to know that others knew how good my father was.

It wasn't until I got a bit older that I started to understand the truth about my father. I realized that my father had a problem, and I realized why my mother left—at least to a certain extent. But I never let it become my focus. What my father chose to do did not matter, as long as I was playing baseball and pursuing my dream.

But I will admit that my father got in the way of my ability to make and keep friends. I had friends, but most of them were on the teams that I played on. I was self-conscious about bringing anyone over because of my father's yelling, swearing, and drinking. A part of me didn't want anyone to see how I lived. The truth is, those that did come over, well, they didn't often come back anyway. I assumed they were afraid to come over, or they told their parents about what it was like over at my place, and their parents wouldn't let them come back.

For instance, one of my friends from elementary school named Adam, also stopped coming around. At one of my birthday parties, my father let me invite a few of my friends over. We had a barbeque and had a home run derby with some wiffle balls in my backyard. We also took some batting practice in the cage. My father was pitching to Adam, and my father almost hit him. He wasn't throwing particularly hard or anything, and he never did hit him. But Adam ducked out of the way and he scraped his knee. It turned out that Adam told his parents that my father almost hit him, and that he was drinking a beer while he was pitching. His parents called my father and there was an argument. When it was over with, Adam was no longer allowed to come to my house anymore. I was still allowed to go to Adam's house, but I only went a couple of times after that, and it was only when some of my other friends and teammates were there. I never went there by myself or was never personally invited. These were some of the sacrifices I had to make because of my father.

The positive side of some of my friends not being able to come to my house, was that this didn't stop some of them from inviting me over to their home. The parents of some of my teammates would invite me over to spend time with their family, have dinner, and even spend the night. I think, as I got older, they could tell how talented I was and how much potential I had, and in a way, they wanted to take care of me. I think they knew I was destine for great things and they wanted to pitch in.

My father didn't mind too much when I went to spend time at a friend's house, but he did remind me that I would have to make up any lost time of training the next day. Honestly, sometimes I did wish I had homes and families like my friends, but this was often when my father was being especially hard on me. But I knew I was all he had.

Early on, my parents hung around with a couple named Doug and Karen, and they had a son named Tyler—he was one year younger than me. They would come over and my mother and Karen would chat, my father and Doug would drink beer, watch sports, and grill in the backyard. Doug was the only friend that I remember my father ever having.

Tyler and I would play like kids do. We would play baseball, or if we were at his house, we would play with his toys and his Nintendo. I don't have many memories of them because they stopped coming over after my mother left. I did go over there a few times but that didn't last. They were just more people that were once close, but eventually faded away from my life.

Nonetheless, baseball is what got me through. And it's what got my father through. I always imagined that everything would be perfect once I made it to the major leagues. I truly believed it. I had to. That's what my father believed, and well, that's what I believed. Sometimes for some people, baseball is more than just a game.

Growing up, I may not have had many close friends, but I did have a best friend named Jacob Cooper. Almost everyone called him Jake. His parents and teachers were the only ones that called him Jacob. He hated it. Naturally, I would call him Jacob when I wanted to tease him.

I met Jake in my second year of T-Ball. He was smaller than me, but he was good. Other than myself, he was the best player on the team. I found out that he lived just down the street from my house, and in no time, we became best friends.

We spent a lot of time playing baseball and trying to hit towering home runs over the "Green Monster," and when we played at his house, we would try to hit it over his house which was much bigger than mine, and we called it the "White Ghost." Originally we called it the "White Monster," but we wanted to be more creative, so we decided on the "White Ghost." It didn't really make sense, but that didn't matter. Him and I hit a lot of home runs, lost a lot of tennis balls, and had a lot of fun together. We both went to the same elementary school, middle school, and high school. We also walked and biked to and from school together. We often played on the same teams growing up, except when we got a little older, Jake never grew much. He was still a good ball player, but he often got overlooked because of his size. I always hated when coaches would pick the biggest players only because they were big. There were so many times that I would have these big oafs on my team that had no talent, would strike out a few hundred times, but would get lucky and hit a long home run once and awhile. It was so unfair to good ball players like Jake. Even Ozzie Smith was overlooked until someone believed in him, and we all know how that turned out.

Mr. and Mrs. Cooper were the model family. They went to church every Sunday, they ate supper together every night, and they were pretty strict on what Jake could and could not do. Jake always had to do his homework and they made sure he got good grades. Jake's parents may have been strict, but Jake was still pretty spoiled and he got a lot of cool things. He would get things like the newest sports equipment, video games, TVs, and Mr. Cooper would take him to St. Louis Cardinals games. They were not much different than my family early on, but then my family became the complete opposite of theirs. Their family gave me a glimpse of how I should have been raised. Seeing their family, I realized my family life was much different. Even though we had different lives, we were still two kids that loved baseball, and we spent all the time we could together.

After losing a few friends and hearing them talk about my father, and since my house was smaller than others, I didn't like to bring other people to my house. Things were different with Jake, however. Jake's house was so much bigger and nicer than mine, but he always suggested that we go to my house. We would spend most of our time outside anyway, and for two kids that loved baseball, my backyard was pretty awesome.

My father was always overly nice to Jake. Sometimes this would upset me because my father was so hard on me. I never understood why he would be super nice and encouraging to Jake and so mean and critical to his own son. Sometimes I would get jealous, especially when Jake would get encouragement that I never received. Either way, I knew since Jake was not his son, my father knew he couldn't speak to someone else's kid the way he spoke to me. Another thing both of them would do is tease me, and they thought it was hilarious. My father didn't really have a sense of humor, but he did when he was around Jake. I think Jake just had that effect on people. At the time I didn't like getting teased, but I was glad that Jake and my father got along, because my father didn't get along with many other people, especially when he was drinking.

As we grew older, Jake started to understand what I was going through—notably when my mother left. My father was hard on me while she was around, but after she left, there was no one to keep his behavior in check. My father could do what he wanted, which was mostly drink beer, and push me as hard as he possibly could.

A lot of parents will tell their kids to do something and when the kid asks, "Why?" the parents will reply, "Because I said so." When my father told me to do something, or when I asked, "Why are you making me do this," he would reply, "Because it will help you get to the big leagues." And that was the end of the discussion. To me, that was a good reason to do what he told me to do.

On more than one occasion, Jake said he wished that he had a father like mine. I think Jake thought it was cool that I had a little more freedom than he did, and he got a kick out of how my father swore all the time. It was probably a nice vacation from the life Jake had at home. The funny thing is, I often wished I had a father like Jake's. Regardless, Jake was a great friend. He was the type of person that would do anything for me. I was lucky to have someone like that in my life.

I remember one time when Jake and I were in grade six, we were taking batting practice at a ball field close to our homes. When we got tired of hitting in my backyard, we would head to that field with a bucket of balls and we would hit, then pick up all the balls, and switch. On this particular Saturday afternoon, two older kids—that must have been in high school—walked onto the diamond.

Jake and I were busy out in the field collecting the balls after I was done hitting. I noticed from the outfield, that one of the older kids picked up my glove. Jake and I both walked in, and as we got closer, these guys looked bigger and scarier. One was smoking a cigarette. They looked like trouble.

Jake and I walked up to them and stopped a few feet away. The one that was holding my glove looked at his buddy and said, "Hey man, look at my new glove. It's pretty nice isn't it?"

"That's my glove," I said calmly. "Can I have it back?"

"Nope. It's mine now."

"My dad gave me that glove."

"Look at this baby. 'My dad gave me that glove,'" he said trying to mimic me in a baby voice.

Jake was a lot smaller than I was, but he was brave. He grabbed the bat I was holding. "Give me back my friend's glove or I'll hit you in the f-f-f-fucking face with this," Jake sputtered out.

I had never heard Jake swear before and you could tell it didn't come out naturally. His threat didn't hold much power.

Both of the scary high school kids started laughing.

"And if you hit him with that, I will stab you with this," the other one without the glove said, as he pulled a knife out from his pocket.

Now things were more serious. I was hoping a cop would drive by, or an adult, or someone. But there was no one to be seen. I finally gave up.

"Alright, take the glove and leave us alone," I said.

"Wait!" Jake said. I wanted to tell him to shut up. But he continued talking. "How about you have a home run derby, and whoever hits the most home runs gets the glove. Look how much bigger you are than he is, and look how short the fences are."

They both looked at each other without saying anything and then the guy holding the glove said, "Alright, you have a deal. But if I win, I get the bat, too."

"Sounds good," Jake said. "I'll pitch. Unless your friend wants to."

"Forget it. Do I look like I play this stupid sport?" the one with the knife said.

No, you look like you rob kids and live behind a dumpster. I wanted to say, but wisely chose not to.

I wasn't sure how good the other guy was, but he was bigger than me, and it was a peewee diamond. I couldn't help but feeling nervous. There was more at stake than losing a game.

"Who wants to hit first?" Jake asked.

"He can go first," my opponent said, and pointed at me.

"Alright, Oz, let's do this," Jake said. I could tell he was more confident than I was.

We used some basic home run derby rules. We would get ten outs each, and any non-home run counted as an out.

With my first couple swings, I hit a ground ball, then a pop-up to second base. I heard the guy laugh and say, "Looks like I'll be getting a new glove and bat today."

But the next three pitches, I hit over the left field fence. The next swing went off of the right field fence, and the following one was a towering shot straight to center field. "Holy shit!" I heard the non-ball player say.

While I was in my groove, a car pulled up. It was Mr. Cooper coming to tell Jake it was time to go home for supper. He got out of his car and walked towards the backstop where the two would-be thugs were standing. I hit a couple more home runs.

Mr. Cooper yelled, "Looking good, Ozzie! What do we have here, a home run derby?"

I turned around and Mr. Cooper was almost right beside the two thugs. They were both watching me hit and didn't see Mr. Cooper walk up. Mr. Cooper must have startled them and they immediately took off running.

"What was that all about?" Mr. Cooper asked.

"They were trying to steal Ozzie's glove. One of them had a knife," Jake said.

"What? Do you know who they were?" Mr. Cooper asked sounding confused and concerned.

"No. But Jake saved the day. Jake challenged them to a home run derby instead and they went for it. You must have startled them when you walked up," I said and noticed my glove was gone. "Ah man, they took my glove."

"Here it is," Jake said. "It was only a few feet away. One of them must have got scared and dropped it."

Jake was the hero that day. His quick thinking and his ability to weigh a situation was a lot better than what I was able to do. Or maybe he was just braver than I was. Either way, my only talents were what I could do on the field.

Mr. Cooper showing up also probably saved us. Those guys would have probably taken the bat and glove anyway. After that incident, we weren't allowed to go to the field alone anymore, unless Mr. Cooper was available to check up on us more often.

When I told my father the story of what had happened, he didn't really say much. He actually scolded me for leaving my glove unattended. I thought it was a serious situation, especially in a young kids life, but it didn't seem to concern my father. It made me even more grateful that I had the Cooper's in my life. It was comforting to know that they cared. Throughout my life, they continued to be there in ways that my father never was.

Chapter 10

Jake and I would ride our bikes everywhere. I believe I developed a lot of leg strength and speed from riding my bike every day. Once I started to grow, my father wouldn't buy me a new bike, and he told me to ride my mother's bike that she had left behind. The worst thing about it was that it was purple. Sometimes, mostly at night, it was such a dark purple that it could pass for a dark blue, but in the sunlight it was clearly purple. I hated that bike, but according to my father, it was a perfectly good bike and it got the job done. I didn't agree.

One day I finally had enough. I went into the garage and I found a can of green spray paint. I decided I would spray paint the bike and this would solve the issue that I had with my mother's bike. I imagined that after I was finished, I would be able to ride my bike in public and not be worried about being made fun of, which happened more than I would have liked.

I brought my bike into the garage and I put a bunch of newspapers down on the floor. I opened the garage door and began spray painting my mother's bike. I realized right away that there was an issue. The paint I used was a dull green. I'm not sure what it was used for or where it came from, but it definitely did not look good on the bike frame. But I kept on painting because I thought anything looked better than that purple color. There was another problem, however. As I sprayed along trying to cover up the frame as much as possible and make it look as good as I could, I ran out of paint. I was left with a half painted bike. It looked like someone had vandalized my bike more than anything. And that's what I decided to tell people when they asked. I would rather ride a bike that had been vandalized than a purple "girl bike."

My father was not impressed when he saw it. "What the hell happened to your mother's bike?" my father yelled.

"I tried to paint it," I replied.

"Why would you ruin a perfectly good bike? Now you're definitely not getting a new one," he said.

It was a little embarrassing, but he wasn't as angry as I thought he would be. I think it actually made him happy because he had an excuse to not buy me a new bike.

When Jake saw my bike he teased me about my paint job, but then offered me his old bike. His old bike had a faulty front brake, but it was a nice bike, and it was perfectly fine otherwise. Jake's parents simply bought him a new one instead of fixing it. Jake was the type of kid that got everything new all the time. He always had the best of everything.

We biked over to Jake's house and Mr. Cooper was outside. Mr. Cooper asked what happened to my bike—he thought someone had vandalized it.

"Dad, do you think Oz can have my old bike?" Jake asked.

"If he gets the break fixed he can. I don't want him injuring himself," Mr. Cooper replied.

Mr. Cooper wouldn't let me ride it until I got if fixed, even though it still had the back break. I figured he was concerned for my safety and didn't want to be responsible. He put it in the back of his truck and drove it the two blocks to my house and dropped it off.

That night, I asked my father if he could fix the brake on my newly acquired bike. He took a look at it and said he had to get a few parts, but other than that, it should be an easy fix. He said I had to ride my mother's bike until then. He ended up taking a few weeks before he went to the store for parts. I think he did that on purpose, so that I had to suffer with riding my terribly half-painted bike for awhile.

Eventually he fixed it, and I had a bike I was not ashamed to ride. But, I mostly had the Cooper's to thank for that.

Chapter 11

My father may not have been the most outwardly affectionate or caring person towards me, but he was there for me in his own way. He wore his coveralls every day and would come home fairly dirty with grease—it was a far cry from the major league superstar he could have been—but he worked hard and still had the energy to teach me about baseball.

My father could have been a great coach, but he didn't have the heart to teach the game to others. He would only coach me and that was it. He believed in hard work, and I'm sure other parents would not let their kids be coached the way my father coached me. It was go hard all of the time. His drills were meant to make me the best I could be, even if they took their toll on me mentally and physically.

It's a shame my father didn't do something with the game. Even after the opportunity to be a player was gone, I believe my father still could have been a general manager in the major leagues. Still to this day, I believe he knew more about baseball than anyone I had ever met. And this is coming from someone who has met a number of players, coaches, and owners, at every level of the game in my short career. My father knew things that most did not. My father knew what to do in every situation and he could read almost any pitcher, and batter. He picked up on everything by playing the game, and studying the game like a scientist. He taught me everything he knew. He would quiz me when we watched ball games together. He would tell me how to read pitchers and then would quiz me on what the pitcher would throw. He taught me when a team should bunt, steal, and hit and run. He taught me how to read teams by where their players were positioned. He taught me how to work every angle. He was training me to have an edge over everyone else, in any situation. Now that I am older, it breaks my heart to think that he was stuck fixing tires. My father's skills should have been put to better use. I know he felt like a failure. But as he also taught me, sometimes you need to fail in order to succeed.

Chapter 12

Baseball is a game of failure and so is life. No matter how good you are, you will let yourself, your team, and the fans down. All you can do is try and be the hero more times than not—and remember those moments—and completely forget about the failures. It's not easy teaching someone the mental side of the game. How do you teach someone about forgetting your failures? Well, first off, you have to fail. Unfortunately, my father had a lesson for everything to do with baseball—including, teaching me how to be a failure.

The lesson of being a failure is the hardest one my father ever taught me. His methods were not always orthodox—as you saw from the way he taught me how to not be afraid of being hit by a pitch. But that was physical pain. I healed from that after a few days. Mental and emotional pain takes a long time to heal. To be honest, I don't think I ever healed from when he made me know what it felt like to let everyone down.

It was the summer of 1994, and I was twelve years old playing Little League Baseball. We had a very talented team, and we had a chance to win the state championship, hopefully win the regional tournament, and head to the Little League World Series.

In the state championship tournament, I was on fire. There was no doubt that I was going to be the MVP of the tournament. I was hitting over .500 with 6 home runs and 14 RBIs. We cruised through the round robin, won the semis, and eventually were one game away from winning the state championship. This was something that Columbia had never done before.

In our hotel room before the game, my father told me that if they were to pitch to me, I had to strike out every time. He also told me I had to make at least one error. If a groundball got hit to me, I had to let it go through my legs. I was appalled. I did not understand why my father would do something like this.

"Why would I let down my teammates? The coaches? The fans? I can't do it," I said, on the verge of tears.

"Yes you will, or you will have to find somewhere else to live. You will learn how it feels to let others down. Once you do this, you will no longer fear it. You will be able to focus on what you need to do, what you will do, and not what you might do. Remember this is for you. No one else matters. Everyone else is not going where you are going."

I didn't know how to respond. I felt like this was going to be the hardest thing I would ever have to do in my life. Seeing my teammates and how excited they were, it made it so much harder for me to let them down. I may have let them down anyway, but to purposely try and let them down? That made me sick to my stomach. For someone who was playing as well as I was in that tournament, I had all the confidence in the world, but because of my father, I felt completely helpless.

He was harsh and I could tell he meant it. I had to do what he told me. This Little League state title may be one of the best moments of a kids childhood, and it would have been one of my top moments, but I had to throw it away to learn a lesson that was supposed to help me in the future. It was a selfish thing to do, but it had to be done. I had no choice. Even without my bat, and an error or two, we still had a chance to win the series. I may have helped to get us there, but I would not help win it. My father had me doing the opposite. All I could do was pray to the baseball gods that we would still win the game.

Everything about that day was hard for me. My warm-up suffered, and my head was not in the game. I dreaded the moment that the umpire would yell, "Play ball!" This was something I had never felt before.

During my first at bat, there was one person on base. I was hoping they would walk me so that my father's plan would be ruined. But the pitcher decided to challenge me. He threw one right down the middle of the plate. It took everything I had to go against my instinct to swing, and I watched it go by. Strike one. The next pitch was a good curve that started in the zone and then dropped. I let that go by as well for a ball. I just saw his fastball and his strike out pitch. I knew that if he threw another fastball I would have hit it somewhere hard—preferably over the fence. The next pitch was a fastball on the outside corner. I would have easily taken it the other way, but again I let it go by. The count was now 1-2. I didn't even swing the bat. I knew what was coming next. It was either a waste pitch, which a 12-year-old pitcher did not normally do, or his strike out curve. He threw the curve, almost identical to the first one, and I swung and missed. I went down swinging—in order to make it a little more realistic. I knew from here on out, as long as he was in the game, I would not get walked. He challenged me, and defeated me. At least he thought he did.

It was only the first inning, but holding back and striking out felt terrible—especially since I was seeing the ball so well. Sometimes I think that when we are the most relaxed—when there is no pressure—that's when we are in the best condition to hit the ball well. Maybe I did learn something from this experience. Maybe there some method to my father's madness?

Surprisingly, and unfortunately, the first ball that got hit to me did not happen until the third inning. I was hoping to get it over with earlier, so that it didn't matter as much. Instead, it happened when our pitcher was struggling. He walked the leadoff hitter and the next batter hit a double that moved the leadoff hitter from first to third. Normally the runner on first would take second base due to indifference, but our catcher had already thrown out three would-be-base-stealers in the tournament. On top of that, since there was a left-handed batter up, it was my bag, and it was no secret that I had one of the strongest—if not the strongest arm in the tournament, so we knew they weren't going to challenge my arm if our catcher decided to take the runner at second.

The next hitter popped out. There was one out with runners on first and third. In these situations, I would hope to get a groundball so we could turn a double play, and get out of the inning without any damage. As fate would have it, the next batter hit a hard, but easy, low ground ball right to me. It was perfect for a double play. It was exactly what we wanted. As soon as he hit it, I felt sick. I bent my knees, had my glove in the middle of my body, the ball was about to travel right into my glove, but then I lifted my glove before it did, and the ball ended up in left-center field. One run scored and the runner that was already moving towards second base on the pitch, made it safely there with a large round to third. It was now a tie game, 1-1, and there was only one out. My teammates were upset. I saw my coach and his hands were on his head. I could tell he couldn't believe it. The fans looked like they were in shock. I heard someone yell, "It's okay, Ozzie, just shake it off."

Knowing that I didn't have to make any more errors, I begged to the baseball gods to give me another chance to redeem myself. I didn't get that chance. The next hitter singled, then the next kid up hit a home run. We were now down 4-1. There was a pitching change and our next pitcher walked the first batter he faced. I couldn't help but thinking, *Are you kidding me?* This was like being in a nightmare. Thankfully our new pitcher managed to strike out the next batter, and the following kid grounded out to our second baseman. The inning was over, but the damage was done.

What made matters worse was that I was due up again the next inning. Ideally this would be my chance to hit it over the fence and put us back in the game. But again, I couldn't do anything about it. I wanted to fake an injury, but I knew my father would not fall for that. He was teaching me a lesson. A lesson I would never understand. A lesson I would regret.

We ended up losing the game 7-2 and a number of my teammates, who were poor sports, said I blew the game. They were right, however. If it wasn't for my error, and my strike outs, we would have had a good chance to win the state title.

After the game, we drove back to Columbia, and I didn't say a word to my father. It was the longest drive of my life.

"Just forget about today, Son. Put this game behind you as quick as possible. If you can do that, the next game you play, you will be better than ever."

I was so pissed off I didn't even have the courage to say anything back to him. I stared out the window and tears fell down my face. *There's no crying in baseball,* I thought. *But this isn't baseball. Or is it?*

The next day there was an article in the Columbia Daily Tribune that said I had a great tournament, but was off in the final game. They said my lack of performance may have been due to all of the pressure. In other words, the great Ozzie Shaw was a bust in big games. I went to my room and cried some more after I read that article.

From that day forward, I never wanted to ever feel like that again. I don't think my father's lesson worked in the way he initially intended—that it was meant to soften the feeling of being a failure—I don't think anything could—but it may have motivated me to work even harder, so that I would not fail if I was ever in a similar situation again. For years to come, I had nightmares reliving that moment when the ball went through my legs, and I would wake up in a cold sweat. No matter how many times I made that play in real life, that dream still followed me around. Those were the kind of nightmares I would have— nightmares about a game.

Chapter 13

The next year we lost a lot of our best players to high school, and we never did make it to the state championship. It was disappointing that I couldn't redeem myself in a game for the state title. But I told myself that these Little League games didn't matter to future major-league-players like myself. That year before I started high school, my focus needed to remain on my training.

I didn't start lifting weights until I was in high school, and even then, I didn't do much because I didn't need to. At a young age, I started doing push-ups, sit-ups, the plank, and bodyweight lunges and squats every day. The summer before high school, I could do just over 100 push-ups, 150 sit-ups, and 250 squats all in a row. I could also plank for over 3 minutes. There was also a branch on the "Green Monster" that my father would have me do pull-ups on. By the time I hit high school, I could do 20 in a row. That may not sound like much, but if you haven't done them before, good luck getting past five.

I also swung a metal bat that my father filled with sand. It strengthened my wrists and forearms. Another thing I used to have was a bat with a towel taped to the barrel. The bat was regular size, and it felt natural, but when I swung, the towel would open up and there would be wind resistance. I was all about getting stronger, and to be honest, I loved the challenge.

When I went to high school as a freshman, I may not have been the tallest, or the heaviest, but my muscles were defined and I was strong. To my benefit, with my size, I could be very deceiving when I had my uniform on. Everybody that saw me play, would often be surprised when they saw the ball clear the fence with such ease—pitchers especially.

Growing up, I lived and breathed baseball. Everything I did, had to be related to baseball in some way. I was always learning and always getting better physically and mentally. Besides what my father taught me, the mental part of my training came from books on baseball, but most notably: *The Science of Hitting* by Ted Williams. That book was like a bible to me. When I was in middle school, I would read my father's old copy over and over again. I brought it to school with me and anytime we had silent reading, that was my book of choice. Any time I found a particular passage that was useful, I would hand it over to Jake and let him read it, too. Whatever I learned, I also wanted my best friend to learn.

My father's copy was old and it had passages that were underlined, highlighted, and had stars beside. It's as if my father had to stress the importance of those passages every time he read them. Whereas Mr. Williams wrote the science of hitting, my father should have wrote the science of baseball. I still think that my father's understanding of the game was unmatched by anyone else.

But when it came to hitting, my father always told me to read *The Science of Hitting*. I remember reading what Ted Williams wrote about taking so much batting practice, he had calluses on his hands, and there I was just a kid, I would look down at my calloused hands, and think I was just like the greatest hitter that ever lived.

When I was younger, I didn't need a lot of things that could be found in that book quite yet. At that point, I was still too young to have a favorite pitch, and pitchers weren't that good—most of the time I tried to hit everything as hard as I possibly could and it worked—but the older I became, I would turn to that book and study it and learn from it. It was always there on my journey all the way through my baseball career. Sometimes I would look at those faces at the back of the book and imagine myself being placed beside them someday. *Maybe I would even write my own book on baseball?*, I thought. I ended up writing a book related to baseball, but as you can tell, it is much different than how to play the game.

My father told me I was the type of kid that learned how to walk before everyone else. I would push myself to try and stand up and take steps and no matter how many times I fell, I would get up and keep trying. Before I was one years old, I had a never give up attitude. This was a great quality to have for baseball, and for life.

As we move on from my childhood years, I want to mention that my childhood was not as "normal" as some others, but for the most part, I didn't mind. I was a kid that loved the St. Louis Cardinals and I loved baseball. All I wanted to do was play ball, and in a way, I grew up in an environment that allowed me to do just that.

I also had a best friend that loved baseball and we had a lot of fun. I remember being a pretty happy kid. I didn't have a care in the world—other than baseball.

And that was my early childhood. I would take everything I learned and everything I experienced, and I carried it with me to probably the most important four years of my life: high school. I still lived and breathed baseball, but as it often does for many people, love entered my life. It may have been the best thing that ever happened to me. But my father would say love was nothing but a distraction.

Chapter 14

The only thing that I was excited for entering my first year at Rock Bridge High School, was the baseball team. The way I looked at it, I had four years until I got drafted. These were important years as a ball player; I didn't even consider the academic side of school. As far as I was concerned, school was just something I had to do in order to be on the baseball team. As you could have guessed, I was never strong academically. I got by, but it was never a priority to me. I believe that the only reason I did pass my classes is because I received half of my mother's genes. She was all about school. Which according to my father, was the very thing that ruined his life. If she wasn't so persistent on going to college, he would have went straight into the major leagues. My father wasn't going to let me make the same mistake.

My father often reminded me that school wasn't important. He told me that there was no sense working hard at school, since I would be going into the major leagues anyway. In other words, an education would not be needed where I was going.

Therefore, college was never part of the plan. Baseball was to be my only focus. My father homeschooled me about baseball—formal school is only a place I had to go. I'm pretty sure if my father could, he would never have put me in school, he wouldn't work, and he would train me to become a baseball player all day long. I thought that would be fine with me. Until I saw her.

I started high school in August of 1996. Jake and I walked to school together. I remember it being a hot and sunny day. I was wearing red Nike shorts and a grey Cardinals shirt that my mother had sent me for the new school year. That was my idea of dressing up for my first day of school. I was glad I never had a family that sent me to school in dorky clothes for the first day. I was a ball player, so I was going to look like one. Jake was not so lucky.

I remember laughing to myself when I saw him come out of his house. He walked out with these beige dress shorts, and a stark white polo. It was the type of shirt that you were going to get dirty by the end of the day, no matter what. You would be worried about it every second, especially when you ate. I knew Jake for a long time and I could tell he did not want to wear that outfit. There was no doubt Jake's parents made him wear those clothes. It was one of those things that his parents made him do—there was no way around it. Just before I was about to tease him about it, Mrs. Cooper followed him and said, "Good morning, Ozzie. You're looking sharp today...are you ready for your first day?"

"Yes, Ma'am," was all I was able to say before Jake butted in.

"If he looks so good wearing what he's wearing, why can't I go put my Cardinals shirt on, too?"

"Oh, Jacob, you look really cute in your outfit," she replied.

"Cute?...I don't want to look cute...I'm a dead man..." he said trailing off.

I laughed. He was such a funny kid. Then to mine and Jake's reluctance, Mrs. Cooper took a picture of Jake and I on our first day of high school.

After the picture, we said bye to Mrs. Cooper and headed down the path from his house.

I put my arm around Jake and teased him, "Awe! You're so cute, Jacob."

He pushed me away and told me to "Shut up," while we

both laughed.

As we walked to school, the conversation quickly turned to baseball. Tryouts wouldn't be for months, but Jake was already nervous about making the junior varsity team. I think deep down he loved baseball more than I did. Jake was the type of player that coaches loved once he was on their team, but he often got overlooked during tryouts if they didn't know who he was. It was often his size that threw coaches off. He was still small and he didn't throw very hard, but he was a good ball player. He could play anywhere—besides first base due his lack of height. His passion for the game could not be matched by anyone else. I decided I would do what I could to help him make the team. While Jake was worried about tryouts for the junior varsity team, my only concern, was if I would make the varsity squad as a freshman. The guys on the varsity team were bigger than the kids I played against last year, but that didn't scare me away. I saw it as a welcomed challenge; just like when they put adults out in the field back in T-Ball. If everything went well, I would make it on the varsity team, and in two years, Jake would be there to join me.

Jake and I got to school and it was pretty overwhelming. It was a bigger school than what we were used to. There were kids all over the place and the hallways were packed. Everybody was trying to figure out where their lockers and classes were. I recognized a few guys from my ball team, who came up to give us a high five, and to make fun of Jake's outfit in the process. Other than that, there were a lot of new faces. A lot of new, beautiful female faces. Jake hit the nail on the head when he said, "This place is a gold mine." Right when I was about to agree, I saw something better than gold.

Just like when my father first saw my mother, I know every detail of the moment that I saw Elizabeth. Jake and I were walking down the hall trying to find our first class, when we saw her. She was wearing a flowing, light-blue sundress. The sunlight from the windows in the hallway danced on her perfect, wavy, dark brown hair while she walked. She beamed her perfect smile, and then, I locked eyes with the most beautiful eyes I had ever seen. Her eyes were greenish/blue, and with her dark hair, they instantly drew you in. I know as a young teenager, my hormone levels were sky-high, but to me, she was the most beautiful person in the world. As she walked past, I quickly found out, many others thought so as well.

Every head in the hallway at the time, male or female, turned and followed her until she disappeared. But for me it was love at first sight. I knew love at first sight, because I heard my father describe it so many times before. I remember being in a sort of daze. I felt like I was up to bat, and a pitcher threw a knee-buckling curve, that got me looking like a deer caught in headlights. At that moment, it was strike three and I was out of this world. The only difference, is that I didn't feel the shame of striking out. I felt ecstatic like I was headed to the world series. It felt like I was going into the big game. At that moment, there was more to my life than baseball. I snapped out of it when, Jake being Jake, sighed and said, "I think I'm in love."

"So am I," I uttered.

But I meant it. And I didn't even know her name.

Chapter 15

The next time I saw the girl of my dreams, is when Jake and I, along with a few of my old teammates, went out to check out the ball diamond after school. When we got to the field, we saw the tennis courts and again something caught our eye. We walked right on past the ball field, and headed towards the court, as if some force was drawing us in. And there she was. She was wearing a white, one-piece tennis dress and she looked like an angel from that distance. As we got closer, she was even more beautiful than the first time I saw her. And she was athletic! I heard a few of the ball players we were walking with say, "Hey, look it's Liz...she is so hot." And we all stopped to gaze at the goddess playing tennis.

"Her name is Liz?" I asked.

"Yeah, Elizabeth Fielder, but a lot of people call her Liz," one of them replied.

From that moment it was official. Her and I were meant to be. Both of us had a "Z" in our names. I remember thinking Oz and Liz. Ozzie and Lizzie. That sounded perfect.

We eventually made our way back to the ball field and I stopped and took it all in. This would be my playground for the next four years. The outside wall, on the right hand side of the dugout, had a giant bear painted on it, and on the inside there was "Bruins" written in big yellow letters. My job was to be the best Rock Bridge Bruin baseball player in school history. Ever since day one, I knew that my experience in high school would determine my future baseball career.

The first few months of high school were mostly uneventful. All I was looking forward to was the baseball season in the spring. I went to all my classes and my father and I would practice every day after school. Jake and I would throw the ball around when we could, and at the school there were a few training sessions and practices throughout the winter. As for Elizabeth, she was not in any of my classes, but I would see her once in awhile in the hallways, and on the tennis court. Even though it was love at first sight, at the beginning of my first year of high school, I could only admire her from a distance.

Chapter 16

Within the first few months of high school, there were a couple of other notable things I remember that should be mentioned. Like usual, I watched as many Cardinals games as I could. But this time, these games were even more special to me, because it was Ozzie Smith's last year. Earlier in the season, he announced that the 1996 season would be his last, and from then on, I watched and studied him as much as possible. I wanted to learn as much as I could from the Cardinals' greatest shortstop in history—the one I shared my name with.

Ozzie Smith was honored at Busch stadium on September 28th, 1996, before a game against the Cincinnati Reds. That was the game that the Cardinals organization officially retired Ozzie Smith's number 1 jersey. That day had an impact on my future. I decided I had to choose a new number because I always wanted to be number 1 just like my hero, but if I were to make it to the Cardinals one day, I would have to choose a different number. Therefore, from that day forward, I decided that I would be number 11.

That October, my father, Jake, and I, watched every game of the playoffs and we watched the Cardinals make it to the NLCS. I remember thinking about how amazing it would be if Ozzie won the World Series to end his career. There could be no better ending.

But game 7 of the NLCS was the Wizard's last game in the major leagues. It was a complete blowout and the Cardinals were defeated by the Atlanta Braves 15-0.

When Ozzie Smith walked to the batter's box for his last at bat in the 6th inning, the away crowd in Atlanta gave him a standing ovation. Seeing him be honored by so many people was incredible.

After Ozzie flied out in foul territory on the first pitch, my father, Jake, and I, sat there quietly and watched him raise his helmet to the crowd, and walk off the field for the last time. It was an emotional experience even just watching it on TV. It sent shivers down my spine, and tears welled up in my eyes. I took a glance at my father to make sure he didn't notice. What I saw shocked me. There was—and I thought I was mistaken at first— a tear that was falling down his face. He quickly wiped under his eye with the back of his hand. But it was too late. I knew what I saw. I felt like calling him out and saying there was no crying in baseball, but I decided against it. That was probably a very wise decision.

It's hard to know exactly why my father was crying. Was he crying because his favorite player had just played his last game in the major leagues? Or was he crying because my father missed out on a professional baseball career? Maybe it was a little of both. I will never know for sure.

I was sad that the Cardinals came up short in the NLCS, but the Wizard had an amazing fifteen years in St. Louis, and a nineteen-year major league career. It was my dream to one day have a long career with the St. Louis Cardinals, just like Ozzie Smith, and to be honored by so many people at the end of it all, just like he was.

It was rare for a kid at my age to think about how I wanted my career to end. But ever since that day, I knew I wasn't going to simply make it to the majors, my career was going to be honored and celebrated.

The 1996 major league season was officially over when the New York Yankees defeated the Atlanta Braves to become

JESSE A. MURRAY

World Series champions. Once the season was over, my focus turned back to training hard for tryouts in the spring.

66

Chapter 17

The Spring of 1997 was soon approaching, and the tryouts I had been thinking about for months, were finally going to take place. I couldn't have been more ready. But one thing about trying out for the varsity team as a freshman, I was going to be stealing someone's spot. This was not something I thought about, until I met the likely candidate. There was one player on the team the previous year that sat on the bench a lot. He was there for his speed, and mostly only got into a game to be a pinch runner. But when he did get in the game, his position of choice was shortstop.

The starting shortstop the previous year had graduated, so I had a good chance of securing a starting spot on the roster. But word must have spread that a young freshman was trying out for the team as a shortstop, and I quickly found out one guy was not too excited about it. I was a threat to his spot on the team.

On the first day of tryouts I found out that his name was Mark—he was a tall, lanky kid that ran like a deer. I may have been shorter, but my legs moved quicker. When we had a sprinting drill, much to his dismay, I proved to be faster. For the rest of the tryout he gave me a hard time. He did what he could to throw me off of my game. When we were lining up to take groundballs, he would be right behind me and would be saying things like, "Don't miss, don't miss, don't miss," or, "I hope you get this one in the teeth," in order to scare me from staying down on the ball. I was there to prove myself and that's what I did. I didn't say a word until it was time to hit.

Like I mentioned before, with all my workouts and training, I was small but strong. The best place to show this was in batting practice. It didn't take me long to hit one out of the park. I could tell the older guys were surprised by my power and I'm sure the coaches were too. I hit everything hard that day. Right after batting practice, I did something I instantly regretted, but I was frustrated. I walked past Mark, that tall, lanky kid that was giving me a hard time, and said, "Let's see you top that." I could tell I rattled him. He went up there and made a fool of himself. He was swinging out of his shoes trying to hit the ball hard, instead of making sure he made contact. The only thing that he hit that day was a few squibblers. I didn't like how I said something right before he went up to bat, and I felt bad about it. I wanted to prove myself with the way I played, and I didn't need to try and throw someone off their game.

In the locker room after my first tryout, Mark was obviously frustrated, and realized how likely it was that I would be taking his spot. He came up to me and shoved me against the lockers. "You little piece of shit...you can't come here and take my spot. It's my senior year."

A big kid, who I recognized as one of the catcher's trying out for the team, stepped in. "Get off of him!" the catcher yelled, as he yanked Mark off of me. The catcher had legs like tree trunks, and was built solid.

"You better watch your back," Mark said to me, as he walked away.

"I swear if you lay a finger on our starting shortstop...you'll have to deal with me," the catcher yelled back.

Mark went off and didn't say a word. He wouldn't have stood a chance against my protector, who introduced himself as, Aaron Ackerman.

Aaron was only one year older than I was, but he was already built like a man. If I hadn't seen him at practice already—with his few days of stubble growing on his face—I could have easily mistaken him for a teacher or a coach.

"Don't worry about that kid. I got your back," he reassured me.

"Thanks, man," I replied, as I proceeded to get myself together. I hadn't been in an actual physical confrontation like that before. I was grateful that someone was there to intervene. I liked Aaron right away, and he instantly became sort of like a big brother to me.

I continued to have strong outings throughout the rest of the tryouts. Mark never said another word to me. And just like my new friend Aaron predicted, I did become the starting shortstop for the varsity team.

A few years later, I ended up seeing Mark after one of my games during my senior year. He would have been three years graduated at the time. He came up to me after the game and apologized.

"Hey, Oz, I don't know if you remember me, but I gave you a hard time at tryouts your freshman year...you ended up taking my spot, and well, you deserved it. I'm sorry, man. I thought I was hot shit back then, but I was never meant to be a ball player," he said.

"It's Mark, right?" I asked and he nodded. "I appreciate it. I wish you all the best."

"You too," he said.

And that was it. I ran to catch up with Jake.

People did treat me differently and tried to be my friend when they realized how good I was and that there was a good chance I was going places. I'm not sure what Mark's motive was, but I appreciated that he came up to me that day and apologized. It was a short interaction, but it changed the way I remember the guy. From that experience, I realized that a simple apology can go a long way.

Chapter 18

From the onset of tryouts, I noticed that everything about the game was quicker than the year before. The pitchers, runners, and the ball coming off the bat were all faster. However, it didn't take me long to adjust. When my father hit infield practice, he would hit the ball hard. When he pitched, he pitched hard. That's the way we practiced, and it helped push the limits of my ability. I came into my first season on the varsity squad ready to play.

My first at bat in my first game of high school baseball, I was a little nervous when I walked up to the batter's box, but that only lasted a second. A lot of the players that I was playing against were bigger than I was, and in particular, their starting pitcher we were facing was a monster. It was man against boy. He had a beard, thick arms, and was tall. It almost didn't seem fair. He threw hard, but it was mostly his appearance that was intimidating. But so was my father when he was on the mound. All I had to do was trust in the fact that I was probably more prepared than any player out there.

I got in the box, did my regular routine, and waited for the first pitch. I let the first pitch—which was a fast ball—go right by for a strike. The next pitch was a good curveball that I didn't want to swing at. It wasn't my pitch and it went by for another strike. It was now 0-2. The pitcher smiled. He shook off the catcher twice and threw another curveball. This one he left up and I mashed it to the gap in left field. I easily made it to third with a stand up triple. A home run might have been better, but that's exactly how I wanted to introduce myself to the league. I wanted to show them that I could play.

When I was standing on third, I was taking big leads. The pitcher no longer had a smile on his face. He was visibly pissed off. I didn't know if it was me he was pissed off at, or himself for serving that one up. That inning, I was left stranded on third, but the rest of the game, I ended up walking, and hitting two singles. It was a solid 3-3 day.

Ever since that first game, I was playing well. To my benefit, I saw a lot of good pitches my freshman year. I think a lot of these older guys still wanted to challenge me. They didn't want to be beat by this young and small kid, but I won those battles more often than not.

For the most part, my new life in high school was pretty good. My grades were not the best, but that didn't matter. I continued to excel out on the field and everything was great. I thought I couldn't be happier.

I should mention, that back in January, when the second semester of school began, I was elated to find out that I had two blocks of classes with Elizabeth. I would see her every day in class, around the school, and I saw her walking on her way to the tennis courts from time to time. I still hadn't said a word to her. But I thought about her a lot. I noticed she never came to any of our games. I must admit, I looked for her, and hoped I would see her, but I never did.

To be honest, I didn't know much about relationships, or how to get a girlfriend. Sure I wanted one, but I didn't know how to go about it. My father never gave me advice about girls, except to not let them get in the way, or ruin my life. I never had an older brother that could give me advice. The only thing I learned about girls was from movies, and locker room talk. These were not the best sources of information on relationships.

In high school, it was harder for me to get away with having a limited social life. When I was younger, if I was going to hang out with friends, we would play baseball and that was the way it was. Baseball was my life and I didn't want to do anything that didn't involve it.

In high school it was different. There was drinking, parties, and girls. My friends that would be just as excited to play baseball all day, every day, now had other things on their mind. I was not fun for them anymore. But I still tried to hang out and go to parties once in awhile.

I couldn't believe the parties that people had in high school. There was people drinking, smoking marijuana, and doing a bunch of other crazy things. Since I was sober all the time, I noticed the effects that alcohol had on other people. Usually when my father drank, he yelled a lot more, repeated things, and sometimes he would slur his words. With my father being my prime example, it was hard for me to see the fun and exciting side of drinking. But at these high school parties, I did notice that shy people turned talkative, and talkative people became even more talkative. People would also fight more often, and just do things that didn't make sense to me. It was a new world. A world I really wasn't ready to be a part of.

I knew drinking would cause problems with baseball, so I had no need for it. Unfortunately, when you are one of the few sober people at a party, it's not always enjoyable. Some of my teammates would act stupid and it was hard to watch. I knew I didn't want to be like that. I didn't want to be liked because I partied; I wanted to be liked for how good I was at baseball. I knew what I wanted, and I didn't want alcohol to get in the way of that.

Sometimes I would have a couple beer at parties, but I would never get out of control. I mostly tried to sip on the same beer for as long as possible, and more often than not, I would put it down somewhere without anyone noticing. I honestly did not enjoy the taste. I probably should not have drank at all, but I did it to fit in, and to keep some of my older teammates from bugging me.

Being the youngest player on the varsity team, led to an interesting social life for me. I ended up hanging out with older people, rather than the friends I grew up with. Jake and I were still good friends but he didn't always come out when there were parties. His parents wouldn't let him. Most of the time I would have to go out alone or with Aaron.

A lot of my teammates tried to get me to do things that I wasn't comfortable with. It was pretty easy for me to get away without drinking or doing drugs, but one thing I couldn't avoid, was the attention from girls.

Getting attention from girls was a new experience for me, and it was uncomfortable at first. It was uncomfortable for me because I was only fourteen years old, but the girls at these parties that gave me attention were seniors, and were nearly adults already. It's not normal for senior girls to be interested in a freshman, but since I was one of the star players on the varsity team, it was my reputation as a ball player that attracted them to me. For the most part, I was shy and quiet, and honestly didn't say much, but that didn't matter. I was the star and they treated me like one.

Some of the older guys said they would get me laid and stuff like that, but I had no interest in that yet. The truth is, I was scared. I wouldn't know what to do, and frankly, I didn't want to be with an older girl. Most of the girls they tried to set me up with would shower me with attention, but they were always drunk at parties. They would come up to me and surround me and say things like: "Awe, look how cute he is. He is just a baby!"

I never knew if that was a compliment or not, but no male ever wants to be called cute, and definitely not a baby. But, they would hang on me, and make me follow them around. I didn't really have a choice, and I couldn't really complain too much. It could be overwhelming at times, but it was better than being alone at these parties, when almost all of my teammates got shitfaced.

There was one particular party that I remember the most in my freshman year. It took place after one of our Friday night games. A very beautiful blonde girl named Carrie—who was a senior at the time—had the party at her parent's house. It ended up being a popular party spot that year, but on this particular night, it was my first time being there.

Aaron, Tom—our third baseman—and Ryan—one of our pitchers—and I, showed up at this party and it was packed. It was mostly juniors and seniors, and I was probably the only freshman there. Like always, there was a lot of drinking going on.

The guys and I made our way to the kitchen. We found a spot next to the keg and Tom handed Aaron and I a beer. I didn't want one, but I had to take it. *I'll just have one,* I told myself.

"Oh my god! Is that Ozzie?" I heard a girl shriek.

A group of three beautiful girls came walking up to me in the kitchen. All three of them had a drink in their hand. These were the type of girls that were the hottest and most popular girls in the school, and they knew it. Everybody knew it. I've seen them around school—they were hard to miss—and I knew all their names—the blonde was Carrie—the tall brunette was Sydney—and the shorter brunette was Vanessa. I knew them because they were often the topic of conversation for my teammates. But it surprised me that they knew who I was. They were the groupie type girls that can be found chasing athletes. In the minor leagues these type of girls would be known as "Ball Girls" or "Cleat Chasers."

I remember leaning up against the cupboard and I felt the heat rise in my face.

"Hey, Ozzie! You played *amazing* tonight! Didn't he ladies?"

Carrie said. She was wearing a tight fitting red dress, that accentuated her cleavage. It was hard not to look, but with an outfit like that, she wanted people to look. It was hard to take your eyes off of Carrie, but all three of them were bombshells.

"So *amazing!*" the other two said in unison.

"Thanks," I said.

It's not like I was going to say anything else, but before I had a chance to, Carrie put her arm around me. "You're coming with us."

"I can't leave my friends," I said trying to resist and looked at Aaron.

"Go!" he said. I thought he also mouthed, "Don't be an idiot." But my brain may have imagined that.

They dragged me around the party and they all kept saying how cute I was. They would stop and get distracted, talk to some of their friends, and then we would move on so they could refill their drinks.

When the focus was back on me, I would hear them whispering things to each other like, "I wonder how he is in bed?" and they would giggle.

Sydney was even blunt enough to come out and ask me. "Have you been with a girl before?"

I didn't know what they meant exactly at the time.

"I'm with three right now?"

"He is definitely a virgin," Sydney said and they all laughed.

"We could change that. Couldn't we ladies?" Carrie said. She was stroking my arm.

If I thought I could feel the heat in my face rise before, now, I was sure it was on fire.

"Look at him blush! He is so cute!" Vanessa said.

All night they were very hands on, and even though it wasn't necessarily sexual touching, I still thought it was pretty awesome. I was also quite aware every time that Carrie's breasts would rub up against me, and even though I felt my face turn red, the majority of my blood was heading elsewhere.

At one point, all four of us ended up sitting on the stairs. The attention was all on me and that is when I had my first real kiss.

"Have you ever kissed a girl before?" Carrie asked.

I thought about lying, but I shook my head no.

"Would you like to?" she asked. Her face was a mere inches from mine.

I couldn't speak I was so nervous, but I was also excited. I could smell her perfume. I didn't say anything, I just shrugged my shoulders. She moved in very slowly and kissed me really gently on the lips, and then put more pressure on my mouth. I don't think I did much, if anything at all to reciprocate, but it felt great.

"Hey! My turn!" Sydney said.

She was a lot more aggressive. She grabbed the back of my head and pulled me towards her. Her kiss didn't start gentle, and I felt a tongue enter my mouth. It was a lot wetter and longer than the kiss with Carrie, but they were equally as exciting.

"Vanessa, do you want a turn?" Sydney said. "He's a pretty damn good kisser."

I remember being shocked by that. *I'm a good kisser? I didn't even do anything.* I mostly sat back as they put their face and lips against mine. Maybe that was the key—sit back and let them do the work? Or maybe they were just drunk.

"Sure!" Vanessa said.

I remember being in a sort of daze of hormones and nerves, but here I was about to kiss another amazingly, beautiful girl. If anything, this was going to be great practice.

"Holy shit! Look at our man Oz," Derek—our center fielder—said as he broke away from a few of my teammates, and headed up the stairs, just before Vanessa was about to kiss me. He sat down on one of the steps and put his arm around Sydney and Vanessa. "Let the man breathe, ladies," he said.

The girls were completely distracted with the sudden interruption, as drunk girls often are.

"Fine we have to get drinks anyways," Sydney said and they got up and they headed down the stairs.

I was afraid of what may have happened with these girls after those kisses. I was not going to lose my virginity with a drunk girl, or girls, for that matter. I wouldn't know what to do anyway. This may have been every man's fantasy, but I was still a boy. Knowing Derek was probably drunk and was coming to get in on the action himself, when he interrupted us, to me, it was as if he came in and rescued me.

We both walked down the stairs following behind the three girls.

"Real smooth, D," Aaron said to Derek as soon as we got the bottom of the stairs.

"Yeah, way to cock block our man Oz," Tom added.

They continued to give Derek a hard time that night, but not long after he interrupted my time with the girls on the stairs, the party got broken up, and we all went home.

On the Monday after the weekend, Jake and I were walking down the hallway at school, and sure enough heading our way, was Carrie, Sydney, and Vanessa. When they saw me they waved and said, "Hey, Ozzie!" and giggled as they walked past.

"What was that all about?" Jake said, and I could tell he was in awe. "How do they know you?"

"Oh, them? I kissed the blonde one and the brunette on the left on Friday night," I said as if it was no big deal.

"Shut up. Serious how did they know you?"

"I did. And I was about to kiss the brunette on the right, but a guy on my team cock blocked me." *More like rescued me.* I should have said. But it's all about keeping up appearances sometimes—even to your best friend.

"You are a god," he said and I could tell his mind was imagining what it must have been like. He wanted to hear the whole story, but much to his dismay, he had to wait for me to fill him in after class.

When I told him the story, once again he said I was a god. I may have come across that way to a fellow ninth grader, but that wasn't the case with my older varsity teammates.

For a long time after that night, guys on my team would make fun of Derek for "cock blocking me." But after a few more parties, and after more attention from girls, they made fun of me for not sleeping with girls that clearly wanted to.

They called me a "pussy," for well, not getting any. To a certain degree they were right. I was scared and I didn't want to do it. But as a ball player you always want to look tough, so you will say things that are not true.

"I would have, if Derek didn't come in and ruin it all," I said one time after some razzing I received from a few of the guys. I put the attention on Derek and it worked. At least I thought it did, until they made a pact to make it up to me and not let Derek interfere this time. *Oh, great!* I thought.

"Why don't you set me up with someone my age...like Elizabeth Fielder," I said. *Shit. I can't believe I said that out loud*, I thought as soon as it left my mouth. At the time I wasn't happy that I said it, but later I was glad I did.

"Consider it done!" Tom yelled.

"Not a bad choice," Tim—our first baseman—said.

"Good! Now you won't be stealing our senior girls," Derek said.

"Shut up, Derek. He wasn't stealing anything you could get anyways you fucktard," Tim said.

But Tim was wrong. About a month later, Derek was dating Sydney and he told us all about the type of things they did in bed, in his car, and on her parent's couch together, in a lot more detail than most of us would have liked. Hearing those stories, true or not, I was super glad I never got more than a kiss from her.

Anyway, from the moment I let it slip that I wanted them to set me up with Elizabeth, it didn't take long for word to spread. I'm sure that in a matter of days, she knew about it. These types of things do not stay quiet in a high school.

For the next few days, my teammates, and other guys in my grade, were trying to get me to ask Elizabeth out. I couldn't believe how much they were trying to set us up. They were determined. I wondered why they didn't use some of this determination to try and get her for themselves—or any other girl for themselves—since that's all they seemed to talk about. But I was thankful they stayed away from Elizabeth. She was out of their league. She was in a league of her own. But somehow, I won her over.

Chapter 19

Every time she walked into the classroom, I would fall in love with her all over again. I still hadn't even said a word to her. Luckily, there was one key moment that got the ball rolling. It was in science class, and we needed to partner up with someone. Without me knowing, some of the junior varsity ball players that I had played with growing up, went up to Elizabeth and said that I wanted to be her partner. All of my usual partners, ended up partnering up with each other, and refused me when I asked them if I could join. Even the odd man out partnered with someone they would not have partnered with in a million years. I was confused and didn't know why the hell they were acting so strange. Then Elizabeth came walking up to me.

"So?" she said.

My face immediately turned red. Was she talking to me? I looked around sort of confused and asked, "So what?"

"Well I heard you wanted to be my partner. Aren't you going to ask me?"

"Who told—" I stopped myself before I shot myself in the foot.

"Would you like to be my partner?" I asked feeling my face grow even hotter.

"Sure!" she replied.

We sat down beside each other. I was hesitant when I pulled out my books because I didn't know what was going on. Was this actually happening? To me, she was ten times more beautiful than Carrie.

I looked at some of my old teammates across the classroom, and some gave me the thumbs up and others were making obscene gestures. Periodically, I saw them look over at me, whisper something to their partner, and laugh. I couldn't hear exactly what they were saying, but I knew it was about Elizabeth and I. I also knew what type of comments they must be, since they were ball players after all. It's the same thing you hear in the locker room. That I could be sure of.

I was kind of upset that I was her partner for a project in science. I never liked science. Why couldn't she be my partner in, well, gym class? That's where I could truly show off.

I watched her while she read over the assignment sheet and she looked focused. I could see why she was so smart. She paid attention to detail and took it all in and processed it. I usually struggled to even read over the entire assignment before I would lose interest, and my brain would wander to baseball, or as of late, to Elizabeth—the girl that was sitting right beside me.

It's safe to say that Elizabeth did most of the work on the assignment that day. But she wasn't letting me get off easy. She would push me to find the answers and made me write them down. She was almost like a tutor. And to be honest, I tried my best so that she wouldn't think I was too stupid. I knew I wasn't going to impress her, but at least I wouldn't scare her away. Regardless, I was the luckiest person in the world.

Something strange happened after that day, Elizabeth and I started partnering up all the time in science class. Whenever we had a lab or anything like that, she would come and sit beside me like we were best friends. I didn't even say much and I wasn't that smart, so I wasn't really sure why she wanted to be my partner. The only thing I could think of, was that she actually liked me. I couldn't be happier. The more time we spent working together in class, the more we talked, and the more familiar we were with each other. This carried over to other classes and we would talk for awhile when we saw each other in the hallways. Slowly, but surely, we got to know each other better.

But it was on a Wednesday afternoon in April, that our relationship moved to the next level. After school, we were walking out of class, and we continued chatting down the hall until we reached my locker.

"I hear you are a pretty good baseball player," Elizabeth stated.

"I'm not too bad," I said.

"A freshman on the varsity team. I think that's better than 'not too bad,' " she said with a laugh.

"I guess." I didn't know what else to say.

"So how does one go and watch a baseball game."

"What do you mean?"

"Well do you need a ticket? Is it free? Where do I sit? Do I need to get invited by someone?"

"Yeah, it's free...anybody can come, and you can sit any place you like. They have stands there."

"Stands? Oh, I thought you said I could sit anywhere," she said.

"No you...." then I realized she was just teasing me and I started to laugh. "I never thought about that before...you sit in the stands? That's kind of funny."

This time we both laughed together.

"I've never been to a baseball game before," she said.

"What! Really?"

"No, sir, I have not."

"Well, you should come sometime."

"You have a game on Friday, right?"

"Yep."

"That's a shame, I have nothing to do on Friday," she was looking at her foot twisting it on the ground. Then she looked at me and fluttered her eyelids. Then I finally clued in that she wanted me to ask her to come watch me play. I was embarrassed that she set this whole thing up. I was too afraid to ask her out, but this was her way of getting me to ask her to come watch me play baseball, which was a step in the right direction.

"Elizabeth," I said with a delay.

"Yes?" she kept looking at me with her beautiful blue eyes.

"Would you like to come watch me play baseball on Friday?"

"I would love to!" she said with a huge smile.

It wasn't necessarily an official date, but I remember what a great moment this was for me in my life.

She was always one step ahead of me. If she wanted something, she would give me hints and make me figure it out for myself and make me do the work. She was teaching me life skills. She was a great teacher and I started to get the hang of things the more time we spent together.

I went off to get ready for practice and I was on top of the world. My teammates could read something was up right away.

"What's up, Ozzie? Why so happy?" Aaron asked.

"Wait, Oz, my man...did you get laid?...did you and Elizabeth bang?" Tim asked. There were many of them that were virgins but they sure liked to talk about all things sex. I guess teenagers like to talk about what is on their mind, and sex is on everyone's mind it seems.

"No, I did not *bang* her you idiots. She is coming to Friday's game though," I replied.

"Oh, my little Ozzie, so excited cause a girl is coming to watch you play," Tim said teasingly.

"Shut up, Tim. All of us are excited that she is coming to watch us play," another player said.

"I'm not, I feel like throwing up...I don't want her out there, I won't be able to concentrate!" Tom who was set to be the starting pitcher added, with an eruption of laughs from the others.

"You guys are ridiculous," I said as I grabbed my stuff and

headed out to the field.

While I was taking batting practice, my arms felt light and the ball was flying off my bat.

"Jesus Christ, Oz! Are you on the juice or something?" Coach Gilmour said after I hit a few long ones in a row over the fence.

"He's on the Elizabeth Fielder juice, Coach," Tim said while he was warming up to hit next, by swinging two bats. A few of the guys who were in ear shot laughed.

"Hey, Oz, you should share with Tim. He sure as hell could use some after last game," Coach Gilmour said.

"Ahhh common, Coach. I told you I got dirt in my eye during that pick I made in the first inning," Tim said.

"What does dirt have to do with hitting muffins barely out of the infield?" Coach asked with a big smile.

"Muffins? I hit one to the warning track in the 5th inning," Tim replied.

"Tim has nothing but warning track power," Tom yelled from where he was throwing a bullpen session.

"Go fuck yourself, Tom! Do these look like muffins, Coach?" Tim said as he dropped both bats and started flexing his biceps.

"Alright, Oz, two more good ones and it's Tim's turn. He talks less when he hits and my ears could sure use a break. All our ears could use a break," Coach Gilmour said.

Tim started to sing some country song that no one had ever heard before. He had a terrible singing voice, he knew it, everyone knew it, and that's why he did it.

"For heaven sakes, Tim, will you shut up!" Coach Gilmour yelled.

"I love you, Coach!" Tim yelled, before going back to his song.

Tim and Coach would go back and forth all day. Tim could be a handful to most adults, especially the teachers, but Coach

Gilmour was a good guy that could joke around with the best of them. The most important thing was that he knew when to be serious and he knew when he could joke around. He ran his team with the right balance which made us all respect him. We did what he told us to do, we worked hard, and we won games. That's the way it is supposed to be.

I was hitting especially well that day. I don't know what it was, but maybe Elizabeth did have something to do with it? Maybe the more time I spent with her, the better I would get? I couldn't wait until that Friday to find out.

Chapter 20

I remember the night that Elizabeth came to watch me play for the first time like it was yesterday. When I was on shortstop I looked into the stands to see if she was there. When I saw her, she was looking right at me, we locked eyes, and she beamed a smile. That feeling of knowing that she was there to watch me is a feeling that I will never forget. I've played a lot of baseball games growing up, but this game was different. I was playing for her that night.

For probably the first time in my life, I was nervous to play baseball. I didn't have an off game very often when I was younger, but it was still possible. I prayed to the baseball gods that I wouldn't have an off day. My prayers were answered.

That game, I went 4 for 4 with a home run, a double, and two singles. I also turned a beautiful 6-4-3 double play, and made a diving catch up the middle behind second base. I couldn't have played much better. The "Elizabeth juice" must have been real.

I had a great game but we only managed to win 4-3. It was a close and exciting game throughout. It was an important game because we took over first place in the division. But having Elizabeth there, meant more to me than winning that game.

After the game was over, I met up with Elizabeth. She ran up to me excitedly and gave me a big hug. That was one of the first times we had any physical contact. I know it may sound pathetic, but you have to remember that hugs are a big deal for someone in grade nine.

"That was so exciting! You were amazing! Who knew a baseball game could be so much fun!" she said.

"You liked it?" I asked

"I loved it!"

"Well, how about you come more often."

"I will come to as many as I can," she said. "Just to watch you!"

"I almost forgot," I said reaching in my ball bag. "I have something for you. My coach gave me the game ball, and I want you to have it." I handed her the ball.

"If your coach gave it to you, I can't keep it," she said, as she held it in her small hand.

"How about you hold on to it for me for luck?"

"I could do that," she said and smiled.

We stared into each other's eyes. Every time, they drew me in. She leaned in and kissed me on the cheek. I don't think I could consider that our first kiss, but it was still one of the greatest moments of my life. All that mattered, was that I was with the most beautiful girl in the world—and the baseball field was in the background. I couldn't be happier.

I walked her home as we talked about the game. She had so many questions to ask me. She seemed to be interested and I couldn't believe how amazing she was. I knew at that moment, she was going to be a big part of my life.

Elizabeth came to a few more games before I worked up the courage to officially ask her out. It probably would have taken me much longer, if my friends and teammates didn't keep pressuring me to do so.

After another one of my games, she met up with me like she always did to tell me what a great game I had. This time I finally asked her the question that I had wanted to ask since that first game back in April.

"Liz, would you like to go out with me sometime...like on a

date?" I asked nervously.

"I would love to!" she said.

"I know it's soon, but are you free tomorrow night?"

"Tomorrow night is perfect."

After our plans were set, I walked her home like I normally did. I remember I had a huge smile on my face the entire time.

Once we got to her house, she gave me a hug, kissed me on the cheek, said "See you tomorrow night," and went inside.

I walked home feeling on top of the world. That feeling lasted all night until I fell asleep.

The next morning, I woke up worried about how my father would react to me hanging out, and going on a date with a girl. As soon as I told him, I quickly found out that he was against it.

I had to cancel on Elizabeth on the day of our first official date, because my father was in one of his moods, and he said I had to practice. He would not let me leave. Sure I could have disobeyed him, but I knew I had to take my relationship with Elizabeth slowly—for my sake, and for my father's sake. When I cancelled on Elizabeth I felt terrible. I called her and told her I wasn't feeling well, which was a lie. She had concern in her voice and said she hoped I would feel better soon. I imagined her getting all ready, being her excited self, only to be let down when I called to cancel. As quickly as my relationship with Elizabeth started, I was sure I had ruined it just as fast. Or more accurately, my father did.

But that wasn't the case. I found out later, that Elizabeth came by my house to see how I was feeling and she brought me a little care package, consisting of soup and a Sports Illustrated magazine. She was the sweetest person in the world.

She rang the doorbell and knocked, but no one answered and then she heard the commotion in the backyard. She looked through a small hole in the fence, and saw the life I had at home.

Crack. "Good."

Crack. "That a boy!"

Crack. "Take those ones the opposite way!"

Crack. "God damn it..." my father said before throwing the next pitch right at me.

I turned and took it right in the back.

"Ow! What did you do that for?"

"You weren't listening! Take those ones the opposite fucking way! Stop trying to pull the ball...now try again."

Crack. "That's better."

Crack. "There you go."

And on it went. That was just a typical night. But Elizabeth was horrified. She couldn't believe how hard I worked and she mostly couldn't believe my father threw the ball at me. I never really thought about it. I was used to it. It's not like he ever hit me with his hands or anything.

Elizabeth was no longer upset that I lied and had to cancel on her, and she went home concerned for me. Later that evening, I called Elizabeth to apologize again for cancelling on her, and that's when I found out that she stopped by and had seen my practice. She accepted my apology and said that everything was okay.

But that night, she saw how hard I had to work; she saw the pain behind the excitement and greatness on the field; she saw that all those people cheering for me and singing my praise at my games, came at a price. She said she was worried about me and wanted to take care of me. She was the sweetest, but it was strange to hear her say that.

I never thought that much about my situation except when I went and visited a few of my friends. But that night on the phone with Elizabeth, that's when I realized that I had a different life than others. However, that did not bother me, because everyone else was not going to make it into the major leagues.

Sure there were times that I would have rather been doing something else, but the truth is, I loved to hit. I could sit in a cage all day and be happy. Just me, a bat, and a bucket of balls. There is always something to work on. And plus, no two pitches are ever the same. I would hit low ones, high ones, outside ones, inside ones. I would visualize being in certain situations. I would make it as real as possible by imagining scenarios in complete detail. Was it a day game or a night game? Who was on the mound? What inning was it? Was it a regular season game or a playoff game? And so on. This would be something I would do every time I stepped into the cage. I wasn't swinging the bat for the fun of it. No matter what, I was swinging with a purpose.

I had the same attitude when it came to developing my defensive skills. I practiced with a purpose. My father would have me practice diving and getting to my feet as quick as possible. This would help on any play that was nearly out of my reach. Most people did not simply practice these things, it was more of a reaction, or a last ditch effort. But for me, I had drills designed for them. My father would yell, "To your left" and I would pretend there was a groundball to my left and I would take a few hard steps then dive for it, catch the imaginary ball, and then hop to my feet as quick as possible, plant my feet, and pretend to throw the imaginary ball to Crow. My father would switch off calling out balls to the left or right. After we did a few of those, then he would hit the ball far to my left and right, and I would practice catching the ball on a dive, getting up and throwing it to Crow. I would be putting it all together. These drills allowed me to perform some of the plays that amazed the people that watched me make them. They would say I made the impossible plays look easy. They may have looked that way to others, but there was a lot of practice and a lot of pain to get me to the point where I could make those plays look easy.

Nearly everything I did in my baseball career, there was a story of how I practiced for that moment. But I was so busy learning and practicing for baseball, that I didn't practice for other areas of my life. The game may have looked like it came easy to me, but everything else didn't. That was the cost of training to be an elite athlete.

As for my relationship with Elizabeth, I couldn't practice for that, I had to learn as I went.

Chapter 21

A few nights later, Elizabeth and I finally had our first date. I couldn't think of anywhere to take Elizabeth, but I knew I needed to make up for having to cancel on her. How did I decide to do that? Since I was such a Casanova, I decided to take her to a local pizza place close by. I was only fifteen at the time, so my options were limited. Most importantly, it had to be somewhere we could walk. There was no way I was going to ask my father to take me somewhere so I could go on a date with a girl. The place I chose was close enough for me to walk to her house, pick her up, and walk to the restaurant. It was the only place I could think of. It was the only place that could work.

You always see in the movies how a boy will bring a small gift to the girl on their first date. This might be flowers, chocolates, or some other small gift. I had no idea what to bring Elizabeth. It felt weird going to buy any of those things, so I went and bought her something that was more up my alley. I bought Elizabeth a Rock Bridge Bruins baseball hat. I imagined her wearing it to my games and the idea seemed perfect. Come to think of it, I was buying this gift for myself, just as much as for her. Either way, I put it in a small gift bag, and carried it along with me to her house.

I was dressed in my favorite St. Louis Cardinals T-shirt and a black Cardinals hat. Like always, I looked like a ball player. I did think about wearing something a little more "date appropriate," but I couldn't find anything in my closet. Plus, she liked me for who I was, so why would I wear something different?

In baseball, you could put me into the most important situation in the most important game, and I would feel comfortable. I welcomed the pressure, because I knew I was the best person for the task. This was not how it was on our first date. I was a mess.

When I got to her house the nerves hit me. I had walked her home a number of times before, but I had never been inside and I hadn't yet met her parents. I think every male has experienced this exact feeling. It's all a part of the courting process.

I walked up her walkway, up the three steps, and rang the doorbell. I remember wiping my palms on my shorts just before Mr. Fielder answered.

"You must be Ozzie," he said putting out his hand. I took it and shook it.

"Nice to meet you, Mr. Fielder," I said.

He invited me in and we had that awkward moment while we waited for Elizabeth to come meet me at the door. In the mean time, Mrs. Fielder came from the kitchen, introduced herself, and also shook my hand.

"Lizzie tells me you are a very talented basketball player. I think she said something about you playing on the varsity team already. Is that right?" Mrs. Fielder said.

My face got warm. And just before I could correct her, Mr. Fielder added an observation that made things worse.

"Gee, Ozzie, you must be very talented if you're on the varsity basketball team as a freshman. You are not very tall, are you? Honey, aren't basketball players supposed to be tall?" he asked his wife with a serious tone.

This was not going well at all. I was very uncomfortable that Elizabeth told her parents the wrong sport I played, and I was insulted by her father's remark about my height. It was a sensitive subject—I was counting on a growth spurt that seemed to take forever to come.

"Don't listen to them, Ozzie," Elizabeth said from half way down the stairs. "They are just teasing you. They know you play baseball."

I was so embarrassed by the basketball and height comment, I didn't even notice she was there.

"Sorry, Son. We just wanted to ease the tension," Mr. Fielder said with a large grin. "We know how tough it can be to meet a girl's parents for the first time. You should have seen when I first met Linda's parents. My knees wouldn't stop shaking."

"You guys are so mean," Elizabeth said with a smile. I could tell she thought it was just as funny as they did.

Mr. Fielder said something else, but I didn't make out what it was. I was in a trance. I couldn't take my eyes off of Elizabeth. She was wearing a light-blue colored sun dress that fell a few inches below her knee. I knew that dress. It was the very same dress she was wearing the first day I saw her.

As she continued down the stairs, her dark brown hair glistened in the sun that entered from the front window. She took my breath away. It was love at first sight every time I laid my eyes on her.

"You look beautiful, sweetie," Mrs. Fielder said.

"Thanks, mom," Elizabeth said. "You ready to go, Oz?"

"Sure," I said. "It was nice to meet you Mr. and Mrs. Fielder."

"It was nice to meet you too, Ozzie," Mrs. Fielder said.

"You too, Ozzie. You kids have fun," Mr. Fielder added.

Elizabeth and I walked outside and Mr. Fielder shut the door behind us.

"I'm sorry about my parents," Elizabeth said. "But you have to admit, it was kind of funny."

"They got me good that's for sure," I said. "Liz, you look really beautiful."

"Thanks, Ozzie," she said and smiled. "You look beautiful too."

"Hey now!" I said.

"You look handsome, better?" she said and swatted the brim of my ball cap.

Playful hitting from the opposite sex. Even I knew that was a good sign!

It took us around ten minutes to get to the restaurant. It was a beautiful, spring day and everything was going well. I don't remember what we talked about on the way exactly. We joked about her parent's little gag, talked about school, and she teased me some more.

Once we got to the restaurant, sat down, and looked at each other from across the table, that's when I became incredibly nervous. I didn't know what to say or what to talk about, but I didn't like the silence. So what did I do? I talked about baseball. I blabbed on about the Cardinals, about hopefully setting some school records, and mostly trying to impress her. Since I was nervous, I found myself talking non-stop.

When I finally took a break to drink some water, I found out our date was not going as well as I thought.

"Can't you talk about anything besides baseball?" she said clearly annoyed.

"Umm, no, not really?" I laughed awkwardly.

I was confused. I realized for the first time, that I couldn't talk about anything besides baseball, because I didn't know anything else.

"There is more to your life than baseball, isn't there?" she said sounding genuinely curious.

I was stumped by her question. The only thing that had been going on outside of baseball besides my time spent with Elizabeth, was the experience I had with Carrie, Sydney, and Vanessa a few weeks before. There was no way I would tell her about that. I remember feeling ashamed and I hoped that Elizabeth wouldn't find out. I doubt she would have agreed to go on a date with me if she had.

Finally I thought about something clever and beamed a smile. "Well...you could be something other than baseball...in my life, that is."

It didn't sound as smooth when it came out of my mouth, as it did when I thought it.

Elizabeth smiled, then looked down and said almost to herself, "I guess I could." Then she looked up at me and said excitedly, "Here's what's going to happen, Mr. Ozzie Shaw. I'm going to start teaching you things outside of baseball. That is what I am going to do for you. Do we have a deal?"

"I guess," I said not really excited. "Just make sure it doesn't interfere with baseball," I added with a chuckle.

But I was serious. I knew my father wasn't going to like this whole learning-things-other-than-baseball idea. I didn't even think he would like the idea of me spending time with Elizabeth in the first place.

The pizza finally came, and we chatted a little while we ate, but things went so much better than how it started. Instead of talking about baseball and trying to impress her, I let her talk, I asked questions, and she asked questions. We talked about our families, and I found out more about her that night, than I had about anyone else in my life. I started to realize how selfish and self-centered of a person I was. This was something I never considered before.

When I first saw her, it was love at first sight, but I knew nothing about her. However, on our first date, I loved listening to her talk. I would stare at her while she spoke and her eyes would draw me into whatever she was saying. When she spoke it was almost mesmerizing. She was so smart and she had so many things to talk about. She had travelled the country and had much more life experience than I did. It was thrilling to hear her stories. I felt like I had been living under a rock my whole life, and she was telling me about things I could never imagine— simply because the only thing I thought about was baseball.

She told me about how her father was a university professor and his job took her family all around the country. She told me about living by the ocean in California, and seeing alligators in Florida. She told me about how peaceful the sound of the ocean waves were at night, and how beautiful the moon was when it reflected off the water. She said she never felt grounded until she looked at that moon, and that reminded her, that at least one thing would always be the same, no matter where she ended up.

She told me of past friends—friends that she would never get to see again. She told me how much it hurt to leave the ones she cared about. She told me about how she had trouble getting close to anyone, because she knew she would probably have to pack up and move away again.

She also told me how she loved to read and play tennis. These were two things she could do all by herself. In the future, she wanted to go to college somewhere near the ocean—where she could play tennis and get an education. She also planned on never putting her kids through the pains of moving all over the country. After she got her degree, she was going to find a small town to settle down, and plant her roots in for her kids, and her grandkids. She told me that was the life she dreamed of. She was fourteen years old, but knew what she wanted. She was unlike anyone I had ever met.

As she opened up, I was able to tell her my dreams, and we always had this bond, knowing that both of us would have to pack up and move away. We were like stepping stones. We would support each other on the journey to where we needed to go.

On that first date, she said we couldn't get too close to each other, but we would help each other until it was time to move on and go our separate ways. This pact we had, sounded perfect. But we failed to realize that this pact only made us closer.

We talked for a couple hours and then I had to walk her home. I remember I felt like I was floating as we walked. I couldn't be happier.

When we got to her house, she hugged me and kissed me on the cheek like she always did. Even though we said we wouldn't get too close, I still wanted to kiss her right then and there. But I couldn't.

Nonetheless, after this night, we would only become closer. Baseball was no longer the only thing in my life. I wanted to know everything about Elizabeth. I wanted to study her like I studied baseball. I wanted to pick up cues of when she was happy, mad, or sad, just like I picked up the cues of a pitcher when he would throw certain pitches. But the truth is, it wasn't that easy. I found out that baseball is a lot easier than getting to know everything about a girl.

Chapter 22

In my first year of high school, I was kissing girls, going on dates with the girl of my dreams, and playing varsity baseball. Since I was on the varsity team, I was growing up quickly and learning a lot from the older guys. For instance, the first time I tried chewing tobacco was after one of our practices, when a few of my teammates and I decided to stay longer to get some more swings in.

As soon as the coaches left, a couple of the older players pulled out their cans of chew. Tim asked Aaron and I if we wanted a dip. I knew that so many ball players do it, including those in the major leagues, so I decided to give it a try. I watched all the guys take a pinch, and then I took one and I placed it in my lower lip, just like everyone else. Then I got in the cage, and Doug, one of our pitchers, was throwing BP. I only took a few swings before I started to feel light headed. I reached in my mouth and pulled out the tobacco, and spit out as much as I could.

"You alright, Oz?" Doug asked.

"I think I'm going to throw up," I replied.

Those that were in earshot started laughing.

"Little Ozzie, you not quite man enough yet?" Tim asked mockingly.

I sure wasn't. Tim took my spot in the cage and I went to rinse out my mouth with a water bottle. Aaron, who was also trying chewing tobacco for the first time, tried to tough it out and didn't spit his out early enough. He ended up vomiting a few feet from the cage. Tim thought that was awesome.

I was lucky enough not to vomit, but I still vowed I would never try to chew again. Nonetheless, I would try it again a few times throughout the years, but always with the same result. With that said, I have no more desire to ever try to chew in this lifetime.

Surprisingly, Aaron ended up trying not long after, and soon enough, he decided he liked it very much. It was not uncommon to see Aaron walk around with a soda bottle, or cup, or juice box that he could use to spit into indoors. He developed quite the habit. He was a ballplayer, and he already looked like a man. His new habit made him even more intimidating to those that didn't know him.

We finished third in our division my freshman year, but I was not too concerned about it. The way I saw it, we would increasingly get better over my high school career; especially when the players I grew up with, moved up.

My freshman year we had a lot of players with talent, but we couldn't put everything together. We had a couple good pitchers, but when they weren't in, it was difficult for us to win. Most of all, we had a lot of strikeouts that year. Guys like Tim could hit the ball hard, but he wasn't consistent. To tell you the truth, I think a lot of the seniors got caught up in the party scene too much, and baseball was not their first priority, as it was for younger guys on the team like Aaron and I.

I still learned a lot that year and I had a lot of good things in my life. When our season ended in May, I only had a few weeks to focus on training before the summer league started. I was also planning to spend more time with Elizabeth and Jake.

Once baseball started in the spring, Jake and I didn't see each other that often. We were both busy with our own teams, and between my training, spending time with Elizabeth, and the odd party, I didn't get to see him as often as I would have liked.

I missed my friend. I couldn't wait until summer league so we could be on the same team, and spend more time with each other.

That summer, Aaron, Jake, and I all became really good friends. All three of us practiced whenever we could and we spent a lot of time together as a group. It must have looked funny when Aaron, Jake, and I would hang out, since we looked so different. Jake looked like he was 12, instead of 14 going on 15; I was a bit bigger than Jake, but I more or less looked my age; then there was Aaron, who was turning 16, but looked like he was in his 20s already. We were all friends, but we could have easily been labeled the kid, the teenager, and the adult. Even so, all three of us loved baseball and that's what brought us together.

Through Elizabeth, however, I was able to build a life outside of baseball. Each day we spent together, she became more important to me.

That summer after my freshman year, I even brought Elizabeth over to meet my father for the first time.

It was a terrifying experience.

Chapter 23

My father knew that I had a girlfriend, but I was putting off introducing him to Elizabeth. I was afraid of what he might say to her, and I was also afraid of what Elizabeth might think. I didn't want my father and my life at home to scare Elizabeth away. Her parents were educated, and they had a good sense of humor. My father was rough around the edges, drank, and was very serious and to the point. But I knew I couldn't keep Elizabeth away forever.

It wasn't until summer break that Elizabeth came over for the first time. We both walked in together and I introduced her to my father, who was sitting in his chair in the living room.

My father got up, smiled, and was polite. That was a huge relief. He didn't take up much of our time. The introduction happened, he went back to his chair, and that was it. The thing I was dreading for weeks, was over in a minute.

I took Elizabeth outside and I gave her a tour of my back yard. I showed her the batting cage, and the "Green Monster." I had to explain to her that Fenway Park is the home field of the Boston Red Sox, and that there is a high wall in left field that is named "The Green Monster." It was funny to me that I actually had to explain things about baseball to someone. Baseball was so much a part of my life, that it was hard to imagine that someone didn't know everything about it, like I did.

Elizabeth picked up a ball and threw it into the netting. Then she walked around looking at things, while I explained to her what they were.

She picked up the bat with the towel attached. "This is clever. I know what this is for. Oh boy, it sure is hot out here!" she said, as she pretended to towel off her forehead.

She was so funny.

"Not exactly," I said still laughing and I grabbed it from her. "This is what it's for." And I proceeded to swing the bat. "It adds resistance to my swing, so I can work on my bat speed."

"I see. But you can still use it to towel off if you needed to, right?"

"I guess I could," I said laughing again.

Then she found something else that caught her eye. "Who's your friend?" she asked.

I didn't clue in until I looked to see where she was looking. "Him? That's Crow."

"Crow?"

"Yeah, short for Scarecrow."

"Hey, Crow," she said to him with a wave. "Your friend is rude. He didn't wave back."

"That's because he doesn't have arms."

Then she started to giggle so much and she slowly filled me in on her new realization, "Wait a second—" she said and started to giggle some more.

"What's so funny?" I asked, laughing at her laugh.

"His name is Scarecrow and your name is Oz? Where is Dorothy, Tin Man, the Cowardly Lion, the witches, and the rest of the cast, Mr. Wizard of Oz?" she finally said. It was hard to understand her through all the giggling.

"I never thought of that before," I said as it hit me.

And for some reason we both found it so funny, we could barely breathe.

"Oh, my cute little Wizzy," she said, once she caught her breath.

"Hey, don't call me that!"

"Why not?"

I explained how my aunt Amy used to call me Wizzy, and I told Elizabeth the unfortunate story behind the nickname. We both continued to laugh.

I was getting teased by Elizabeth about playing baseball with the cast of *The Wizard of Oz*, and then she was calling me my old nickname my aunt gave me when I peed my pants, but I didn't mind. I loved how Elizabeth could make me laugh.

"I'm sorry for teasing you. But I'm calling you Wizzy from now on."

"Oh, great."

"Look how red your face is."

"Well, I just told you an embarrassing story."

"It's okay, Wizzy. I think it's cute," she said as she moved closer, and wrapped her arms around me. "You're still handsome when you blush."

We locked eyes and they instantly drew me in like they always did. She moved in and kissed me nice and gently on the lips. That was our first kiss. It was perfect.

I could have stayed in that moment forever, but Elizabeth had to leave shortly after.

When she left, I went inside and asked my father what he thought of Elizabeth. I was afraid of his response.

"She is beautiful, Son. And she seems nice."

I was elated. But he wasn't finished yet.

"But I don't want her to be a distraction, Oz. Trust me, pretty girls like that can be a distraction. Remember the focus needs to be on baseball."

"She won't be, Pop," I said.

He didn't say anything else, but I'm sure he knew better.

That summer, I realized how lucky I was to have so many good people in my life. The times when I felt alone, when I had a hard day, when I was tired, I had people like Elizabeth, Jake, and Aaron to cheer me up. They were my sense of normalcy.

They were my sense of joy outside of the game of baseball. They are the type of people that everyone should have in their life, but sadly, a lot of people don't. They were not distractions like my father said they were. They were the best things in my life.

With that said, something else also happened that summer that changed my life as a ball player—I hit my first major growth spurt.

Chapter 24

My father may have been a hard-ass, but he was nurturing when it came to eating healthy foods. We always ate well because my father wanted me to grow and be healthy, so I could perform at the top of my game. To my father, what I put in my body, meant just as much as my practices. Not only did he prepare me healthy meals, he also had me supplementing my meals with smoothies and protein shakes. You should keep in mind that these were homemade protein shakes. My father would go to the health food store and buy a big bag of whey powder in bulk. This stuff was completely natural, but it smelt and tasted like feet. This was before commercial protein shakes became a regular phenomenon with all different brands and flavors. I would choke these awful homemade shakes down with little resistance. I did what I had to do, to be the best.

Height wasn't really something you could control, however. The men on my father's side were all tall, and I was hoping I would get some of their genes. But I didn't want to grow too much. If I grew as tall as my grandfather Shaw, who was six foot six, I would have to switch positions. That was a real concern for me. I didn't want to give up playing shortstop, but if I was a giant, I would have to. Yet, I had no say in the matter.

Jake, on the other hand, didn't care how much he grew, as long as he grew. His biggest fear was that he would stay small forever. For both of us, we knew that a growth spurt would help us develop in all areas of our game.

It wasn't until the end of the summer, before my sophomore year, that I finally hit my growth spurt. I grew four inches, which put me up to five feet and ten inches tall. I still wasn't the tallest person for my age, but to me, it made the world of difference.

Mr. Fielder observed one day when I was over there visiting, "Hey, Ozzie, did you grow overnight? You could be on your way to being a basketball player after all." I was glad he noticed that I grew, but I was still scared that I would grow too much.

But over the next couple years, I slowly grew a few more inches and topped off at six foot one. I remained three inches shorter than my father. I was completely happy with my height.

Jake still hadn't grown much, but at least he grew a little. He was five foot six in grade ten, and still had plenty of time to grow before he moved up to the varsity team. His goal was to grow a bunch before his senior year, so that we could be stars together. We often imagined and talked about what it would be like if we both got drafted. It killed him to know that his size was the only thing holding him back from being a great ball player. It was hard for me as well. I wanted him there beside me just as much as he wanted to be there. But there is a fine line between good and great, and sometimes that line is nearly impossible to get over. Sometimes it's out of our control.

When school started, I worked hard in the fall and winter months to put on some muscle mass that would compliment my growth in height. This is when I started working out with weights a lot more, and the gains in muscle started to escalate fairly quickly during this growth period.

I was filling out, and on my way to becoming the top athlete in the school. And my only competition meant the world to me. My only competition was Elizabeth.

Chapter 25

Football and basketball were big sports in Columbia, but I never played or paid much attention to any sport besides baseball. Being with Elizabeth, however, I started to learn a lot about tennis. I loved to watch her play. She worked hard and was an inspiration to me. That sophomore year she improved greatly and became a very notable tennis star at Rock Bridge. We both had our training for our sports, but we also made it work so we could train together.

We would head to the tennis courts and Elizabeth would practice her serves, while I tried to catch the tennis ball, and lob it back over the net. I would have to quickly dart to my left or right, and work with the spin she put on the ball. This activity helped me work on taking short-hops, high-hops, and it helped me develop soft hands. It was also great practice for my reflexes and getting a good jump on the ball. The more Elizabeth improved and the harder she could serve, the more practice I would receive. We made a good team.

When she was working with someone else, sometimes I would set up the ball machine and have it shoot the ball to me, while I worked on my footwork, and ball transfers from my glove to my throwing hand. I don't think many ball players trained the way I did on the tennis court, but I know it helped me improve defensively.

One particular time when we were grabbing some water, I picked up Elizabeth's racket and turned it around and observed it.

"Look at this thing," I said. "It's huge! How hard can it be to hit a tennis ball with one of these? This is probably the easiest sport in the world."

"Oh, quiet you!" she said.

"Seriously! Try hitting a ball with a baseball bat. There isn't even a flat surface on a bat. Now that's a sport."

"How about we play a game?"

"You want to play me? One on one? Me and you?

"Yup!"

"Naw. I don't want to embarrass you."

"Oh, we're playing!" she said, and handed me a racket and went to get another one.

"Okay, fine."

I knew she was going to beat me, but I thought it would be fun to have a little game.

She explained some of the basic rules to make sure I knew what I was doing.

"I'll serve first," she said, and bounced a bright yellow tennis ball a few times.

I bent my knees and got into a ready position. Instead of catching her serves, I simply had to hit them back over the net with this giant racquet, and keep the ball within the singles lines. *How hard can this be?*, I thought. She threw the tennis ball up in the air and smashed it to the corner on my right. I darted over and took a swing and the ball flew high and deep to the right. If I had been playing baseball it would have landed way foul into the seats. But since this was tennis, it landed a few courts over and interrupted a doubles game that was taking place.

Thanks to my horrible attempt of returning Elizabeth's serve, I attracted the attention of the other tennis players that were out there that day. They decided it was probably safer to watch us play, rather than continue on with their practices or games. Ozzie Shaw the great Rock Bridge baseball star and

Elizabeth Fielder the tennis star, now had an audience. Most of them were cheering for Elizabeth, but I heard a couple people say, "Let's go, Ozzie!"

The next serve she smashed it over to my left this time—forcing me to hit it on the back hand. I took a couple hard steps to my left, I swung as best as I could, but the ball flew way to the left and landed on another court. I was never a good switch hitter. Every one there was laughing at me. That never happened when I played baseball.

Elizabeth served again and this time I knew I was going to hit it and show everyone how good I was. She served it over to my forehand just like the first serve. I wound up and smoked it way over the fence. Everyone that was watching turned and watched it go.

"Home run!" I yelled.

Everyone laughed except Elizabeth. I walked up to her and said, "Okay, you win. Tennis is a lot harder than I thought, and you are way better than me."

"Thank you," she said.

"But did you see how far I hit that last one? I think that might be some kind of record."

She slapped me lightly on the stomach with the back of her hand. "And now you have to go get it."

From then on, I never challenged her to another game of tennis. We decided it was best that we stuck to our practices.

The more I watched her play tennis, the more I appreciated the sport. I remember one time Elizabeth had a match against an opponent that was ranked higher than she was. It was a battle that went back and forth each set. But there was one moment that Elizabeth proved that she was better, and from then on, she couldn't be beat.

Her opponent was serving and the score was 15-15. She served and hit the net twice in a row. Elizabeth went up 30-15. I found myself getting deeply into it. I was saying to myself,

"Come on babe, you can do it!" I really wanted to cheer her on.

Her opponent managed to smash her next serve over the net and Elizabeth was able to return it. Her opponent returned it back, and Elizabeth hit it deep to her opponents backhand, and she was barely able to get to it, but got enough of the ball to loop it over the net. Her opponent was in trouble since Elizabeth was running up to the ball to hammer it back. But at the last second, Elizabeth pulled her racket into her side, and lobbed the ball just over the net for a point. It was masterful. A perfectly executed deceptive shot. It showed how talented she was. It showed how she could hit the ball hard, or completely change speeds when she needed to. The score was now 40-15. Tennis was a lot more like baseball than I thought. Simply changing speeds could be the most effective weapon of a great pitcher. The same goes with a great tennis player.

One thing that I came to really admire about singles matches in tennis, is the fact that it is a sport that you have to win or lose on your own. You can't blame things on a teammate or a coach. There are no excuses. The harder you work, the better you will get, and the more matches you will win. In baseball, sometimes you can be the best in the game, and still be on a losing team.

Elizabeth ended up winning her match that day and after that she rarely lost. She was talented and she worked hard. I couldn't have been more proud of her. I was her biggest fan. And there we were—two of the top athletes in our school.

Chapter 26

Elizabeth was the type of girl that would spend her lunch hours in the library—a place I never spent much time in. It's ironic to me that there is the misconception that nerds and people that have nowhere else to go, spend their time in the library. In reality, it is the people that are going somewhere that spend their time in there. Elizabeth was not a nerd. Elizabeth was the total package—smart, beautiful, funny, athletic, and very loving. She was only in high school, but she knew what was important in life. She was wise beyond her years.

It didn't take me long to start doing something that I would never imagine myself doing—I was spending time in the library to work on my school work. The only reason I did it was because of Elizabeth and we always went together. But after a while, I started to go by myself. Mostly to impress her, and make her proud of me, but I also enjoyed the quiet. Sometimes I would go to have my own space to think about my future without anyone being there. I couldn't do this around my teammates and I couldn't do this around my father. I could do this with Elizabeth, but I always felt sort of stupid talking about it with her. I needed to do some of my own thinking. I needed to try and figure out what was best for me. It was in the library that I actually started to write. I would write down my thoughts, but I would never show them to anyone. Often, I would simply throw what I wrote away, but some writings I would keep in a folder that I stuffed underneath some old clothes in my closet. I think my love of writing started out from my time in the library, but I never picked it up seriously until I was in recovery from alcohol, much later on in life.

Sometimes you hear of the smart girlfriend doing homework for the dumb jock. It was never like that with us. Elizabeth would never do that for me. She wasn't with me to get a reputation. She never needed that. Elizabeth would make me do my own work so I would learn and be a better student. She didn't want me to get away with things because I was talented on the field. She wanted to make me better in all areas of my life.

In grade nine, I used to have teachers hold me back after class and ask me why I didn't hand in certain assignments, or scold me for not putting any effort into my work. It was annoying because school wasn't important to me and I had my father to back me up on that. But once I started going out with Elizabeth, that all changed. I started to put more time into my school work, and I surprised myself when I got good grades and praise for something other than baseball. Nonetheless, I had to be careful not to let Elizabeth or school interfere too much with my dream, and my father's dream.

After I started hanging out with Elizabeth more often and doing things like getting good grades, this upset my father. He would remind me to focus on my goal and get rid of any distractions. When he felt I wasn't listening to him, he started throwing batting practice harder than he ever had before. I could tell he was doing it out of anger. When I couldn't hit his pitches, he would say I used to be able to before I started dating Elizabeth.

One time I argued back by saying that he was throwing too hard and he was giving me pitches I couldn't hit. But he said I was weak and unfocused. Finally he threw the ball against the ground, and said weakly, "Fine, go be with Elizabeth. Then you can end up just like me."

When he threw the ball and went inside, I didn't want to let him down, so I stayed outside and hit off the tee until I couldn't swing anymore. Part of me did it out of anger, while a part of me did it for him. He didn't have anything else other than me, and his dream of doing whatever he could to get me to the majors was his only purpose.

I knew he was hurt and that's why he pushed me so hard, but I never knew he was hurting that much. I knew I had to make it in the major leagues for my father. No matter what. I owed this to him. I needed to make him proud of something in his life. I wasn't going to let him down. But at the same time, I think I was falling in love with Elizabeth.

My father drank his beer every day, but now and then my father would take his drinking too far. It was hard because he would get angry and do things that were embarrassing, hurtful, or simply annoying. As I grew older, and the more I was used to his behavior, it became mostly an inconvenience.

On nights when he got bad, I would go off into my room and do as many push-ups and sit-ups as I could. Sometimes I would hit hundreds of balls off the tee, and sometimes I would go for a long run. I took some of that anger and frustration and turned it into something positive—in the form of pushing myself to train even harder to get out of there.

I was lucky in a sense, however. You hear stories of people that have physically abusive fathers. That's scary stuff. My father was harsh with his words sometimes, but he was never violent, and other than the odd bean ball, he never hurt me physically. But when it came to Elizabeth and the things he said about our relationship, at times it was too much, and I had to get away.

Chapter 27

It was hard for me when Elizabeth and I started to get closer because my father did not approve of it. My father started to notice that my priorities were changing. And so did I.

One day about two months into our sophomore year, Elizabeth was over and we were working on an assignment for school together. I was learning so much from Elizabeth in such a short time, and my grades were improving significantly. After we were finished our assignment, I decided it was time for me to teach Elizabeth something that I was good at, so I took her outside to my backyard.

The leaves had started to change on the "Green Monster," and they turned to a beautiful red and orange. Some leaves had littered the ground and others were caught up on the top of the netting of my hitting tunnel. It made my backyard look like a picturesque training facility. Even I could admire its beauty.

I always loved hitting in the fall. When my father and I would go out there to do some hitting, the leaves would fly up in the air when I hit one on the top of the netting. The harder I hit, the further the leaves would fly up in the air. Most would land on the ground, but others would land back on the top of the tunnel; until I knocked them all off.

"Alright, Liz, today is your lucky day. I am going to teach you how to hit a baseball," I said, as soon as we got outside.

"I thought you said it was my lucky day? I can't hit a baseball."

"That's why I am going to teach you."

"But I'm scared of the ball. What if you hit me?"

"I won't hit you. I promise."

"Fine, I will try," she grumbled.

I handed her a bat.

"Let's see your stance," I said. She got in her stance and I couldn't help but laughing. "Not bad. But move your right hand on top of your left hand."

"But I always have my right hand at the bottom when I play tennis."

"This isn't tennis, Liz."

"Fine. Like this?"

"Perfect. Now let's see a practice swing."

She swung the bat weakly.

"Okay, okay," I said. "Don't be afraid to swing hard. You can't hurt the ball."

"Like this?"

She swung again.

"Much better, but you need to twist your hips and not just swing with your arms."

"I think you should come help me."

I did what I was told. I came up behind her, wrapped my arms around her, and held my hands over hers on the bat. "When you swing, you have to swing with your arms and rotate your hips at the same time. It also helps to pivot your back foot. Pretend you are twisting your foot to crush a spider."

"Ewww! I hate spiders. I don't want to step on a spider."

"Fine, how about a cigarette butt."

"Ewww! I don't smoke."

"You are ridiculous! How about let's pretend there is a nail right through your foot and you can only twist the ball of your feet from side to side."

"You're such a mean teacher! Why would you want to put a nail through my foot?"

"You Elizabeth, are un-coachable."

"That's rude! I am just going to pretend I am a ballerina and I have to twist my toe a little bit to begin a spin, but then stop."

I chuckled. "That works, I guess. I don't think I'd use that if I were teaching a boy how to hit, though."

I was still straddling her and we practiced a few more swings.

"I kind of like this baseball thing actually. You should teach me more often," she said, and twisted slightly to look back at me. She moved her mouth towards mine and we kissed.

Being a teenager, straddling my beautiful girlfriend, and now kissing her, it was starting to become too much and I had to separate myself, before there was a little baseball bat poking her in the back. We were not quite there in our relationship, yet. I went back to being the pitcher.

"Okay, let's see what you got. Remember to keep your eye on the ball, and when you swing, watch the bat hit the ball."

I threw the ball nice and slow underhanded. She swung and missed.

"Good try. It's okay to miss," I reassured her. "Let's try again."

I threw another one and she swung again, and missed.

"I'm trying to keep my eye on the ball, and do a little ballerina twirl with my back foot. This is too hard...I need my tennis racket," she said clearly frustrated.

"You're thinking too much. This time keep it simple. See the ball and hit the ball."

I threw another one, and she got a little piece of it and fouled it back.

"I ticked it! I ticked it! Did you see that? I ticked it!" she shouted gleefully.

"I did! You were so close. And it's called a foul *tip*, not a foul *tick*."

"I prefer *tick*, thank you very much."

"Okay, then," I laughed. "Let's try again. I have a feeling you will hit this one. Just see the ball and hit the ball."

"Okay, I am ready."

I threw another one and this time she made solid contact and hit it over my head. She stood there stunned.

"Now you have to run!" I shouted.

She started running and I cut her off, and wrapped my arms around her—just like my father did to my mother years ago.

If you had someone as beautiful as this...you would never want to let them go. But he did.

"Let me go! Let me go! Help!" she shouted as she tried to wiggle away.

"I never want to let you go."

She instantly stopped wiggling and looked me in the eyes. "You promise?" she asked.

"I promise," and we kissed again. I loved her so much and I never wanted to let her go.

"Oh, shoot," Elizabeth broke away. "I have to be home for dinner."

We kissed again and we went and grabbed her bag from inside and I led her to the door. She said she would call me later. I was on top of the world. But that did not last. My father must have witnessed what took place outside. My guess is that he remembered a similar scene he had with my mother.

"Oz, I saw you two out there. It looks like you and Liz are getting too close. We can't have anyone distracting you from our plans," my father said. And then he came out and said it. "Are you two having sex? I think it's time we have a little chat..."

My face turned red. "No, Pop, we are not having sex. And we don't need to have a talk about it. We learn all that in school."

"What I'm going to tell you is not what you learned in school...Don't have sex, Son. You don't want to risk ruining your future like—" he caught himself.

"Like what, Pop?" I was angry and hurt. I knew what he was

going to say.

"Like so many talented ball players do."

"I know you were going to say like you did," I was overwhelmed by a feeling of so much hurt. "I'm out of here."

I stormed out of the house and slammed the door. I didn't know where to go. How could I go from feeling so amazing with Elizabeth, to feeling like shit seconds later with my father?

Without having a plan, I found myself walking towards Jake's house. I walked up to the door and knocked. Mrs. Cooper answered. They were all getting ready to sit down for supper.

I must have looked upset. "Are you alright, Ozzie?" Mrs. Cooper asked.

"I'm fine, I just..." I said, and then stopped. I didn't want to talk about it.

Mrs. Cooper must have known not to press the subject. "Have you eaten?" she asked. But before I could reply, she turned and yelled over her shoulder, "John, set Ozzie a plate."

I walked into the house, took off my shoes, and went and sat down at the table.

"Hey, Ozman," Jake greeted me.

"Hey, pal."

"I hope you brought your appetite. We're having my mom's famous roast beef."

It smelt fantastic. During dinner we talked about baseball and the Cooper's didn't mention anything about my unexpected visit. Their home was a place where I always felt welcome...no matter what.

After dinner, Jake and I went into the basement to play some *Major League Baseball featuring Ken Griffey Jr.* on his Nintendo 64. We just called it "Griffey," as in, "Want to go play some Griffey?"

When we were downstairs, I told him that my father and I had a fight and I told Jake what it was all about.

"Wait, wait, wait. Back up, back up. You were in the

backyard kissing Liz?"

"I was. I think I'm falling for her, man."

"I fell for her a long time ago," Jake said.

"No, but I mean...I think I am really in love with her."

"Are you not listening to me? I am *really* in love with her."

I punched him in the arm. "Shut up, man."

"See! Look at that smile. I cheered you up, didn't I? I still love her though," he said laughing.

Jake could always cheer me up. He was so sarcastic and said ridiculous things all the time. Sometimes it was hard to know when he was joking or not, especially for people that just met him. But since I've known him so long, I could tell when he was sarcastic and when he was not. He could always lighten the mood and he even made adults laugh. He taught me it's important not to be so serious all the time. I should have learned a lot more from him.

Jake and I played video games for awhile until I had to go home. When I went home, my father was in his usual spot in the living room with a beer in his hand. I walked on past without saying anything and went to the backyard. I spent the next couple hours hitting off the tee and swinging my heavy bats until I stopped thinking about what my father said earlier, and I was completely exhausted.

I knew that no matter what happened, tomorrow would be a new day and things would most likely go on as usual. My father was always someone I looked up to and trusted, but he was starting to piss me off. It's hard to say if it was because I was a teenager, or because I was starting to realize, that maybe, he didn't always have my best interest in mind. I still loved him and I still trusted him, but after that night, I started to have my doubts. It was clear that my relationship with Elizabeth started to create a wedge between my father and I.

I was only fifteen years old and I already had to decide what was more important to me: love or baseball?

Chapter 28

Grade ten was a lot different for me than the year before. It was only a year difference, but I felt so much older, and life was on its way to becoming more complicated. Most of all, I was changing. I was gaining even more attention at school from the way I performed on the field; I had better grades; and I was with the most beautiful girl in the school. I didn't need attention from groupie-type girls like Carrie, Sydney, and Vanessa anymore—even though this didn't stop some girls from trying to lure me away from Elizabeth. But my focus was always on Elizabeth. She continued to blossom every year and was truly heart-stopping. I didn't want anyone else.

Whenever Elizabeth walked into a room, you could see people do double takes all over the place. People would be writing in their books, or reading, and when Elizabeth walked in, they would look up real quick, then back down, then back up again, and their eyes would follow her wherever she ended up. If she happened to look their way, they would quickly avert their eyes, and their face would be red because they had been caught staring. I know all of this because I used to be one of these people. But now I was walking right beside her most of the time. Somehow she was mine, and I couldn't help but thinking how lucky I was.

She was smart, beautiful, and understanding. She was always positive and had this amazing outlook on life. She knew things that most people our age did not. I loved watching her speak.

Her eyes would light up and she would smile while she spoke, which captivated anyone who was listening. She worked hard at whatever she did, and she was always there to help others. Just being with her made me a better person. How could I not love her?

I must admit that when I "should" have been thinking about baseball, I was thinking of her. I was scared of losing her. I often thought about what would happen if she did have to move again? I could not imagine losing her. But we talked a number times about how we would eventually go our separate ways. In a way, she was the perfect person for me; she couldn't get too close, so it wouldn't be that hard to leave her behind someday— at least that's what I told myself. But deep down I knew I loved her and I knew I would never want to let her go.

Sometimes I would try and talk to my father about Elizabeth. But he never gave me the advice I wanted. When I would come home upset or try to talk to him about relationships, all he would say was, "Remember, Son, you can't bring her with you, to where you're headed." I understood this for everyone else, but not Elizabeth.

One night I asked him why I couldn't bring her with me once I got drafted. He told me that she would only make me distracted and lose focus on my goals. He even said that I would get soft and weak, and this was something I could not afford to do if I was going to make it in the big leagues. I tried to tell him that Elizabeth actually made me feel stronger and that she supported me. He told me that this was only a false sense of strength. He said it was a weak strength. *Weak strength?*, I thought. *What the hell is weak strength?* Sometimes I wondered where he came up with these things. When I got older, I realized he was trying in his own way to protect me from the hurt he felt when he left baseball and when my mother left him. He tried to do it through the only way he knew how. He tried to make me the person that he wanted to be. The person who he thought he wanted to be.

What he didn't realize is that there was no better motivation in the world to pursue my dream, work hard, be my best self, than for Elizabeth. I wanted do what I could to be good enough for her. I was still motivated by my father, but Elizabeth's impact on my motivation was even greater. I wish my father understood this. And maybe he did. Maybe he was too afraid to admit it. Maybe he was afraid of losing me. Maybe he was afraid of losing his purpose.

Chapter 29

My sophomore year flew by. I was excited for the new ball season in the spring, but when it came along, our team wasn't as good as it was the previous year. The season before, we had a lot of players who focused on partying and girls, but they also had a lot of talent. When we lost those guys when they graduated, I thought a lot of the juniors would step up and we would have a better team, but I was wrong. My new team worked harder in general, but they just didn't have it. Hard work can only take you so far.

I didn't let being on a losing team discourage me, however. With the lack of pitching we had, I ended up pitching quite a bit that season. In the first half of the season I was 5-1 as a pitcher. My father didn't let me focus on pitching at home, but he was okay with me getting some innings in on the mound during games. He explained to me that it would help me understand hitting on a deeper level. By being a pitcher, I could see where hitters hit certain pitches, and I would have more insight into how pitchers pitched, and what their patterns might be. It was another way to ultimately improve my game as a shortstop and as a hitter. And honestly, pitching was a lot of fun.

Pitching was something I did when I was younger, but most of the time I got up there and threw as hard as I could. Since I was throwing much harder than most players my age, I was able to be successful with little effort. But in high school, there was more talent and hitters could hit. I became good at switching speeds—I used the curveball my grandfather Shaw taught me (the best damn hook you ever saw), and a circle changeup to get hitters out.

Also, when I would watch baseball on TV, I would study what the pitchers threw, how they threw, and what they threw in certain counts. I would then take this information and use it the next time I pitched. I improved greatly, and I ended up getting four wins in a row and I finished the season 9-1 as pitcher. I had a pretty solid record and I could have probably been drafted as a pitcher if I wanted to. But I didn't want to give up hitting. In high school, as a pitcher, you are still able to hit, so I didn't have to worry about missing out doing the thing I loved the most about baseball. Ultimately, as much as I enjoyed pitching, I knew I was destine to be a shortstop—it was in my namesake.

As for hitting, I was doing nothing but improving. I set another school record with 12 home runs and 52 RBIs, and that would be the peak in my four seasons with Rock Bridge. After that season, I wasn't seeing as many good pitches. My name had spread around the league, and pitchers started to pitch around me. The only good thing about being walked so much is that I would break the school record for stolen bases. I was going to be a threat no matter what.

That season we struggled to hit the ball, and when I wasn't pitching we lost a lot of games. We finished third in our division, but I knew we would improve significantly my junior year.

My sophomore year we may not have been the best team, but Elizabeth came to every home game, and her, and a few of her friends would travel together when we were on the road. Having her there to watch me was one of the best things about playing baseball. Every play I made, every pitch I threw, and every at bat was for her.

Chapter 30

My junior year was probably one of the best years of my life. The pressure had not reached its peak yet, and I was playing great baseball on a championship caliber team. For the first time Aaron, Jake, and I were on the same team. We had so much fun together. We trained hard, we played hard, and we won a lot of games. When you win playing baseball, everything in life seems better. It felt like my life was on the right track. I continued to grow taller and stronger, and I was developing my game to new levels. No longer was I simply the wonder boy—I was on my way to becoming a man.

The team we had in my junior year was something special. Aaron was one of the best offensive and defensive catcher's in the district. He was quick, had a strong arm, and could block anything. It makes a huge difference when a catcher isn't afraid to call a pitch in the dirt with runners on base—especially in scoring position—but Aaron would, because more often than not, he would block the ball. He practiced blocking the ball relentlessly and he took a beating in the process.

Aaron would also practice flipping through pitch signs with his fingers anytime he wasn't playing baseball. He would constantly be flipping through signs while he drove, during a movie, or while we sat at a restaurant. He made it a habit and it became a part of him.

But one thing that could not be taught or practiced was Aaron's ability to call the game. The coaches and pitchers completely trusted Aaron. He had a phenomenal memory and he knew what to throw each batter. Aaron would call the game, and we would win. He was a great team leader.

One of the best things about that team my junior year, was Jake being there. He played second base most of the season, and him and I became a great pair. We knew what each other could do, where each other would be, and this made us probably the best shortstop and second base combinations in the league. Jake didn't have the strongest arm, but at second base that didn't matter as much. Him and I turned some of the nicest plays up the middle, and it was the best feeling to have him there with me.

Jake didn't hit with power, but he would hit everything. Even the fastest and best pitchers rarely put anything past him. He might end up grounding out or popping-up, but he took pride in knowing that not many pitchers could strike him out.

We also had Troy Abernathy, a senior that grew four inches in the offseason, who became our ace. He was also a solid outfielder. He would go on to set the school record for most wins, most innings pitched, and most strikeouts. He was an all-state pitcher that would go on to play Division 1 ball at the University of Mississippi.

Jason Morrison was our second pitcher in the rotation—who also became an all-state pitcher that year. He too went on to play Division 1 baseball, but he stayed right at home in Columbia and went to the University of Missouri.

With those two guys in our rotation, we were a hard team to beat. We had the pitching, the defense, and we could hit. It didn't take us long to become the number one ranked team in the state. With all our talent, scouts were at a lot of our games, and they had a plethora of players to watch. We were winners and everybody knew it.

Coach Gilmour had three seasons under his belt at Rock Bridge, and we were all comfortable with him, especially me.

This was my third year playing for him, and I couldn't have asked for a better coach. He developed our team into champions, and built a very successful baseball program at Rock Bridge. He was able to deal with a bunch of talented players, pressure from scouts and recruiters, and keep the team focused on winning. He was a big part of why we were successful that year.

We started the season off with seven straight wins and it felt like we would never lose. We were just too good. We destroyed other teams in Columbia that were our rivals. We beat the Battle Spartans high school 10-1 and I went 4-4 that day. Then we beat the Hickman Kewpies 9-0, and I was 2-2 with two home runs, and I was walked my last 3 at bats.

We didn't get our first loss until we faced the Liberty North Eagles in a non-conference away game. It was a pitching duel that we ended up losing 1-0. We couldn't buy a hit that day. Their pitcher threw a complete game one-hitter. We probably had a better team, but their pitcher had everything working for him. It happens.

That game didn't stop our roll as we beat the Kearney Bulldogs 13-1 in our next game.

When we didn't have games, I practiced a lot with Jake and Aaron. My father and I didn't spend as much time training together. I took everything he taught me and I was doing a lot on my own. My father still threw me BP when I was at home, but he wasn't pushing me as hard, simply because I was already pushing myself. He just didn't have the need to push me anymore. But I think the more I was off doing my own thing—and the less I needed him—the lonelier he became, and the more he drank.

Sometimes he would show up to my games clearly drunk, and other times he wouldn't even make it at all. I would come home after my game and he would be passed out in his chair. It made me feel like he didn't care anymore. It hurt.

LOVE OR BASEBALL?

Outside of baseball, I found myself spending more time over at Elizabeth's house, Jake's house, or Aaron's house. In a way, my father was becoming the distraction.

Chapter 31

As a junior, I started to receive letters and calls from college recruiters—more than a year before I would graduate.

When I first started to get these letters and calls, I was excited. But that did not last long. My father quickly reminded me that college was not a part of the plan. Even though he took most of the excitement out of these letters, it still felt like I was closer to my dreams, and it was a great feeling to know that I was wanted by so many people. I felt like those letters were a testament to my talent and my potential. And they made me feel better about working so hard and focusing so much on baseball. Still, every time a letter came to the house or a phone call came in from a college, my father would simply throw out the letter and hang up the phone. I never even got a chance to read any letters or talk to any of those recruiters to see what they had to offer.

I think this made colleges try harder to get my attention. They started to show up at our home, only to have my father tell them, "We aren't interested!" followed by the slamming of the door. Eventually, they knew better not to come to my home and they found other means to try and get my attention. They would send letters to Coach Gilmour and he would have a stack for me in his office. But I knew better, and I threw them away after he gave them to me.

Schools also did their homework. Elizabeth started getting letters of her own—recruiting her for tennis—but some of them offered to bring us both out as a packaged deal. Elizabeth thought this was a great idea and she often tried to convince me to go to college with her. A part of me wanted to, but I often thought about my father and mother, and I didn't want to make the same mistake my father had made. I was amazingly stubborn, but who could blame me? Ever since I was born, my father instilled in me that I was to train to make it into the major leagues, and nothing else mattered. There was no way that I was going to spend four years in college. But my mind was constantly on Elizabeth. The battle of deciding what to do was weighing me down and it wasn't getting any easier.

I couldn't talk to my father about anything, and with his increase in drinking, I didn't like being at home. Between the Fielder, Cooper, and Ackerman households, I had a sense of what a normal life could offer. However, I knew that normal didn't usually lead to greatness. My circumstances were out of the ordinary, and they had to be in order for me to pursue my dream. Yet, I wanted to be with Elizabeth. But whenever I had an off game, my father blamed her, and I think a part of me did too.

Before a practice, while Aaron and I were getting ready, I asked him for his advice. I looked up to Aaron. He was only one year older than me, but he was always like the older brother I never had.

"Hey, man," I said. "Can I ask you something?"

"Maybe," he laughed. "What's it about?"

"Elizabeth. College. The Show. What I should do."

"Shit. Pretty heavy stuff for a Tuesday afternoon."

"Seriously, man. I don't know what to do. It's stressing me out."

"What are you stressed about?"

"My father keeps telling me that Elizabeth is getting in the way of my dream, and that I won't make it to the Show if I stay with her. And Elizabeth is trying to get me to go to college with her. I feel like I have to choose one or the other, and I don't know which one I should choose."

"You're going to make it to the Show, either way," Aaron said reassuringly.

"And what about Elizabeth?" I asked

"What about her?" he replied.

"Is she going to come with me?"

"Do you want her to?"

"I don't know...I love her. At least I think I do. But my dad keeps saying that she is a distraction and that she will make me unfocused and weak."

Aaron pulled a can of chew from his back pocket, snapped it a few times, opened the lid, smelt it, took a large pinch, and put it in his bottom left lip. "Unfocused on what?"

"On making it to the majors."

"I already told you that you're going to make it. Look how good you are and look at all the schools that want you already, and all the scouts that come to our games. You've been with Elizabeth for two years now. Did she make you unfocused and weak?"

"I don't think so. But what if I could have been even better without her?"

"And would that make you happier? Would you have rather been alone the last two years just focusing on baseball?...Did you ever think that maybe you would have been worse off without her, and you are better with her in your life?"

"No, I haven't. My...my dad just always makes me think that she is holding me back from the player that I could be."

"She's not going to hold you back."

"How can you be so sure?"

"Cause she won't hold you back unless you let her. She loves you, man. She has been nothing but supportive. Maybe it doesn't have to be one or the other. Maybe you get drafted, follow your dream, like you were planning to all along, and just bring

Elizabeth with you."

"What if I hold her back? Is that fair?"

"That's a tougher one. I guess you will just have to talk to her about it and see what's more important. Your career or hers."

"Yeah. You're probably right. She has a history of moving around a lot, though, and I get the feeling it is taking a toll on her. A part of me doesn't want her to have to move around following me in my career, just like she had to follow her father."

"You're reading into things too much. Shit, maybe your dad was right, maybe she does make you unfocused. " He punched me in the arm, spit a large brownish gob of tobacco juice between his legs, and stood up. "Let's go get refocused."

We both got up and made our way to the field.

Aaron was right. I was reading into things too much. Elizabeth made me happy and so did baseball. Why couldn't I have both? If Elizabeth wanted to go to college, I could go there with her, play my four years, and get drafted from there. Or if she wanted to come with me when I got drafted out of high school, then I would let her do that. No matter what I chose to do, Elizabeth would be with me. I was not going to make the same mistake as my father, but I was still going to choose love and baseball.

Chapter 32

Our team continued to go through the schedule as if we couldn't be beat. We had a couple tough loses, but they were usually close, or happened when we gave our top pitchers a break during less important games.

Everyone was excited for the playoffs, and the buzz going around school and in the newspapers was that we were on our way to the state championship. A lot of people believed in us that year.

One thing that's challenging about having such a good team is that there is a great deal of pressure to win. The other teams we faced had nothing to lose, whereas we had everything to lose, and many people were waiting for that underdog team to upset us. But the further we went in playoffs, the better we played.

The first stop was the district tournament and we breezed through the competition. We went undefeated and took the district title against the Holt Rams by winning the final game 8-2.

In the state championship tournament, we were playing against some of the top teams that we hadn't seen before. That was going to be our biggest challenge.

We ended up winning our first game 2-1, but our offense was finally shut down for the first time in a long time. We ended up scoring the winning run in the 7th inning, on a double from Aaron that knocked me home from second base. We were so close to going home, but we managed to pull it off.

It wasn't until the next game that we were back to being more patient at the plate, and having better at-bats. We made pitchers work for their outs, and our bats lit up again.

We won the quarter finals 9-2 against the Kickapoo Chiefs. In the semi-finals we faced the Staley Falcons. Jason Morrison got hit around in the first two innings, but eventually battled back. He threw an outstanding complete game, including an extra inning, and we won 8-7 in the 8th inning. It was a hard fought battle, but we had made it to the state championship, against the Francis Howell Vikings.

With Troy—one of the best pitchers in the state—starting the game, we knew there was a good chance we were going to win. The only concern was if he could go the distance, since he had pitched so many innings already that season. But Troy was always ready to compete. He would sacrifice his arm for the team if he believed it would get us a state championship. That's the type of player he was. He was a winner.

With home runs by Aaron and I in the 2nd inning, we gave Troy a 3-0 lead early on. From there Troy threw a complete game, two-hit performance. He only gave up one unearned run and we won the game 7-1.

In the bottom of the 7th inning, Troy got two outs right away on a strike out, and an easy ground ball to Jake. The next hitter singled, but we still had a comfortable lead. The fourth batter of the inning battled Troy to a 3-2 count and he popped up on a changeup down in the zone. The ball sailed into the air between third and second, and I knew as soon as the ball came off the bat, that we were state champions. I camped under the ball and it landed in my glove. As soon as I caught the ball, my whole team rushed towards me, they threw off their gloves, and we jumped for joy in one big circle that eventually ended up in one big pile.

We dominated that game like we had done all season. It was a great feeling, and I could not have been surrounded by a better group of teammates.

We were presented with the trophy, and after some pictures were taken, the celebrations continued. After we finally gathered ourselves to continue the celebration in the locker room, I went and picked up my glove. In it was the ball I caught to win the state championship. I took it out, looked at it, and smiled. As good as I played, I knew it didn't belong to me. I made my way to the locker room, walked up to Troy, and handed him the ball.

"Hey, man," I said. "Here's the game ball. You won us this championship."

"Thanks, Oz," he said, and gave me a big hug. Then he went over and cheered with the rest of the team that were screaming and spraying water and pop everywhere.

Troy was the ultimate team player. I could have learned a lot from him about being a leader, and winning, no matter the cost. Instead, I handed him that ball because I felt it was beneath me to hold on to it. My goal was to make it to major leagues, and to me, a high school championship didn't matter. It did feel good when we won, but that didn't last. I had to focus on what was next for me.

My teammates were champions and they acted like any other championship team would. People were talking about parties afterwards and where they were going to celebrate. I sat there thinking that this would be the pinnacle of the baseball career for many players on that team. But I knew this was only something small for me in the grand scheme of things. It didn't matter much to me. I didn't feel like a champion.

I packed up my gear, and left the locker room, hoping no one would notice.

Chapter 33

When I walked out, Elizabeth was out there waiting for me. She ran up to me, wrapped her arms around me, and kissed me.

"Congratulations, babe! You did it!" she said. She looked around and asked, "Where's the rest of your team?"

"They are still celebrating and making plans for the night."

"Well, what are you doing out here? Shouldn't you be with your team?"

"This was just a high school championship...it means nothing," I said.

Elizabeth had a look of disappointment on her face. "Ozzie, this is a big deal. You guys worked hard as a team and you are the best team in the state. *You* may go on to bigger things, but you need to be there with your team. You need to live in the moment. It should mean something to you, that it means something to them. You need to go back in there with them. I will wait for you. Go find out where everyone is going tonight and we will both go celebrate with them, together."

Like always she knew something that I did not. She knew that it was important for me to celebrate with my team and my friends that I grew up with.

I went back to join my team. That night we went out and talked about all the plays and favorite moments we had that season, and we gave each other so many high fives. It was good to bond with my team and share so many happy moments with them. Many of these guys I would never see again, but I will never forget them and what we accomplished that year.

That team we had when I was a junior, was the most talented group I had in my high school years. We had four players from that team that made it all-state including Aaron and I and two of our pitchers—Troy Abernathy and Jason Morrison. We also had Jake, who was a solid day in and day out, and could play anywhere. He was above average, but just based on his size, he would never be considered great. Either way, it meant a lot to have my best friend there with me.

I remember feeling sad knowing that this would be the last year I would play with Aaron. He played a major role in my life the past three years and I was going to miss him. I felt like I was losing a brother. But I had to remind myself, he couldn't go where I was headed anyway.

The night we won the state championship, Elizabeth taught me how important it is to celebrate all the accomplishments you achieve in your life—even if they don't seem that significant at the time. That was one of the many lessons I would learn from her; but I did not realize the importance until later in life—when I happened to lose everything that once mattered to me.

Looking back now, I realize how right she was. I could not imagine not having the memory of winning that high school championship and not being there to celebrate with my teammates. It is one of the best memories that I still look back on today.

Without Elizabeth, I would have missed out on so much in life.

Chapter 34

After the high school baseball season was over, there was this war going on inside me, and at times it was hard to tell who was winning. My father would bombard me with the idea that I was going to get drafted, go into the major leagues, and have a great life. He would continue to constantly remind me that no one could go where I was headed. But, then there was Elizabeth. She was so loving, and everyday my love for her grew stronger. She would do things that would only bring us closer.

For my seventeenth birthday, she bought me a ticket to the Cardinals versus the Montreal Expos in St. Louis that June. It was the greatest gift that anyone had ever given me. It was so thoughtful of her. She wrote in the card:

> *Happy Birthday my Wizzy! Ha Ha*
> *Now you can see the Cardinals play in person*
> *and watch the team your father was once drafted by.*
>
> *I hope you have a wonderful day, and I look forward*
> *to sharing many more years with you.*
>
> *Love,*
> *Liz.*

My first trip to go to a St. Louis Cardinals game was special in so many ways. Elizabeth got permission from her parents to spend the night in St. Louis. Her argument was that she didn't want to drive home at night after the game. Her parents agreed, but said we had to sleep in separate beds. They probably knew we wouldn't, but they were still good parents, and at least made the attempt. I told my father that Elizabeth bought me a ticket to watch the Cardinals play the Expos, and that we were spending the night. My father didn't say much about it, so I just assumed I had his permission to go.

Elizabeth had another surprise for me, but she didn't tell me until we got to St. Louis. We checked into the Sheraton Westport Plaza, which was a really nice hotel. It was around twenty miles away from the stadium, but she chose it for a reason. After we checked in and settled in the room, we went down to get something to eat at the hotel restaurant before we were off to the game, and there it was: Ozzie Smith's sports bar and grill. Not only was she taking me to my first Cardinals game, she made it more special by choosing a game against the Expos, and she went out of her way to find Ozzie Smith's restaurant, which I didn't even know existed. It was clear that she cared and loved me more than anyone else in my life.

When we went down to the restaurant, I stood and marveled at all the Cardinals memorabilia, but, what caught my attention most of all, were Ozzie Smith's thirteen Gold Gloves that were there on display in a big glass case. A feeling of awe swept over me, followed by an eagerness to win one of my own someday.

We finally got to our table, but I still found myself looking around the restaurant. Elizabeth just sat there with this little smile on her face. She was completely happy, that I was so happy. That's all she ever wanted. I looked at her as if I was seeing her for the first time. *How can a person be so loving?* I thought. At that moment, I loved her more than anything.

"I love you, Liz. This is the nicest thing anyone has ever done for me."

That was the first time I said I loved her and I meant it with all of my heart.

"I love you too, Ozzie," she said, and smiled even bigger.

We were officially in love, and I couldn't help but feeling that I was the luckiest person in the world.

After our meal, we asked the front desk to call us a cab to take us to Busch Stadium. We headed there nice and early so we could take in the entire experience of going to our first major league baseball game together. If you have never been to a major league baseball game in your life, and you pull up to a stadium for the first time, it's hard to explain—especially when you are a kid playing at ball parks that only hold a couple thousand people. Pulling up to Busch Stadium for the first time felt like the equivalent of pulling up to something similar to the Roman Coliseum; it felt like I was in the center of the universe.

We got out of the cab, and I just stopped and stared. "This is where the Cardinals play?" I said, not really asking anybody.

"It's huge!" Elizabeth added.

We slowly walked up, and there were people with Cardinals jerseys, shirts, and hats walking towards the stadium. Some venders were selling water, peanuts, and cracker jacks. I've heard the song "Take Me Out To The Ball Game" many times, but it was funny to me to actually see those things from the song, first hand.

We strolled around the building and I walked up to the statues of all the legendary Cardinals players, and I read the plaques on each one. I stopped and stared at Ozzie Smith—who was frozen in time as he was making a diving catch—and I thought: *Maybe I would be out here someday?*

As soon as we walked in through the gates, I walked straight through the concourse to get a glimpse of the field. What I saw was hard to comprehend. Everything looked perfect—as if it was divinely created—with the seats, the rows, the fences; the field with its flawless lines; and the greenest turf I had ever seen. It was the biggest baseball stage I had ever laid my eyes on, and it's hard to believe, even to this day, that the field was no bigger than the ones I played on in high school. It's the entire surrounding and the environment of the stadium that's larger than life, and you can't help but thinking, "This is the Show."

We went and found our seats that were about twenty rows off to the right, behind home plate. I was excited to be close enough to see everything. We were there early enough that we got to watch some of the players take batting practice. That was something else. You see all the players that you recognize on TV, and it's almost disappointing when you see them get ready for the game. You see these major league baseball players stretching, playing catch, and warming up, and you realize for the first time that these people that you always thought were superheroes, are actually human. You see them stretching like you stretch, playing catch like you play catch, and running sprints like you run sprints. You start to think, "I can do that. I could play here." And for me, I was thinking: *I will play here.*

But then something happens when you watch certain players take BP. It looks different, it sounds different, and it feels different. Everyone around stops what they are doing and watches that player hit, and you are completely awestruck. Then you realize, "Maybe I can't do that."

After BP, when the grounds crew came out to get everything all set up for the game, Elizabeth and I went and walked around the stadium. We went to the team shop and Elizabeth bought a white and red Cardinals shirt and a red hat. I was already wearing my Cardinals jersey and Cardinals hat, but with Elizabeth's new purchases, we were now the perfect Cardinals couple. She never looked so beautiful.

The closer it was to game time, the more people started to pour in. I've never seen so many people in my life, and they were mostly all Cardinals fans. I was surrounded by red and white. This is where I belonged.

When the game started, I soaked in the experience. When

you sit behind the plate, you can see the pitchers throw 100 MPH; you see the off speed stuff; and you see the movement. You see hard shots come off the bat and you see fielders make the play like they have a few thousand times before, and it all looks so easy. The game looks easy. I tried to notice every detail. I watched what the players did in the field; I watched their pre-pitch routine; I watched what they did on the on-deck circle; I watched how they behaved in the dugout; I watched the coaches give signs at third base; and I predicted pitches. I pointed out all these little things excitingly to Elizabeth. Even though I was there for fun, it was still a part of my training. Elizabeth sat there and clutched my arm and seemed to watch me with a smile on her face, more than she did the game.

The cheers were loud when the Cardinals did something right, and the boos for the other team, or the ump, were equally as loud. You could feel the collective nature of the entire stadium filled with over forty thousand people. It was a remarkable experience. *How can this not be more than a game?* I wondered.

The Cardinals won the game 6-5 in the bottom of the ninth on a two out double to right field. It was an incredible game, but I remember being happy just to experience it with Elizabeth. She made everything so much more enjoyable.

After the game, we went back to the hotel and I was on cloud nine. This was the best night of my life, and it only got better.

So far that day I told Elizabeth I loved her for the first time, I went to my first Cardinals game, and that night, we had sex for the first time. When we got back to the hotel room, we kissed, slowly undressed each other, and made love. We weren't nervous, we had no doubts, and it felt like our love for each other guided us that night.

We spent the night in bed together with our Cardinals gear in small scattered piles on the floor. Eventually she fell asleep on my chest and I held her. I was completely content until I dozed off. It was a perfect night of love and baseball.

The next day I woke up and my life felt different. I felt even closer to Elizabeth. She meant the world to me. She was still sleeping, and like they often say, she looked like an angel while she was asleep. In that moment, I was perfectly happy. I didn't need anything else—not even baseball. And you know what? That didn't bother me. I wasn't afraid. All I knew was that I wanted to be with her. That's the only place I needed to be.

When she woke up, she looked at me, smiled, and whispered, "Good morning."

"Good morning," I said smiling back. But I must have had a weird look on my face.

"What?" she asked.

"Nothing?"

"What's the big smile for?"

"I'm just happy, I guess." I moved in and kissed her.

On the drive home, I felt like Elizabeth was meant to be in my life forever.

But, sadly, I have never felt that feeling I had that morning, ever again. I guess I was never completely content and happy—like I was on that first trip to St. Louis.

Chapter 35

In August of 1999, I started my senior year of high school. It was a big year for me in all areas of my life. Elizabeth was starting to win the fight to become my top priority. Consequently, I was forced to make some of the toughest decisions of my life that year. There was so much going on that I never had time to stop and take it all in. This would happen more often the older I became.

That year, Aaron had gone off to college, and Jake took over Aaron's role of guiding me and giving me advice. Elizabeth was now a woman, and I fell deeper in love with her. My father and I got in arguments more often, because he started to realize that Elizabeth was having the same impact on me, that my mother once had on him. I was almost an adult now, and I felt I could make my own decisions. That didn't stop him from trying his best to convince me to keep my eye on the prize—the prize being a career in the major leagues.

As much as my father tried to remind me that Elizabeth could not go where I was headed, he still did things that surprised me. I think he also had a battle going on inside of him. This became apparent around Christmas time of my senior year.

Elizabeth had given me so much during our relationship. Her parents were well off and she was able to afford things that I could not. She spoiled me and I was starting to feel bad about not being able to give her much in return. I wasn't allowed to work, so I had to rely on my father to give me money for whatever I needed. But when it came to gifts for Elizabeth, it was tough for me to ask my father for money. I knew that he would ask what the money was for, and I thought that if he knew I was using it to buy a Christmas gift for Elizabeth, he wouldn't give me the money. I believed he would never help me with my relationship with Elizabeth. But I was wrong.

One night, around a week before Christmas, I finally worked up the courage to talk to him. I walked into the living room and sat down on the couch.

"Pop, I need to talk to you."

"What is it?" he said dismissively.

"I need to get Liz a Christmas present, and I have no money, and I have no idea what to get her."

He looked at me, then looked back at the TV. That made me angry. I thought he was ignoring me. Suddenly he got up and walked to his room. He came back out and tossed me a little box shaped gift, that was wrapped in shiny red wrapping paper.

"Just give her that," he said, and sat back down in his chair.

I was dumbfounded. *Where did he get this from?* I wondered.

"Pop, what is it?"

"It's a pair of diamond earrings I bought your mother for her birthday. She left before I could give them to her."

"I can't give Liz a gift that was meant for mom."

"Why the hell not?" he asked. "They are worth far more than anything you can afford right now, and they have been sitting in my room all these years. They will look beautiful on her. Trust me."

In that moment, I realized that even when he wasn't the nicest person to my mother, and even during all the arguing before my mother left, my father still loved her so much.

"Thanks," I said. He gave me a nod without taking his eyes off of the TV. I got up and went to my room to open up the gift I was to give Elizabeth for Christmas.

I didn't know much about diamond earrings, or care that

much, but when I opened the box and saw the earrings, even to me, they were beautiful. I knew Elizabeth would love them. I just had to decide if I would tell her where I got them from.

It was a relief that I had a nice gift to give to Elizabeth. It felt good to know that I could give her something she deserved, but I felt guilty knowing the earrings were not exactly from me. I felt like I may have been taking the easy way out. I decided to get her something else as a backup plan. And once again, I was stressed about what I could get her on a limited budget.

But a great idea eventually came to me one night while I was hitting off the tee in my backward. I remembered something Elizabeth once told me when we first started dating. She told me about this one thing that her father and her used to do when they had to move around a lot when she was younger. Elizabeth and her father had this tradition where they would find a used book store in the town or city they moved to, and they would buy books together. They would try and find books that they had never heard of, and ones that caught their eye and seemed interesting. But even if those books happened to not be interesting, those books would at least have the story of where they came from. I thought it was sort of silly at the time when she told me, but as I was getting older, it made a lot of sense. In her room, she had a bookcase full of all these old books, and in a way, they told the story of her childhood.

The next day I was excited to head out on my new adventure. I looked up used book stores in Columbia, and found one downtown. When I got there, I didn't know where to start. I had never been in a book store before. It was a little overwhelming to see the thousands of books stacked on the shelves.

The lady working at the front desk asked if I needed any help. I told her I wanted to find a few interesting, old books, that were not necessarily the most popular, but something that someone might not know about. She sort of gave me a weird look, but pointed out the sections, and suggested I should look around and see whatever caught my eye. I made a mental note of where the sports section was, but wanted to find books for Elizabeth first. I was in there for almost an hour, wandering, pulling out random books, and wondering if Elizabeth would like them. Eventually I chose three books that I thought were the most interesting, and if they weren't, at least they had the story behind them. I took comfort in knowing it was a win-win situation.

After I found books for Elizabeth, I made my way to the sports section and took a quick look. Immediately a book caught my attention. It was *Wizard* by Ozzie Smith. I opened it up and there was a stamp from the St. Louis Public Library on the first page, and there was still a library card inside with a bunch of names and dates on it. I felt like this book was meant for me. Not only was it a book written by Ozzie Smith, but it was from St. Louis, and here I was buying it in a used book store in Columbia, MO. In a way, Elizabeth brought me to this book and I felt like I was destine to find it.

I brought my books up to the front, and I was shocked to find out all four books cost me less than twenty dollars—even less than what I budgeted for. I was all set for Christmas, and I even bought something for myself.

On Christmas Eve, I was invited to Elizabeth's house for dinner, just like I had been the last two years. Ever since my mother left, I had always spent Christmas with my father at home. It was always just him and I. My father would cook supper and we would just hang out. As much as I wanted to spend Christmas day with Elizabeth, I always vowed to never let my father spend Christmas alone.

At the Fielder's house on Christmas Eve, we had a nice dinner, and that night I gave Elizabeth the earrings. I remember watching her gently peel off the red wrapping paper that I rewrapped her gift in. I was still unsure if I was going to tell her that my father actually bought the earrings for my mother. Elizabeth opened the lid to the little box and her eyes lit up.

"Oh my god, Ozzie! They are so beautiful," she said. She was so excited I immediately felt guilty. "Ozzie, you shouldn't have!"

I could have easily said something like, "You deserve them," or something like that, but I had to tell her the truth.

"Well, Liz, I sort of didn't buy them—"

"What do you mean?" she asked concerned. "You didn't steal them did you?" she said jokingly.

"No, I didn't steal them, and I didn't buy them either. Liz, I wanted to get you something special, since you always spend so much money on me, but I had no money. I asked my father for money and he gave me these instead. My father bought them for my mother, and she left before he could give them to her. I can give them back to him if you don't want them," I said, and I felt bad. "It was stupid I know, I'm sorry, Liz, I—"

"It's okay, Oz. Do you not know what this means?"

"No?" I said, not sure what she was getting at.

"Your father telling you to give these to me means a lot. It's almost as if he is giving his blessing for us to be together. Of course I am going to keep them," she said, and looked back down at the earrings in her hand. "Plus, your father does have great taste!" she added, probably only half joking.

I wasn't sure what my father had intended when he gave me those earrings to give to Elizabeth, but maybe he *was* giving his blessing for us to be together. But I knew that was probably wishful thinking.

"I got something else for you too," I said handing her the heavier box of books. "These, I actually did pick out and buy myself."

"I was wondering what the extra gift was for," she said. "Now who is spoiling who?"

She unwrapped the second gift, opened the box, and pulled

out each book one by one and sifted through them.

"I remembered how you and your father would go to used book stores where ever you were, and I wasn't sure if you had gotten any books from Columbia yet. But now you do. I was in there for over an hour, and these are the ones I finally picked out."

"Ozzie, these are—" tears filled her eyes and she wiped them with the back of her hand. "This is the sweetest gift anyone has ever given me."

"Gee, for a second I thought you hated them."

"I love them, Ozzie. And I love you. You are the most thoughtful person in the world," she said, and she got on her knees, leaned over, and kissed me.

"Now it's your turn," she said handing me a small, rectangular-shaped gift wrapped in shiny blue wrapping paper.

I opened it up and it was one of those fuzzy jewellery boxes; similar to the one the diamond earrings came in. I opened the lid and there was a gold necklace with a gold baseball pendent, that had "#11" engraved in the middle of the baseball.

"Liz, this is awesome!" I said taking it out.

"Here, let me help you," she said. I handed it to her and she got up and went behind me, and put it around my neck. "Now you will always be number eleven, no matter what, Mr. Ozzie Shaw."

"Thanks, Liz. I love it," I said, holding it in my hand and looking down at it.

I still wear it to this day. The ironic thing about it, is that every time I look at it, it reminds me of how there is more to life than baseball.

We sat there basking in the happiness we were both feeling that Christmas Eve.

"Promise you won't tell anyone the real story where I got the earrings from?" I said, later that night.

"I promise," she said, and she leaned in and gave me a long

soft kiss to seal the deal.

"And, Liz, it's probably best you don't wear them around my father for awhile."

"Okay," she said, and I could tell she understood.

Looking back on this is painful, especially since it wasn't that long after, that my father told me I needed to break up with her.

Chapter 36

In the spring, my grades started to slip, and baseball once again became my main focus. I felt like I was so beyond high school. I had a cocky attitude that I carried with me until the end of the school year. Regardless of the influence Elizabeth had on me in the last couple years, I knew I was going to be drafted, and I just did not care about school anymore. And once my final season started, the real pressure began.

In my senior year I started using a wood bat full time—when I practiced and during games. Since there was a good chance that I wasn't going to go to college, I didn't think using a metal bat would be beneficial to me. Sure I could have hit more home runs, and maybe even contributed more to win games, but if I was going to be in the big leagues, I needed to learn how to hit with a wood bat, and show the scouts that I could. A few times I would break my bat during a game and some of my teammates would get pissed off because that could have been a hit if I used a metal bat. I may have been letting them down, but these high school games didn't matter to me. It was probably selfish, but I also felt it was necessary.

That season was a bit overwhelming for me. Scouts were coming more often than ever, and people started to recognize me around Columbia, and I was in the newspaper more often. Everyone seemed to know that I was something special, and they wanted to be a part of my journey to the major leagues. It was common for my teammates' parents, teachers, and even strangers to say: "Ozzie, if you need anything, anything at all, don't hesitate to ask." It was strange to me, but I always dismissively said, "Thanks," and walked on, knowing I didn't need help from anybody. The offers continued, nonetheless.

We lost a lot of talented players the season before, so we were not as good of a team as the previous year, but we still had a lot of pressure to continue to have a successful baseball season. But even when we were losing, I was drawing in most of the attention.

With the loss of Troy and Jason when they graduated, I was back to pitching more often at the beginning of the season, but my father put an end to that. This was my senior year, so my father said I had to choose if I was going to be a shortstop or a pitcher. I decided I would only pitch when my team really needed me, and I would only come in for an inning or two in relief. Truth be told, I didn't mind too much. As much as I liked to pitch and control the game, shortstop was still my position.

We started off the season with three straight wins, and then we lost five in a row. Our defense struggled, but it was mostly our pitching that couldn't keep the games close. Greg Wilcox was our third man in the rotation the year before, but was forced to move up to the number one spot this season. He threw hard, but was wild and flat. When he was "on" we had a chance to win, but when he wasn't, we struggled. To be honest, even though he was considered our "ace," I never liked the guy. He was lazy and his main priority was smoking pot. Eventually he got bumped down the rotation, and a junior named Kevin Jones stepped up and became our number one guy. Kevin was the opposite of Greg; he had great control, but didn't throw very hard. His success came with his curveball and his ability to hit the corners. Once we made the transition of putting him at the top of our rotation, we started to get back on track. But in high school, it is often the team with the best pitchers that win the most games.

At the beginning of April, the Jefferson City Jays were in town to face us. Their starting pitcher, Chris Kowalski, was one of the fastest pitchers in our division. He was clocked at 92 mph and some even said he had hit 95 mph a few times. That's the equivalent to some pitchers in the major leagues. Like many kids that could throw hard, he didn't always have control. That was an issue in itself and sometimes that led to his success. He didn't have great secondary pitches, but he had the intimidation factor working for him. Some of the players on my team were openly scared to stand in the box, and I don't blame them; I would have been too, if I didn't have a father that threw hard, and literally beaned the fear of being beaned out of me.

Elizabeth was at the game, and before the game started she came over to talk to me, and she heard Chris warming up on the other side of the field, "How is anyone going to hit that? It sounds like a gunshot. Aren't you scared?" she asked.

Great motivational speech there, babe, I thought.

"It's not that fast," I said, trying to act nonchalant. "Plus, the harder they throw, the further the ball goes when you hit it."

Every year, you learn about players like Chris pretty early on in the season. Word spreads amongst the teams: *"Did you hear the pitcher from the Jays throws 95?..."; "I heard he's fucking wild too..." ; "I heard he throws so hard that he broke some guys arm on a changeup..."*

And on it goes. Every season you would hear horror stories about pitchers like him, but the ones about Chris were actually true. Nonetheless, true or not, some guys that heard these stories were already defeated before they even got to the plate. When you faced pitchers like Chris, the first at bat was the most nerve wracking. You would stand up there and you didn't know if you were going to get the "Wild Chris" or the "In-Control Chris." You had to stand in there to find out for yourself.

Luckily, for our safety, but not for our chances to hit, on that day, we had the "In-Control Chris," and he mowed us down one-two-three. Our first two guys K'd, and I popped up in foul territory just beyond third base. I was ahead of it. I saw the ball well and I knew I would be able to hit him hard if he gave me a good pitch the next time I was up.

Chris continued to shut down our lineup. The next two innings were three up and three down, and in the first nine outs he had seven K's already. But in the fourth you could see he started to lose some control, and he walked the first batter. Our next hitter struck out, and I was up to bat with a man on first.

I dug in, and I was ready to hit. The first pitch was high and inside. I had a split second to move out of the way. This rattled me a bit. I doubt it was intentional since he walked our first guy, but you never know.

The next pitch was low and inside. He was definitely losing it, which was good, because I knew he had to come over the plate with one. The next pitch was right down the middle. It was all automatic from there. I swung and hit one hard over the center fielder's head. He was playing pretty shallow since he hadn't seen a ball all day; and anything that was hit, wasn't hit very far. Our guy that was on first scored and I managed to make it to third for a triple. We were up 1-0.

Our next two hitters got out, but they battled, and fouled off a bunch. They made Chris work and this tired him out. We knew their pitcher was not the same one that started the game.

That was the turning point. Chris started to get frustrated and the more frustrated he got, the harder he tried to throw; and the harder he tried to throw, the less control he had.

In the bottom of the inning, they ended up scoring a run on a sac fly to tie the game 1-1.

When Chris came out in the fifth, he was tired, and his control and speed both went downhill. He walked the first batter of the inning, and their coach came out and made a pitching change.

All game we were eager to hit, and when they made a pitching change, we saw that the new pitcher didn't throw as hard. Often a significant change in speeds can throw a team's timing off, but for us, it was right where we needed it to be. We welcomed the slower pitcher by putting another guy on base, and I hit a long home run to put us ahead 4-1. We ended up winning the game 5-2.

My father said I had a great game. He said I had good at bats and he could tell I was seeing the ball well. "You see how quick your hands are, Son? Doesn't that feel good to know you can hit major league speeds? If you keep working and keep getting stronger, you will be able to hit 100 mph, no problem."

It did feel good, and that was enough motivation I needed to keep working hard.

Speed doesn't always mean a pitcher will win games. Control and a good off-speed pitch is what separates a successful pitcher, from a pitcher that stands out simply because he throws hard. But Chris did nothing but improve the rest of the season, and he finished with an 11-1 record. We faced him again in the district tournament and he threw seven innings of shutout baseball. He was the star that game, but they only ended up getting a run on a passed ball, and they won the game 1-0. It could have been anyone's game that day, but Chris deserved the win.

We were still a great team, but Chris and the Jay's dominated the league, and proved it by eventually winning the state championship that year. He was the best pitcher I faced in high school. He had a lot of interest from major league teams, but he went on to play college ball at the University of Texas in Austin. I followed his career after high school, and he spent some time in the minors in the Toronto Blue Jays system after college, and they tried to make him a relief pitcher. He had a few injuries and his velocity slowly decreased. He never did make it to the Show.

After our first game against Chris, the next night the Cooper's had me over for supper. It was one of the last suppers I would have with the Cooper's while I was still in high school.

And it was one of the last normal things I did, before everything changed.

Chapter 37

As soon as Mrs. Cooper put the food on the table, I realized how much I missed having family suppers. I sure needed it. Thankfully, I could always feel at home with Jake and his family.

"That was quite the game you had last night, Ozzie," Mr. Cooper said. "That game winning home run you hit in the sixth, must have been one of the longest I had ever seen. I didn't think anyone could have hit one that far."

"Thanks," I said, and I couldn't hold back a smile even if I tried. "It sure felt good."

I never knew what to say when it came to accepting praise and I always felt embarrassed. In my mind I also thought, *that's what I am trained to do,* as if I was a robot or something. With the help of my father, a lot of the emotion was taken away from the game. But yet, I always felt a lot of pressure, because I didn't want to let everyone down. I knew I was good, but what if I wasn't good enough? Or what if I blew it somehow, then what would everyone say? He's just like everyone else? He is nothing special? I came here to watch this? These were all thoughts that I had in my mind the closer it was to draft day. I was just human after all, wasn't I? Maybe then, I was not a robot, maybe some of the joy for the game was lost. On the other hand, Jake had nothing but joy for the game.

"I sure wish I could hit like that," Jake said.

The table went silent. No one knew what to say for a moment.

"Not everyone can hit like that Jacob or else everyone would be in the major leagues. Some people are better at some things than others. That's life. But everyone is good at something. It doesn't have to be sports. Some people are good academically, some are good with their hands, some are good at being creative, and some are good at helping others. I am proud of you for the way you help Ozzie practice, and how you're there for him. You're a great friend Jacob," Mr. Cooper said.

"I wouldn't be where I am without you, Jake," I said, and I meant it.

Their whole family gave me a sense of belonging and a sense of a normal life. I owe a lot to them, and I vowed right then and there that I would pay them back some day. It was little things like feeding me and just letting me relax at their home that meant a lot to me.

"I can always come with you and help you practice next year," Jake said.

"You're going to college, Jacob," his father replied, before I could.

"I was only kidding. But wouldn't that be something, Oz?" Jake said.

"I would love to have you there, pal," I replied.

I knew that the minor leagues had their own training staff and I didn't think they would accept a tag-along. I knew he was just joking, but I think only half-joking. The Jake I knew, would come anywhere that close to the majors in a heartbeat.

There were so many people trying to get close to me and be my friend, because they knew I was going to the major leagues some day. Some just wanted to be a part of my journey, and I'm sure others wanted to act like my friend, in hopes that I would give them something when I became a rich baseball star. The Cooper family were one of the few families that truly cared about me. They didn't care if I made it or not, they just wanted me to be happy, and they just wanted me to be a good person.

Throughout my life, their support helped more than they will ever know.

After dinner, Jake and I went to his basement to watch baseball, and as it often did during the last few months of high school, the topic of my future came up. Without Aaron being around, I often turned to Jake for advice. Jake was an easy person to talk to. He was always positive and he could always cheer me up. Whenever I brought up the tough decisions I had to make, he told me exactly what I should do.

"Man, I didn't think it would be so hard to make decisions about the future. It was so much easier when we were younger, wasn't it?" I said, as we watched the game.

"What kind of decisions are you talking about? Your future's golden, bud."

"You don't understand. My life's pretty stressful."

"What are you talking about? You have the best life. Your dream is about to come true. When we were kids, all we ever talked about is making it to the Show, and pretty soon you're going to. How is that stressful?"

"I guess. But what should I do about Liz?"

"What do you mean?"

"Do I break up with her?"

"What are you talking about? Why would you break up with her? Are you drunk?"

"No, I am not drunk." I laughed. "My father says no one can go where I'm headed, not even Liz. And she wants me to go to college with her, so she can go to school and play tennis. Or she wants to come follow me around the minors."

"So you're not joking, and you're not drunk right now?"

"No, buddy, I'm not joking, and I'm not drunk."

"Well, what's gotten into you, man? It's simple. You should be with Elizabeth and play baseball. Having those two things in your life, Ozman, no matter where you end up, you will be happy...how could you not be? You're the most talented person

I know, and Liz is like the most beautiful girl...ever. And you two are perfect for each other. You're lucky, man. Never forget that," Jake said.

Everything was so simple to him. If he had my size, with his passion, we both would be going to the majors together. That's something I didn't want to lose sight of. I wanted to make it for guys like Jake; guys who loved the game so much, but just did not have the talent or the genes. As for Elizabeth, Jake couldn't believe I was even considering the idea of breaking up with her. But Jake didn't have to live with my father.

Looking back, it is amazing that the young people in my life were the ones that knew the most. They were wise beyond their years. I was lucky to have them in my life, but I wish I would have listened to them a lot more.

It was on nights like this during my senior year that I was excited to get drafted, but I was afraid to leave everyone behind. I had so many decisions to make, and it was hard to not get stressed about everything that was going on. I didn't want to lose Elizabeth and Jake.

I wished they could come with me to where I was headed.

Chapter 38

I haven't talked about him much, but Coach Gilmour and I had always got along well. He was a good coach, and he did everything he could for me. He wasn't an old and seasoned coach like so many schools had, and I could tell he was still learning. But he worked hard, and he knew how to win. Having a kid like me on the team put a lot of pressure on him. He had to deal with the media, college recruiters, scouts, and he had to make sure he did everything by the book. For an up and coming coach, this was a gift and a curse. There would be an eye on his program at all times because of me. Regardless, he was able to take it in stride. The first meeting we had as a team back in my freshman year, I remember him saying that his goal was to win games, and help us move on to the highest level we could play. It was never about him; it was always about his players. Coach pushed me in a different way than my father did. He guided me in the right direction, but often asked for my opinion, and tried to make sure that I was going to do what I wanted to do. But, that didn't matter. Because what I wanted to do, was what my father wanted me to do. Or so I thought.

In my senior year, coach Gilmour called me into his office one day. We were just over halfway through the season, and I was in the midst of one of the busiest and most stressful weeks of my life. I think he could tell that I was stressed and overwhelmed. I had been pestered by all types of recruiters, and everyone felt like they had to stop and talk to me everywhere I went. I also had where I was going on my mind, and the thought of those I had to leave behind was weighing me down.

I went into Coach's office and he told me to take a seat. I pulled out the chair in front of his desk and sat down. He just sat there for a second and looked at me. The little delay was enough to make me feel uncomfortable.

"How are you doing, Oz?"

"Fine," I said, not knowing what this was about.

Noticing that I was not going to do the talking, he started to speak.

"Listen, Oz. I know you are under a lot of pressure and I want to talk to you, and all I want you to do is listen. Things are going to be moving very fast for you in the next little while, and I bet it has already started. Soon you will be forced to make a lot of decisions that will impact your future. A lot of people are going to try and influence these decisions. This may sound a little scary, but it is the truth. I want you to understand, that it is *your* life, and it is up to *you* to decide what is best for you. I know your father is tough on you and has pushed you very hard, but you have to remember this is *your* life. You cannot make your decisions based only on what your father wants. He is a good man, and he wants the best for you, but what he thinks is best for you, might not be what is actually best for you. You understand?"

I nodded in agreement. I had never heard anyone else say that my father may be wrong, and I think I needed to hear it.

"*You* are the only person that can make the decision about what you are going to do. And Oz, you will also have to make a decision about Elizabeth. I know many schools have been sending her letters for tennis. But I have seen you two together, and you two are great for each other. I don't think I have ever seen a more talented and special couple. I know it will be hard to leave her behind, but that is something you will have to decide on your own. I don't want to get too involved, but I think you two should try and stay together for as long as you can."

He paused to make sure I heard what he said. "And that's all I have to say. If you ever want to talk, I am available any time. I want to let you know that I am in your corner whatever you decide to do."

I know he was being sincere, but I felt like he added to all of the pressure. And why did my coach bring up Elizabeth? I understood he would give me baseball advice, but relationship advice? What I didn't realize then, was that so many people saw that Elizabeth and I had something special. Yet, I was still concerned with what my father thought.

I left Coach Gilmour's office more overwhelmed. I had so many voices in my head that I could barely think. When I got overwhelmed, I would always try to go and hit, and that is what I did. I called up Jake and he met me at the field to come and throw to me. Hitting always took my mind off of everything. Hitting was my therapy. Hitting was what I loved to do—what I wanted to do.

Chapter 39

What was I going to do about Elizabeth? The plan all along was for us not to get too close, just in case she would have to pack up and move at any time. But we had been together for over three years, and now, I was the one that was going to leave.

I knew where my father stood; I had, *No one can go where you're headed,* engraved into my mind. But Jake, Aaron, and Coach Gilmour all seemed like they thought that Elizabeth and I should stay together no matter what. Most of all, I wanted Elizabeth to come with me. But I had my doubts—created by my father—that I didn't know if she should. What did Elizabeth want? This was something we had always avoided—our future.

One night in the midst of the season, Elizabeth and I got together and watched a movie at her house. We hadn't been hanging out as much because I was busy with baseball, and Elizabeth was studying a lot so she could get accepted to any school she wanted. But she already received so many offers for tennis, that her grades probably didn't matter. Elizabeth still took pride in her school work. I did the opposite; and it was unfortunate that a lot of the time, the attention was still put on me. She was just as, or even more deserving of praise from others, than I was.

I remember sitting there on the couch watching a movie with her and thinking about how grown up we had become from when we first met. I remember looking at her and wondering how she seemed to get more beautiful every year. I sat there and knew that I wanted to be with her forever.

I don't even remember what movie we were watching—we ended up talking through most of it. At one point she asked me, "Why do you love baseball so much?"

"Is that all you can talk about is baseball?" I joked.

"Shut up," she said, and nudged me with her elbow. "Seriously, I want to know. I give you permission to talk about baseball…just this once," she giggled.

"You give me permission, do you? I don't know. It's hard to explain."

"Just try. I'm curious."

"I don't know. I've never really thought about why I love baseball. I just do. It's something I have always done ever since I was a little kid. I think I've always loved the competition. Someone throws you a ball, and you have to hit it. Or someone throws you a ball, and you have to catch it. And if you do, people will compliment you for it. It's no different now that I'm older. I love when I am up to bat and it's me against the pitcher. I love the feeling when I hit the ball…I mean hit the ball as solid as I can, and everyone sees the ball fly, and they cheer. I love making plays in the infield that no one else can make. I love knowing that any ball hit near me, there is a good chance I will get to it, and throw the runner out. I like making things that are difficult for other players, look easy. But I also love the little things. I love going up to bat with a plan. I love picking up clues that might help me know what the pitcher is going to throw me. I love that every pitch, every at bat, and every little action can have a purpose," I said, and I looked away from Elizabeth for a moment to gather my thoughts. I looked back at her. "I guess most of all, it probably sounds corny, but I feel good out there. I feel like I have a purpose. I feel like I am special."

"No, it's not corny at all, Ozzie. You are special. There is a reason why so many people are talking about you. Why so many people come out to watch you play."

"Another thing, is that I don't think when I'm out there. I'm not worrying about anything at all. Not school, not my parents, not my future. Nothing else matters. It's so easy for me to get completely lost in the game."

"Do you think about me when you are out there?" she asked, but then quickly added, "Forget it, you don't have to answer that."

"It's okay, I can answer that. I do at times, yes. Not when I'm at bat, or when I am making a play. But when I'm in the dugout or I am standing at short, or on the on deck circle, I look up at you. I think about you. I probably shouldn't, but I do. I love having you there. Every time I look at you or think about you, I smile. There may be a bunch of people that come to watch me play, but you are the only one that matters to me. I want to make you proud. I want to do things so you will think, 'Did you see that? That's my boyfriend out there.' "

"You do make me proud, Oz."

I smiled. That's all I ever wanted to hear.

"I love you, Liz."

"I love you too, Oz."

"Liz, can I ask you something?...Never mind, it's stupid."

"Ask me! You know you can ask me anything."

"Fine. Liz, why do you love me?"

She didn't even bat an eye. "I love you because you are such a sweet person. I love the way you look at me. When you look at me, I can tell it's always with love in your eyes. You are talented, you work hard, and you have a lot of passion in your heart."

"What about times that I have let you down. Like when I had to practice instead of spending time with you."

"Sure it upset me a little. But I understand. I understand that if you had the choice you would be with me. I know you're doing what you feel is right, that's all."

She did understand me.

"All I want to do is be with you, Liz. Even when I'm stuck

167

training and working my ass off, I'm always thinking of you."

"I know you are."

We kissed. She was the only person I could talk to like this. We could completely open up to each other. We were completely in love.

What I didn't tell Elizabeth is that she was the one I played for. I wanted to be great at baseball, so I would feel worthy enough to be with her. If I wasn't a great ball player, or a great anything, I knew I wouldn't deserve someone like Elizabeth. It's the game that brought her into my life. If I didn't have the game, I wouldn't have her. It's true that I loved baseball and always would, but I worked hard and wanted to be the best for her. I never told her this, however. And I sure as hell wouldn't mention this to my father.

I left Elizabeth's house that night knowing that I wanted her to come with me after I got drafted.

When I got home, I walked in the front door and was headed to my room.

"Did you break up with that girlfriend of yours yet?" my father said, as I walked by the living room. I stopped to answer him.

"Nope, not yet."

"It'll be easier for both of you if you get it done sooner, rather than later, Son. Remember, no one can go where you're headed," he added as I walked to my room.

Just when I thought I had made up my mind, my father crept into my life, and was back to influencing the decision I had to make. Why couldn't he leave me alone? Or why couldn't he support my relationship with Elizabeth? I knew the answer to both of these questions—he didn't want me to make the same mistake he did.

Regrettably, he eventually got to me, and I started to push Elizabeth away.

Chapter 40

There was so much going on in my life during the last couple months of high school, that my brain was sort of in a fog. During this time, I started to treat Elizabeth the way my father once treated my mother. I didn't drink, and I wasn't aggressively mean, but I would shut down and emotionally distance myself from Elizabeth. I also did things that I am not proud of, and I wasn't there for her when she needed me.

The biggest turning point in our relationship happened on her 18th birthday. She wanted me to go out for supper with her and her family, but I had a game the next day, so my father wanted me to take some swings with him, and he made me stay home. As the draft approached, he was harder on me than ever, and it was difficult for me to say no to him. When I called her to explain why I couldn't be there on her birthday, she was just as understanding as she always was. So I thought.

"It's fine," she said, after I told her that my father was making me stay home.

"Are you sure?"

"You have a big game tomorrow so it makes sense you should go practice."

"You sure you're okay with it?"

"Yes, it's fine...go."

"Thanks, babe. I love you."

"I love you, too."

I loved her. I really did. I wanted to be there for her. But at that time, with the help of my father, I felt like I was doing the right thing. There was going to be many scouts at this game, and it could have a big impact on my future, and specifically, it could have an impact on the round I would be drafted in. Little did I know, if I went out with Elizabeth, it may have had a different kind of impact on my future. I may have had a different life. A happier life.

When I was in my room resting after my father and I finished hitting in my backyard, I felt bad for not being there for Elizabeth, but I couldn't help but thinking how amazing she was. She was always understanding, and she truly was supportive. What I didn't know is that it wasn't *fine* that I missed her birthday. I should have known better, but I didn't.

I called her later that night to apologize again for missing her birthday. I was surprised to hear she was very upset.

"Hey, Liz," I said when she answered the phone. "I hope you had a good birthday. I'm so sorry I couldn't make it tonight. I feel terrible."

"You feel terrible? I feel terrible. I thought you loved me, but you are always choosing baseball over me. You never cared about me. I should have saw it sooner. How could you go practice instead of coming out for my eighteenth birthday?"

"Wait, I thought you said you were fine with that," I said. I was confused.

"Here's a lesson to you. When a girl says it's fine. It's not fine. It's the opposite of fine."

"Well how was I supposed to know that? You were the one that said you were *fine* with it."

"Why would I ever be fine with you missing my birthday? You can be so selfish sometimes."

She was right. I was selfish. There was nothing I could say that would make up for that.

"I'm sorry."

"Well it doesn't matter now."

Click.

The next day, I hit three home runs, and played one of the best games of my life. Elizabeth was still upset, and she didn't come watch. I resented her for that. After the game, my father noticed I was down—even though I played so well—and he guessed why, and used it to his advantage. "Son, you played the best game of your life in front of all those scouts, and Elizabeth wasn't there. You said she supported you, and made you stronger. I think you got your answer tonight."

It was harsh, but I was upset, and I felt he was right.

Things after that were never the same between Elizabeth and I. There was a distance that was felt by both sides, but I was the one who was responsible for it. I held a grudge. I was just like my father.

Chapter 41

Elizabeth felt bad about missing my game, and she did her best to make it up to me. She bought me a St. Louis Cardinals jersey, and she had my last name and the number eleven stitched on the back. She did it to say she was sorry. I was the one that missed her 18th birthday, but she was the one that put the effort into making things right between us. She became more loving than ever. I wish I had done the same. But just like a costly error late in a game, the damage was already done.

When my father saw my new jersey, he asked, "I'm guessing Elizabeth got you that?"

"She did," I replied.

"Don't be fooled by her, Son. Remember what happened when she didn't come to your game...you played better than ever."

I loved the jersey Elizabeth bought me, and I forgave her—even though she wasn't the one that needed to be forgiven—but still, my father had a point. A point I couldn't get out of my head.

I could tell that Elizabeth was growing more concerned about our future. She would bring up a number of options of what would happen after we graduated. I never brought up our future, because I was still unsure of what to do.

One night, we were hanging out on her bed in her room. We were both on our backs with our feet on the wall, and I was tossing a baseball up in the air towards the ceiling, and catching it on its way down, while we talked.

"I love you, Ozzie. After high school, I hope you know that I want to go wherever you go."

"What about tennis?"

"I don't need to play tennis, all I need is you."

I tossed the ball up in the air, and caught it right at my chest.

"But you're so good. You could go to any college that you want to."

"That's the thing, I don't want to go to any college if you're not going to be there. I thought about it and I decided I could always take classes in the offseason, and in the spring wherever you are playing."

I tossed the ball up again, but this time I caught it in front of my face.

"You have to go to school, Liz, and play tennis. You've been offered so many scholarships. You love tennis, and you're too good and too smart to just give all that up"

"I don't love tennis, I love you."

I tossed the ball up again, but this time it sailed back out of reach above my head, and it landed on the floor with a loud thud.

"Be careful, Oz. You'll break something."

"I still can't let you give it up," I said as I rolled over, got off of the bed, and picked up the ball.

"Why not?" she asked, and sat up to look at me.

"Cause."

"Cause is not a reason."

"I'm done talking about this," I said.

That was something my father would say.

"You're such an asshole sometimes," she said, visibly upset.

"Yep."

I put the ball back on her night stand, and left.

And that's how things were. We started arguing because I would often shut down. I didn't want to think about losing her, and I was fighting a battle inside my own mind—inside my own heart. I would love for her to follow me around in my career. But was that the right thing to do? It hurt to think of all this, so I wanted to avoid it as much as I could. Yet, all I was doing was giving into what my father wanted me to do. I wouldn't even give love a chance.

Chapter 42

After all the pressure my father put on me, and all the mental battles I had with myself, I decided that I didn't want to make the same mistake as my father. I decided not to go college, and I decided not to bring Elizabeth with me on my journey to the major leagues. I loved her so much, and it hurt to let her go, but I couldn't let her give up tennis and the college education she deserved. I have been reminded of how that can turn out, every day of my life.

A few days before my 18th birthday, I went over to Elizabeth's house unannounced. Eight years earlier, my mother walked out of my life, and now I was the one about to do the same thing to someone I loved.

I went into Elizabeth's room and everything looked normal, but I already felt different. Glancing around the room I saw so many "souvenirs" of our relationship. I walked across the room and sat on her bed. Folded neatly beside me was the green Rock Bridge Bruin sweater she took from me. She would wear my green sweater whenever she came over, and eventually she took it home, and I had to ask my coach for a new one.

I stretched out and grabbed the baseball that was sitting on her night stand. It was the same ball I had given her at the first game that she came to watch me play. I held it in my hands and thought of the events of that game. I was so young then, and so proud to have my first girl there to watch me. I remember stepping up to the plate and looking over and seeing her there.

I've never felt so much pride and a sense of accomplishment in my life. I also had never felt so nervous in the batter's box. I looked at her and she smiled at me and watched me with those amazing eyes. The nervousness disappeared. I knew I could not fail; would not fail. With her, I never could fail, and, I was about to give that up.

Elizabeth walked into her room and smiled. Her hair was pulled back in a pony tail, she was wearing black running shorts, and a blue tank top. *She is so beautiful,* I thought.

"Hey, I didn't know you were coming over today. I was just out for a run," she said. She must have saw the look on my face and her smile disappeared. "What's wrong, Ozzie?"

"Your mom let me in and told me I could wait in your room," I said, not answering her question. I could see the sweat beading on her forehead and they reminded me of tears. I had to look away. I have never broken up with anyone before, so I started the way people always do on TV.

"Liz, we need to talk."

She grabbed a towel, patted her forehead with it, and sat down beside me. "About what?" she asked.

"Liz, we can't be together anymore," I said, and my voice cracked.

"Stop fooling around, Ozzie," she said with a smile, with the hopes I would smile too. But when I didn't smile, her face changed. "Your father put you up to this, didn't he?"

"This has nothing to do with my father."

"Oz, I know you and I know your father. This has everything to do with him. You're not a child, Oz. You can make your own decisions. I love you, and I know you love me too. I know you are going to get drafted, I know that's what you want, and I am coming with you."

"You don't understand, Liz, I have lived with the pain of seeing my parents despise each other. My father blamed my mother everyday for him giving up on his dreams and for having such a miserable life. I owe it to him to not make the same mistake he did, as harsh as that sounds. Most of all, I don't want to be the one you blame for not following your dream. We have to go our separate ways."

"We won't end up like them. I promise. You can't live your whole life afraid because of the way your parents turned out."

"I have to."

"No you don't! Their case is unique. No relationship is the same and no life is the same. I will follow you wherever you go. If baseball is that important to you, I will be there every step of the way. My dream is to be with you. My dream has never been to play tennis."

"I can't let you do that."

"Yes you can!"

"No, I can't, and I won't."

"Don't do this."

"This is the way it has to be. There is no other way. I am going to go off and play baseball and that is the only thing that matters. That is the only thing I can focus on."

"Ozzie, there is more to life than baseball."

"Not for me. Know that I will always love you, Liz—"

"But not as much as baseball..."

"Exactly."

"Please don't do this."

"I have to."

Those were the last three words I said to her and she burst into tears. It was the harshest thing I have ever said or done to someone. I patted her on the back—a half-ass thing to do to someone you love. And then I walked away from the most amazing thing in my life. I was too much of a coward or too much of an asshole to stay there with her, or even to hold her and console her. I just left her there crying. I was holding in the tears myself. And that was it.

Why could I not see it then that she was right? There is

much more to life than baseball. If only my father had understood this as well. So much misery could have been avoided.

When I got home, I slammed the door as I entered the house. My father who was in the living room turned from his chair and asked what was wrong.

"I broke up with Liz."

"You did the right thing, Son."

I didn't believe it then, and I still don't believe it now.

Chapter 43

When Jake found out about Elizabeth and I, he was very upset. He asked why I broke up with her. I explained that I had to focus on baseball, and I didn't want to hold her back. He thought we were perfect for each other, and he couldn't believe I could give up someone so beautiful, smart, and caring. I told him there would be plenty of girls to choose from when I made the Show. Looking back, I was such an asshole. I was hurting and I covered it up by being someone that I was not. Maybe it was my father in me.

Did I actually believe I would find someone better than Elizabeth? The answer is no. But I did believe that Elizabeth could find someone better than me. I knew I wasn't the best at relationships, and I didn't treat her the way she should have been treated. But I asked myself, *Didn't she deserve to be with someone that was going to make it in the major leagues?...Wouldn't every girl want that?* The only thing that disproved this notion was the thought that I wouldn't make it if I stayed with her. Still, if I made it to the major leagues, I could have given her everything.

What it all came down to, is that I had to convince myself that I did the right thing. I did this by being hard on myself. I told myself that I was the one that didn't deserve her. I was scared that if I didn't make it to the Show, that I would have resented her and blamed her just like my father blamed my mother. After mentally beating myself up night after night, eventually I came to the conclusion that I had made the right decision. It was for the best. Baseball was the only thing that mattered.

But with her, it was the only time I could truly be myself. Sure I loved being a ball player and I believed the confidence from the game is how I got Elizabeth in the first place, but she didn't buy all that. She wasn't with me because I was a ball player. Being a ball player may have been my in at first, but she wanted to know who I was outside of the game. She pushed and prodded until she got to know who I really was as a person. That was something that no one had ever done before. I could talk to her about things other than baseball, I could share my concerns, and she would listen. But most of the time when I was with her, I would forget about any issues in my life. I forgot about my father's drinking; I forgot about how my whole family left me; and I forgot about any doubts I was having when it came to baseball.

Most of all, with her, it was that feeling of being loved—the same feeling I have been chasing my entire life. At first it was through the game, but Elizabeth taught me a sense of intimacy that I wanted more than anything. Her love and acceptance was worth more than having millions of fans. I believe that love is what life is all about, the major issue is that I didn't know it at the time. I found something that would have given me a lifetime of happiness, but I lost it—more like pushed it away.

After I ended our relationship, I was a mess. We lost out early in the district tournament, and the last few weeks of school were a blur. I desperately wanted time to speed up so I could get drafted, head to camp, and start playing ball again. I missed a lot of classes, and I didn't even go to prom. I also found out that Elizabeth did not go to prom. The most beautiful girl didn't go to prom because she was heartbroken. It hurts to think about that. And I didn't go because I didn't care about high school anymore. I was waiting impatiently for the draft in June.

So my friends, teammates, and people that had been

supporting me and following me the last few years, didn't even get the experience of seeing me at prom or graduation. I felt like I had no reason to go, and my father never even brought it up. Jake and I could have hung out, and I feel ashamed that I didn't at least go for my best friend. But who would I go with? Any girl would have been overjoyed if I had asked them to prom. I couldn't do that, however. I would never go with anyone other than Elizabeth. Thinking back on it, I was selfish. I could have created great memories for the people in my school and city. I could have helped them in a way. But it wasn't my responsibility, was it? Many people may have looked up to me, but I was still just a kid.

In the month of May, I spent most of my time alone. I continued to practice in my back yard with my father, and I went for long runs every day. It helped me take my mind off of things.

Other than that, I didn't go see Jake, I was no longer with Elizabeth, so I just sat and watched TV with my father and waited until the draft. I was hurt, sad, and impatient. But, it was soon to all be worth it.

At least I hoped so.

Chapter 44

On Tuesday June 6th, 2000, all of the hard work and sacrifice in high school finally paid off. In the Major League Baseball June draft, I was the thirteenth pick overall in the first round by the St. Louis Cardinals. It was a dream come true. That was five spots ahead of my father, which was an accomplishment in itself. To me, my father was always bigger than life—I never believed I could possibly be better than him. I'm not sure if I ever became better than him, but I did get drafted higher. That should at least count for something, right?

For a boy from Missouri to get drafted by the Cardinals was a big deal. The odds of that happening were slim to none. Once I made it to the Cardinals, it would be like playing for my home town team—even though I grew up around a hundred and twenty miles away. There was only one shortstop picked before me—the rest were pitchers, outfielders, and one first baseman. So in the year 2000, I was viewed as being the second best shortstop prospect. Not bad for a kid right out of high school.

In the last few years, the amount of money first round draft picks were getting as a signing bonus was astonishing. I knew I was going to be getting a lot of money, but the exact number was not important to me. I trusted my father and I trusted my agent that my father chose, Vince Michael, and left them in charge of the negotiations. But to know I was going to be a millionaire almost overnight, was an incredible feeling. Truthfully, it was almost hard to comprehend. It was only six months earlier that I didn't have any money to buy Elizabeth a Christmas gift. Now I couldn't help but thinking about all the gifts I could buy Elizabeth—if we were still together.

After I got the news that I was drafted, I instantly wanted to call Elizabeth, but I had to repress the urge. She was still the first person I wanted to tell. Regardless of our break-up, I believed she would be excited for me, but I couldn't bring myself to do it. I knew where I was headed, and I knew she couldn't come with me. But it was still hard for me. I felt like she was part of the reason my dream came true—even though I would have to pursue it without her.

I believe that if there was more time between the draft and being sent to my first assignment, Elizabeth and I may have patched things up. We could have possibly gotten back together, or I could have at least said goodbye. But since I had to move right away, I didn't even have the chance to do so. Well, I could have made an effort to see her, but I chose not to.

Packing up my things was a wakeup call. It was sad to see how little I was actually taking with me. All I had was my ball gear and my clothes—along with everything that my father taught me. That's all I would be taking with me on my journey through the minor leagues for the next few years. No longer would I have a home. No longer would I be rooted in one place.

When I got drafted, there was no celebration with my friends, and there was no going away party or anything like that. I didn't call anyone to tell them. What would be the point since no one could come where I was headed anyway? That was the attitude I had. I knew they would eventually find out. I had to leave everything behind, and move on.

Regardless of getting everything I wanted, I still felt alone. I felt like something was missing, and deep down I knew it was Elizabeth, but I tried my best not to think about her. I kept reminding myself what my father told me, "She can't go where you're headed." I repeated this to myself in order to comfort myself—in order to convince myself.

Three days later, on Friday June 9th, 2000, I grabbed my stuff and headed to St. Louis. I didn't say goodbye to anyone. My father and I drove down together to meet all the necessary people within the Cardinals organization, and to sign my contract.

The last time I was at Busch Stadium was with Elizabeth. All of those memories came flooding back. It seemed like everywhere I went, there she was. But instead of sitting in the stands like I had one year before, I was in a boardroom overlooking the field. The St. Louis Cardinals were out on the field taking batting practice, and some pitchers were throwing a bullpen, while others were shagging flies. It was surreal to think that I could be playing with those guys someday.

Mr. Robert Calvin—the team's owner—introduced himself. He was a nice man that had a strong passion for the game. I couldn't be happier that I was drafted by the Cardinals. Everything was happening just like I imagined. He said he was excited to have me as a part of their organization and that they were looking forward to helping me make the transition from the minors to the majors as quick as possible. That sounded perfect to me.

I can't remember what was all said during that initial meeting. It didn't seem real and everything happened so fast. All I had to do was sign my contract that made me property of the St. Louis Cardinals, and I would receive a bonus of 1.85 million dollars, pending a physical. With a quick stroke of a pen I was a professional baseball player and a millionaire. They told me that in a couple days I would be off to Johnson City, Tennessee, to report to my Rookie League team where my stint in the minors would begin. *Was this actually happening?* I thought.

After all the paper work was completed, Mr. Calvin had one more surprise for me that day. He asked me if I wanted to take a few swings with the Cardinals. After I agreed, he had his assistant take me down to the clubhouse, where I was introduced to Len Garfield—also known as "Lenny"—the clubhouse manager. I was nervous to be in the Cardinals clubhouse, but Lenny was friendly and he made me feel at ease.

"Hey there, Ozzie. I had been expecting you, right this way," he said, after Mr. Garfield's assistant introduced us. "You know when I heard you were coming, I was excited to have another Ozzie in the clubhouse. I didn't think I ever would, especially another shortstop. But word has been going around that you could be better than the Wizard. They say you hit for more power than he did, and your glove is just as good. You must be pretty special."

"You knew Ozzie Smith?" I asked. "My father named me after him."

"I sure did. He was a spectacular ball player. One of the best. I've been with the Cardinals for twenty-six years. I have known a lot of great players that have walked through this very clubhouse," he said as we reached a locker. "This one's yours today."

The nameplate on the locker had "Shaw" already on it. In the stall, there was a white, Cardinals jersey with my last name and the number 11 on the back. They *really* had been expecting me. Lenny let me enjoy the moment, before he told me to get dressed and asked me what size my feet were, and what size of bat I liked. I told him I was size eleven and that I normally swung a thirty-one ounce bat. I put on a pair of white baseball pants, and a red warm-up shirt that was hanging there for me. Since it was just batting practice, I didn't know if I should wear the jersey or not.

Lenny came back with three different bats, and said I could bring all three and decide which one I liked. He also came back with two pairs of brand new red Nike cleats. One was low-top and the other was a mid to high-top. He brought several different pairs of batting gloves and told me to pick some that I liked. I picked a brand new pair of Franklin Tri-Curve batting gloves. I couldn't believe the way I was treated. I showed up with nothing, and I was immediately all set up with brand new cleats, a bunch of new bats to choose from, batting gloves, and warm up gear. Not to mention, my new jersey.

"Mr. Garfield?—"

"Call me Lenny, Oz."

"Lenny, should I wear this jersey for batting practice?"

"It's up to you. You can take it with you after you're done. It's yours either way. I'll let you get ready and if you need anything I'll be just over there, and if you're good to go, the tunnel to the field is that way," he said, pointing straight ahead to what looked like an equipment room, and then to my right to a hallway that I saw a few players exit out of already.

I put on the jersey to see how it fit, and to see what it felt like to wear an official Cardinals jersey with my name and number on the back. It felt good. It felt just like the one that Elizabeth gave me.

There were a few other players coming in and out of the clubhouse and I recognized a few of them. None of them were wearing their jerseys, so I decided to take my jersey off before I headed to the field. I wanted to act like I belonged.

I still remember the damp smell in the hall to the dugout, and how it opened up to one of the most beautiful things I have ever seen. I stood in the Cardinals dugout and looked out at the field in awe. I was there one year earlier as a fan, but to be at field level as a player, was something else entirely. I will never forget that moment.

I looked around and saw all these familiar faces that I always saw on TV. They looked different when they were not in their uniform, but most of all, I noticed their size. These were not the boys that I was facing against just over a month ago. These were grown men—grown supermen.

I walked out carrying my bats, and a few players introduced

themselves. *Like they needed an introduction!* I had been watching them on TV all season already. Jerry Atwell their manager, and the hitting coach Casey Munroe, also introduced themselves. Then I heard it.

Crack!...Crack!...Crack!

It was the sound of the Cardinals big, muscular first baseman, Tony "The Crusher" Campbell, hitting BP. I have heard people hit a baseball before, but it never sounded like that. The Crusher was a three time home run champion and I could almost guarantee there were more to come. This guy was a beast. A guy I often marveled at and rooted for to hit a home run when I watched him play. There he was—standing six foot three with 230 pounds of pure muscle—absolutely destroying the ball, and hitting it ungodly distances. All I could think was: *Wow.* I remember thinking how far Aaron used to hit balls in BP, and then seeing the Crusher—Aaron did not even compare.

The hitting coach said I was up next and should go take a few swings to warm up. I didn't stretch, I barely had a chance to get ready, and I was supposed to hit after Tony "The Crusher" Campbell? I went and swung a few times and stretched as best as I could. Then I went and stood beside a few guys that were watching The Crusher hit. One was Russell Page, the Cardinals starting third baseman, and the other was Brian Benitez, their right fielder. Brian made a costly error a few nights before, and my father cursed him out through the TV. Now I was standing next him. I was still nervous, but the thought of that put a smile on my face.

"Hey, kid, won't be an easy act to follow today," Russell said.

"I've never seen anything like it..." I said, still in awe.

"Neither have we, kid...neither have we," Brian added.

We sat there in silence and listened to the crack of the bat. The Crusher yelled out in his deep voice to the pitcher, "Two more and I'm good." He proceeded to hit the next two far into the stands. After he was done, The Crusher walked my way, made eye contact, and said with a big smile, "Feels good today," as he continued on past me.

"The kid's up!" the coach yelled in my direction.

"That's you," Brian said to me. "Good luck."

I walked up to the left side of the plate and settled into my stance. I took a few lazy swings just to loosen up my arms. The pitching coach said, "Let me know when you're ready." I did my usual routine, tightened my batting gloves, took a deep breath, and then nodded, "Ready."

It is an understatement to say that I was nervous. My knees were shaking. It was only batting practice, but I didn't want to screw up. I knew that they wanted to see who they just spent 1.85 million dollars on. I wondered if the other players would laugh if I swung and missed? I was reading into things more than I needed to. I took a few deep breaths and reminded myself that it was just batting practice and everything would be fine; I have prepared for this moment since I was a little kid. There may have been a massive arch peeking over the stadium beyond left field, but I dug my cleats in, and imagined I was in the backyard with my father.

I looked at the pitcher behind the L-Screen. He threw me a pitch and I let it go by. I didn't care. I just wanted to read the ball and see how well I could pick it up from his hand. He showed me the next ball he was going to throw, as if to say, "Here it is." When he released the ball from his hand, I loaded, my instincts took over, and the best possible thing happened; I swung and the ball jumped off my bat and cleared the left field fence. The pitcher turned and watched it go. Even The Crusher who was joking around with a few players and paid no attention to me, turned and watched. All the nervousness was gone in an instant. I felt right at home. I felt like I belonged. All it took was one swing. I dug in and waited for the next pitch. The same thing happened—it sailed over the left field fence.

After a few more pitches which resulted in some hard line

drives and a few more home runs, I was done my first session hitting at Busch Stadium. I had broken the ice, more like shattered the ice, and it felt great. I know that it was just one session of BP, but it couldn't have gone any better. I walked out of the batting cage and I saw Mr. Calvin and my father sitting in the stands of Busch Stadium. There my father was—watching his son at his favorite team's stadium—with a smile on his face. That was something. I felt like I had finally done it. But I still had a long way to go.

I went back in the clubhouse and undressed. Lenny came up to me and brought me a ball bag, and told me to keep everything he gave me that day. I thanked him and he said he hoped to see me sometime soon. He was such a nice man. I left there vowing that it would only be a matter of time before I would be back.

The next day I had to complete a physical with the team doctors so my contract would become official. Everything checked out and I had a clean bill of health. I was all set. Everything was going according to plan.

The following day, my father and I caught a plane from St. Louis to Knoxville, TN, where we rented a car and drove the rest of the way to Johnson City. It was a quiet drive for the most part. I couldn't help looking out the window and imagining playing with the Cardinals. I was still a kid with a kid like dream. Aren't we all in way?

There was one thing pressing on my mind, however, and I had to ask. "Hey, Pop, do I tell Mom I got drafted?"

"It's up to you, Son. When's the last time you talked to her? If you feel she needs to know you can call her. But I'm sure she will find out on her own sooner or later."

It had been a couple years since I talked to her. The last time I heard from her she was remarried to someone I had never met and had a son and a daughter. She was moving on with her new family. So I decided I would too. I decided not to call her.

In Johnson City, my father stayed at the hotel, while I got

settled in with the team, and the host family I was going to be living with. My father was around for only a couple days and then he went back to Columbia.

For the first time, I was on my own.

Chapter 45

I was eighteen years old, and over seven hundred miles away from home. From mid-June until September, I played for the Johnson City Cardinals in the Rookie Appalachian League. Rookie ball is a chance for younger players—especially those coming right out of high school and those from other countries—to get some time in to develop, and get some experience before they move on to a full-season minor league team in the spring.

A few of my teammates and I were placed with a host family that we would be able to stay with when we were in town. Mr. and Mrs. Nelson were a couple in their sixties, and they were some of the nicest people I have ever met. They had three grown children that no longer lived with them, and they had a nice home that they wanted to put to use. Mrs. Nelson was a wonderful cook. Coming back from the road after eating fast food, to her homemade cooking, was always much needed. Unfortunately for Mrs. Nelson, ball players are known for being bottomless pits, but she never seemed to mind feeding us all. We didn't have a lot of time to spend with the Nelsons—since we were only there for a couple months, and half the time we were on the road—but we often joked, that the way she could cook, it would be hard for us to leave after the season was over.

Mr. Nelson was a big baseball fan and he loved helping young ball players. He told us a few times that he had a tryout with the Texas Rangers when he was younger. I could tell he was proud of that fact and that's why he told us more than once.

He played one season in the minors, met the future Mrs. Nelson, was released from the team, and settled in Johnson City, where Mrs. Nelson's father got Mr. Nelson a job working for his flooring company. "You see, you boys, I went from swinging lumber, to laying floorboards, and swinging hammers. But I made a pretty nice life for myself," he said the first time he told us about his baseball past. "But I wish you boys luck in pursuing your dreams."

Mr. Nelson didn't seem to have any regrets in not fulfilling his dream of playing major league baseball. But maybe that wasn't his dream after all. I didn't think about it then, but Mr. Nelson was another great example of there being a life outside of baseball.

I got along well with the three other ball players I was living with. There was Matt Hamilton, who was our center fielder, Mackenzie Wilson, our third baseman, and Leroy Hernandez, our catcher.

Normally a team will try to place you with other position players, or if you are a pitcher you will stick with the pitchers, but a couple weeks into the season, a pitcher named Scott Anderson came to stay with us as well. He was a tall and lanky kid at six foot six and 180 pounds. He was very friendly, and most of all, he loved baseball. It's all he could talk about. Naturally, Scott and I got along well, and we stuck together quite a bit that summer. The Nelson's took him in after Scott was having issues with his last host family. There was young children in the home and Scott and two other pitchers couldn't get any rest, and they even tried to make them babysit. They knew they couldn't last in that place, so they talked to the coaches, and the coaches made arrangements for them to be placed with other host families.

My second home, other than the Nelson's, was Howard Johnson Field. I remember my first time seeing it, and wondering what the hell was out in right field. There was a hill that was in the park, with a high home run fence behind it. This meant that the hill was in play. I remember thinking, *Thank god I don't play right field.* I couldn't imagine running for a ball past the warning track and up onto a hill, or even playing a ball that rolled down the hill.

Some may say a baseball field, is a baseball field, but this is not the case. Whatever position you play, you have to deal with a variety of factors. Outfielders have to deal with different distances of fences, different walls, obstructions in foul territory, and so on. Infielders have to deal with turf, natural grass, dirt, and the various combinations of all three. There is a reason why some fielders are more successful than others in certain parks. Often the home team advantage is a real thing, not just because of the energy the fans bring to the game, but because of the familiarity of the playing field.

Even the way pitchers are able to warm up in the pen can make a difference. Some fields have their bullpen right in foul territory where someone has to go out and protect pitchers from any balls that are hit their way. Pitchers may have trouble focusing on their warm up when so many people are watching, and they also have to worry about getting hit by a foul ball. It all has an impact. But it's all a part of the game.

All of us in rookie ball were in a new situation, but it wasn't easy going from a high school league, to a minor league team in just over a month. It was a different atmosphere all together. In high school, I had a bunch of fans and scouts out to watch me, and now, nobody knew who I was. The competition increased and it didn't feel like many were in my corner. I had to remind myself that I needed to focus on playing ball and improving, and nothing more.

In one of the first practices we had as team, our manager Bruce Green gathered us around. He went through his rules and guidelines and what he expected from us as players and as a team. It's the typical thing you would hear from every coach at the beginning of a new year.

He finished up his speech with, "We have to work really hard in order to come together as a team by next week, when the Elizabethton Twins come to town."

"What did he just say? Who is coming to town?" I asked a player sitting beside me.

"The Elizabethton Twins," he replied.

So much for focusing only on baseball, I thought. Elizabeth was everywhere. I felt like the world was trying to tell me something, but there was nothing I could do about it. I had made my decision, and now I had to learn to get out of my own head.

Chapter 46

Baseball is a game of focus. But there are a number of reasons why it might be tough to focus on baseball. If your life outside the field starts to seep into your mind, it can impact the way you play. Or, sometimes during a game, people will make it their job to try and distract you from the task at hand, and throw you off of your game. We call these people hecklers. For the most part, they are just assholes. But the bigger the asshole they are, the more effective they tend to be.

My first experience with a heckler in the stands happened my first time on a road trip as a professional baseball player. We were playing the Bristol White Sox in Bristol, Virginia. It was my first at bat in the first inning. I remember it being a hot, but cloudy day, and I was eager to start the road trip with a hit.

I walked up to the on deck circle and I heard someone yell, "Hey, Cocksucker!"

At first I wasn't really paying attention and I wondered to myself, *Did I just hear what I thought I heard?*

"Hey, Cocksucker!"

Yup, I sure did...there it is again.

I was curious to see if there was a fight in the stands or something, so I turned and looked in the direction where the voice was coming from. I made eye contact with a middle aged man with a beer belly. And now he was laughing in delight, because, turns out, the cocksucker he was talking to, was me.

"Hey, look everyone, he is a cocksucker! I yelled 'Hey,

Cocksucker!' and he turned and looked right at me," the heckler said, and laughed some more.

Some people laughed and others looked horrified. I was appalled when I saw a boy that looked to be about five years old sitting a few seats away from this man. How can a grown man act this way in public, especially in front of young children? I didn't say a word, but I turned away and made a mental note, *never look towards the fans again.* I was eighteen years old, I just signed a contract with a 1.85 million dollar signing bonus, but all I was to some people was a cocksucker. That was my unofficial welcome to professional baseball.

The next time I was on the on deck circle in the third inning, I never heard a peep. I broke my mental note of not looking towards the stands and took a quick glance to where that man was seated, and noticed it was empty. My guess is that someone complained and he got kicked out. Either way, I noticed he never returned

That guy was the first heckler I had as a professional, but it sure wasn't the last. Having fans yell horrible things at you is an unfortunate part of baseball that all players have to get used to; and tuning the fans out is just another skill a baseball player has to learn.

The good thing about being sent right to Rookie League is that everyone is in the same boat as you. It was a new experience for everyone. If I was nervous, if I was getting heckled, or whatever, it didn't matter, because everyone else was going through the same thing.

I didn't play as well as I wanted that season, but I was still above average. For getting drafted as high as I did, I wanted to play much better, and I knew I could improve.

I think my issue was that I found it hard to get comfortable. Everything was a new situation and I didn't know anyone. These excuses shouldn't count because everyone else was in the same situation, but I think it still had an impact. Or maybe I just put too much pressure on myself.

Not having my father there was also a different experience for me. In high school, my father was always there to tell me how I should improve my game. In the minors, I had to do things on my own.

I still watched ball games on TV every chance I had. I continued to study pitchers the way my father taught me. That never stopped. I knew I would be facing these pitchers someday, and I wanted to be prepared. Something else I did, which a lot people didn't think of doing, was I studied my own pitchers just as much. I wanted to see what they threw and when, and this helped me to be able to get great jumps on the ball at short.

That season I started off slow, but I started to pick it up at the tail end of the schedule, and I finished off on a ten game hitting streak. Just as I was picking up steam, the season ended. I finished with a .276 batting average in 214 at bats. I had 7 home runs, and 33 RBIs, with 15 stolen bases. I also had 11 doubles and 2 triples. Thanks to my ten game hitting streak, my batting average increased a few points right at the end.

I put up pretty solid numbers that year, but coming from high school and having over a .700 batting average and rarely striking out, it was hard not to be upset. Still, I was at least able to show off a bit of everything. I showed that I had some power, could drive in runs, steal bases, and do the little things. But the major problem I had with that season, is that I had 37 strikeouts. That was more than I had my entire high school career combined.

Something else that I wasn't used to was being on a losing team. We finished the season well under .500, with a 26-42 record. But my time in rookie ball flew by, and in September I was headed back to Columbia. I found myself thinking, just like I did every new school year in high school, I couldn't wait until spring.

Chapter 47

On a scorching September day, when I was back in Columbia, I headed out on a nice, long run. I ran past the school, circled around to the baseball field, the tennis courts—where I had so many memories only a few months before—and headed back towards my house. It was so hot out that I ended up stopping at the store quickly to buy a Gatorade. Part of me wished I hadn't. I wasn't ready to see the person I ran into inside.

I opened the door to the store and instantly felt the refreshing air conditioning hit my sweat covered face. I went down an aisle to get to the refrigerators in the back, and Mrs. Fielder turned the corner and I almost ran right into her. I was sweaty, thirsty, and out of breath.

"Hi, Ozzie! How are you?"

"Good," I said trying to catch my breath, "was just out for a run. Sure is a hot one out there."

"It sure is! I've been trying to avoid outside as much as possible. It's good to see you, Ozzie! How are you doing? It's been too long. I saw your father a few weeks ago and I heard you were in Tennessee playing ball. Are you back now?"

"I'm doing good. I was in Johnson City, Tennessee for a couple months playing rookie ball. I had a good experience out there and learned a lot. Now I have the winter off until spring training in March. So yep, I'm back at home for a little awhile."

"That's good to hear, Ozzie. I'm glad you're doing well. I was sorry to hear about you and Lizzie. You two made such a great pair."

I felt horrible. I loved Elizabeth and I loved her parents. They meant so much to me and they would never know how much I missed them. I missed them a lot more than I could have imagined. I wanted to ask about Elizabeth, but I was nervous to find out where she was.

"How are you and Mr. Fielder doing? Is he still busy with school?" I asked, simply delaying the question that I really wanted to ask.

"Oh, we are doing fine. I'm still working and Jeff is still busy, as always, at the University. We're trying to keep occupied because it's still strange to us not having Lizzie at home."

"That must be tough," I said, and I'm sure Mrs. Fielder saw the pain on my face. If I still missed Elizabeth, and her parents missed her as well, I wondered how Elizabeth felt about being on her own. It hurt to think about it. "Well, I'm going to grab a Gatorade and head back out to continue my run. It was nice to see you, Mrs. Fielder," I said, turning to head to the cooler.

"You too, Ozzie." I heard her say.

Then I stopped myself and turned back around. "Mrs. Fielder!" She stopped and faced back towards me. "How is Liz?"

I was still afraid to ask, a part of me didn't want to know, but I had to.

Mrs. Fielder smiled. "She is doing well. I talked to her on the phone yesterday. She is still getting settled in. She likes her classes so far and she said her roommate seems nice."

"That's good to hear. I haven't talked to her since we bro—" I couldn't finish what I was going to say. It felt weird talking to the mother of the girl I broke up with. "Since I moved away...where did she decide to go to school?"

"She accepted a full ride athletic scholarship to Stanford University."

"She always liked being by the ocean, didn't she?"

"Yes she did," Mrs. Fielder replied.

Then it hit me, and I almost broke down right there. "I guess she decided to be a Cardinal...just like me."

"She did," Mrs. Fielder said, and smiled.

When Elizabeth was trying to convince me to go to college with her, one of the things she said was that we could both go to Stanford and be Cardinals together. I told her a Stanford Cardinal wasn't the Cardinal I wanted to be. I almost felt like it was a sign. Elizabeth could have went anywhere. She had letters from Duke, Vanderbilt, the University of Florida, and many other schools that had great tennis programs. But she chose to be a Cardinal. I wanted to call her up right then, and tell her I missed her and I loved her. Maybe I could even go fly out and see her?

"Anyways, Ozzie, I have to get going. It was really great to see you. And since you're in town, Jeff and I would love to have you over for dinner sometime. You still have our number, right?"

"Yes I do. That would be great," I said, and I thought it would be, but I knew I would probably never be able to bring myself to call or go over there. "It was great to see you, too. Tell Liz I say hi," I added, and I immediately felt stupid as soon as it left my mouth.

"I will," she said. "I could give you her number if you want, Ozzie."

"I'll get it from you when I come for that dinner!" I said, knowing that I never would.

"Sounds good. Have a good run! And don't work too hard."

"Don't worry I will," I said with a laugh as I walked away.

I got my Gatorade and walked home from there. I couldn't bring myself to run anymore that afternoon. I felt winded. I walked home in the heat thinking about Elizabeth the entire way.

When I got home, I plopped on the couch in the living room.

"What's with you?" my father asked. "You look like you fell in a lake."

"She's a Cardinal, Pop."

"What are you talking about?"

"Liz went to Stanford. She chose to be a Cardinal, too."

"Oh," he said. "You want a beer, Son?"

That was the first time he ever offered me one. "No, I'm good," I replied.

I got up and went outside in the backyard. I spent the next half-hour hitting balls off of the tee until I was completely exhausted. I had to take my frustrations out somehow.

When I moved back in the offseason, things were different. My father and I trained like we always did, but it didn't take me long to realize I couldn't stay there. Outside of baseball, I didn't have much to do. My friends like Jake and Aaron, and a few of the other ball players I grew up with, had all gone off to school. Some of my old teammates that were still in high school tried to get me to go to these high school parties. I went with them once, but I did not like the attention I got. Girls would swarm around me just like they did my freshman year.

Here I was, eighteen years old, complaining about getting attention from girls. What was wrong with me, right? Well, I still missed Elizabeth. None of these high school girls could compare to her. Elizabeth was special. She was always mature for her age and she taught me so much. There would be no one that could ever replace her.

When I went out to restaurants, or anywhere out in public, people would recognize me and try to come talk to me. They were always overly friendly, but would all ask me the same questions. It was exhausting.

I told my father that I couldn't stay in Columbia anymore. Everyone had seen my picture in the newspaper the last few years and there were too many people that knew my face. My father suggested that I could go live with my uncle Frank, who lived in Evansville, Indiana, which was only about a four-and-a-half-hour drive away. Evansville was a similar size to Columbia, but there, no one would recognize me unless they were die hard baseball fans. I decided it was probably my best option. It was my chance to continue focusing on baseball.

I hadn't seen my uncle in probably five years, and I didn't know him that well at all. He ended up getting married to a girl from New Mexico—who became my aunt Susan—and had two kids, Lisa who was four, and Samantha who was two. So I was going to live with these people that were basically strangers, but at least they were family. I was excited and nervous to meet my auntie and two cousins for the first time.

When I got to their house, it reminded me of what my home used to look like. They were a family—they were all together—and they seemed happy. I was excited to become a part of it.

We sat down and had dinner as a family just like I did at the Cooper's and Fielder's. The thing I enjoyed the most about it, was that they did things together—just like my family did when I was younger. I didn't necessarily miss my mother or father, I missed having a family. Being around my two young cousins was also a new experience for me. They were the cutest little kids I had ever met. I had never been around kids much in my life, so having them follow me everywhere I went was new to me. It was a welcomed distraction, however, and I loved entertaining them.

Evansville was a good place for me. I could go anywhere without being noticed. It was a nice feeling. For awhile I felt like a normal human being. But it didn't take me long to start getting into a strict training routine. Out in Evansville, I did things on my own. The first thing I needed to do in the offseason was strengthen my arm in order to increase my velocity. Players were a lot faster at the professional level, so I needed to be able to throw them out as quick as possible. The first few weeks I was there, you could find me out in the field with a bucket of recently made "heavy balls." I would throw long toss without a partner until my bucket was empty. And then I would go and throw them back. It was like playing fetch all by myself. My only goal was to strengthen my arm. I couldn't do this during the season because I couldn't afford injuring my arm or tiring it out. In the offseason, I could throw until I couldn't lift my arm and then let it rest for a few days and repeat. After a few weeks I could already see the results. I was able to throw those heavy balls further than I ever could, and when I picked up a regular ball, it felt as light as a feather. My arm became like a whip and the ball would travel on a line wherever I needed it to go. I couldn't wait to go home and test it on Crow. *I would probably put a hole right through him,* I thought.

After a while, I realized that I needed a place to hit and work on other areas of my body. A place I found was called the Sports Acceleration Program. It was a gym in a warehouse, developed to train athletes, to make them faster and stronger, and their specialty was baseball. It was perfect. They had batting cages, advanced treadmills, actual weighted baseballs, and all types of rubber bands. During this offseason I got into the best shape of my life. Everything was timed and calculated. After it was all said and done, I was more explosive, faster, and stronger. The stats were there.

The reason a person gets drafted, especially out of high school, is that a team is banking not on the player that you are, but the player they hope you can be. I was doing what I could to be the best.

After about a month, I finally convinced my father to come out and visit. Like me, he had never met his brother's wife and their two kids. When he was there, we went out and trained together, and he hit me more ground balls than I had ever taken in my life. He noticed right away that I had been throwing harder. When I took BP the ball exploded off of my bat. He kept saying, "Looking good, Son...looking real good." That meant the world to me. It was great to have my father there, and having a semblance of a normal family life felt good as well. My dad seemed to enjoy himself, but I did see a few things that made me feel like he was still hurting. I wondered if it was because he was witnessing a life that he missed out on—a life he used to have.

One night all three of us boys were sitting outside. They were both drinking beer and I had an iced tea. My father said to my uncle Frank, "It's good to see you're not such a prick anymore, big brother."

My Uncle laughed. "It's the women in my life, they softened me up...and you know what, I couldn't be happier."

We just sat there in silence for a moment.

"Ain't that something," my father said, almost to himself. I never knew what he meant by that, but he looked like he was deep in thought. My uncle Frank broke the silence by asking my father if he needed another beer.

I still remember that moment. My father was a smart man, and he had a good mind, but he didn't seem to use it too often for anything besides baseball. This was one of the few times I had seen my father deep in thought about something, what I assumed, was something outside of the game.

My father stayed for a week and then he went back home. I felt bad after he left, knowing that he was all by himself. I never thought that my father was lonely, but I could tell he enjoyed being around his brother's family. When he left, he told me to keep working hard, and he said at the rate I was improving, I would be in the Show in no time.

This was a fairly happy time in my life. I had a semblance of family, I didn't feel alone, and I was making a lot of progress. Everything was going well. It felt like my life was on the right track. Most of all, I couldn't wait to report to spring training. As good as this time was, I still wanted to get out there and play baseball. Being an athlete, when you improve and get stronger,

LOVE OR BASEBALL?

you can't wait to show it off and use it where it matters.

Chapter 48

I had barely travelled outside of Columbia, and now I was going to be traveling all over the country. The first stop in 2001 was spring training in Jupiter Florida—from there, I would be assigned a minor league team for my first full season in the minors. The Cardinals organization had teams all over the place from New Jersey, to Illinois, to Connecticut, to Virginia, to Tennessee. The next few years would be an adventure and a battle to make it to St. Louis.

I reported to spring training ten pounds heavier in muscle. The improvements I had made were night and day compared to the high school kid I was several months before. I never expected to make it to the Show right away. I felt like one year in Single-A, one year in Double-A, and one year in Triple-A would be my ideal time frame to get to the majors. If I was called up earlier, that would be a bonus, but anytime longer would be a disappointment.

I was never nervous when I was sent to Johnson City in rookie ball. It felt like I was sent away on a traveling all-star team or something. The season was short and I knew I would be back in Columbia in a couple months. It wasn't until spring training that I actually felt like I was starting my professional baseball career. I was excited to begin my career, but it was also a little nerve wracking. I wasn't worried about being on the field, it was everything else I was uncomfortable with—like living arrangements, meeting people, the routines, and unspoken rules.

What I set out to experience was new, and it was hard to know what to expect. The learning curve outside of the game, was the only curve I was afraid of.

My plan was to focus on baseball and let that guide me when I was feeling stressed or unsure of myself. Another thing that helped, was that I thought of Elizabeth and how she moved around to all those different places when she was younger. She got to see so many things, and she learned so much from those experiences. If Elizabeth could do it, so could I—I just needed to focus on the positives. We were no longer together, but she continued to have an impact on my life. I still thought about her every day. How couldn't I? I still loved her.

Sometimes I would look at the moon from my hotel window, like she used to, and it also helped to ground me. I pictured that big, old moon as the great baseball in the sky that would be there no matter what. At least I'd always have that.

I remember my first day at camp like it was yesterday. I was so excited to finally be that much closer to my dream. It would be an understatement to say my excitement diminished a little that first day. Once you get a group of future prospects all together at the same time, you start to see the talent you are up against. So many players are just like you—doing whatever they can to make it to the Show. Everybody there could hit, run, throw, and catch the ball. What you were trying to show those that were watching, was how much better you can do these things than the other guys out there. It wasn't just the fact that the players at camp were good, they were always working to improve.

I came to understand quickly, that the other players at training camp were not like my pal, Jake. They are either trying to get a spot on the team or protect their spot. It's rare to find someone that would go out of their way to help you. I remember when I was younger and my father said, "There are no friends in baseball," and this couldn't be more true in the minor leagues. From the day you step into training camp, until the day you find out if you're on the team or not, you have to give it everything you have. Spring training was only a short pit stop to find out what path we were headed on to our futures in the game. There was no point of getting close to anyone, since many of us would be sent on our separate paths at the end of March anyhow.

The guys I hung out with and played catch with were mostly guys I roomed with back in Johnson City. Scott and I would go out for supper and talk ball during our down time. But other than the friendly conversation here and there, I didn't get close to anyone else. When I wasn't with Scott, and when I was off the field, I spent a lot of time alone. Even though it wasn't easy to feel lonely, I tried to remember my father's words, "No one can go where you're headed."

On the field, I had a solid camp. I didn't have issues with my defense, and I hit well. In the intrasquad games I continued to hit, and I put up some good numbers once the preseason games began. But that wasn't surprising. I played how I always did.

After Spring Training in 2001, I was sent to Peoria, Illinois to play for the Peoria Chiefs. The Chiefs were a Class A team in the Midwest League. Class A ball is the first time you have to play that full, grueling schedule. In one year, I was facing a much different level of play than I was the year before. All I could hope for was that I improved enough to get noticed.

Beyond rookie ball, you start to see how many different types of players there are in the minor league system. Some guys have been playing in the minors for several years, and some like me, are making their first attempt at a full season of baseball. In Class A, you play more games, get more at bats, and you see a lot of raw talent. The pitching there is good, but still not great. Pitchers are throwing hard, but many are still working on finding their secondary pitches that will help complete their arsenal, which will get them to Double-A and beyond.

LOVE OR BASEBALL?

What it all comes down to is that the minor leagues are the apprenticeship of a baseball player. Regardless of what position you play, you learn many things, on and off the field.

Chapter 49

My life at home growing up was not always the easiest, but it didn't compare to my life in the minor leagues. That first year in Class A ball, I learned a lot of lessons about being a ball player. The minors can be a real wakeup call. Travelling and sleeping on busses, sleeping in lousy hotels, and the poor quality of the meals will wear a person down. The bus rides are always an awkward situation—especially when you move to a new team. It's tough to know the dynamics of who sits where, and who gets to sit alone, and who doesn't. Players will trade goods—such as a bottle of booze, or cans of chew—and even pay those with seniority in order to acquire an empty seat next to them. Still, it's always bad for the new guys on the bus. It doesn't matter how high you got drafted, or how much of signing bonus you received, you will still feel like Forrest Gump walking down the aisle, when all the other players are already in their seats. They give you dirty looks, they shut you down, and it's a terrible feeling. All you can hope for is to find your "Jenny," but unfortunately, your Jenny will be a six foot four and 230 pound hairy man-child with chew spit dripping down his chin.

I don't think a lot of people realize how hard it is on some of these long road trips, where you travel around on these busses with little to no sleep, and then you have to play a game the next day. But it doesn't stop there. Immediately after that series, you hop on the bus to the next city for the next game the following day. There were days that you just wanted to crawl into a bed and sleep for days, but instead you had to go play another nine inning game. But like everything else, it is all a part of the job. It's all a part of the apprenticeship. It's true that we were playing a game we loved, but it wasn't an easy life. And unfortunately, many people do it for a long time, and they may never make it to the Show.

As a player trying to make it, the only thing you could do was try your best, not complain too much, and try to keep focused. For me, I tried to look at the minors as being one more necessary step to get to where I was going. I was fortunate enough that I did have a lot of money, so if I wanted certain things, I could go buy them. Other guys were not so lucky. There were many players in the minors that barely had enough to feed themselves—let alone their families if they had them. Some of the sacrifices you see in the minors can be hard to believe. There were players on my team that were in their thirties, still trying to make it, and balancing their lives and families outside of the game. It was early in my journey, but I could never imagine how hard it was for some of my teammates.

The social aspect of being a professional baseball player can be a challenge. When I was growing up it was always easy for me to get along with my teammates. Once they saw how good I was, they often treated me with respect. In the minor leagues it's different. Your teammates come from many different walks of life, and many are just as good, or even better than you are. There are also many different social dynamics at play in baseball. For the most part a lot of the younger guys will stick together, and the veterans will stick together. People from certain countries or who speak a certain language will also stick together. There is also further separation between position players and pitchers.

In baseball, especially at the higher levels, pitchers can be some of the weirdest people you'll ever meet. They are a part of their own little world. I honestly think that since they are not everyday players, they simply have too much time on their hands. I guess it comes with the territory. They say being on the mound is one of the loneliest places in the world. So I guess it makes sense that some pitchers end up a bit strange.

Being a kid in the minors, it can be an eye opening experience. You can be on the same team, but that doesn't mean everyone gets along. What you see in your day-to-day life also happens on a baseball team. There will always be little groups and cliques in baseball—just like there will always be little groups and cliques in life. Even though we are supposed to be a team, a variety of different personalities can be found—you have the leaders, the respected, the popular ones, the clowns, the cocky, the tough guys, the jerks, the quiet types, and so on. On a team there is racism, clashing of personalities, some players will sleep with another player's girlfriend or wife, and some players are just assholes. As a result, arguments and fist fights do happen. Probably more often than you think.

In my experience, I found that the veterans, or the older players, were the ones that were the nicest. They are older, wiser, and have been around the game much longer than you. I think a lot of times they are more settled in the game and in their lives, so they can afford to be nice. They have been around, and you can tell that the little things do not bother them anymore. And, some of them play for so long, simply for the love of the game.

Mostly, I was the quiet type. I never had a direct incident with anyone. I would hear of guys talking behind my back, and some would even say things right to me. But I never let it get to me. I tried to be friendly to everyone, or keep my mouth shut. I was there to focus on baseball. If I did have a bad game and someone said something, I would try to forget it, and put it behind me as quick as possible.

Sports are all about proving yourself, and because of this, you spend a lot of time comparing yourself to others. Other people compare you to others as well. It is right there in the open for everybody to see. It can take its toll on you, if you choose to allow it to. But I never bothered myself with the thought of other players. I mean, I was still competitive, but I never compared myself or worried about what someone else might be doing. I never felt I had to. I just knew that I had to work hard, and one day I would be in the Show. It wasn't that I was cocky, I just did not have any doubts. My father knew the game, and he was never worried that I would not make it, so neither was I. Since the day my father brought out Crow, and told me to hit Crow in the chest, and if he didn't catch it, that was his problem, I knew that I should never worry about what the other guy did, or failed to do. Worry about yourself, is what my father always told me. So I believed, that if I followed what my father taught me, it was inevitable that I would make it someday.

That year, I also found out that the minors could be a lot of fun. But they could also be too much fun. Partying in the minors can take its toll on a player, and consequently, players that get caught up in the party scene may miss out on their chance to make it to the big leagues. Their level of conditioning usually is the first to drop, and then their numbers. It will all catch up to you if you let it. There are a lot of talented players that you will never get to see because of bad decisions. The minors are not just another beautiful day at the park. It is work, and you have to do what you can to survive, and make it out on top.

For the most part, Class A ball was an introduction to learn how to survive in the minor leagues as a teammate, and as a competitor for the limited spots available. Another part, was learning how to survive on the field.

Chapter 50

There are a lot of things that happen outside of baseball that people don't talk much about—including the fights between teammates, and other personal issues. But there are also the things that happen on the field: the fights, the bench clearing brawls, and the bad mouthing. Things often get heated when guys are in competition with each other. There are a lot of egos and testosterone (natural and unnatural) flying around. Insults travel around the field just as much as the ball does. For some people, part of their game is trying to get in the other player's head. I was never like this, except for a few isolated incidents, but it happened to me a lot. Most of the time you have to try to ignore the people that are trying to get in your head, but sometimes it's easier said than done.

My first bench clearing brawl happened in my first year of Class A ball. It happened in a game against the Burlington Bees, and I was 3 for 3 with a home run. It was over half way through the season and you could tell that the life in the minors was starting to wear on players. For many it is a longer season than they are used to, and with all the traveling, and with the overall conditions, ball players get moody.

I was having a great day, and I walked up to plate in the top of the 8th. I got settled in the batter's box the same way I always did, and the catcher said to me out of nowhere, "You're a big fuckin' pussy, aren't you?" I didn't say anything, and so he added, "That's what I thought...a huge fuckin' pussy."

I called time and backed out of the box, looked at him, shook my head, and said, "Really?"

The catcher stood up and lost his shit. He started calling me every name in the book. The ump stepped in and gave the catcher a warning. The catcher was a short and stocky, brick shit house. I didn't know what his problem was. He must have been just mad at the world that day.

I got back in the box, and the first pitch was right at my head, and I didn't have time to move. It hit me right in the helmet, my helmet flew off, and I dropped to the ground. It all happened so quickly and must have looked way worse than it felt. I was thankful for my helmet because I hardly felt anything. Getting beaned in the head was not enough for the catcher, and he stood over me and spouted off more insults. The ump motioned that the pitcher and the catcher were tossed from the game, but it was too late. As soon as I got hit, my team ran out, so did theirs—both bullpens included. I was angry because they could have seriously injured me, and for no other reason than the fact that I was having a good day. There was some pushing and shoving, but it was basically a big pile up right around the plate. It took awhile for everyone to settle down. Eventually, I got to take my spot on first base, while they brought in a new catcher and a new pitcher. Our next hitter ended up getting out and that was it for the inning. We won that game 13-2 and I reached base all four times, scored twice, had four RBIs, and almost got my head taken off. Not a bad day.

Another incident early on in my career happened when I slid hard into second base. The second baseman happened to be standing right on top of the bag and I ended up clipping his ankles with my cleats. It wasn't a dirty slide, he just happened to get in the way. That didn't stop him from saying, "If you slide like that again, I will put this ball through your fucking teeth."

No one has said this was a gentleman's game. Or have they? Nonetheless, these were not isolated incidents. Things like this happened quite often, and they happen in all levels of the game. As far as I am concerned, it's okay to show emotion out there, and situations do get tense, but it's not okay to try and hurt someone. Baseball is meant to be fun, and you can't play and have fun if you're injured.

For a lot of players, however, they would say most of the fun happened off the field.

Chapter 51

When it came to enjoying life as a ball player, I did make the most of my situation when I first started out. Come to think of it, the beginning of my minor league career was a lot like my freshman year in high school. I was hanging out with older guys and I tried to fit in. When I was with Elizabeth, I didn't need to party or chase girls. But since I was now on my own, I didn't have anyone to keep me in check, and because of this, I made a few mistakes.

One of those mistakes happened to be a girl named Kayla. After the first few weeks of the season, I was playing well and was leading the league in batting average, stolen bases, and I already had four home runs. After one of our games, a few of my teammates made me go out with them to a bar in Peoria. I still wasn't of age, and technically I couldn't go out to any bars, but since ball players often receive special treatment, they didn't even bother asking for ID.

When we got there, someone bought a round of beers and I felt like I had to have one to fit in. As the night progressed, I had a few more beer, and I was feeling pretty good. The other guys were having a great time drinking beer, doing shots, and letting loose.

After awhile, I went to the washroom, and when I was walking back to our table, a girl came up to me and stopped me.

"Hey, handsome! You're Ozzie Shaw, right?"

"I am."

"My name's Kayla. How about you buy me a drink."

"I would love to, but I need to get back to my friends," I said, trying to be polite.

"Wouldn't you rather hang out with me tonight, instead?"

She had a point. She was a pretty girl, but she seemed to have an edge to her. I decided she was more sexy than pretty. It had been awhile since I had even talked to a girl, so I decided what the hell. She was so forward, and I didn't have much choice, either way.

We went to the bar and I bought her a drink and one for myself. Then we went to a booth and chatted. It turned out that she was a baseball fan and knew a lot about the game. I must admit, that was quite the turn on for me.

I didn't have any more to drink, but since I wasn't used to drinking, I was already feeling drunk. At this point in my life, I was a lightweight.

Kayla and I had a good time, talking and laughing, and after awhile, she invited me over to her place. Part of me wanted to just go back and hang out with my teammates, but a stronger part of me wanted to go home with her. So I did.

I waved to my teammates as we passed by to let them know I was leaving.

"Have fun, Oz!" Leroy our catcher yelled.

Thanks for that, bud, I thought.

When we got back to her place, it was a small little home, but it was nice. Kayla said she was going to go get more comfortable and that she would be right back. I wandered around her living room and looked around. I felt awkward because I was not used to these situations, and I didn't know what I was supposed to do. I could hear her rustling around in the bedroom from where I was. I spotted a table in her living room that had a bunch of pictures of her and several players that were on the Cardinals at that time. I picked one up that caught my eye.

"Holy shit, you know Tony the Crusher Campbell?" I said loud enough for her to hear.

"I've known a lot of ball players that have come up through Peoria," she replied from the bedroom. I remember thinking that was pretty cool at the time. "Maybe I'll have a picture of you someday, too," she added.

That sounded good to me.

Kayla came out wearing nothing but black lingerie. She walked over to me and practically jumped my bones, and then dragged me back to her bedroom. She knew what she was doing. It was clear she brought me back to her place for one reason, and one reason only.

It was the first time I was with someone besides Elizabeth. And I will tell you, after the deed was done, I did not feel good about it. Why does that always happen? Why do we not feel good about things, always after the fact? Sometimes I wish we didn't feel good about it before the fact, so that we could avoid doing it in the first place. But that is rarely the case.

"You really knocked it out of the park tonight," she said breaking the awkward silence. Now this might sound like a good thing, and normally it could boost someone's sexual confidence, but the way she said it, it sounded like she had said that line many times before. After she said that, I felt terrible, and I rolled over to try and fall asleep. But I stayed awake thinking about Elizabeth. I went from the greatest girl in the world, to this? To having a one night stand with someone I didn't even know? I felt ashamed.

A couple days later in the locker room, my teammates, however, congratulated me about going home with Kayla.

"I heard you were with Kayla the other night...she's one of the most famous cleat chasers. A real superstar fucker...just so you know," Max Lawrence our first baseman said. "Her claim to fame is that she slept with five guys that are currently making it big in the Show."

"I fucked her last night," Andrew Simon one of our starting pitchers said, and received some high fives from a few teammates. "She was pretty good, hey Oz? Did you knock it out of the park too? Looks like we're on our way to the Show," he said, trying to give me a high five.

I weekly slapped his hand. I was feeling sick to my stomach. Two guys in three nights? Who knows how many others. Then I thought about all the pictures she had in her living room. I tried to remember how many, but had to stop myself. And then I thought about The Crusher. That was something I did not want to imagine.

Sleeping with girls that took turns being with any ball player they could find, was not something I ever wanted to do. There are a lot of players that welcomed girls like that, but I was never one of them. I hated myself because of it.

I couldn't let this affect me, however. I had to learn from it and put it behind me. I knew I didn't want to do anything that might interfere with baseball anymore. I had made so many sacrifices already for the game, and I had to keep focused no matter what. Baseball was to be my only priority. I didn't care if guys bugged me because I didn't party and sleep with girls as much as they did. As far as I was concerned, all that mattered, was that I was going to make it to the Show.

But for a lot of my teammates, it was sex and baseball. Adding more notches on the belt was like a side game to many ball players. My teammates wanted to hit home runs on and off the field. Before you get angry and try to contradict me, yes there are exceptions. It's just that when you are a part of a team that's the type of things you talk about. Ball players love to hear and share stories. That's how they pass all the down time. When your life is playing a game, other things also become a game. We feed off of each other. I was pretty timid compared to others, but I followed for a time—we all followed. It's just the culture of being a ball player. But it all depended on how you were raised. Sure some came from different cultures, or from a very religious family, so they did have different beliefs and attitudes. But for a lot of us young guys that were on our own for the first time, we wanted all that this life had to offer—the parties, the women, and the game. Being significantly sheltered my whole life, part of me was ready to join in. I was ready to have fun. I was ready to be a ball player. I wanted to pull pranks, drink beer, go out, and do all the things that a lot of other guys were doing. But deep down I knew I shouldn't do those things. And I did my best not to. That was another sacrifice I made for the game. And I believe I continued to improve on the field because of it.

But how did some of these other ball players succeed when they seemed to focus on other things besides baseball? For some, I think the answer is all in their routine.

Chapter 52

One thing that amazed me is how naturally talented some players were. Some players would drink all night, be hung over, but they would still play well the next day. You would think they wouldn't be able to perform, but they would go 4 for 4, or have some other ridiculous day at the plate. I never knew if the coaches could tell their starting player was drunk or hung over, but if they did, they must have known they could still contribute. Yet, some players spent hours and hours practicing and doing all the right things, but could not make it to the level of some of these guys that didn't give a shit—simply because they didn't need to. I didn't understand how some players could head to the field feeling like garbage, but once the game started, they were on. It didn't seem to matter what their condition was a few minutes before game time. It amazed me, but it almost made me a little sad.

Was this the game I loved? Were some of the players I grew up watching, just like this? Then it made me think, if I had to work so hard to get here, should I be playing baseball? Maybe this game was meant for the ones with inconceivable talent? These are some of the things I thought about, and I talked to my father about some of these concerns. He said that the lifestyle of these players would catch up to them, and they would be the ones not making it, and chances are they will look back on their life and regret not giving it their all. Sure enough he was right. Many of those guys often didn't get out of Double-A ball. Sure they could compete with those in the minors, but they would never be able to do it consistently in the majors, and keep up with the best players in the world, day in and day out.

But there were still some of these players that would party, not work as hard as others, but would still perform and succeed against all logic. What I noticed was that many of these players would have the same routine, and many were superstitious. No matter how lousy they were feeling on game day, they would dress the same way, warm up the same way, do the exact same thing every time they were on the on deck circle, and up at the plate. Some pitchers and other defensive players would have the same little routine before every pitch.

What I came to understand is that with the same routine, you will have the same results, which you want to be good results. So when I was playing shortstop, I learned that I needed to develop the same routine and drill it into myself by doing it over and over again. After I did the same routine, I would be prepared for any ball that came my way. When you watch games on TV, you often don't get to see what a fielder does before the pitch, since the camera is often on the pitcher, the batter, and the catcher. You don't see what is going on behind the pitcher. However, when you watch a game live in person, you will see a variety of routines. Some guys play with their gloves, they may take it off, put it on, take a few baby steps as the pitcher is in their windup, and then get set with their knees bent ready to move to their left or right, forward, or backwards. Some infielders will time their pitchers and jump up in the air as their pitcher throws the ball, and when they land they are ready to move in any direction. This little hop allows these fielders to literally get a good jump on the ball.

Now if you watched me play shortstop, you would notice I did the same thing before every pitch. I would take my glove off, wipe my hand on my pants, put the glove back on, look at it, turn it over once, turn it back, then when the pitcher is set, I would take one slow step with my right foot, then as he makes his move I would take a small step with my left foot. When the pitcher released the ball, I would do a small hop, and get set. It depended on the pitcher and the timing—sometimes I would slow it down a bit, or speed it up, and it also depended on whether he was pitching from the full windup or stretch—but it was always the same: "Right, left, little hop, set." It became the routine I did all throughout my professional career. It was second nature, and once I did it, I would be in the zone on every single pitch.

Hitting is no different. You will see players do the exact same thing every time they are up to bat. Some will tap their cleats a certain number of times, some will do up the straps on their batting gloves, and others will tap the plate a few times, or various combinations of other things. It is all a part of their routine, and it has to be done in order for them to be comfortable and ready.

Having a routine was one of the most important things I learned in the minors. With a routine it didn't matter what team I was playing for, where I was playing, how I was feeling, because once I completed the same routine each game, and before every pitch, it would help me focus. Sometimes a routine can be the secret to one's success.

Yet, a routine can only take you so far. I knew I had to continue to work hard and do things to separate myself from every other player. With the way I worked, it's hard to believe that I had the same amount of talent as others that did not have to work as hard. I may have had the tools to learn and grow and become a great ball player, but it was a lot of hard work, and without that hard work, I would not have made if very far in baseball.

But one thing that I did have that gave me an edge over every other player that I was competing against, was a father that could teach me more about the game than anyone else.

Chapter 53

When I was in the minors, I would call and talk to my father whenever I needed to. He would never ask me how I was coping or anything like that, we would only talk about the game. He was my baseball coach and that was it. I would tell him how I hit that day, the plays I made, the score, and other things baseball related. Most importantly, he would always try and help me work out any issues I was having. In a stretch of games in the middle of the season, I was having trouble with being behind on the ball, and when I tried to fix that, I over compensated. When I called my father, he reminded me to go back to the basics. "Try and hit the ball back to the pitcher...look to hit it up the middle, " he said. "Once you get that down, then you can try and start pulling the ball again. Go back to what I taught you. Go back to all the things I told you in the backyard. Keep it simple. Quick hands, and up the middle.

"And remember, get to know the pitchers. Where is his arm in the glove? Does he fidget? Is there any tell of what pitch is coming? Wait for your pitch to hit. Visualize that you will get your pitch and wait for that one. Anything resembling that pitch hit it. If not, let it go. Once you are down to two strikes then you have to protect. Hit anything close. Look for patterns. What's his strike out pitch? What did he get you out on last time? Know these things. If you don't have time to do this, or you never faced this pitcher before, look for your pitch. Your pitch is a fastball just on the inner half. Wait for that. And if he gives it to you, drive it like you can. He doesn't know you either, so it's a fair battle. You'll win this battle if he gives you exactly what you have been looking for. Fight him off until he gives you what you want."

After I was done talking with my father, I would pull out *The Science of Hitting*, and Mr. Williams would tell me the same thing.

My father also taught me to study my own pitcher when I was playing shortstop. One thing I needed to do when I played defense was to know what our pitchers threw. I would even get the signs they used, so if I was playing more up the middle, I would be able to see what pitch was coming, and based on where the catcher was set up, I could anticipate where the ball would be hit. I believe this is the exact reason why many said that I could get to balls that would normally be a base hit. I studied everything, because that's what my father taught me to do.

Other than my father, I didn't have anyone else to talk to outside of baseball. Jake and I tried to catch up as much as we could, but that eventually faded away. We were both busy and we had different lives. It became more apparent that we wouldn't be able to see each other since our schedules were so different, and when I was home, he was in school. It's amazing how quickly you start to develop new lives and separate from the people you were close with. You start to realize that for many people life goes on without you, and you go on without them.

What I had to do, was truly forget all the people that I left back home. I needed to focus on the here and now. Nothing mattered but my baseball career. I realized I had to become a machine that only did what he had to do to improve his game. That was my goal. That's what motivated me. But yet, those times alone, especially at night, my mind would wander off, and I would think about all those that I had left behind. I would think of the life I had outside of baseball. But mostly, the life I wished I had outside of baseball. This empty feeling I had always remained just that—empty.

I wanted to believe there was more to life than baseball, but I didn't know where to begin. I was lonely, confused, and unfulfilled. There was something missing, but I told myself, the only thing that was missing was my spot on the Cardinals.

But deep down, I knew it was Elizabeth who was missing from my life.

Chapter 54

It would be a lie if I told you that I never thought I would get back together with Elizabeth. In my head, I would concoct entire scenarios of how Elizabeth and I would get back together. I would imagine that I made it the major leagues, I signed a huge contract, I am leading the league in slugging, and I am on my way to winning yet another Gold Glove award. Then one night, while I am sitting alone in my big house, I call up Elizabeth to see if she wants to meet up sometime. When we do, it's just like we were never apart. We laugh, smile, and cry tears of joy together. I wouldn't risk wasting any more time, so that night I ask her to marry me, and she says "Yes." We create a beautiful family and we live happily ever after.

Or another scenario I would think about would go something like this: I would be up to bat, something in the stands would catch my eye, and I would look into the crowd and there Elizabeth would be, with her Cardinals hat on. She would stand up and say, "Hey, Oz! Hit me a home run!" and I would go up to bat and hit one far over the fence just for her. Then after the game she would run up to me like she used to, and we would hug, and kiss. We would proceed to tell each other how we love each other so much, and we can't live without one another. She would move in with me, we would get married, have kids, and have a wonderful life. When I finally retired, I would be able to watch my kids grow up, and enjoy every moment with the love of my life.

In these scenarios, I always fast-tracked everything, because all I wanted to do is be with her as soon as possible. But I didn't just want to be with her, I wanted to be with her forever. I wanted to have a family with her. I visualized everything in so much detail that I could almost believe it would happen someday. I would never imagine that she had moved on without me. I always pictured her waiting just for me after all these years. It's probably the reason why I never found anyone else. The girls I did meet, I was always careful not to let them get too close. It's like I was waiting for when I could be with the girl I loved.

I would be so deep in these fantasies, and then I would snap out of it, and say to myself, *Focus, Oz, focus!*. And then I would think about something related to baseball.

Until the next time Elizabeth entered my thoughts.

Chapter 55

Near the end of the season in Class A ball, I remember sitting on a bus that smelt like a combination of dirt, sweat, and tobacco juice. It was the smell of a ball team that got it's ass kicked for the tenth game in a row. Road trips are painful as it is, and to add nothing but losses, that was the ultimate "fuck you" from the baseball gods. It was tough on everyone. Coaches' jobs were on the line, starting positions were up for grabs, and anyone could be traded or dropped at any moment. During times like that, it would be expected that things would need to be shaken up. It was hard. It was hard because there were so many factors at play. We wanted to be a winning ball club, but we never knew how long we would be on this team, and all we wanted to do was move up. We were never able to mesh together as a group. But we were all in a place that could make or break a career. The truth is, it was not glorious in any sense. It's not easy to make a name for yourself when you are on the losing end of things. You only get looked at when things are going well. The attention that we were receiving was not positive attention. It was hard for anyone to believe that we were the future of the game.

When we got back to Peoria, a lot of my teammates did what they normally did when things were going wrong: they went out and got shit-faced in order to let off steam. They did this, almost as if hoping, that in an drunken stupor, one would determine the meaning of our slump, or it was one last ditch effort to turn everything around.

My teammates tried to get me to come out with them, but I did what I always did—I went back to my room and thought about what I could do to make my game better. We were losing, but I was still playing well. I decided I needed to develop my leadership skills. Some guys were champions on every team they played for. They were the type of players that could turn a team around, and make everyone play better in the process. A good example is Troy—the pitcher we had when we won the state championship in high school—he was a leader and a champion. I wanted to be that type of player.

I called my father to ask him how I could be a leader. He told me that was a foolish idea. He didn't want me to make other players better. He wanted me to be the star and keep doing what I was doing. He said that if I wanted to be a leader, I could be one when I made it to the big leagues, and had already proved myself. Until then, I needed to keep working only on myself and the way I played. There were so many things that I wanted to do, but I ended up getting shut down by my father. Many times, I should have followed my instinct.

We finished the year with a lousy 48-90 record. Besides some of the long losing streaks we had, for me it still felt like it was another good year. It was a good season for me because my hitting greatly improved. I had 462 at bats, with a .303 average, 16 home runs, 76 RBIs, and 37 stolen bases. This year I only had 52 strike outs, which was only 15 more than Rookie ball, in over twice as many at bats. I was way more comfortable at the plate and the results showed in my numbers.

In all honestly, it didn't matter to me that the minor league teams that I was on didn't always have a winning record. Sure being on a winning team was always a good thing, and in my heart I always wanted to be a winner, but I still believed that a World Series championship was the only championship that counted. I always believed my day would come that I was helping the St. Louis Cardinals win. That's all that mattered.

After that season, I went back to Columbia for a couple weeks to spend time with my father, and then I headed back to Evansville to live with my uncle Frank and his family. I further separated myself from the life I once had in Columbia, and baseball was my only priority.

My offseason was a lot like the year before—I continued to work hard, so that I was ready for spring training.

Chapter 56

So far in my baseball career, everything was going well for me. I had another great spring training and was promoted once again. It wasn't the promotion that I wanted exactly, but at least it was something. In 2002, I was sent to Potomac, Virginia to play for the Potomac Cannons, who were a Class A-Advanced team in the Carolina league. My goal was to prove myself and hopefully make a jump to Double-A sometime during the season.

I was on another losing team in Potomac, but I kept improving and showed that I was better than a lot of others in A ball. I was the Carolina League's player of the month in May, and a couple weeks into June, I got the call to say that I was moving up to Double-A in New Haven, Connecticut, to play for the New Haven Ravens. They had a winning record and wanted me to come up and help the squad when their shortstop got called up to Triple-A. I moved to Connecticut, and continued to stay hot for the rest of the season.

Once I moved up to Double-A, it was different. I could tell that players were a lot more serious. Of course there were still the partiers and jokers, but those guys could be found at every level. In Double-A, I knew I needed to step my work ethic up a notch. Life outside of baseball went to the way-side a little in Class A, and I had to make up for that. There were still distractions in Double-A, however.

The minor leagues were not the Show, but they could be pretty damn entertaining. There was such a diverse group of guys, some would make it and some would not, and others would hold on to their dream for as long as they could. Players were always joking with each other, being vulgar, and playing practical jokes.

I like to think that there is so much tension, heartbreak, and stress in the minors, that ball players will do what they can to ease that stress and keep things as light as possible. For instance, players that fell asleep on the bus before everyone else, would be prime targets for practical jokes. Not only was it hard to sleep on a hot, smelly, and cramped bus, but you also had to learn to sleep with one eye open.

When I was in Double-A, a lanky pitcher named Seth Lancaster was the second guy in our rotation. He was slotted to pitch the next day, and he needed his rest. Unfortunately for him, he was the first to fall asleep on the bus and some of my teammates were trying to decide what they should do to him. Some guys suggested shaving his eye brows in order to distract the batters the next day. They decided against it because he would wake up by the sound of the electric razor. Instead, they decided to draw on his face with a permanent marker.

Seth didn't realize anything happened to him until we got to the field, and he had to spend the time he needed to warm up before his start, scrubbing the permanent marker off of his face. He got most of it off but his face was red and raw from all the scrubbing, and you could still see the faint lines of what was once there.

When our manager saw Seth, he demanded answers. He asked the usual suspects, and Jared Lyons, our relief pitcher, said, "All we did was draw a bat with two balls on his cheek. We all love baseball, right?"

Everybody was cracking up. You could tell that our manager was even trying to hold it in, "A bat and two balls going into our starting pitchers mouth...just letting everyone know he loves baseball? Give me a break," our manager said, and then there was an explosion of laughter. Let me tell you, they did not draw a bat and two baseballs. I'm confident you can guess what it actually was.

In the minor leagues you could get away with this stuff because games were not televised. But if this happened in the Show, there would be some serious consequences, and probably some pretty hefty fines. But in the minors, stuff like this was a common occurrence. There may be small fines involved, but to the guys that did it, they usually thought it was well worth it. All you could hope for was that you wouldn't be the first to fall asleep on those dreadful bus rides.

We finished the season 82-57 and it felt good to be winning games again—mostly because everyone is in a much better mood when they are a part of a winning team. By the end of the season, I was starting to become the star player that I once was in high school. The right people were noticing me, and I continued to excel.

Chapter 57

In 2003, I had another good spring training, and I was sent to Knoxville, TN, to play for the new affiliate Double-A team for the Cardinals, the Tennessee Smokies, who were a part of the Southern League. I played mostly a full season there, minus fifteen games that I played in Triple-A. I got pulled up to Triple-A for a long road trip in June, while their shortstop was on the disabled list. I continued to prove myself, but I was sent back down when their shortstop returned.

Back with the Smokies, we finished the season with a 76-63 record. I continued to put up good numbers and my average was still over .300. My power started to increase dramatically, however. I had 33 home runs, including 3 that I hit in 15 games in Triple-A. I also had 42 stolen bases, which made me a major threat up at the plate and on base. It was hard for teams to put me on, since there was a good chance I would put myself into scoring position, so I saw a lot of good pitches. I was hoping they would bring me back up to Triple-A, but all I could do was continue to play my game, and I knew it would happen eventually.

That year I felt like I was deep into the routine of the minor leagues. I knew all the ins and outs of being on a new team, and I was able to focus strictly on baseball. It's hard to take everything in when you are a minor league player. A lot of cities, restaurants, hotels, and ball parks, all seem the same. I spent a lot of time in a lot of different cities, but I can't tell you much about any of them. A bus would drop you off at the field or hotel and take you to a restaurant and that was it. We did not go to many other places. Many of these places all seem to blur together. Even many of the games, at bats, and plays I have made are hazy. But I think that's the way life is—some things become a routine, and you only remember the things that stand out.

Scott Anderson stands out the most in my memory of the minor leagues. Him and I remained close in Double-A. His heavy fastball and pin-point command were winning us a lot of games that year. But one game that I remember more than any other game, in my entire baseball career, is the complete game no-hitter that Scott threw that July. He had 13 strikeouts, was getting tons of ground balls, and I made five plays that day. I remember feeling like I was witnessing something magical. Scott dominated the entire game, and I knew he was ready to move up.

Scott was so talented, but he was always extremely hard on himself. There were times he would be so down after a bad game, that I thought he would pack up and quit, and he did threaten to do just that several times. I think a part of his attitude made him such a good pitcher. He was a perfectionist. He always wanted to do better no matter how good he was that day. I learned a lot from him, and our long discussions about baseball. Baseball was our life and that's why we got along so well.

Scott ended up hurting his elbow towards the end of the season, and he had to miss a full year after he had Tommy John surgery. A lot of pitchers come back better than ever, but he never did. His velocity returned, but he lost his accuracy and stamina. He ended up making the transition to the bullpen, like many pitchers do, but he went up and down in the minors for years. He would never make it as a full-time player in the big leagues. He was one of those remarkably talented players that people would never get the pleasure to watch. Not very many people will know of him, but he pitched the best game I have ever seen. As our careers went in separate directions, we lost touch with each other. We had our time in the game and that was it. I never heard from him again. But I guarantee from time to time, he still thinks, "What if?" It's one of the saddest parts of this sometimes, elusive game.

Another thing that is challenging about the minors, is that a lot of the time players want to play hurt, because they do not want to lose their spot. If someone takes your spot and excels, well, you might have just put your future in jeopardy. There is also the risk that you could injure yourself even more, and naturally this also can put your future at stake. All of a sudden you realize that it's extremely difficult to make the right decision. When you see so many great players come and go, you start to understand that luck, and being at the right place at the right time can make or break someone's career. But you have to push things like this out of your mind and continue to work your ass off, regardless.

In the offseason of 2003, I started to feel like I was reaching the prime of my athletic ability. I felt like I was ready to be in the major leagues. In the past three years, I had learned a lot about the game, and I kept on getting stronger. At 21, I was six foot one and 190 pounds. I was older, more mature, and no longer felt like a kid. That was the first time I felt like I had grown up.

I spent some time with my uncle Frank—like I always did— but this time I went back to Columbia for a longer period of time than usual. No longer was I afraid of being home. I didn't care who I ran into. I could handle all the attention, and I could handle seeing anyone that I may not have wanted to see a couple years earlier. Time had gone by and I was a different person. I think a part of me had a feeling that I would not be back for awhile. I felt like it would be my last year in the minors, and sooner than later, I would be starting a life in St. Louis. I treated this offseason as my last visit before I moved on to bigger and better things.

When I got back to Columbia, my father looked great.

"Pop, there is something different about you," I said. "You look younger!"

"Well, I stopped drinking, Son. I haven't had a beer in six months," he said. "I have no need for it anymore."

In all the times I called him when I was away, he never told me he was planning to stop drinking, or that he had been sober for that long.

"Good for you, Pop!"

I didn't know what else to say.

Now that I was so close to the Show, maybe both of our lives would change for the better.

Chapter 58

I knew I was one of the best players coming out of spring training in 2004. The Cardinals sent me to play with the Triple-A Memphis Redbirds—who were a part of the Pacific Coast League—to see if I could continue to perform at the highest level of the minor leagues. I was a few weeks away from turning 22 years old, and I was on the door step to my dream of making the major leagues. In Memphis, I got to see more of Tennessee, and I truly enjoyed my time there. I was finally playing in a big city, and our road trips took us all over the country to other big cities. I got to see New Orleans, Sacramento, Las Vegas, Colorado Springs, Oklahoma City, Nashville, and many others. The road trips were still not easy, but they were a lot easier than the lower levels of the minors. In Triple-A, we would take a plane to places further away, and if it was within driving distance, we would often have two busses, so everyone could have their own section. The equipment managers would handle everything. No longer did I have to pack my bag, drag it to and from the bus, unpack, and do it all over again. I know it seems arbitrary, but little things like that can make a big difference. It was one less thing you had to worry about.

The jump to Triple-A was all business. I was playing with and against players that would be called up to the majors at anytime, players from the Show that were on rehab assignments, and players that had been up and down throughout their career. At that level, we were all so close to our dream, yet so far. I felt I had to push even harder to prove myself. I was the first one to the field and the last to leave. I would train constantly, and hit until I couldn't hold a bat anymore. I would throw until I couldn't throw anymore. It got to the point that my coaches pulled me into their office, and told me to slow down. They said I was no good to anyone if I was sore, or got hurt from over doing it. The thing is, the harder I worked, the better I felt. I slowed down a bit, but I was still always working on my game. A few players resented me, but those that mattered admired my work ethic. I wanted to separate myself from everyone else, and it didn't go unnoticed.

We started off the season taking 10 of our first 12 games, and that got the ball rolling. In the first few weeks of the season I put together a 16 game hit streak, and already had two multi-home run games. I had 7 homeruns during that stretch. My teammates joked around that I would hit over 100 home runs at the pace I was going. We were the best team in the league at that point, and everyone on the team seemed to feed off of the joys of winning.

Early in the season, there had been rumors that the starting shortstop for the Cardinals, Luis Rios, would be traded. He was a good player, but he was prone to injuries. If he got traded, I was hoping they were planning on bringing me up. But he never did get moved to another team, and I continued to work my ass off in Triple-A.

In Memphis, we played at AutoZone Park that had around a 14, 000 spectator capacity, and sometimes it would fill up. It was good to have fans that would support us, and it felt like a different level from where I started out in the minors. Fans actually knew who you were, and there was more media exposure involved.

But the cool thing about being in the Pacific Coast League was that our rivalry with Nashville made things interesting. Every game between us was the battle of Tennessee. One of our starting pitchers went to Vanderbilt before he got drafted, and he still knew a lot of people in Nashville. A bunch of his friends would make the trip to Memphis when we played the Nashville Sounds, and it could get up to around ten thousand fans when we went to their park.

Nashville, Tennessee is country music's breading ground of superstars. Even the Nashville Sounds' scoreboard was shaped like a guitar. There was not much room for baseball amongst all the people there to enjoy music, and that's probably why they never got a professional team. But when we were in town, a lot of my teammates would go down to lower Broadway, which is also known as "Honky Tonk Row," to see all the live music, and all the beautiful tourists who were there to do the same. Or sometimes, my teammates would head to Midtown where the college bars were—Vanderbilt girls and cold beer was an ideal night for a lot of guys on the team.

Most of the time on road trips, I didn't go out with the rest of my teammates, but I was always curious after I heard a bunch of stories about Nashville. Finally, one afternoon, I decided to check out downtown Nashville with a couple other players.

And I met a girl.

Chapter 59

I met her at Legends Corner on lower Broadway in Nashville. She was on stage with an acoustic guitar, she had blonde hair, and was wearing a simple, black sundress. I was never a big country music fan, but something about her captivated me. Her name was Lindsay Lock, and she sounded like an angel. After her song, she came off the stage, and went around to collect money in a big, tip jar. She sat down beside me, and asked us if we wanted to give her any tips.

"I'll give you more than just a tip," Phil Letowski, our loud mouth second baseman said.

She immediately hopped down from the bar stool and called him an asshole.

"Nice work, you fucking idiot," Blaire Morgan, our first baseman said to Phil.

We were there for awhile, and I went to the back to use the washroom. When I came out, the girl that had been singing up on stage was now sitting at a table by herself, and was looking through some papers. I don't know why, but I felt like I had to apologize.

I walked up to where she was sitting, and she looked up at me with a little smile. "Sorry for my friend back there. He... he's an idiot," I said.

"Don't worry about it," she replied. "Singing in bars, I hear stuff like that all the time. You sort of get used to it."

I knew exactly what she meant. She had to stand up there

and perform day in and day out, and not let any distractions bother her or get in the way. I realized that being a singer, is similar to being a ball player.

"Well, I just wanted to say that you were amazing up there," I said. "I don't know much about music, but I can tell you will become someone great someday."

"Thank you darling," she said. "I'll be back up on stage soon after my break. Ya'll should stick around for awhile."

I said I would, and I went back to my spot at the bar.

We ended up watching a couple more songs, but the guys that I was with wanted to move on to see what else Honky Tonk Row had to offer. That afternoon we made our way to Tootsies, The Stage, and a few other places on Broadway before we went back to the hotel. But I wish we would have stayed at Legends Corner.

After the first time I saw Lindsay, I couldn't get her out of my mind. I had to see her again. We had a series back in Nashville a couple months later, and this time I drove down early by myself. That was the nice thing about Nashville—it was close enough that some of us would take our own vehicles, or car pool together, which gave us a break from the bus, and gave us a little more freedom.

I went back to Legends Corner on a Wednesday afternoon, hoping Lindsay would be there. But this time I was alone—I didn't want any of my teammates to get in the way. When I walked in, she was up on the stage wearing white shorts and a black top. She was just as beautiful as last time. After a few songs, she came around again with that big, tip jar, but surprisingly, she remembered me.

"Hey, you're back!" she said, and jumped up on a bar stool beside me. "I thought you looked familiar when you walked in. This might sound weird, but there was something about you that I kept thinking about later. It's that look in your eye," she put her tip jar down on the bar. "Do you remember when you said I would be great someday? Well looking at you...I want you to know, and I don't know what you do, but I can tell you'll be someone great yourself."

"Thank you," I said with a smile.

I couldn't believe that she remembered me, and hearing her say that she kept thinking about me, made me feel something that I hadn't felt in a long time.

"My name's Lindsay, Lindsay Lock," she said, and held out her hand.

"My name's Ozzie Shaw," I said, and I took her hand and shook it.

She said that she had to go back to collecting tips, but she hoped that I would stay awhile, so we could talk during her break.

During her break, we had a few more minutes to chat, and I liked her even more. I felt like she could see right through me. I don't know how she did it. Maybe it was because we were on similar paths in our lives—we were both working hard to become somebody with our given talents; we were living through tough times just to make it big; and we were both paying our dues. Either way, we had a connection, and we both felt it. I don't know where I got the confidence from—maybe it was because I was more mature—but I asked her if she wanted to go for dinner after she was done with her set. She said she would love to.

I continued to watch her perform, and the whole time I was drawn to her. She was beautiful, she was talented, and she had so much confidence when she was up on stage.

After she finished her last song for the day, she circulated the room with her tip jar, and came up to me last.

"So, where do you want to go tonight?" she asked.

"You know what, I 'm not even sure," I replied with a awkward chuckle. "I'm not from here, so I don't know anywhere good to go. Any suggestions?"

"We'll find a place," she said. "I just need to grab my things."

She grabbed what she needed, including her guitar, and we walked out together.

"If we go out somewhere, I don't want to haul my guitar along with me, so do you mind if I go drop my stuff off at my place? You could follow me there. I don't live far and there are some good restaurants nearby."

"That sounds great to me."

"And do you have a cell phone? I will give you my number just in case you get lost."

"I do," I replied. I pulled out my cell phone and put her number in.

I went and pulled my truck around to her vehicle, and let her lead the way. I was able to follow her to her place without any issues. When we got there, she ran in and dropped off her guitar, and came out to meet me. From there, we were able to walk a few blocks from her house to the restaurant. I hate to admit it, but as we walked to the restaurant, I thought about my first date with Elizabeth. I needed to get out of my own head, so I started to ask Lindsay questions.

"Are you from Nashville originally?"

"No, I have only been here a couple years. I moved here from South Carolina to follow my dream of becoming a country music singer."

"Well, like I said before, you're going to be great someday. But what I saw this afternoon, I think you already are."

"Thanks, Ozzie. You're sweet," she said. "So where are you from? What brings you to Nashville."

"I'm originally from Missouri, but I play baseball for the Memphis Redbirds. We have a game tomorrow night against the Nashville Sounds."

"Ahh, a ball player. That makes a lot of sense. Those guys you were with last time must have been your teammates, I take it?"

"They were," I said with a smirk.

"I've heard plenty of stories about ball players," she said. "But I can tell, you are one of the good ones."

When we got to the restaurant we were seated at a table near the window. The restaurant wasn't fancy or anything, but it was small and cozy, and Lindsay said the food was delicious. We looked at the menu, and then continued on with our conversation.

"So, what's the Memphis Redbirds? I mean, what league would that be?"

"It's a Triple-A team, in the minor leagues," I said. "It's one level below the major leagues."

"You must be pretty good then," she said, and took a sip of her water. "My older brother played baseball growing up. My parents dragged me to all his games. So I know a little about baseball. What position do you play?"

"I play shortstop."

"That's what my brother played! He also pitched. Do you pitch?"

"Not anymore, but I used to. Once you get to this level, we usually stick to one position."

"That's too bad. I always liked to watch him pitch. It was more exciting than seeing him stand there only to get a ball hit to him once or twice a game."

"I agree. There is a lot of standing around. But I love to hit. When you are a pitcher, you don't always get to hit."

"Are you a good hitter?"

"I think so."

"Do you hit a lot of home runs?"

"I do. I am currently leading the league in home runs."

"That's exciting!" she said. "You said you played tomorrow night in Nashville?"

"Yep, at seven o'clock at Herschel Greer Stadium."

"Maybe I will come watch."

"Have you ever been there before?"

"No. But I didn't have anyone to go watch before."

Everything was going better than I imagined. We already had plans for the next night, and our meal hadn't even arrived yet. As we ate, I asked her more about herself. I liked her and wanted to get to know her. I liked how she understood what it was like to leave everything behind to pursue one's dream. I also liked how she knew a little about baseball, but thankfully, not as much as someone like Kayla.

After dinner, I walked Lindsay back to her house. I told her she should come watch me play the next night, and she said she would. I went back to my hotel still feeling something that I hadn't felt in a long time—and now I knew what it was—I liked a girl. And for the first time in years, I was excited for a girl to come and watch me play baseball.

The next night Lindsay came to my game with two of her friends, but I wasn't able to talk to her until after. We won the game 5-4, and she said she had fun. I went 2-4 with a double and a single, but she jokingly said she thought I was going to hit her a home run.

"If you come back tomorrow night, maybe I will," I said.

"You play again tomorrow?"

"And Saturday and Sunday, and then we have three games in a row against the Sounds back in Memphis."

"That's a lot of baseball."

"It sure is. We only get about two days off a month."

"How do you do anything else other than baseball."

"I don't."

"I see."

"What are you doing tonight?" I asked, mostly to change the subject.

"My friends and I were thinking of going to Winners or Losers."

"What did you just say to me?"

"They're names of two bars in Midtown," she said with a giggle.

"Gotcha."

"You should come with us."

"I don't think I should. I shouldn't be out too late, and I need to get something to eat."

"I wouldn't mind getting something to eat with you."

"I would love that."

That night we went to a cool, open-air restaurant and bar called South Street in the Midtown area. We could hear all the noise coming from the college bars, and I was glad I chose not to go. All I wanted was to spend more quality time with Lindsay.

We had another nice meal together, and later that night, she invited me back to her place. There was nothing I wanted more, but I didn't accept her invitation. I told her that I had to go back to the hotel, and I did not want to risk breaking curfew, which was true, but I knew I could have easily gotten away with it. I'm not exactly sure why I didn't go home with her. Maybe I was just nervous. But back at the hotel, I stayed awake regretting not spending the night with Lindsay.

The following night, Lindsay came out once again to watch me play. This time I hit her a home run, but we lost the game 4-2. We made arrangements to go out after the game, and I suggested the same restaurant as the first night we went out.

That night we continued to talk about our lives, our goals, and our dreams, until the night was coming to a close.

"Does the offer from last night still stand?" I asked.

"What offer was that?"

"The offer of you inviting me to your place."

"What about breaking curfew?"

"You're worth it."

We went back to her house and spent a lovely night together. For the first time since Elizabeth, I didn't regret being with another woman.

From that weekend on, Lindsay would come to Memphis when she could, to spend time with me and watch me play. She would book gigs for when she was there, and I would go and watch her perform as well. I liked her, but since we were both so busy, we didn't get to see each other often. Maybe that was a good thing, because she was never that big of a distraction. But in a way, I felt like I was growing up, and maybe I was ready for a distraction.

Chapter 60

Every day, I felt like I was becoming a better hitter and fielder. I was making plays that many people couldn't make, and I was continuing to be a viable threat at the plate and on the base paths. There didn't seem to be many holes in my game; if any at all. The only remaining test to see if I was ready for the Show, would be if I could keep playing well once they pulled me up. I just needed the opportunity. I knew it would happen in a matter of time, but I was still enjoying being on a winning team, and I was having a lot of fun with Lindsay. But, on one home stint in Memphis against the Iowa Cubs, everything changed.

My cell phone rang and I saw it was Lindsay. I remember being excited every time she called. It was a great feeling.

"Hey, Ozzie, I'm playing a few gigs at a couple bars on Beale Street again, and was wondering if you had time to come watch me sing on Friday."

I told her I would. I was looking forward to seeing her. I had been away from Memphis for quite awhile, and I missed her.

When that Friday came along, I went to the bar she was playing at around noon, but I could only stay no more than an hour, because I had a game that night. Lindsay was already playing a set when I walked in. She looked and sounded as beautiful as ever. She smiled at me when she saw me, and I smiled back. She made me happy.

The bartender asked if she could get me anything, but I only asked for a water. I sat there and watched Lindsay like I had done the first time I met her. I sat there thinking about her, and I started to realize how much she meant to me. There was no doubt that I was starting to fall for her.

After her set, we moved to a table in the back where it wasn't as loud. "You look beautiful. And you sounded so amazing today," I said. "Not that you don't normally, but...you know what I mean." I laughed awkwardly.

"Thanks, Ozzie," I noticed her demeanor change, and her eyes filled with tears.

"What's wrong, Linds?"

"Ozzie, I wanted to tell you in person that we can't see each other anymore. What we had was a lot of fun. But I can't do it anymore."

"What? Why not?" I asked. I felt sick to my stomach.

"This was just a fling, Oz. The two of us meeting up every once in awhile...it was fun...but both of us are on our own paths," she said trying to explain. "Truth is, I met someone in Nashville. And I think I am in love with him. I'm so sorry, Ozzie."

I knew we weren't officially dating or anything, and I knew she may have been seeing other people, but this came as a blow.

"It's okay," I said, trying to keep my composure. "I'm glad you found someone that makes you happy."

I stood up.

"You're not going to stay?"

"I have to go get ready for my game tonight," I replied. "Come here," I said, motioning for her to give me one last hug. I squeezed her tight in my arms, and broke away. "Remember, you're going to be someone great, Lindsay Lock."

"So are you, Ozzie Shaw," she said, and smiled at me one last time.

I turned and walked straight out of the bar. I may have acted strong in front of Lindsay, but I was pretty shook up. I cared about her, and it didn't feel good to be rejected. When Lindsay ended the relationship we had, it felt like it came out of left field. And then I understood how Elizabeth must have felt—even though Lindsay and I were not in love like Elizabeth and I were.

I was happy for Lindsay, but at the same time part of me wished it was me that she was in love with. She was just another person that would no longer be in my life. Only this time, I wasn't the one that had pushed her away.

I headed to the field not knowing how I would play that night. I had a lot on my mind. But as soon as I picked up my bat, I forgot about the events of that afternoon. That's all I ever needed—with a bat in my hand, I knew everything would be alright. Without that bat in my hand, I felt incomplete—just like when I was a kid.

That night I ended up going 2-3 with two home runs and a walk. I guess that afternoon didn't have an impact on my game. Or maybe it did—maybe it made me play better.

Yet, from that day forward, it got to the point that I wondered if I would ever be with anyone. It didn't seem like there was anyone in the world that could go where I was headed. It was impossible to find someone when I was afraid that I would hold them back, and at the same time I was afraid they would hold me back. It was a lose-lose situation. But I also didn't want to end up alone like my father.

I often wondered, what type of woman would be good for me? Someone with no ambitions? Someone with no dreams? Someone who didn't want to settle down? Someone who could just follow me on my journey? I started to question what kind of wives did players have in the Show. This was something I never really thought about before. My father basically always said that everything would fall into place once I made it there.

I would also think about what kind of father would I be? Would I have to move my family around like Elizabeth's father had to? Make it so my kids were scared to get close to anyone because I would get traded, and they would have to move again?

Or what about the fact that I wouldn't be around very often. As a ball player, I would be on the road a lot. Is that the type of life I would want? I thought about these things, and realized I would never want to put my kids through that. But, when I think of Elizabeth, even though her family moving around a lot caused some pain, it also made her the amazing, and confident person that she was. She was great at meeting people; she had so much to talk about and so many experiences; and those were the things I loved about her. Our life experiences are what make us who we are, good or bad.

I was so close to the Show, but I was starting to think more about finding love, and having a family. I always tried to focus on baseball, and forget about everything else, but for some reason, these thoughts would still creep up into my head sometimes.

After Lindsay ended things with me, I couldn't wait to be called up. I was enjoying my time with the Redbirds, but after Lindsay was no longer in my life, it was time to move on. There was nothing for me down in the minors anymore. I wanted to get to St. Louis and begin my life there once and for all. I vowed there would be no more distractions until my dream came true.

On one ordinary day when I was taking BP, our manager called me into his office. He looked at me with his stone cold face. *What's this all about?* I thought.

"There has been an injury," he said. And then he broke out into a big smile. "You have been called up. You're meeting the Cardinals in San Diego."

"Jesus, Coach. You scared me."

"Congratulations, Oz. You deserve it. Now go up there and make us proud."

"Was it Rios who got injured?"

"It was. I think they said it was his hamstring. Go grab your stuff...they want you out on the next flight."

"Thanks, Coach."

"It's been an honor, Oz. Good luck up there."

And that's how it happens in baseball. One man's misfortune, is another man's opportunity. It could happen at any time. Just like that, I had to drop everything and fly out to San Diego to play a three game series against the Padres.

There was no more time to prepare.

But I was ready.

Chapter 61

I packed up what I needed, and I called my father to let him know I was being pulled up by the Cardinals, and that I was heading to play my first series in San Diego. I told him that he should fly out and come watch me play, but he said that he couldn't get off work with such short notice. But he said he would check the schedule and try to make it out to watch me play as soon as possible. I wished he could have come out, but I understood. He still had other obligations. I decided that once I signed a major league contract, I would tell him to quit his job, and come watch me play whenever he wanted.

I had no one else to call to share the good news with. I thought about calling Lindsay, but she had someone else to be happy and excited for. It's ironic how I got drafted not long after I broke up with Elizabeth, and now I was called up a few weeks after Lindsay ended things with me. It's almost as if those relationships had to end for me to be able to move on with my career. Why did I need anyone to be happy and excited for me anyway? Why couldn't I just be happy for myself and be content with that?

The Cardinals set me up with a first class flight from Memphis to San Diego that night. I was a plane ride away to California and the major leagues. It didn't take me long to wonder if Elizabeth still lived there. I was about to play my first major league series, and I couldn't help but wonder: *Maybe Elizabeth would be watching?*

No matter what I did and accomplished, no matter how much time had passed, she was always right there on the forefront of my mind. I was on my way to the Show, but a part of me wished I was on my way to California to see her. But either way, in less than twenty-four hours, I was going to be stepping on the field with the best baseball players in the world. I was determined to prove that I belonged—that I was one of them.

The Cardinals had a car waiting for me at the airport, and it took me to the Omni hotel, where the rest of the team was staying. I checked in at the front desk, and there was already a room reserved under my name. The front desk agent asked me if one of my bags was my ball equipment and she told me to leave it there with them, and said someone would take care of it for me. I got my key, and took the elevator to my room.

When I opened the door to my room, I was immediately drawn to the window. I had a beautiful view that looked towards the harbor, and the ocean beyond. The same ocean that Elizabeth used to talk about—the sea salt, the waves, the humid air, and the endless mass of possibilities that felt like a metaphor for my future. It was all there in front of me. The phone rang in my room and it was Jerry Atwell the Cardinals manager. He told me to come up to his suite, so I could meet some of the coaches, and have a little chat.

I went to Jerry's room, and Sam Leary, the bench coach, and Adrian Thompson, their new hitting coach, were also there. I was introduced to everybody. At first Jerry made small talk. He asked me how the flight was, how my room was, congratulated me on having a good season so far with Memphis, and then we got down to business. Jerry said that they were excited to have me up, and that there was a good chance, if I performed, that I could be up for the rest of September, and the playoffs. It was confirmed that Luis Rios, their starting shortstop, had a badly pulled hamstring, and he was going to be out for awhile. All I could think about, was that if I proved myself, shortstop would be mine for the rest of the season.

In moments like these, it's hard to take it all in. I was there in San Diego with the big club, whereas earlier that day, I was taking BP with my team in Memphis. This goes to show that you have to be ready for your chance, because it can happen at any moment.

Jerry filled me in with the schedule for the next day: when I should be at the park, and other small details. I wouldn't have to worry about catching a bus or commuting, since the Omni had a pedestrian Sky Bridge connected to Petco Park. Jerry left off by saying, again, that they were all happy to have me join the club, and that if I needed anything to help me get settled in, all I had to do was ask.

I liked Jerry and the rest of the staff immediately. I knew that he didn't have to call me to his room when I got there, and he didn't have to welcome me and fill me in on their plans for me. Some managers may have just let me show up to the park and do my job. But Jerry, as I would come to know, was a player's manager—he was very personable, and he was the type of manager you will give it your all for, because he makes it known that he will do the same for you. I think that's a major reason why the Cardinals are so successful—they know how to treat people, and they know how to win. That's the type organization *of* that everyone dreams of playing for.

I left Jerry's room feeling pretty lucky about my experience so far. I was hoping that the players would be just as welcoming as Jerry and the other coaching staff.

When I got back to my room, it was hard to fall asleep. I had a huge day ahead of me, and I needed my rest, but that's never how it goes, does it? When you are anxious or excited for something, against all logic, your brain will keep you up. When I would finally doze off for a little while, my brain would wake me up, and this continued all night. It was a very restless sleep, but I was wide awake at the crack of dawn. I was running on pure excitement and adrenaline. I was awake to see the shades of orange and the golden sun come up over the ocean outside the window. This was officially my first day in the Show. I will never forget that moment. It felt like the beginning of a new life—the life I always dreamed about.

I showered, and headed down to the restaurant to have breakfast before I headed to the park. I saw a couple of players down in the restaurant sitting at a table together. I recognized them, but had no idea if they knew who I was or not. I wasn't going to just invite myself to sit down with them. I wasn't a part of the team yet. I know some of the more outgoing guys I played with in the minors, probably would have got a kick out of making themselves right at home in situations like these. They would have introduced themselves, cracked a few jokes, and would have been accepted before anyone knew what just happened. But that isn't me. I have never been one to put myself out there, plus, you hear so many horror stories while you're in the minors, and some say the best advice about being called up is to speak only when you are spoken to, and make sure you don't step on anyone's toes. In other words, stay out of everyone's way, and do not interfere with their routine.

I sat at table in the corner by myself, and thought about the day I had ahead of me. I was filled with so much excitement, and I couldn't wait until game time.

After breakfast, I made my way back to my room. I stopped in front of the elevators, pushed the button, and patiently waited for the doors to open. When they opened, I walked in and pushed the button for the 9th floor. When the doors started to close, I heard a woman's voice yell. "Wait! Hold the door."

I stuck my arm out to activate the sensors to stop the doors.

"Thanks!" a blonde woman—who I assumed was in her mid-thirties—said. She had a young boy around five or six years old with her, and he had a San Diego Padres hat on covering most of his blonde hair.

"No problem," I said. "What floor?"

"Seven, please," she said, and I pushed the button.

"Mom, are we going to the ball park now?" the boy asked.

"The game isn't for a few more hours. We are going to the zoo to see the hippos, giraffes, and the monkeys, remember?" she said trying to peak his interest, but to little avail.

"But I want to go to the ball park. I want to see Michael Sharp, Steve Armstrong, and Bo Monroe hit home runs and beat those Cardinals 10-0...because they stink!" he said full of energy and child like excitement.

I couldn't help but laughing. *I sure hope not, kid*, I wanted to say. That sure would be something if the Padres beat us that bad my first game. But I couldn't help but smiling at the young, little guy. I would have been the same way if my mother had taken me to a Cardinals game when I was a kid. I had to admire his innocence and his pure joy for the game.

"Do you play baseball, little man?" I asked him.

"Yep! I just started this year!" he said looking up at me. Somehow he must have sensed that I was a ball player. "Do you play baseball?"

"I do. I'm actually on that team you think stinks. Well, today is actually my first game playing for the Cardinals."

"You mean, you're in the major leagues! What's your name?" he asked, impressed.

"My name is Ozzie Shaw. What's your name?"

"My name's Joey Morton," he said proudly.

"Nice to meet you, Joey," I said.

"Joey, maybe you should ask politely for his autograph. I'm sure he will give you one," his mom said.

"Oh yeah! Can I have your autograph?"

"Joey! What do you say?" his mom reminded him.

"Please," he said unenthusiastically.

"Of course you can, big guy," I said. His mom searched in

her purse for a pen and pulled one out and handed it to me. "What do you want me to sign?" I asked Joey.

He looked disappointed for a second. Then a flash of brilliance lit up his face. "How about my hat?"

"Are you sure you want a stinky St. Louis Cardinal to sign your Padres hat?" I said with a chuckle.

"Yep! I'm going to cheer for you today, too! You're my new favorite player. You and Michael Sharp."

"Thank you, Joey. That means a lot," I said.

He took off his hat and I signed it Ozzie Shaw. I didn't know what number I was going to be that day, so I decided to write my usual "#11." Just as I finished, we reached their floor.

"Have fun today, champ," I said.

"I will!" he said.

"Thanks, Ozzie. You just made his day," the mother said. "And hey, good luck in your first game tonight."

"Thank you," I said.

"I can't wait to show dad..." I heard my new number one fan say as the elevator doors were closing.

I hadn't even played one game for the Cardinals yet, and I already had a fan—a converted Padre fan, nonetheless. In moments like these, you know exactly why you love this game so much.

That experience in the elevator made me even more excited for the game that night. I wanted to get to the field right away. I left my room once again back towards the elevator. I had figured out where the Sky Bridge to Petco Park was before breakfast, and started to make my way there. As a fan, the experience at the Omni and Petco Park would be amazing. As a ball player, it was surreal. There I was, crossing the Sky Bridge to my future in Major League Baseball.

As I was walking over, I heard a voice behind me, "Hey, Oz! Off to the park bright and early?" it was Sam Leary the bench coach. I stopped and waited for him to catch up.

"Good morning, Coach."

"Pretty cool, isn't it?" he asked as we looked towards Petco Park. "Have you been here before?"

"It sure is...and no, I haven't," I replied.

"Well, you're in for a treat. This park is brand new this year, and it's probably the nicest facility out there. Not a bad welcome to the big leagues," he said.

And he was right. As the guard let us in the entrance with the help of Sam's ID he showed—I briefly wondered if they would have let me in if I didn't have Sam with me—and we walked into the concourse, and I could see part of the field. It felt like I was walking into something magical. In a matter of hours I would be down there playing in front of thousands of people. I wanted to keep walking and check out the field in its entirety, but instead, Sam led me to the visiting team's clubhouse so I could get settled in.

The clubhouse was bigger than any clubhouse in the minors— each person had a large locker assigned to them, there were leather couches, TVs, tables, and so much open space. This was the visitors' clubhouse, but there were nameplates for all the players on the Cardinals already in place, and every player's things were unpacked in each locker. Sam pointed to an area and said my locker should be somewhere in that direction. Then he took off and let me settle in on my own.

My locker was right on the end of the row near the showers, and it had my last name on a nameplate above it. It was beside Donnie Wood, the young, Cardinals third baseman. The bag I had left at the front desk the night before, was all unpacked in my locker. And, hanging up right in front, was a Cardinals away uniform with Shaw stitched on the back, right above my number 11. I picked it up and held it out in front of me. This was my jersey. At that moment, that's when I knew I was a Cardinal.

The Padres clubhouse assistant came over and introduced himself. He asked me if I had everything, and told me that if I needed anything to let him know. He pointed out the lounge and said I could grab some breakfast if I wanted, but I told him I already ate. I kept on being blown away by how much everything is taken care of for players in the Show. There are so many people ready to do all the little things, so you have nothing to worry about except getting ready for the game. It's the complete opposite of the minors. In the minors you have to fend for yourself and perform at your top level. In the big leagues, your only concern was playing your best.

I walked around the clubhouse area, and checked out the lounge, and the weight room. Then, I walked down a hallway that led to the manager's office, a trainer's room, an indoor batting cage, and eventually it took me to the visitors' dugout. I walked out into the dugout and took in the magnificent sights of Petco Park. It's hard not to be amazed at all the empty seats— that would be filled in a few hours—the large screen in left field, the skyline, the green grass, and the perfect symmetry of all the lines created by the edges of the grass and the warning tracks that surround the field. Everything is perfect. You don't have to be a player to realize what a beautiful game baseball is.

There were only a few other people out there around the field doing some maintenance, but none of the players were out there yet. I was left standing there with nothing but my thoughts and a smile on my face. I remember thinking how cool it was to see a guitar in the outfield at Grier Stadium in Nashville, but that did not even come close to my first experience at Petco Park. The stadium was mind blowing. This was the Show. This was what it was all about. After I soaked it all in for a couple minutes, I turned around and headed back into the clubhouse.

I didn't know what to do to pass the time, so I decided to ride a bike for awhile in the weight room, and then I went to the cage to hit off a tee. At first I was the only one in there, but after awhile, players started to trickle in, here and there.

It's hard to make yourself right at home on your first day.

I've played for a number of teams already in my professional career, and the first few days, and even weeks, are not easy to get settled in. You don't know what the routine is; you don't know where to go, what to do, and who is who. It's hard to feel comfortable because there are so many things that you have to get used to. When more players started to show up, I watched what they did in order to try and follow their lead. Some guys had breakfast, others sat around on the couches watching TV, others went in the weight room, some went in the cages, some showered, and a few players got some work done in the trainer's room. That morning, I managed to meet a few more people such as coaches, trainers, clubhouse assistants, and a few players that were willing to introduce themselves. But I spent most of the day trying to look busy while I waited for batting practice to start.

After batting practice, I felt great. I was smashing the ball all over the field, and I managed to put a couple into the stands. Other than the day I signed my contract in St. Louis, that was only my second time taking batting practice in a major league stadium.

Before the game, I had to be filled in with the offensive signs for hitters and base runners by the third base coach. Since I was starting at short, I also asked the Cardinals catcher, Casey Wells, what our starting pitcher Jeremy McNeilly threw, and I got the situational defensive signs from him as well. I wanted to be prepared as much as possible. After I covered the necessary details, I still had my own routine for warming up, and getting ready for the game. I knew that once I was on the field, it was still the same game that I had been playing my entire life.

When it was time to get suited up for the game, I went to my locker beside Donnie Wood. He introduced himself, and was friendly right from the start. This was his first year in St. Louis— he was traded from Atlanta, where he played two seasons. He was having a breakthrough season in his first year with the

Cardinals—he had 22 home runs and 77 RBIs, with around 30 games still to go in the regular season.

Before I was set to get changed into my uniform, I took a shower to cool down, and wash off the sticky sweat accumulated from the hot, San Diego sun. Once it was time to put on my jersey, I savored every moment. I wanted everything to look perfect. I checked myself once, twice, and three times in the mirror. It was crazy to me that there was a St. Louis Cardinal staring back at me. I was ready for my first game.

No matter what, there is always a sense of uneasiness when you are playing for a new team. You want to get that first defensive play out of the way, and of course, your first hit. Until then, you are nervous and anxious standing out there on the field, and in the batter's box. I felt this way, to some extent, on every new team I had ever played for since I was a kid. But once I got those two things out of the way, everything always fell into place.

In the majors, however, I found that everything is way more amplified. There are thousands of people watching you. A large number of fans want to see you fail, because you are wearing the wrong jersey. Other ball players want to see you fail, so they are successful. One thing about sports, is that others have to fail in order for you to succeed, and vice versa. All you can do is play the game like you know how, and not worry about anything else. The worst thing you can do is think that if you fail, someone else might be there waiting to take your spot. But this is always much easier said than done.

I was penciled in to hit in the ninth hole, and I didn't get up to bat until the 3rd inning. But I was lucky to get my first defensive play out of the way in the 1st inning. Their first batter, Michael Sharp, struck out. The second batter was right handed Jose Avila. Our pitcher, Jeremy McNeilly, went up in the count 0-2. He threw a hard slider just outside that Avila didn't swing at. The next pitch was a hard, inside fastball, and Avila swung and made solid contact, and hit it into the hole between Donnie Wood, our third baseman, and where I was playing at shortstop. I got a great jump and took a few hard steps deep in the hole, I slid on my right knee, the ball took a nasty hop over my head, and I managed to reach up and grab it at the last second. I then popped up on my right foot, planted it, and gunned the speedy Jose Avila out at first. I did it all in one motion, and I must have made a tough play look really smooth. The fans of course booed, but I knew it was the type of play that I would see again on ESPN. From that moment forward, I was on. I was ready for any ball headed my way.

In the 3rd inning, the game was still scoreless. I was the second batter due up. What's it like to have your first at bat in the major leagues? Let me tell you. You can't help but notice that pit in your stomach. You are sweating and breathing heavily. You force yourself to take a few deep breaths while you walk up to the plate, and one last big one while you settle yourself in the box. You are still anxious, but how can you not be? You have been dreaming of this moment your entire life. Those that say baseball is just a game, don't realize how physically and mentally strenuous it can be on a person.

I stood there prepared. As prepared as I could be at the moment, but even so, I knew the odds were against me. They always are in baseball. I may strike out like I have a few hundred times before. I may hit the ball, but it may be a pop-up, or an easy ground ball. Or I may hit it hard, but right at someone, or someone might make an amazing play. Every time you are at bat, it is the ultimate underdog story, and that's part of the game's allure. That's part of the reason why people have been fascinated with it for over a century.

My first at bat in the majors, I struck out. It was a combination of a number of things. Their pitcher, Bobby Fletcher, was a 20 game winner the season before, and that current year he was two wins away from doing the same thing.

He threw me a first pitch fastball—I had good hack on it—but I fouled it off. He threw a good changeup that I swore actually went into reverse at one point, and then continued to move forward on the outside corner for a strike. I let a high fastball way out of the strike zone go by for a ball, and then the next pitch, a dirty slider, caught me looking. I wanted that fastball again, but I never got it. And that was the majors—if you get a good cut on a pitch, even if you don't hit it, there is a good chance you will never see it again, at least for that at bat.

I popped up my second time at bat in the 5th inning. It wasn't until my third at bat in the 6th, that I got my first big league hit. I hit a 3-2 fastball that was on the outside corner, over the second baseman's head, and I drove in a run in the process. I was able to make contact and go the other way. My father must have been proud.

Running down to first base, rounding the bag, and having the fans in the background—even though I was on the away team—it was a surreal feeling. When you are standing there and the crowd is enormous around you, it's a challenge to actually be able to focus. I wanted to stand there and take it all in for a few minutes, but I couldn't. The pitcher was set, and I had to take my leadoff. The next batter grounded out to the shortstop on the first pitch, and that was the end of the inning. But it was a big inning, and we took the lead 4-3, because of my RBI single with two outs. After that hit, I felt right at home. The adrenaline was still there, but I was able to take a few deep breaths, and I was able to concentrate on playing baseball. You have to remind yourself that the magnitude of the stadium may be enormous, but the dimensions of the ball field are still the same. I took comfort in my regular routines in the on deck circle and in the batter's box, and my same old routine before every pitch when I was at shortstop. It's a psychological thing—you have to trick yourself that you are in no different of a situation than you normally are.

My fourth at bat I ended up getting a walk. I finished my first game in the majors offensively with a .333 batting average, and an on-base percentage of .500. Defensively, I also caught a pop-up, got two routine ground balls, helped turn a 4-6-3 double play, and didn't make any errors. We won that game 5-3.

I wasn't able to take things in until after the game. When I took off my jersey with my number and name on the back of it, that's when realized I had just played my first major league game. No matter what happened, if I played one game in the major leagues or one thousand, I would always know that I was once a St. Louis Cardinal. That was a very special moment for me. I remember thinking about how I couldn't wait until the next day, when I could put that jersey on a again. This was one of the most exciting times in my life. I was living my dream.

I had a decent game my first day in the majors—it wasn't amazing, but it wasn't terrible, which was a relief. I remember going back to my hotel and sitting there alone. I ordered room service, and called my father while I waited for my meal to arrive. We talked about the game, and it was a very short conversation. I do remember he told me, "Hell of a game, Son. Keep up the good work." And that to me, was the equivalent of him saying he was proud of me. After I got off the phone, I sat there alone thinking of my first game, and I was still riding high from all of the adrenaline.

After dinner, I sat there on the bed and watched the highlights of the defensive play that I made in the 1st inning, and my hit that drove in the winning run in the 6th. Watching myself on TV as a Cardinal, was also hard to believe.

At about midnight the phone rang. I thought it would be one of the ball players or coaches, since no one else had the number to my hotel room. I picked up the phone and answered.

"Hello?"

"Hi, Ozzie." It was a female voice. Elizabeth's voice.

"Elizabeth?" I was dumbstruck.

"Yes, it's me," she replied. "Sorry for calling so late. I just wanted to tell you that I watched you play tonight on TV...I'm so proud of you, Oz."

Her saying that she was proud of me, was the best thing anyone had ever said to me. My eyes filled with tears of joy.

"Thanks, Liz," I said, and my voice cracked.

"Are you okay, Ozzie?" she asked.

"I'm fine. Better than fine...I'm just so happy to hear from you."

"I miss you, Oz."

"I miss you too, Liz."

And then I snapped out of it. I had to stop imagining Elizabeth appearing back into my life. I sat alone on my hotel bed and sobbed. Some dream I was living. Wasn't I supposed to be happy once I made it to the Show?

The following day, we won the next game 6-2 and I went 1-4. We lost the third game of the series on Sunday, but I went 2-5 with a single and a double. *There you go Joey, your Padres won at least one game*, I thought after the last game. I had played three games, and already had four hits. When I was on the field, I felt great.

Chapter 62

After San Diego, we had a three game series against the Los Angeles Dodgers. We checked into another hotel, and this time I was placed in a room with Donnie Wood. This was a good thing, because I would be able to ask him some questions, and find out what life was like as a big leaguer. I would also be able to follow his lead, and this made the transition easier for me.

We swept the Dodgers, and I continued to play well. In the third game of the series, I went 3-4, and after the game, I had my first major league interview. When I got back to the hotel, I called my father, and we talked about the game. Then I asked with a smile on my face, "Hey, Pop...did you see my interview?"

"Yes I did. You sounded like a dumbass like the rest of them."

"I knew you'd like it," I said and laughed.

When my father would watch any major league baseball game on TV, he always hated how players would be asked stupid questions after the game. As a baseball fan is it actually important to hear a player's take on a certain play, or on losing, or winning a game? If you ever hear an interview they are all the same. The more you do it, the easier it gets to deflect the questions, and answer them as quick as possible, so you can head out on your way. My father could not stand when a player would be asked, "What were you thinking when you made that play in the sixth inning," or "What was going through your mind when you stepped up to the plate in the bottom of the ninth."

These questions would drive my father crazy and he would yell and swear at the TV, "He wouldn't be thinking anything if he was fucking doing his job." And he always wished for someone to answer: " 'My mind was completely clear and I was relaxed. I did what I was supposed to do.' Done that's it. That's all you fucking having to say!"

Another one of my father's favorite questions was about a pitcher: "What do you think about your starting pitcher Matt Johnson's performance today?" Again my father would say, " 'He did his job and he did it well.' That's fucking it! But here is the answer you have to give. 'Johnny had a great game today. He had a lot of movement on his fastball, and uhh, great command, and his curve and changeup were working well. He's a great pitcher and uhhh, he had a great day today.' Wow, powerful stuff, isn't it? That interview meant so much to those listening...fucking waste of time."

That was my father. So whenever I would hear one of those useless questions I would laugh inside. These interviews were a part of the job, nonetheless, and to be honest, I always got a kick out of it whenever I did one. I always pictured my father losing it in his living room whenever he heard me say some bullshit answer that they wanted to hear. For that reason, every interview, I always welcomed those ridiculous questions.

After the series against the Dodgers, we caught a flight back to St. Louis. I was going to be playing my first series at home against the Houston Astros.

In St. Louis, the Cardinals set me up at another hotel. This time I had a suite, but it was weird to know that the rest of my stuff was back in Memphis for another month or two. Regardless, in the next few weeks I would be on the road some more, and then it was playoffs, so there wasn't any opportunity for me to settle in at all. Moreover, the only place I needed of my own, was in the Cardinals clubhouse.

I had been in the Cardinals clubhouse four years earlier, but now I had my own locker with my name plate sitting above it, for more than one day. This time I was able to settle in and try to get comfortable. Lenny helped with that. It was great to see him again, and he was just as friendly as the first day I met him. He let me know that if I needed anything that I shouldn't be afraid to ask. He gave a tour of the place, and everything was bigger and better than anything I had ever experienced—from the cages, to the equipment in the weight room, to the hot and cold tubs, and the video room. I knew I would spend a lot of time in that video room. I had spent a lot of time watching pitchers that I may end up facing in the majors, but now, all that information was at my fingertips. Any at bats I had, I could re-watch at any time, even during a game. I had full access to whatever I needed.

Our trainers were also welcoming, and they let me know if I needed anything taped, or if anything was sore or tight I should let them know right away. So many people on staff were there to help in any way they could. That's what they were there for.

One of the best things about being on the Cardinals was that my father was able to come and watch me play my first series at home in St. Louis. That first home game of the series was something special. It was the first time he was able to watch me play in years. I was hoping that he would be proud of me, and see how much I had improved since the last time he had watched me play. I was no longer the 17-year-old high school baseball player he watched before I got drafted.

My father drove down from Columbia, and booked a room at the same hotel that I was staying at. I was excited to have him there, and it meant a lot to me. That night, I ended up hitting my first, and second major league home runs, and my father was there to watch it all from the stands. The first one I hit was a deep shot to center field against Ricky Molson, the Astros number one starter. It was on a 3-2 count on a hard fastball that got a lot more of the plate than he wanted. I made him pay for it. That solo shot put us up 1-0 in the 2nd inning. I ended up hitting a single in the 4th, a two-run home run on a curveball in the 7th, and I struck out in the 9th. We won the game 6-2, and I drove in 3 of our 6 runs.

After the game my father and I had supper together at our hotel. I could tell my father had softened up quite a bit, and I think it was because I had made it, and he didn't have to push me, or yell at me anymore. Or maybe he finally saw me as a man. Or maybe he was a different person now that he was sober. Either way, I was happy to have him there, and I think he was happy to be there.

My father said I played well and that I looked good out there. "You have come a long way, Son. At least one of us Shaw's made it somewhere," he said, and slapped me on the back.

"Thanks, Pop."

I always wondered what he *really* thought about being there with me. I wondered if he was proud of me. But mostly, I wondered what he was thinking about. I wondered if it pained him to sit there in the stands in the very place where he always dreamed of playing. Instead, when the weekend was over, my father would head back to Columbia all by himself, and he would go back to another work week at Big O Tires. I felt bad for him, and I suggested that once I signed a contract with the Cardinals he should quit his job, and come move to St. Louis, but he refused. I think he wanted me to have a life of my own, and I think a part of him just needed to keep himself busy with work. Columbia was home to him, and that's where he would stay.

My name was in the newspaper the next day, and there was a nice article written about me. I was known as a hometown kid from Columbia, MO, that came up in September, and had already put up great numbers in my first few games in the big leagues. The media was optimistic that if I continued with what I was doing, and with the lineup we had, we would have a good chance to win the World Series that year.

My first few weeks in the major leagues were like a dream. I went through the grind of the minors the last few years, but it still felt like I was just a kid in high school the day before. It was almost hard to believe, and truly appreciate it at the time. Still, I had achieved my goal once and for all. But once you achieve a goal, you will find yourself creating other goals. I wanted to win the World Series, break records, and be one of the best players of all time. There was no modesty involved when it came to my plans for my career.

Everyone around me was just like me. I was no longer a standout, and I was playing with the best of the best. But we all lived and breathed baseball, and I felt like I belonged. I knew that if you can stand out from a league of standouts, than you are truly special. And that's what I aimed to do.

One thing that my father's practices prepared me for was my work ethic. It was not uncommon for me to take BP after games, even the ones that I hit well in. I heard some of my teammates talk about going out and hanging out together, but I didn't partake in too many gatherings outside of baseball. The way I looked at it, while some of those guys went out, I was doing what I could to be the best player I could be. I didn't even consider the benefits of going out and bonding with my team. Truthfully, I didn't want to do anything that would jeopardize my spot on the team. I wanted to play so well that when Luis Rios came back, then the Cardinals would have a tough decision to make about who should start.

In the next series against the Arizona Diamondbacks, I hit my second multi-home run game, in game two of the series. I hit two home runs—the first was a three-run home run in the 5th inning, and I hit a two-run blast in the 8th. I was the talk of the town in St. Louis, and I felt like everywhere I looked, I was seeing my picture on TV and in the Newspaper. It didn't take me long for others to compare me with some of the top players in the league.

We remained in first in our division, and I was proving I belonged. Not only was I hitting home runs, I was also stealing bases. Jerry moved me up to the two spot in the order, and as a result, I ended up seeing a lot of good pitches, and I scored a lot of runs when I got on base. We were a team that seemed like we couldn't be stopped, and I did my best every game to make sure we couldn't be.

Chapter 63

I knew after the first few weeks that I joined a team that was special. Not only were we first in our division, we had the top record in the National League. I hadn't even been on the team for a month, and I was already going to be playing in the first post season of my career. I couldn't help but imagining that we may win the World Series—which was a real possibility. It was hard to believe, but everything was happening right in front of me. I was accepted as part of the team, and it was awesome to see everyone with a smile on their face and joking around in the clubhouse. Everything was very lighthearted, and I believe because of this, we kept on winning. There is nothing like weak morale in the clubhouse that can bring a team down. I lived through that in my first few years in the minor leagues.

Like I mentioned earlier, playing in the major leagues, everything was a lot more amplified. Now the same rang true for the playoffs, but the amplification is greater in all areas. The crowds are bigger and louder; and each pitch, each hit, each defensive play, and even each decision, means so much more. Everything in the playoffs is analyzed by so many people on a much larger scale. A manager's job is probably the most stressful of them all, but for players, you still have to perform. Slumps in the playoffs can make a whole season seem worthless. Any error can erase every nice play you made all year. Many players throughout history have suffered in the playoffs, and it has defined their career.

For the most part, I felt like I was along for the ride in those two months, and it was hard to concentrate on anything else. Baseball was my only focus, and I was happy.

On October 5th, 2004, we started the National League Division Series (NLDS) at home at Busch Stadium, against the Los Angeles Dodgers. Just like we had done a few weeks earlier, we ended up sweeping them in three straight games. We won the first game 7-2, and the second game 2-1 in a pitching duel. Then we headed to Dodger Stadium and beat them 6-4. I hit a home run in the second, and third game of the series. I was still riding high. We all were.

We didn't use a lot of pitching in that first series, and we continued to be on a role. We felt like it was our time, and there wasn't much doubt that we could win it all. But in the back of your mind you still understand, that in sports, you never know what could happen. A lot of people have mixed thoughts about sweeping in the playoffs. Some will say it's good to give players a few extra days rest, especially the pitchers, but others say you may cool off in that time, and it's the teams that stay hot that end up winning it all. Either way, a lot of it is just based on opinion.

The National League Championship Series (NLCS) against the Houston Astros, was a hard fought series that took seven games to settle. We battled back and forth, and as soon as one of us scored any runs, the other team managed to answer right back. In that first game, we lost 9-8 in the 10th inning. It was a tough loss, and a tough way to start a series. We knew it would be survival of the fittest, and survival of whatever manager was lucky enough to make the right decisions. Playoffs are especially challenging because the manager has to make decisions he would not normally make in a regular season game, such as: Who should pitch when, and how much rest do they need in between games?; Should you throw in a reliever to save your starter so you can use him sooner in the series, or do you let him go the distance?; When do you play the matchup, pitcher against a hitter?; When do you risk it, and when do you make the change?; And specifically to the National League, when do you put in a pinch hitter and take your pitcher out of the game? Every decision will have an impact, and as a manager you might be a genius or a failure, but you won't know which one you are, until after it's all said and done.

We bounced back in Game 2 with a well-pitched game by Jeremy McNeilly. He went 7 strong innings with 10 Ks, and we gave him a comfortable lead after a three-run shot by The Crusher in the first inning. We padded our lead by adding a few more runs until we were up 6-1 by the 8th inning. But the Astros quickly narrowed the gap when we gave up 4 runs in the 8th. Brent Miller, our closer, was able to get the save in the 9th, and we held on to win 6-5.

Some would go on to say that Game 3 of NLCS was the best game I had ever played. The reporters after the game wanted to know my secret. Did I get a scouting report on the pitcher before the game? Did I study tapes? I've never told anyone about this before, but when I saw Ron Sanford was their starting pitcher, I smiled.

I remember sitting in my living room just a few years before with my father. He sat there and took apart Ron Sanford's pitches, and broke all of them down one by one. "Look at him up there, Son. He does a great job of working the corners, and changing the sightlines of the hitter. But his fastball can be hit hard if you don't fall for his other pitches. And that slider he throws is almost unhittable when he throws it low and outside. But look what happens when he throws a fastball up and in, and then goes back to that slider. Most of the time he gets it down low, and many hitters get fooled by it, even though they know it's coming. But one out of every four times, he will leave that slider up and over the plate. If only the hitter would be ready for it...that mistake should be hit out of the park. All you have to do is look for it. As for his changeup, a hitter won't see it enough to worry about it. You need discipline to succeed against a pitcher like him. With discipline, you won't be beat."

Every time I faced Sanford, I was ready. My father taught me everything I needed to know to be successful against Sanford. I was only in the Show for a month, and I was probably more prepared than anyone else out there. When I faced Ron Sanford in that series against the Astros, I went 5-5 against him—3-3 in Game 3, and 2-2 in Game 7.

My first at bat against him in Game 3, I took him deep on a slider that he left up and over the plate. I walked my next at bat, hit a two-run home run my third time up, and hit a single my forth time facing him. We won the game 3-1, and I knocked in all of our runs. I also hit 3 of the only 5 hits that Sanford gave up against us that day.

The Astros took the fourth game at home on a come from behind win in the bottom of the 9th. We were winning 3-2 in the 8th, but they hit a solo shot to tie it, and in the ninth they managed to put a runner on base, and on an unfortunate error by Larry Toller, our centre fielder, they scored to win 4-3. Games like that can often be heartbreaking, and can totally change the momentum in the other team's favor, which we hoped would not be the case.

But in Game 5 they won again 6-2 on a grand slam in the 7th inning. It was another close game until they blew it wide open, and we couldn't come back from that.

We were headed back to St. Louis, but now it was a do-or-die situation. We could not lose another game—we had to win the next two, to make our way to the World Series.

There are so many emotional highs and lows in the playoffs, especially when you play a full seven game series. Both teams are battling it out, feeling the highs of winning, and the bone-crushing lows from losing. The highs and lows can even be felt from inning to inning, depending on what happens; and Game 6 was a perfect example of that.

Game 6 went to extra innings, tied 7-7, and both teams were making incredible plays to shut the other team down. In the top of the 12th, with runners on second and third with two outs, I made a diving stop on a hard ground ball up the middle, and was able to get the out at first to keep them from getting the lead. We won the game 9-7 in the bottom of the 12th, on a two-run home run by Rick Bellamy, our left fielder. It was a long, stressful game that could have went either way. Knowing we were one run away from being eliminated, was too close for comfort. But we came out ahead, and needed to win just one more game to move on.

Game 7 was a different ball game. We were facing Ron Sanford once again. I knew I was going to have another great game at the plate. This time around, the only strikes I saw were fastballs. I hit a double my first time up, and with 2 runners on in the 6th, I took a high fastball deep over the center field fence. I helped knock Sanford out of the game early, and we went on to win 8-5.

Winning the National League Championship at home, and playing the way I did, was one of the greatest feelings of my life. Nobody could ever take that game away from me. I stayed up all night in my hotel suite, and just held on to that feeling as long as I could. I remember thinking that this was the reason why I chose baseball over everything else.

But not every game will be glamorous—even in the playoffs. There will be days you can't sleep because you are thinking about the game the next day. You're excited, anxious, and you just want the game to begin. You get out of bed, and you still have hours to wait. You may try to do other things to stay busy and pass the time, or you might go right to the ballpark to wait there and surround yourself with the whole playoff environment. Then the game starts. You're excited, you want to contribute, but you may go 0-4 that day. Then what? It can be a real let down, but then you have to put it behind you, and you have to do the same thing that night, and the next day, hoping this time you might do something extraordinary. Yet, no matter how you played all year, the best time to do something extraordinary, is in the World Series.

Chapter 64

Fate would have it, that the first time I would play at Fenway Park, was on October 23rd, which was Game 1 of the World Series, against the Boston Red Sox. I remembered all those days when I was a kid, imagining I was hitting home runs in my backyard over the "Green Monster," and now I was getting my chance to hit a home run over the *real* Green Monster.

In the 1st inning we scored right away. Our leadoff hitter, David Fernandez, struck out; and I singled to left. I stole second base, and Rick Bellamy hit me home with a double on a 3-2 count. They ended up getting two more outs, but we were able to put up a run. We were up 1-0 after the 1st inning.

In the 2nd inning, we scored another run on a solo blast by our catcher, Casey Wells. After those first couple innings, and being up 2-0, it felt like we could sweep the Sox on our way to a World Series Championship. But our momentum was put on hold when their starter, Vernon Martin, shut us down for the next four straight innings.

Then things changed in the bottom of the 6th when they ended up scoring 4 runs, and we didn't have any outs. We made a pitching change, and our middle reliever, Landon Williams, got a groundball for a 4-6-3 double play, and then the next batter popped up to The Crusher at first. Landon got us out of a jam, but the damage was already done. Again, it was another instance where we had blown our lead late in the game. Our pitchers were not able to go deep in games anymore. As it often does, the long season seemed to have taken a toll on a few of our starters.

Some teams struggle all year, but at the end of the season they make a run for the playoffs, and stay hot; others are on top all year and start to cool down by the end. We didn't want to be the team that dominated all year, but lost the ability to win when it mattered the most. But it's tough when a lot of your players are hurt and tired, and it feels like you are running on fumes.

One thing I learned that series, is that the atmosphere at Fenway Park can instantly change the momentum of the game. If the Sox string a few hits together, the crowd comes alive like nowhere else. It's almost as if the energy of the crowd gives the Boston players special powers, and all of a sudden all their hits drop in, and they score runs. It's a terrible feeling to watch it all happen, and know there is nothing you can do about it. We ended up losing that first game, 4-2, and we had to be back at Fenway the next night to try and tie up the series.

When I went back to the hotel, I wanted to get some rest. All of us did. Everyone wanted to regroup, get some sleep, and hopefully come back out the next night and turn things around. We couldn't let the series get out of reach. We knew we had to win the next game.

Chapter 65

In Game 2, I struck out my first at bat, but I made up for it with a two-run home run in the 3rd inning. That at bat was something special, and I will never forget it. I was hoping David Fernandez, our leadoff guy, would be able to get on base, and I was hoping I could hit one hard. Fernandez walked on six pitches, and I studied the Sox pitcher intently. I saw his curveball was breaking hard, but he was leaving it up in the zone. I went up there looking for the fastball, but expecting a few curves. I was standing outside the batter's box, looking out at the Green Monster, and thinking: *It's just a big tree.* It actually made me smile to myself, and all the tension I was feeling instantly disappeared. Moments like this, you realize that you're just a big kid playing a game. But it worked. With the crowd as loud as it was at Fenway, I remember feeling completely at ease.

The first pitch was a fastball on the outside corner for strike one. The next pitch was a low curveball that I didn't swing at. He threw me another curve ball, but this one he left up, and I swung and hit it hard foul into the stands down the left field side. I was angry at myself because that was the pitch I knew I should have put over the fence, but I got too excited, and swung too early. The count was 1-2, and I knew he wouldn't risk throwing another curveball in the zone. He threw another low curveball, and I didn't fall for it, and the count was now 2-2. He threw yet another curveball in the same place as the last one, and I let go by, and the count was full. He gave me his best pitch twice in a row, and I let them both go by. I knew a fastball was coming. I was assuming on the outside corner, but I was hoping he would miss his spot. Sure enough, he threw a fastball on the inner half of the plate, and I drove the ball high and deep over the Green Monster in left field. I did exactly what I wanted to do. I was able to study pitchers in the majors just like my father had taught me. I was going up to the plate with a plan, and I knew what to expect. There is no better feeling than going up to the plate and visualizing a certain pitch, and then seeing the exact same one coming your way. I believe that's what separates great hitters from the rest.

That two-run home run put us up 2-0 in the third. The only minor threat they had, came in the 7th, but I turned a double play on a hit-and-run—I got a great jump on a line drive up the middle, I dove for it at the last second, and managed to catch it in the webbing of my glove, and I got up in one motion, and had all the time in the world to throw it to first for the double play. That is another play I still see from time to time on ESPN.

We went on to win that game 4-0, and we were headed back to St. Louis for the next three games.

The fans can make a huge difference when you are playing at home. The energy in the stadium is often in the home team's favor. But the home team advantage extends outside of the stadium. Some guys are lucky enough to sleep in their own beds, spend time with their family, and relax as much as they can. They at least get the comfort from knowing they can spend some time in a familiar situation. For me, I didn't have that hometown advantage. I was living in a hotel, I was alone, and every game felt like a road trip.

In Game 3 on October 26th, I went to the park early and spent a lot of time in the video room. I wanted to get a good look at each of their pitchers. I wanted to know what I was facing, and when game time arrived, I felt I was prepared.

Being in front of the hometown crowd was exhilarating. I

remember the moment when they announced my name and I ran out from the dugout to the third baseline, and I remember the eruption from the crowd. I was accepted, and I was loved by so many watching that day. I had proved that I could contribute to winning games; I could perform in the playoffs; and because of all that, I was admired by thousands of Cardinals fans. It was a wonderful feeling.

In baseball, there are things that happen, or there are things you do, that feel like they can only take place in a fairy tale story. In the first inning, one of those things happened. Fernandez led off the game with a bloop-single to right field. I walked up to the plate as they announced my name to the 50,000 fans that were there to watch us play. I don't know if I was jacked up from all that energy, but I dug in, and Nathan Mills, the Red Sox starter threw me a first pitch fastball that I jumped on, and sent over the left-center field fence. I was the second batter of the game, and with one swing of the bat, we were up 2-0. The crowd went absolutely nuts when I was rounding the bases. The feeling was electric.

The inning was not over yet. The Crusher hit a solo home run, and we were already up 3-0 after the first. Mills ended up throwing 45 pitches that inning before he could get out of it. Knocking around a pitcher early on—especially in the World Series—can force a team to use a pitcher that they would not normally use. Things were looking great for us.

I popped up in the third, and didn't get up again until the 5th inning. In the 5th, I managed to hit a long line drive single to left field. And in the 8th, I hit a solo home run on a 3-1 fastball. It was the first, and only multi-home run game that I would ever hit in the World Series.

We dominated Game 3, and won 5-1. After the game, I was interviewed, and gave them the same old spiel. They asked the usual "How it feels to hit a home run, and what my approach was," and I told them that I got a pitch I liked, and hit it hard.

One thing they asked me, however, was how did I deal with all the pressure of being pulled up at the end of the season, and playing in my first World Series. I told them that I felt the pressure like everyone else, but more so, I was excited to be there. Being a Cardinals fan growing up, I have been imagining this moment my whole life, so in a way, I've done all this before. Each game, I go out there, and I know I am ready for it.

When you look at what I was doing for Cardinals that year, sometimes it does seem like a fairy tale, but for me, I lived it, I accomplished those things, and it was an incredible time in my life.

In game 4, the tables had turned. The Boston starter, Scott Harlow, pitched an 8-inning 1-hitter, and their closer, Ted Rakes, finished it off. I went 0-4 that day, and we lost 3-0.

We headed into the 5th game tied 2-2 in the series. We all knew it was important to win this game, so we could head back to Boston only needing one win to capture the World Series. This game turned out to be another pitching duel, until we broke the game open with a 3 run 6th inning, to put us up 3-0. They answered back in the top of the 7th, with a two-run home run by their first baseman, Victor Reyes.

We managed to score one run in the bottom of the 7th, on a deep two-out single that sent me home from 2nd base. I had a great jump on the pitch, and I managed to slide under the tag at home. The score remained 4-2 until the 9th.

In the top of the 9th, we put Brent Miller in to close the game, but he ended up putting the first two batters on base. Just like that, the go ahead run was at the plate. After a visit from our pitching coach, Brent settled in, and he managed to get a strike out, and then a ground ball, which we turned into a 6-4-3 double play to end the game. We were headed back to Boston, and we were up 3-2 in the series. If we won the next game, we would be World Series champions.

Game 6 on October 30th in Boston, was a cold, emotional

rollercoaster. We got an early lead with a 2 run double from Rick Bellamy in the 2nd inning, and we put up one run each inning in the 3rd and 4th. We were up 4-0, and it looked like we would win, as long as we held on. But in the 5th inning, our pitcher got into trouble, and the Sox scored 4 runs to tie the game.

We were now tied 4-4, and after a pitching change, they managed to get two more runners on base against our next pitcher, Carl Landry, but he was able to get the last two outs. We were headed into the top of the 7th inning, still tied at 4.

After both teams were shut out in the 7th, in the top of the 8th, their first batter singled on a ground ball to the left side that found a gap between Donnie and I. The next batter bunted down the third-base line on the first pitch, and Donnie couldn't make the play. The Red Sox now had a runner at first and second, with no outs. The next guy bunted on the first pitch as well, but he popped it up to the pitcher. Carl tried to double the guy up on 1st, but hesitated, and didn't make it in time. Our pitching coach made a visit to the mound—in order to give guys in the bullpen more time to warm-up, and to slow things down. A lot of people wondered if Carl was left in too long, he was our set-up guy, and normally only pitched in the 8th, but bringing him in early changed his normal routine. Yet, that's the playoffs, guys are forced to do more than they normally would.

When the game was back on, Carl got ahead in the count with a slider called for a strike on the outside corner. The next pitch was a fastball that just missed down and away. The count was evened up. The next pitch was a fastball on the inside corner that the batter hit hard to left field in foul territory, but Rick Bellamy made a spectacular running catch. We now had 2 outs.

Our manager came out to make a pitching change to bring in a left-handed pitcher, for a lefty-lefty matchup. Their next hitter hit a hard groundball to me, and I scooped it up, and threw it to first for the third out.

There was still no runs scored in the 9th, and we remained deadlocked, and we headed into extra innings.

In the top of the 10th, I was due up second. Fernandez managed to get on base on a 10-pitch at-bat. I walked up to the plate feeling confident. Their pitcher was throwing a lot of pitches on the outer half. I could tell he was being careful. I was ready to take something on the outer half of the plate the other way, and hopefully move Fernandez to scoring position. The first pitch was a low, outside fastball that I let go for a strike. The next pitch was a curveball that I also watched go by for another strike. Before I could even swing the bat, I was down 0-2. The next pitch was another fastball on the outer half, but belt high. I hit a hard line drive right to the second baseman for the first out. Luckily, Fernandez froze, and didn't get doubled off. Our next two hitters got out, and Fernandez who was stranded on first, was the only opportunity we had.

We shut them down in the bottom of the inning, and they shut us down 1-2-3 in the top of 11th.

It was in the bottom of the 11th, that everything fell into place for the Red Sox. Their lead off guy got on base on a four pitch walk, and we were already in trouble with the heart of their lineup coming up. After that four pitch walk, Jerry came out to talk to our pitcher, and he decided to leave him in for one more batter. The next guy singled to right field, and there was now runners on first and second, with a left-handed hitter coming up. Jerry came back out to make another pitching change to bring a lefty in. Our guy did his job, and got the next guy to pop-up in foul territory, and Donnie easily made the catch. Jerry came out once again to bring in another righty. Their cleanup hitter walked, and their number five hitter, who was another major threat, was up to the plate with loaded bases. We needed a strike out, a ground ball to turn a double play, or an infield pop-up. Anything else, and the game would be over.

The first pitch was a fastball that was high and outside. The next pitch was a curveball that was hit hard over my head, and the game was over. The Red Sox won 5-4, and they forced a Game 7.

That Game 6 took a lot out of us. Games like that can crush a team, especially when you come out on the losing end. If you lose a game like that, it's so hard to come back from it. You are completely drained mentally and physically, but the next day, you have to go out there and give everything you have in the biggest game of the year, which might be the biggest game of your life.

In game 7, the momentum was clearly on the side of the Red Sox. We left a lot of runners on base in the first few innings, and we couldn't buy a hit when it counted. The Red Sox chipped away, and by the 5th inning, they were up 5-0. Games like this are extremely tough. You know everyone is doing what they can, but nothing seems to be working out in your favor. Yet, the other team has everything going their way. In the top of the 9th, I was the leadoff hitter, and I hit a solo home run over the Green Monster to make the score 5-1. But it was too little, too late. Rick Bellamy singled, and we left him on base after our next three hitters got out.

When their first baseman caught the throw from third on the last out of the game, the Red Sox stormed the field. All we could do was watch from the visitors' dugout, completely defeated. That could have easily been us out there. We battled all year, and in moments like that, it feels like it was all for nothing. If only we had won the night before. If only we would have not left so many guys on base. *If only, if only, if only.* When you are on the losing side of things, these thoughts will swim around in your head for days, weeks, and even months later.

In the end, they go on to celebrate being World Series champions, and we go home.

But that's baseball.

Chapter 66

When we lost out in the World Series, it was heartbreaking. But as disappointing as it was, I was grateful to be there. As a hitter, I had one of the best playoffs in the history of the game. The 9 home runs that I hit in that postseason, set a record that stills stands today. It's hard to believe that I made a lasting mark on the game in the first two months that I played in the major leagues.

I ended off on such a high note, however, that it was difficult to fall right into the offseason. A lot of players welcome the time off to heal, get back into shape, enjoy other hobbies, and go back home and spend time with their families. For me, I played just as many games as all of them, but I felt like my season was just getting started. I didn't want it to end.

That offseason dragged on for me. I had to pack up my stuff in Memphis, but I still had nowhere to go. I didn't really belong anywhere—I didn't have any friends, girlfriends, or any sort of life outside of baseball. It was strange to me that I just came from playing in the World Series, I set a record with the 9 home runs I hit, but in many ways, I was no different of a person than I was before. I had only played in the major leagues for two months, so I wasn't really a part of the team yet, and I couldn't settle down anywhere. My future was still undetermined, and I still had to wait until spring training to find out if I would make the team at the start of the 2005 season.

Once spring training came along, I was put with the Big

Club right from the beginning. I got to face the high level prospects, and the veterans that were getting ready for the season. My job was to make sure that I picked up right where I left off just over four months before. And right from the start, I showed them my power, I was stealing bases, and I played solid defense.

Luis Rios was back, and there was a lot of talk about what the Cardinals would do. There was some rumors going around that one of us may be making the transition to second base, since Jace Young—the Cardinals second baseman last year—struggled at the plate. Jace was a fantastic fielder, but he only finished the season with a .225 batting average. I didn't want to make the move since I had never played second base before, and I did have the stronger arm, so I was hoping it would be Rios that would have to make the change.

After a couple weeks, they started to groom Luis Rios to play second base. There may have been some resentment on his part, but he never did show it. He did his job, and he worked hard to make the transition. I was excited to be paired with him, and I knew we would be covering a lot of ground in the infield. With both of us, there was no doubt in my mind that we would have one of the most solid infields up the middle.

One of the highlights of that spring training was a walk-off home run that I hit against the Mets to win the game 3-2, in the bottom of the ninth. After I finished running the bases, I remember the veterans in the dugout were all laughing, joking, and giving me high fives. It felt just like it did in the playoffs the season before. I felt like they accepted me. I felt like I was a part of the team. I felt like I belonged.

When the 2005 season began, I was on the starting roster for opening day. That was a great feeling. To make the St. Louis Cardinals right out of spring training, there was no greater honor—especially with a team that had made it to the World Series the year before. It's tough to not let things like this go to your head, but I was now the starting shortstop on the number one team in the National League. It was hard not to think that I was one of the best shortstops in the world.

That first year in the major leagues was different than the season before. If all went well I was going to be up for the entire season, and my entire career. I would be spending more time in St. Louis, and I would have the opportunity to start to figure out a routine for myself, settle in, get comfortable, and hopefully start living the life I had always dreamed about. I felt like I was ready for everything else to fall into place; just like my father told me it would when I was younger. The sacrifices I had made, had to be made, so I could truly be happy once I made it to the Show.

But the thing is, things didn't just fall into place. I still had to work hard at baseball; we didn't have many days off; and we were on the road a lot throughout the season. It was hard to meet friends, girls, or anyone outside of the game. We may have had access to many things that ordinary people did not, but in a way, it came at a price.

Baseball was still the only thing I had in my life.

Chapter 67

The one thing I had admired the most at the beginning of the 2005 season, was playing at all the stadiums I had watched on TV. I managed to play in a handful the year before, but I was more focused on the game—each at bat and each defensive play. But now, I felt like I could take it all in. To me, all stadiums were remarkable, and some were more magnificent than others, but every time I stepped on that field it was a special experience. It was hard to believe that more than fifty thousand people could be there to watch you play, and thousands of others would be watching you play on TV. Every game I took it all in—the sounds of the crowd, the crack of the bat, the smells. Baseball is a beautiful game, and I was always grateful to be there, but most of all, I was ready to play the game I loved.

But it didn't take me long to take things for granted, and begin focusing on what I might do in my career. I didn't have anything to focus on outside of the game, so when I wasn't on the field, in my mind I would always think of things like: "When I break this record...When I win the World Series...When I reach this milestone," and on it went. I would even look at some of the game's most elusive records, and think I could beat them. I would look at Joe DiMaggio's record of hitting safely in 44 straight games, and think I could do better. I would calculate over and over again how many home runs it would take each season for me to be right there in the likes of Hank Aaron and Babe Ruth. What if I only hit this many this season? What if I only played this many seasons? I tried to think of every scenario.

Instead of truly enjoying the life that I had, I always thought things could be better. It was always, "When I do this" and "When I do that." It was good to have goals and something to focus on, but I became too obsessed with these things. The biggest problem I had, was that I always set my mind on one thing, and forgot about everything else. And that one thing was always baseball. This was something I did my entire life.

There would be talk in the clubhouse about issues with girlfriends, wives, and any other concerns outside of the game, but I could never join in. All I had was baseball. I remember thinking back to the first date I had with Elizabeth, when she asked me, "Can't you talk about anything besides baseball?" I couldn't then, and I still couldn't now.

I realized that I needed to make some changes, but I didn't know what exactly, so I did all the things that I thought I was supposed to do. I rented a nice condo near Busch stadium, and bought a brand new, black, luxurious Mercedes SUV. I was still only making the league minimum, but that was more money than I ever had before, and I felt it was time to start spending it, and enjoying my life. I had made it, and I was playing well, but I was ready for everything else to fall into place. I was even thinking of contacting Elizabeth and putting into motion the plans I had thought about so many times before. There were a few times that I did pick up the phone, but I never did make the call. Something was holding me back, and I didn't know what it was. I think I was afraid to find out that she had moved on without me. That she had forgotten about me. Or worse yet, maybe she would think I'm crazy for calling with the hopes of getting back together after all this time. I was on top of the world, and still, there was something missing.

That season I did become friends with Jace Young. Jace was still on the roster as utility player when Luis Rios took his spot at second base. I knew Jace from the minor leagues. He was a couple years older than me, and spent the last few years going up and down from Triple-A and the majors, but last year he was up for the entire season with the Cardinals. He was a great defensive player, but sometimes he struggled at the plate. I considered Jace a great friend, but when I was playing so well and he wasn't, it was hard for us to stay close. I felt bad that I was part of the reason he lost his spot in the first place. I tried to help him out as much as possible, and we put in a lot of hours in the cage together, but he was a left-handed hitter that struggled with left-handed pitchers, and this forced him to lose a lot of playing time. He became a solid utility man when we needed him on defense, but eventually he would be dropped back down to the minors after only a couple months into the season.

We started off the season with the best record in baseball. We didn't lose a series at home, and at one point we had a 11-game win streak on the road. It was still early in the season, but we were the favorite to win the World Series that year; even more so than the season before. Our defense was solid, and our starting rotation was one of the best in the league on paper. Our hitting, with my name now in the number two spot, was a big step up from last year. The Crusher had 24 home runs before the all-star break, and I was right behind him with 20. We also had Donnie Wood, Rick Bellamy, and Casey Wells, who were all in the double digits for home runs. We were going to be a hard team to beat. The media knew it, and frankly, so did we. It would be difficult to not feel confident with the group of guys we had, and with a manager that did nothing but win games season after season. All we could hope for, was that everyone would stay healthy.

Last season, I was all about proving myself and winning the World Series. This year I wanted to excel. I wanted to make the All-Star team, and I wanted to win awards for my offence and defense. I wanted to be the best, and I wanted everyone to know I was the best. How could I do that? By winning the Rookie of the Year Award. That's what I strived for.

In July, Luis Rios got injured once again, and although it was disappointing, I was excited to have Jace Young rejoin the team. He moved in with me in my condo, and it was good to have him there beside me on the field. He was a different player this time around. He found his bat down in the minors, and he never looked back. He also stole a lot of bases, and in no time, it was hard to remember what we were like with Rios in the lineup.

But that did not last forever. When Rios was back, the Cardinals traded Jace for a relief pitcher, and two other prospects from the Padres. It was disappointing, and hard to lose one of my only friends on the team. I think the Cardinals were trying to capitalize on Jace's good play, just in case he happened to lose his ability to hit once again. In my opinion, I think we should have kept Jace. Even though Rios was good, it didn't make sense to keep a guy that couldn't stay healthy the entire season. I would prove to be right when Jace had a breakthrough second half of the season with the Padres, but I couldn't be happier for my friend. I missed him that's all.

I realized that even in the major leagues it was tough to get close to your teammates. Players still came and went, and it was hard to make friends. Donnie Wood and I hung out a bit, but he was on a different level than I was. He had signed a big contract, was on commercials, and was a very flashy character. He was also all over the news surrounded by girls at clubs after games. I don't know how he did it, but he still showed up every day, and his batting average hovered around .300 that season. He was one of those players that were freakishly talented and knew it, and they didn't work as hard as others, because they didn't need to. I always wondered how much better some of these guys would be if they worked as hard as people like me. But it's hard to ever know.

Donnie and I were too different, so we never became close friends. We were still friendly, but we rarely hung out outside of baseball.

Soon after Jace got traded, I was elected—along with four other Cardinals—to represent our team in that year's All-Star Game.

It wasn't until the 2005 All-Star game at Comerica Park in Detroit, that I felt others would be proud of me. I truly felt like I had accomplished something. Being in the majors is one thing, but being an All-Star separates you from the top baseball players in the world, and lets everyone else know that you are the best of the best. Rick Bellamy, Tony "The Crusher" Campbell, Jeremy McNeilly, and Brent Miller were all with me to represent the Cardinals. Being an All-Star alongside them, created a bond that I would not have had without that experience. Most notable, Rick Bellamy took me under his wing. I followed Rick's lead during our trip to Detroit, and he introduced me to many of his friends from other teams, and he guided me through the whole process. I would have been at a loss without him. Through his introductions, I was able to meet the top players in the major leagues, not as a fan, but as a fellow All-Star.

The most memorable moment, was when Terry Cole—the Yankees third baseman, and a 12-time All-Star—said that he enjoyed watching me play the game. "Ozzie, you're a lot fun to watch out there. You sure have a lot of talent. I wish you the best," he said. Hearing him say that, made me feel like I belonged.

On the night before the All-Star game, The Crusher was one of the eight players chosen to partake in the home run derby. He lost out in the first round, but it was cool to witness everyone having such a great time. Players that were rivals all season long, came together to celebrate everyone's talent. For two days, you get the opportunity to cheer for the best players in the league as if they were your own teammates.

The next night at the All-Star Game, I was not on the starting roster, but it felt incredible to be there. I felt like a kid again. It was an honor to be surrounded by so much talent. I ended up getting in the game as a pinch hitter in the 6th, and I hit a single up the middle. We rallied that inning, and Dante Lawrence—a centre fielder from the Cubs—hit me home to make the game 7-5. I walked my next time up, which was my final at bat in the 8th. In the three innings that I played, I only had one routine groundball hit to me. We ended up losing the game to the American League All-Stars, 9-6. Nonetheless, it was an unforgettable experience.

After the All-Star break, I realized that I could learn a lot from players like Rick Bellamy. But probably not for the ways you would think. For one, he reminded me not to take things too seriously.

Chapter 68

Life is still hard when you make it to the major leagues. You live through hell in the minors, and then you finally make it to the Show and everything is perfect, right? It's not. In the Show you are always in the spotlight. You are always being watched. And you have a very small margin for error. Once you get an opportunity, you cannot blow it. There are a lot of nice things in the majors, but the work is strenuous, and the schedule is long. It takes a toll on your body, your mind, and your relationships. For a lot of players, it is not easy.

I don't know what I expected, but I was still shocked when I noticed the social division amongst players in the major leagues. We were on the same team, but not everyone got along. There are certain groups that hang out off the field, and a lot of players do get excluded for one reason or another. Some players are naturally more easygoing and get along with anybody, but some really struggle to connect with others. When you are alone off of the field, it makes things so much harder. These are some of the things that many athletes don't talk about. But baseball can be one of the most lonely sports in the world; especially when you are in a slump and struggling; or if you bounce around from team to team; or if it is difficult for you to get close to people, like it was for me.

For the most part, I was alone. I didn't have much support outside of baseball, and it was hard. After Jace got traded, I had no one to talk to. Everyone used to look up to me in high school, and I had some very close friends, but now there was nobody. The truth is, once you enter professional baseball, you are in competition with everybody, even your own teammates. I think once you have established yourself in the major leagues, you start to earn a lot more respect, but this can take a long time. And this doesn't guarantee you friends. What I didn't understand at the time, was that the game can do a lot of good for somebody, but it's what happens outside of the game that matters the most. Much of this I learned from Rick Bellamy.

Rick Bellamy—a 7-time All-Star left fielder—was one of the most respected players on the Cardinals, and in the entire major leagues. He was a great player and a great leader. He was only 31 years old, but he had already proven himself so much. He was still fairly young, but with ten years under his belt, he had been in the majors for more than some peoples' careers already. He was no doubt a future Hall of Famer. He was a super nice guy— as nice as they come—but he was also a prankster. His pranks were designed to lighten the mood, and ease the tension of being a professional athlete. In the minor leagues, pranks were often straight up malicious—like drawing inappropriate things on someone's face—but pranks in the Show were more sophisticated. Yet, they could be just as funny, and just as embarrassing. Rick's pranks took planning, time, and money to pull off. For instance, at some point during a game, Rick took the clothes out of The Crusher's locker, and replaced them with a new outfit. He had a bright red suit custom made for Tony, who was a large man, which made it even funnier. It was the most ridiculous suit I had ever seen. It was a full, three-piece suit with vest, tie, shoes—everything. Then after the game, The Crusher went back to his locker, and all of his clothes were gone. Only a few people knew about it. All there was left, was a black suit bag hanging in his locker, and a shoe box sitting on his seat.

The Crusher was furious. "What the hell is this? Where are

301

all my clothes."

At this point you could hear a few players chuckling around the clubhouse.

"I swear to god, Bell, if this was you..." The Crusher threatened.

"Just open it!" someone said.

He slowly unzipped the suit bag, and he was greeted by the bright red suit. "Fuck right off," he said.

Rick walked up to him. "I got you these as well," he said, and handed over a little box. The Crusher opened it, and there sat two gold, Cardinals cufflinks. "There, now your outfit's complete," Rick added, and patted The Crusher on the back.

"Seriously, Bell, where's my fucking clothes?"

"Ahhh common, Tony, put the suit on. Be a sport," Rick said.

Someone started a chant, and a few joined in. "Put it on! Put it on! Put it on!"

"Be a team player...come on put it on," someone chimed in.

"Fuck, I hate you guys." He sat down and opened the suit bag completely.

"Yeeeahhh!!!...That a boy," someone else yelled.

The cheers erupted.

We all sat there, and watched him put on the suit. The whistles and cheers continued throughout the entire process. The more he put on, the more some of the guys were killing themselves laughing.

"Come on, guys, where's my clothes? I can't leave the room wearing this."

"You have to! You look great," Rick said, and many others showered The Crusher with compliments.

"You fucking assholes. I'm going to get you back!" he said. He finally gave in.

And it was all in good fun. A bunch of the guys made him leave first, and there were reporters and photographers out there, and everybody complimented him on his suit. He even had to do an interview, and it was hard for him to keep a straight face. He would be on TV for many days, and he was the talk around the league with that suit for weeks. He would get on base and players on the other team would say, "You sure looked sharp the other night," and the Crusher would utter some kind of threat, and then smile.

Everyone would not let it go for a long time. But after a stunt like that, many players were afraid that they would be the next victim of one of Rick's master plans.

Some other common pranks credited to Rick, included replacing a player's workout gear with undersized clothing—making the player wear short shorts, and shirts that would fall above the belly button. They would have to spend the entire practice wearing these outfits. He would also replace someone's bats with kid-sized bats. The equipment managers would be in on it, and they wouldn't give the victim any replacements.

Jerry Atwell and the rest of our coaching staff were pretty good about it, as long as it didn't interfere with the way we played, and our ability to win games. Baseball can be extremely stressful sometimes, and it was important to keep things lighthearted whenever we could. Believe it or not, it is things like this that can bring a team together.

The first time Rick Bellamy stopped to talk to me after a game, I must admit, I was afraid he was going to pull some kind of prank on me. But instead, it was the beginning of a life-long friendship.

Chapter 69

We had just defeated the Cubs at home 9-0, and I had hit my first major league grand slam. My teammates were giving me high fives and congratulating me in the clubhouse. It was an amazing feeling. I was fresh out of the shower and was headed to my locker when Rick stopped me. *Oh, shit, here it comes.* I thought. *Here comes the first prank. Why does he have to ruin the great game I just had?*

"Hey, Oz, what are you up to tonight? A few players and our wives are going to get some food after the game. Want to join?"

"Thanks for the offer, but I think I'm going to head home. I'm beat," I lied. I was on a high, and had more energy than ever. It felt weird to go out with a few players and their wives. Did they not know I wasn't married?

"I insist, Oz. My wife wants to meet you. And I promise you she won't give up until you come out. So if you don't come tonight, don't say I didn't warn you."

It was such a strange invitation. His wife wanted to meet me? What was that all about? Why would his wife want to meet me?

"Alright, I guess I can make it. Where at?" I said not sounding too excited.

"Perfect!" he said, and looked down at his watch and then back at me. "We are going to a new restaurant downtown on Market Street, it's called Jolliet's. You know where that is?"

I nodded my head. "Yep."

"Okay, perfect, we'll see you in an hour or so!"

I didn't want to go. But it kind of scared me that Rick's wife would be after me until I came out. Who was this woman?

I headed back to my locker, and continued to put on my clothes. Just as I was finished, Lenny was walking by.

"Hell of a game, Oz."

"Thanks, Lenny. Hey, can I ask you something?"

"Shoot."

"Rick Bellamy just asked me to join him and his wife, and a few other players and their wives, out for dinner tonight. He said his wife wanted to meet me. I'm not sure if I want to go. It seems kind of weird, no?"

"Oh, Jennifer! She is such a wonderful...wonderful lady! The Bellamy's are probably the nicest people you will ever meet. You should be honored they asked you to join them. You definitely should go," he said, and walked off before I could ask him anything else. Lenny made me think it was not so awkward after all. I felt a lot better about agreeing to meet them. But I still wondered, was this some sort of prank?

I still felt awkward when I showed up at the restaurant on my own. At that moment, I wished I had a girlfriend, or wife, to bring with me. They wouldn't prank me if I wasn't alone, would they?

When I walked up to the restaurant, I could tell it was a nice place—in fact, it was a fancy restaurant, and I felt underdressed. Now that I was a big leaguer, I made a mental note that I needed some new clothes.

I was nervous for many different reasons that night—I didn't know if I was walking into a prank; I felt underdressed; and I wasn't used to being social anymore. As soon as I walked in, the hostess greeted me with, "You must be Ozzie. You had quite the game today," she said with a beautiful smile.

"I guess I did," I said. How did she know I had a great game? And how did she know who I was? Was she a Cardinals fan?

"The rest of your party is already here. You can follow me right this way."

Shit, I thought. *Of course I had to be the last one to arrive.*

When I got to the table, Rick welcomed me with a smile. "There he is. We're glad you could make it. You had us worried for awhile!"

"Yeah, we were about to send Jennifer after you," Steve Malone, our right fielder, said.

"Shut up, you guys. You're going to scare him away," a beautiful blonde woman in a black dress, a pearl necklace, and the whitest teeth I had ever seen said. "Here, we saved you a seat."

This must be Jennifer, I thought.

I sat down in the empty seat across from Rick and Jennifer. I was right beside Jeremy McNeilly, who was there with his wife. It was a group of four couples, and I was the odd one out on the end.

"Ozzie, I'm not sure if you met everyone here, but that's Steve's wife, Nicole, that's Casey's wife, Ellie, that's Jeremy's wife, Barb, and this is my wife, Jennifer. Everyone as you already know, this is Ozzie," Rick said.

"Nice to meet you," I said to each one as Rick introduced them.

"Great game today, Oz. You've really impressed all of us out there so far this season," Jennifer said.

"Thanks," I said.

"Look how modest he is," Jennifer said to the others, and laughed.

My face turned red. What else was I supposed to say?

"Rick talks about you all the time. And I finally told him he had to bring you out."

"Stop freaking the kid out, Jenn," Rick said.

"Well you do. 'You should meet this kid, Jenn, he is going to be something special.' You just told me that the other night," she replied.

"Alright, fine. It's true, Oz. All of us here are impressed by the way you play, and we want to get to know you more. As ball players, it's important to get to know everyone on your team. That's how a team becomes great," Rick said.

"When Rick first started out, Greg Davis, who was a veteran on the Cardinals at the time, invited us out and made us feel a part of the team. Ever since then, Rick and I always vowed to make younger players feel welcome," Jennifer said.

After she said that, I knew this wasn't a prank.

The more Jennifer talked throughout the night, the more I liked her. It's not like I was interested in someone else's wife or anything, but to be honest, the way she talked, she reminded me of my mother. I could tell she loved baseball, and she loved her husband.

The awkwardness I was feeling when I first got there disappeared as the night went on. Everyone there made me feel at ease. They talked about baseball, they included me in the conversation, and they asked me questions. They wanted to know more about me. It is strange to say, but I felt like they cared about me.

I left the restaurant feeling not so alone. I had a great game, and a great night with some pretty amazing people. Maybe things were falling into place?

After that night, Rick invited me out more often. I spent a lot of time with that group, but most of all, with Rick and Jennifer. I could not have imagined my life up in the majors without them. I learned so much from them, and they truly made a positive impact on all areas of my life.

Chapter 70

Just like every hitter that has ever played the game, I went through a slump. In the last two weeks of July, I was 0-12, and game by game, the latter number started to climb. Soon I was 0-16, 0-19, and 0-23. I couldn't buy a hit. I did manage to get a couple walks during that time, and a few lucky RBIs, but it got to the point where I was dreading having to be in the batter's box. I didn't want to know what my father thought of my slump. I imagined him cursing at the TV at every at bat. I was swinging at so many bad pitches, because I was so eager to get a hit, and get out of the slump. What I failed to see, was that I needed to be patient and relaxed at the plate, like I always was before. It's such a difficult spot to be in when you're in a slump—you don't know what is wrong with you. I was hitting well at the beginning of the season, and out of nowhere, for no apparent reason, I was not.

When you are in a slump everything seems different. You go up to the plate like you have thousands of times before, but now you hear the noise of the crowd; you never feel like you can get settled in; the bat feels heavier, and the ball seems smaller; the pitcher's fastballs are faster, and their breaking pitches break harder and sharper, and the movement is unhittable. Yet, the only thing that is different is your mind, and your mind is what impacts your physical response—your heart beats faster, your body is tense, your senses are over-stimulated, and you are unable to relax.

During that slump, I would walk up to the plate, lift my bat to my shoulders, and wonder why my bat felt like it was filled with sand? Why did it feel like there was a jack hammer in my head? And why did my muscles feel like they were in a vice? It's not fun anymore when you step in the batter's box and know that you are already defeated. I would still go up there, and like always, I would know what the pitcher was going to throw me. For example, I would know that a certain pitcher was going to throw hard sliders outside, because he has gotten me to ground out on that pitch before. I would be waiting, and I knew if he left anything on the outside part of the plate, that I would take it the other way. The pitcher would wind up, throw the ball, and I would automatically notice the spin, and realize it was a slider just like I thought. He would leave it a little too far on the plate, and I would swing, but it would cut harder and sharper than it ever had before, and it would avoid my bat by a few inches, but would feel more like a few feet. The next pitch he would throw the exact same pitch, and I would swing and miss a second time. It's as if the ball had grown eyes and could move out of the way of my bat when it wanted to. Then the next pitch would be a fastball high and inside, just within the strike zone. I would watch it go by, but the truth is, I didn't even see it. That pitch could have been a bullet whizzing by, for all I knew. I would have kept standing and waiting for the pitch if I hadn't heard the umpire yell, "Strike three." I would walk out of the batter's box totally flummoxed. I would then wonder what was wrong with me? Even when I knew what the pitcher was going to throw, I still couldn't hit it.

Then, the next at bat, the crowd noise would be drowning. I wouldn't be able to think or focus. I would go up there without a plan, and just try to hit whatever came my way. I would strike out on three straight pitches, and it wouldn't even matter if they were balls or strikes. I wouldn't even stand a chance. Everything would go wrong, yet, there was nothing I could do about it.

Many great players have felt just like I did. That's the only comfort I could try to get out of it, but it's tough when you are in the moment. It's tough when you are standing up at the plate with thousands of people watching, your teammates are counting on you, and the only thing you could manage to do was make a fool of yourself. When I somehow managed to hit the ball it would be an out, or worse yet, a double play. During that slump, the only thing I believed, was that I was cursed.

Some of your biggest fears will take over your mind when you are in a slump: *Will I get dropped down to the minors? Or will I get traded?* When things are going well, you are considered a great ball player, but as soon as things are not going well, people will think you can be easily replaced. The rumors going around don't help these fears. Soon enough, there are always "experts" that believe if they were the owners or managers, they would make these deals that would ultimately make the team so much better. "We need a left-handed pitcher for the rotation, so why don't they trade Ozzie Shaw, so that they have a chance of winning the Series this year? That's what I would do if I was in charge." Thankfully, they are not. People like this think they know everything about the game, but they rarely do. I tried to ignore the rumors and all the "experts" as much as I could.

I spent a lot of time on my own trying to shake the funk I was in. I felt like everyone was laughing at me and talking about me, and this only made matters worse. I would always think, *What if I strike out again? What if I still don't get a hit?*

I tried to take more BP, since that always worked before. I would spend hours in the cage, and our hitting coach was patient with me. But the more I practiced, it felt like the more mixed up I became. I finally talked to my father, and he said, "Know the pitcher, what's his best pitch?...Stay back, quick hands, hit it up the middle," and all that basic stuff he had been drilling into me as a kid. I brought all these things into my mind when I went up to bat, and it still didn't help.

I tried everything to get that part of my game back. I tried new bats—including different lengths, weights, different colors, more pine tar, no pine tar—different batting gloves, no batting gloves, everything you can think of, but nothing worked.

After refusing them a number times in a row, Rick and Jennifer made me go out for dinner with them after another 0-4 game. They wouldn't take no for an answer. It was just the three of us. At first, we talked about things other than baseball, but we mostly ended up in a bunch of awkward silences. Their attempt to lift my spirits didn't seem to be working. Finally I asked, "What is wrong with me?...Why can't I hit the ball anymore?"

"It happens to everyone," Rick said. "It happens to the best of hitters, and trust me, everyone has felt the exact way you do right now...I know it feels like you will never get out of it, but you will. You've hit the ball before, so you know you can do it again."

"You are trying to do too much out there," Jennifer added. "You are trying too hard. You need to be relaxed and be yourself, and you will get right back into a groove. I can see it, you are in the box all tensed up. You were never like that before. The harder you try, the harder it will be to get out of this slump. Relax and have fun. Remember, it is just a game."

"She's right you know. She always is," Rick said.

Jennifer smiled. And she *was* right. Every time I got up to the plate, I felt I had to come up with a big hit. I was trying to do too much, and I wasn't relaxed. What I didn't want to tell her was that baseball was my life—it wasn't just a game—that's why this slump felt like the end of the world.

The next game I went 0-3 with a walk, but I hit the ball hard in two at bats, and just missed in another. I was relaxed and was seeing the ball well. I was comfortable. I knew a hit would come soon, and it did.

In a game in Milwaukee against the Brewers, my first at bat, I hit a 2-1 fast ball in the gap to left-center field. With one swing, my slump ended, and I was standing on second base. I went 2-3 that day—with a double, single, and a walk.

The biggest issue during my slump was that it was hard for me to relax. Every time I found myself doing nothing, I would feel guilty. I was such a different person than I was in the minors. For some reason, I worried about what other players were doing, and I couldn't stop comparing myself to them. I worked hard to prepare and separate myself from others, but with that, came the pressure I put on myself, and the inability to relax. Too often, we forget about the importance that our mind can have on our ability to perform our best. During that slump, I learned that there is such a thing as over working and over thinking. Like Jennifer said, I needed to relax. I needed to have fun. I needed to be myself. I had worked hard to get to where I was, and I needed to get back to enjoying baseball.

When a guy is struggling on the field, it is often because what is going on off the field. The only problem is that many ball players do not see this at the time of their slump, and it takes someone else to recognize what is going on. Sometimes, it takes someone outside of the game to notice these things. I was grateful to Jennifer and Rick, but I wished I had someone of my own that could be there for me, and notice when things were off. Someone like Jennifer. Someone like Elizabeth.

Things changed drastically after my slump. I went from being on the brink of being sent down during my first full season in the majors, to leading the league in batting average. I felt like I was unstoppable. When I wasn't hitting, I was walking and still getting on base. Right around the time I made the turn around, our team started to get hot. We ended up going from the middle of the pack, to being two games behind first place. With a few more wins, we would be at the top of our division, and on our way to clinching a playoff spot.

The ultimate goal for every team right from the onset of spring training is to win the World Series. But the mere length of the season in the majors, really puts a test on teams and their athletes. It's a long journey. A team will go through streaks and slumps, and the team changes—sometimes drastically—as the season goes on. There will be injuries, trades, players will be sent down, and others will be brought up. Faces come and go, and so do certain attitudes. For me, I was up, I was down, and then I was up again. There are many ups and downs in baseball, just like there are many ups and downs in life.

Even though I had Rick and a few other friends on the team, I often found myself home alone. It's hard to admit it, especially since I was a young and rich professional baseball player, but I was lonely, and it hurt. It was on the nights after a game when I was alone, that I felt the worst. I was always fine during the day, because I was busy, and I didn't have much time to think, but when I was alone at night, I felt empty, and I knew that there had to be something else for me out there. But those nights would go by, and I would wake up the next morning, and I would begin my same routine all over again. Keeping busy was the best thing for me.

Chapter 71

One thing that my father didn't tell me, and he probably didn't know about it anyway, was that it wasn't easy to find a girl to start a relationship with, once I made it to the Show. The long, grueling season doesn't give you much time to meet new people, and date girls in a consistent way. It's hard to devote yourself and give someone the energy they deserve—especially when you are first starting out and getting to know each other. You may meet someone great, go on a date, and then have to spend the next few weeks away on a long road trip. Or maybe you meet someone during the offseason and everything goes well, but then your relationship gets put through the ringer once spring training comes along, and the season begins.

So how do you find somebody? Ideally, I believe you have to bring someone with you on your journey—someone that will learn and grow as you do. For me, that person could have been Elizabeth, but I let her go.

I was left with only two others options: I would have to find someone that understands the life of a ball player, or someone willing to understand the life of a ball player. As you can see, it's not easy to find someone, let alone build the foundation that a lasting relationship could grow on. A lot of people don't think about this, but baseball is hard on relationships.

I still had hope that I would find someone that I would spend my life with. There were times when certain things would happen, and I would wonder if they were a result of fate or coincidence. For instance, being constantly reminded of Elizabeth, was that fate or coincidence? Or was I giving meaning to things that had no meaning at all?

When I met Anne for the first time, however, I wondered: *How could this not be fate?*

A few weeks after I broke out of my slump, we had a series in Atlanta. I was nervous for that road trip. I wasn't nervous for our games against the Braves, but I was nervous because Rick and Jennifer wanted me to meet a friend of theirs that lived in Atlanta. Her name was Anne, and Rick and Jennifer said we would be perfect for each other. I wasn't particularly comfortable meeting someone new, but I agreed to meet her. In reality, I knew Rick and Jennifer wouldn't take no for an answer.

We won our first game in Atlanta, 7-0. I hit a three-run home run in the 1st inning, a single in the 5th, and a triple in the 8th. I had a great game on the field, but the real challenge for me, was meeting Anne after the game.

I felt Rick and Jennifer put a lot pressure on me when they said that Anne and I would be perfect for each other. I was excited to meet her, but of course I couldn't help but thinking: *What if we weren't perfect for each other? What if she doesn't like me? What if I blow it?*

Just like when I was going through my slump, I was over thinking things. I needed to learn how to relax. I needed to learn how to enjoy the moment.

After the game, Jennifer and Anne were already at the restaurant, and Rick and I went together to meet them there. On the way, I was still stewing in my own nervous thoughts. Rick broke the silence. "You excited to meet Anne? She's a wonderful woman, Oz. Very beautiful," Rick said. "And you must be feeling pretty good after that game tonight."

I wasn't feeling good at all. I was already thinking of all the reasons why Anne might not like me, instead of why she might. "I'm not excited at all, Bell. I feel like throwing up."

Rick laughed. "Come on, Oz, you'll be fine."

"Seriously, Bell, it's been a awhile since..." I stopped myself. I was feeling embarrassed.

"Since what?"

"Since...since I've went out on a date with someone."

I could tell Rick knew I was serious. Most guys would make fun of me if they heard me say something like that, but Rick was a good friend. He always looked out for me. He cared about me.

"Don't worry about it, Oz. Anne is great, and you're great. Just relax and have fun tonight. Jenn and I will be right there with you. Just let the girls talk, listen, smile, and answer any questions Anne might ask you. Just be yourself, Oz. Jenn and I think you're pretty awesome, and Anne will think so too," Rick said. "Plus, Jenn has already talked you up, and Anne saw the excellent game you had tonight, so you're way ahead already."

I calmed down a bit after he said that. "Thanks, Bell."

"No problem, Oz," he said. "Well, maybe not way ahead, she is a Braves fan."

We both laughed. I was feeling better, and more relaxed as we entered the restaurant. Jennifer and Anne were sitting side by side at a table with two empty seats directly across from them. They both stood up as we approached. Anne was gorgeous. She had golden brown hair, was wearing a stylish, black, loose fitting dress, with a belt around her waist. She was tall, had long legs, and looked like a super model. I could tell she had style, and a lot of class. Jennifer introduced Anne to me, and I smiled, shook her hand, said "Nice to meet you," and we sat down across from each other.

"See, I told you he has a great smile," Jennifer said to Anne.

My face got warm. *Of course Jenn would say something like that to make me blush right off the bat,* I thought.

"Don't worry, Jenn, I already saw his nice smile...when he was rounding the bases after that three run homer in the first against my Braves."

"Sorry about that," I said beaming another smile.

"No you're not," she said.

"You got me, I'm really not," I said, and we all laughed.

The conversation continued on, and it was all very lighthearted at the beginning, which helped me relax. Then as the night progressed, Anne started to ask me more questions about myself as if she was genuinely interested in me.

"What do your parents do?" she asked.

"Well my dad is a tire technician at Big O Tires back in Columbia, Missouri, and my mother left us when I was eleven years old, and I honestly don't know what she does. She has another family somewhere else."

"Oh, I see," she said.

I was kind of embarrassed about my family, so I added, "My father was a great ball player. He was drafted by the Montreal Expos in the first round. Things just didn't work out the way he planned, however."

"What about your parents? What do they do?"

"Jennifer and Rick didn't tell you?"

"No they didn't."

"My father is Roger Westbrook, the ex-Brave."

"Are you serious? Your father is Roger *"The Razor"* Westbrook? He was a twenty plus game winner for 5 straight seasons. He had probably the best cut fastball in the history of the game—"

"His fastball cut so sharp it was like a razor," Anne said before I could continue, and laughed. "Yes, I know, I know. I hear this from everyone."

"This is too crazy. My father actually played with your father back in college in Miami. I can't wait until I tell him that I met The Razor's daughter."

What are the odds that I would end up meeting a girl who's father played with my father back when he was in college? What are the odds I would meet a ball player's daughter? If there was anyone that knew what the life of a baseball player was like, it was Anne. As the night continued, she talked about baseball and about watching her father as she grew up. I was totally drawn in. Rick and Jennifer were right, she was great, and we were perfect for each other.

When we were parting for the night, I didn't want to leave. I wished I had some more time to talk with Anne.

"It was nice to meet you, Ozzie," she said. "Next time you're in town, we should all go out again."

It felt like it was more addressed to me than Rick and Jenn. I took that as a good sign. "It was nice to meet you, too. I'm not sure when we are back, but I would like that," I said.

She seemed nice, and she was beautiful. But I knew better than to get my hopes up right away. Was I even ready for a relationship? Like my time with Lindsay, I decided not to push things, and see what would happen.

I continued to concentrate on baseball, but often, when I got home, I would think about Anne, and I wondered if we would actually meet up the next time we were in Atlanta. I knew I needed to be patient.

One night, in St. Louis, I went home after a game against the Marlins, and my phone rang.

"Hello, Ozzie?" said a female voice.

"Liz?" I replied.

"No, sorry, it's Anne. I hope I am not bothering you. But Jenn gave me your number. I just wanted you to know I watched your game tonight. You played great!"

"Hey, Anne. No you're not bothering me. Thank you, it was a good game," I said. I had thought about Anne quite a bit, but I never expected a call from her.

"I wanted to tell you that I talked to my father on the phone the other day, and I told him I had met the son of a ball player that he used to play with back in college. He said that your father was one of the best baseball players he had ever played with," she said.

"Really? That's pretty cool your father remembered him."

"He also said, 'That Ozzie Shaw is a pretty damn good ball player himself. Now that I know he is Joe Shaw's boy, that makes a lot more sense.' "

"That means a lot coming from The Razor!" I said. As much as I enjoyed the compliment, I still didn't like talking about myself. "How are things with you, Anne?"

"I am doing well, thanks," she replied. "Work has been busy. I just got back from a big sports nutrition conference in Chicago over the weekend. It's good to be home. I looked at your schedule, and I noticed you're back in Atlanta in a couple weeks, are we still going to meet up?"

"Absolutely. I think Rick and Jenn said they would love to all go out together again," I said.

"Sounds good!" she replied. "Anyway, I better let you go. I can't wait to see you. And sorry for calling out of the blue."

"I'm glad you did, Anne. I can't wait to see you, too. Have a good night."

A few days later I called my father, and told him that I had met The Razor's daughter through a teammate. I also told him that the Razor said that my father was one of the best ball players he had ever seen.

"We had a lot of talented guys on that team," my father said. "The Razor wasn't even the best pitcher we had at the time, but he ended up having the best career. So this Anne girl...are you two seeing each other?"

"Too early to tell, Pop. Just met her once, and talked to her on the phone once. We'll see what happens."

"Well, I hope it all works out, Son."

It was strange to hear my father say something like that. Was it because he was sober? But it did feel good that my father finally wanted me to have a successful relationship.

When we were back in Atlanta, I was excited. I was actually

more excited for after the game, than I was for the game. I couldn't wait to see Anne.

After our first game in Atlanta, we all went out for dinner again. We all appeared to be having a nice night, but out of the blue, Jennifer said she wasn't feeling well, and Rick took her back to their hotel room. I figured they planned it so Anne and I could have some time alone. I didn't mind. We had another wonderful night, and the more time Anne and I spent talking to each other, the more I realized how perfect she was for me.

We also hung out the next two nights alone together, and it was disappointing when I had to leave Atlanta. I wanted to continue spending time with Anne. From when I left Atlanta, I talked to Anne on the phone almost every night. She even came to visit me in St. Louis when we had a stretch of home games.

The excitement and anticipation to see her wasn't a distraction. I was playing as well as ever. I knew when I needed to be focused on the field, but after the game, I was excited for something outside of baseball. This was something I hadn't experienced for a long time. It felt good to care for someone, and be cared for. Just as soon as we were enjoying our time together, the postseason was fast approaching, and I was busier than ever. As much as I liked her, I had to focus on baseball.

Chapter 72

The road to the playoffs is never easy. Some of the top teams in the league will hit peaks and valleys all throughout the season. Often, it all comes down to the last few weeks before the playoffs, which becomes known as the playoff race.

I could not imagine being one of those teams that are out of contention early on, and playing the 162 game grind, and the only thing that is consistent, is that your team loses more often than they win. I experienced it in the minors, but it must be hard to be on a team that does not win in the major leagues, since there is nowhere else to go, unless you get traded. This must make for a long season. I was lucky to be brought up to such a successful team.

Making the playoffs is an incredible thing. The long season— with the hard work, injuries, slumps, and sacrifices— finally becomes worth it. All you have to do is continue to give everything you have for a few more games, and you only have to play three more teams. Everybody has been waiting for this moment—the players, the staff, and the fans. The stakes are higher, and the level of excitement increases dramatically.

I remember when we clinched a playoff spot in a home game against the Diamondbacks. I had experienced the same thing the season before, but this year was different—this year I felt a part of the team, instead of an outsider that was celebrating someone else's achievements. To add to it, I hit a walk-off two-run home run to win the game.

There is no greater feeling in the world than hitting a walk-off home run to win a meaningful game at home. You round the bases, and you can see everybody standing and cheering. You can feel the energy in the stadium. Your whole team is waiting for you at home plate to tackle you, or lift you up, or do whatever they are going to do. In that moment, you are the hero. It took a team effort to get there, but in that moment, it is all on you. There is no way to possibly describe that feeling. Only those that have done it, know how it feels.

After we beat the Diamondbacks, we went back to the clubhouse, and everything was covered in plastic. There was champagne and beer in huge tubs in the middle of the clubhouse. As soon as we got there, guys were popping champagne bottles, and spraying and dumping them everywhere. There was only a small amount that ended up in anyone's mouth. The emotions were so high, it is hard to explain. It felt like true happiness. I soaked it all in—literally and metaphorically. If this is what it was like to make it into the playoffs, what would it be like to win the World Series? That feeling of true happiness, that's what you play for. If you have ever experienced it, you know that the only thing you want to do is experience it again.

In the playoffs, a lot of guys like to compare their teammates to brothers, or even soldiers. They talk about going into the trenches together. Your teammates are the guys you grind day in and day out with, and you win or lose as a team. That's what the playoffs are like. There may be things that happen during the season, but it all needs to come together in the playoffs. The teams that bond together and trust each other, are the ones that prevail. The postseason is where the true leaders and true champions come out. Some guys may struggle in one area of their game, but they will do whatever they can to help the team win—it can be with one key hit, or one great play in the field, or even with words of encouragement. Every little thing can make a difference. Every little thing counts. There is a lot of pressure in the playoffs, and the veterans are the guys that have to step up and calm the younger players down, and teach them the ins and outs of playoff baseball. When it comes down to it, you will do anything to help your team win. The only downside, however, is that the other team you are facing is doing the same thing.

Going into that NLDS series against the Padres, a lot of our teammates were no longer with us, and we didn't feel like we were the same team that began the season. Jace Young had been traded, along with a few others, and Luis Rios was injured once again. What made matters worse, was that our best pitcher, Jeremy McNeilly, suffered a strained calf the tail end of the season, and he was not the same in Game 1 of the playoffs.

On the other hand, my pal Jace Young and the Padres came into the series with a 9-game winning streak, and they swept us in three straight games. No one saw it coming. In those three games, I went 6-11 with two home runs, but that didn't make a difference. We put our blood, sweat, and tears out on that field, but came up short. That's the way it goes sometimes.

Once we lost out in the NLDS against the Padres, we knew we had a lot of work to do in the offseason, or else we would struggle next year. We needed to make some big changes, and fill in a lot of holes that we didn't know existed, until it was too late.

It was a disappointing finish to the season, but it didn't bother me as much as it should have. I went into the offseason looking forward to something other than spring training. Now that my season finished earlier than expected, I was looking forward to spending more time with Anne.

Chapter 73

I finished my first complete season in the major leagues with a .304 batting average, 35 home runs, 97 RBIs, and 30 stolen bases. I felt like the sky was the limit for the type of career I would create for myself. Through my performance I was not only showing that I belonged in the big leagues, but that I could become one of the best around. My picture was all over on magazines, newspapers, and the internet; and a number of my highlights were playing on ESPN. I was breaking club records, and my name was mentioned alongside some of the true greats—including Ozzie Smith. There was also a lot of speculation that I was going to be chosen as the National League's Rookie of the Year. It felt good to know that my hard work and sacrifice was paying off. I was finally the ball player that I always wanted to be.

A few days into the offseason, Anne invited me to Atlanta to stay with her for awhile. Time with her was something I needed. We went for walks; she cooked for me; and we went to movies. All those little things that I had not enjoyed since my time with Elizabeth, I was starting to enjoy again.

After my time in Atlanta, I went back to Columbia and spent some time with my father. I continued to be surprised at how well he was doing. He was still completely sober, and we talked about him retiring, so he could come watch me play more often in the upcoming season. He was more open to the idea than he had ever been in the past. He still must have been lonely, but he appeared to be happy.

We took BP in my backyard like we always did, but we did not do much else. It was weird being a major league star, and staying with my father in the house I grew up in. It made me feel like a kid again. I also planned on spending time back in Evansville with my uncle Frank and his family, but I never made it there.

After about a week and a half of spending time with my father, I went back to St. Louis. It was time for me to get settled in, and become a grown up. I continued to stay at the condo I had rented at the beginning of the season, but my plan was to purchase a home in a nice neighborhood where a few of my teammates lived.

At the beginning of November, Anne came to visit for a week, and we had a great time. We did all the things that I never did in St. Louis the entire time I was there. We went to see the Arch and the museum underneath, took walks down by the river, sat in the park, went to restaurants I had never been to before, and we explored old St. Louis together. We did things that couples normally do—that people normally do. I was getting to know Anne, and St. Louis at the same time.

It was difficult to know where our relationship was headed. We enjoyed each other's company; we got along wonderfully; and I thought about her a lot. But I still wondered how we could make things work. We lived in two different cities, and I knew it would have to be her that would eventually have to move to St. Louis. That's if things got serious between us. Now, did I want things to get serious between us? The answer is a resounding yes. I liked her, and she seemed perfect for me. But, I still thought about Elizabeth.

When Anne left, I soon got bored, and I did what I always did—I spent most of my time training for the next season. Through one of our trainers, I had 24-hour access to a facility that had batting cages equipped with pitching machines. This was beneficial for me, since I spent many sleepless nights wanting to hit, and now I could go and hit whenever I wanted.

On November 10th, 2005, I went there to hit around midnight, and I spent a couple hours hitting in the cage and working out. It was an ordinary night for me, but the drive home changed my life forever.

At around 2 am, I was driving along, heading home. It was a twenty minute drive to my condo, and I had made that drive almost every day—sometimes a few times a day. Only a couple blocks from my condo, I was heading into an intersection when the light was green, but I didn't see a black pickup truck blow the red light, until it was too late. I remember that feeling right before I was hit. It was that "Oh shit!" moment that is accompanied with a gross feeling in your stomach. It was the feeling when you know something bad is about to happen, but there is nothing you can do about it. I was blindsided, but luckily the entire truck did not hit my driver side door straight on, instead, he caught more of the front end. I remember the impact and the sound, and the explosion of the air bag. I didn't feel much at first. I was dazed and didn't know what to do. I remember trying to get out, but my legs were stuck under the dash.

I heard voices, and saw some faces that I did not recognize. They came up to my window and asked me if I was okay. I just sort of looked around and was out of it for a few seconds, and said my legs were stuck. A man told me that the ambulance was on the way, and I just needed to hang tight. I couldn't have went anywhere if I wanted to. I reached down and touched my left leg, and I felt a warm substance. I raised my hand up and looked at my fingers, and they were covered in blood. When I saw the blood, that's when I knew I was hurt.

The police arrived, and two officers walked up to my window.

"Hello, sir, can you tell us your name?"

"My name is Ozzie Shaw."

"The ball player?" he asked.

"Yes."

"We need some help over here right now...that's Ozzie Shaw," he said to his partner.

I remember thinking that it was kind of ironic how things gained more urgency when they found out my name. Wouldn't they want to help anyone in this situation? Isn't that their job? But I understand that some people are more important to others. It's how society views certain people. I was a St. Louis Cardinal, so they knew that my career was on the line.

Eventually the initial adrenaline wore off, and my left leg was in pain. I felt that was a good sign. If I didn't feel anything at all, then I would have been more concerned. I was in my vehicle for almost two hours. My legs were stuck, and they had to take all precautions with extracting me. I was fortunate that none of the vehicles were leaking fuel, and didn't pose a risk of catching on fire. Consequently, they were able to take their time. Who knows what would have happened if they had to act more quickly— more damage could have been done to my leg. However, that wasn't a concern then. I was only concerned if my leg would heal for spring training.

While they were studying the situation and planning the extraction, they asked if I wanted them to call anyone. My cell phone was still intact, and I was able to give them the number to call Trevor—the head trainer for the Cardinals—and my agent's number. They called them using my phone, and they notified them of the situation, and told them what hospital I would be taken to. That's when I heard I had been hit by a drunk driver.

"I was hit by a drunk driver?" I asked the officer who wasn't on the phone.

"Yeah, the bastard tried to run away, but a witness grabbed him and held on to him until we got here. He barely has a scratch on him, but he can barely stand he's that drunk. The son of a bitch will pay for this," the officer said.

I was silent. *How could this happen to me?* I thought.

When the officer finished talking to my agent, he asked me if there was anyone else they needed to notify. "No there isn't," I replied.

I thought about getting them to call Anne, but I didn't want to worry her. She was a few hundred miles away, and I knew she would find out about my accident sooner or later. Then I thought I should maybe call my father, but I also didn't want to worry him. I wasn't in serious condition or anything, it was just my leg. I knew that I would be able to call both of them from the hospital, and update them once I knew more.

I had to sit there for another hour, while others worked on getting me out. I sat there thinking how sad it was that I had no one else to call. I could have been seriously hurt, and I had no one that would be able to come to the hospital right away, besides my trainer, and possibly my agent. I didn't have anybody that I was close to in St. Louis. I was a major league star, but I couldn't help thinking: *Some life I had created for myself.* Little did I know, the worst was still to come.

The firefighters brought tools to cut the metal away from my legs. When my legs were free, they lifted me, and put me on a stretcher. There were many people around: paramedics, firemen, police officers, and bystanders looking at the scene from where the officers had blocked off the road. When they put me in the ambulance, they gave me some pain killers and the pain went away, but they told me my left leg was in rough shape. To me, hearing that, was more painful than the physical pain from the accident

At the hospital, they cleaned up my leg, and did x-rays and a CT scan to find out the extent of the damage. I had a badly broken femur, and a torn ACL. It was clear that I would need surgery, and it would be months until my leg was healed. Other than my leg, I only sustained a few other scrapes and bruises, and they told me I was lucky that it hadn't been worse. I didn't see it that way, however. My biggest fear of not being able to play baseball was unfolding in front of me.

After the preliminary tests, it was early in the morning and I was exhausted. When I woke up, Trevor, the Cardinals' head trainer, was there to see how I was doing. He said that the most important thing to do was to get the Cardinals involved, so they could take the best course for me and my career. My agent called and said he was out of town, but he said he would make it there the next day. Trevor and Vince were the two most important people for me at that time.

A few other members from the Cardinals' training and medical staff came about an hour after Trevor. Immediately they started to work on a plan for me. They wanted the best doctors and the best surgeons to fix my leg, and help me get back on the field. Talks with the doctors and surgeons were promising in the sense that they could fix my leg with the help of pins and rods that would bring the bone back together, but they couldn't promise that my leg would be one hundred percent ever again. They reminded me how fortunate I was that the car accident wasn't worse. It was hard for me to see the optimistic side of things. It was all bad news to me. I decided to call my father to let him know what happened, and he said he would be there as soon as he could.

I don't know if it was the pain killers, the trauma of the accident, or both, but I had nothing but nightmares whenever I slept. In my dreams, I saw visions that I would never be able to explain. In my dream I was looking above at the whole scene of the car accident, and when the police handcuffed the drunk driver, the driver had my face. It would scare the shit out of me, and I would wake up. I was left wondering in that hospital bed, did I do this to myself?

There was also one particular reoccurring nightmare that I had many times for years to come. I am at Busch Stadium, and I am walking with a limp up to the batter's box. The announcer announces, "Now batting, number eleven, Ozzie Shaw!" I get in the batter's box, and dig in. But I do not have a bat with me. The umpire looks at me, and says from behind his mask, "Where is your bat, kid?"

"It's right here," I reply, and I start to twist my left leg counter clockwise. After several turns it comes off. I hold it like a baseball bat, and bring it to my shoulder as I am trying to balance on one leg. The pitcher gets the sign, sets, and begins his windup. Right when the ball is released, I fall over, while the whole crowd laughs. I remember the taste of the dirt, and the humiliation. It is all so real. Then I wake up.

When I first had that nightmare in the hospital, I woke up startled and sweating, and my father was sitting in a chair near my hospital bed.

"Son," is all he said. I remember that sad look on his face.

"It doesn't look good, Pop," I tried to tell him, but I'm not sure what came out.

"We'll get the best, Son, don't worry. You'll be back in no time."

The way he said it, I could tell he was not so sure of his own words. But I don't know if I was hearing clearly. I dozed off back to sleep.

The next day, I had a missed call on my cell phone from Rick, and one from Anne. I wasn't ready to call Anne, so I dialed Rick's phone number. Rick said him and Jennifer were sorry for what happened, and that they would come to see me as soon as they were back from visiting Jennifer's family in Savannah, Georgia. It was a very brief conversation, but it was nice to know they were thinking of me.

Then I called Anne.

"Ozzie, are you okay?" she answered with concern in her voice. "My father called me and told me that he saw on ESPN that you had been in an accident."

"I'm okay. But my leg is pretty banged up," I said. "I don't think I'll be playing next season."

I got chocked up from saying it out loud.

"Oh, Ozzie. Everything will be okay," she said. "Do you want me to catch a flight and come down to see you?"

"Thanks, Anne, but I think I will be in and out of surgeries for the next little while. I will let you know when I know more about the plan. Then from there, we will see if there is a better time for you to come down," I replied. "The doctor just walked in. I have to go, Anne. I will talk to you later."

"Okay. Bye, Ozzie."

It was nice of her to call, but sadly, she was the last person I wanted around. I didn't want her to see me when I was down and out.

The doctors decided that they needed to get me into surgery right way. It was becoming more apparent from what the doctors and surgeons were saying, that I would miss the entire upcoming season. I couldn't even say that I was injured doing the thing I love. I wasn't even given that. I was only a year and a few months into my major league career, and I was injured from a freak accident caused by a drunk driver. It was hard to believe that some stranger ruined my life.

While I was stuck in that hospital room, I saw the news report about my accident. The driver was named Lance Smith. The son of a bitch had the same last name as my father's favorite baseball player. The driver was charged with impaired driving committing bodily harm, and they said it would be some time until he was convicted and sentenced. Seeing his face and hearing his name filled me with rage.

What are the odds my career would be ended by someone with the same last name as the person I was named after? Sometimes I think there was a greater force at play here, or it could be the simple fact, that Smith is the most common last name in the United States.

Chapter 74

The next few days, weeks, and months were filled with surgeries, rehabilitation, and a lot of down time. After all that my leg had been through, all I could do was let it heal. I had to rest, which is something I was never good at. You want to talk about loneliness? I should have been enjoying the best years of my career, but instead, for the first time in my life, I was kept from playing baseball. I also hated using crutches to get around, and I hated not being able to use my body the way I could before. After the initial shock, sadness, and depression wore off, I did something that I had never done much of before: I read a lot. Some people had brought me sports magazines, and Rick brought me a bunch of books he still had from his college days. I couldn't handle looking at a magazine filled with sports, so I picked up a book. The first book I started reading was Charles Dickens's *Great Expectations*, and I couldn't put it down. And after I was finished that one, I picked up another one, which happened to be Ernest Hemingway's *For Whom the Bell Tolls*. All of a sudden, I had this deep appreciation for the characters in these stories, and for the authors that created them. They understood love and sacrifice, and, in a way, I felt like I was living the same story. I kept reading, since I had nothing else to do. Much of what I read during that time is what inspired me to eventually write my own story.

Only about a week after my accident, I received some bitter sweet news. I was sitting on my couch, alone, with an injured leg, when I found out I was the National League's Rookie of the Year for the 2005 season. It was an honor, but it didn't mean much to me at that moment. I was still in pain, and I knew I wouldn't be able to play at all the upcoming season. Sadly, it only made me feel worse.

I spent several weeks cooped up in my condo; only leaving for appointments with my doctors and physiotherapists, and when Rick and Jennifer made me go out. In the first little while after my accident, some of my teammates that remained in St. Louis came to visit, but that came to an end once spring training began.

When the accident happened, everything changed. I wasn't the same person anymore. Anne came to visit me when I was recovering from my surgery, and she was such an angel the way she took care of me. But it didn't take long for me to push her away. It was mostly because of my self-pity, and the fact that I didn't think I deserved her while I was injured, and unable to play baseball. I was in a bad spot mentally and physically, and we didn't yet have the foundation to get through something like that. Not for lack of trying on her part, however. The truth is, I didn't have the foundation to deal with any of this myself, let alone be in a relationship. When she went back home, she would call to check up on me, and after awhile I stopped answering the phone. Not because I didn't want to talk to her, but because I didn't want to be a burden. It was my way of distancing myself from her.

For awhile, my father would drive down and come visit me on weekends, but there was not much he could do for me. I wasn't that great of company anyway. We would watch a few ball games together like we always had, but he became tired of my "pissy" attitude. It was not good for our relationship, or my recovery. I desperately wanted to get back to my old self.

After a long healing process, there was still so much I had to do. My goal was to push myself as hard as possible through a rigorous rehabilitation program, so I could get back sooner than expected. Just before I was cleared to start expanding my rehabilitation exercises, the doctors said the healing was going well, but they knocked me down a peg when they said there was still a good chance I would never be a hundred percent. They said I should not expect to play at the level I did before my injury, or be able to run as fast. I was determined to prove them all wrong.

I thought the accident was painful, and the recovery time after the surgeries, but that was nothing compared to the rehabilitation program I had. Building the strength back up in my leg was no routine ground ball. Getting up and putting weight on my leg was a laborious and long ordeal. When I would put the littlest amount of weight on it, pain would shoot through my whole leg. My whole body was affected—my heart would race; my breathing would speed up; I would become light headed; and I would have to sit down again. But I never gave up. Eventually I moved on to a variety of exercises that would help me gain back the range of motion in my leg. Again the pain was nearly unbearable, but I would force myself to fight through it.

Once I started to get motion back in my leg, I was able to start strengthening the muscles that had been completely depleted. My physiotherapists would have me sit on these machines with the littlest bit of resistance, and I would slowly work my strength back up from square one.

My physical therapists, trainers, and doctors were all amazed by my determination. They said I had made gains in the least amount of time they had ever seen. This was some of the best news I had heard in a long time. In everything I did, I had to prove my work ethic and my greatness. That's the way I was raised.

But while I was making significant strides with my recovery from my accident, I also received some horrible news.

Chapter 75

I was sitting alone in my condo, when Rick called me out of the blue about a month before the end of the 2006 regular season.

"Hey, Ozzie. How are things? I heard from the trainers that your rehab has been going well. You have always been a tough son of a gun, haven't you?"

"Hey, Bell. Yeah it's going alright. The doctor's said I can get out there and start throwing in a few weeks. I can't wait," I said. "How's the season going? I saw you boys are in first. And what the hell, man, how are you leading the team in home runs? You must have been hitting the weights."

"I can't explain it. I haven't done anything different. I—" he stopped himself and paused. His tone changed. "Oz, I have to tell you something."

"Sure, Bell, what's up?" I said concerned.

"I'm retiring at the end of the season."

"Retiring? You're only thirty-two years old. You have at least six more years left," I said confused. "Wait a minute. You're messing with me, aren't you? You have to be. I'm not going to fall for that one, Bell."

"I'm serious, Oz," I could tell he wasn't joking. "Jenn is sick. She has been for awhile now. She was diagnosed with breast cancer not long after your accident."

"What?" I said. I paused, and let it sink in. My left leg started to hurt. "Why didn't you guys say anything?"

"I wanted to, pal, but Jenn didn't want me to. You know

how she is. She knew you were going through a tough time, and didn't wanted to give you any more bad news."

"But—" I stopped myself. I didn't know what to say. "Rick, I'm sorry."

This news was hard to comprehend, and I didn't feel much. When you get bad news it's not always easy to turn your feelings on; especially when you don't expect it. Sometimes it's hard to process in the moment.

"How is she? She's going to be okay, right?" I asked.

"She's been getting treatment for it, and she didn't respond well to the chemo. They decided on surgery instead. They removed her right breast. She's been doing a lot better, and the doctors say that the cancer is gone for now."

"Oh my god," I mumbled. I felt so bad for Rick. I felt so bad for Jennifer. I was so worried about my baseball career, while Rick and Jennifer were going through their own battle. A battle for survival.

"That's why I'm retiring at the end of the season," Rick said after I didn't say anything else. "I want to spend as much time as I can with her. With the cancer being gone, she can still live a long, and full life, and we want to spend it together. She has followed me around to my baseball games for so long, and now it's time for me to do something for her. She still wants me to continue with baseball. But my heart's not in it anymore. Every time I am out there, I am thinking of Jenn. It is tough because I am having the best year of my career, but I would rather be in the stands beside her. I made up my mind, and I have told the team already. After the season, we are going to travel, spend some time with my family back in Canada, and just enjoy our lives. Jenn still jokes that if I get bored of her, I am young enough that I can still make a return to baseball."

I admired Rick so much, and his love for Jenn was incredible to witness. As good of a player as he was, and as much as he did in his career, this was a guy that would choose love over baseball every time. I couldn't say anything.

"Ozzie, are you still there?"

"Yeah, buddy, I am. I just...I'm speechless."

"I know this is a lot to take in. But she's doing alright, Oz, and she would love to see you...if you're up for it."

"Of course I am."

"She will be happy to hear that. Well, we have a day game tomorrow. Does dinner at our house after, work for you?"

"I will be there."

"See you then, Oz."

"See ya there, Bell."

After I hung up, I slumped down on the couch. Rick was having the best season of his life as he was going through so much off the field. He was playing well, but that didn't matter. This was a person I looked up to. A person who made the first year of my major league career so much easier, and so much better. And yet, it was what he taught me outside of the game that was important. Rick and Jennifer befriended me when I was alone, and they introduced me to Anne, who was an amazing woman. They tried to get me a life outside of baseball, but instead, I was pushing another person away, because I thought that I needed to focus on baseball. If Rick was in my situation, he would have done the opposite.

I picked up the phone and called Anne. We ended up talking for over an hour. I apologized for the way I treated her when she came to visit and take care of me months earlier. We talked about Rick and Jennifer, and she filled me in on more of what had been going on the last few months. I was ashamed that I was in the dark through it all. Rick and Jennifer were my best friends, and when they needed someone the most, I wasn't there. The only good thing is that Rick and Jennifer were the type of people that had so many friends that loved and cared for them. Still, I felt selfish. I was caught up in my own little world like I always have been, and I was never there to help anyone else.

The next night I went over to Rick and Jennifer's house. I brought them flowers and a bottle of wine. After I rang the doorbell, Jennifer answered. I don't know what I was expecting, but she looked fine to me; she looked like Jennifer.

"Ozzie! Good to see you."

"Good to see you, too. These are for you," I said, handing her the flowers and the wine.

"Thanks, Ozzie, they're beautiful," she said, and smelt the flowers. "And this, we will definitely drink tonight," she added with a smile. "As for you," she said as she put the flowers and the wine down on a table near the door, "I haven't seen you in forever. Get over here."

She opened her arms for a hug. I moved in and wrapped my arms gently around her.

"Come on, Ozzie. I'm not broken," she said, and squeezed me tighter. I reciprocated with a tighter squeeze. I did feel awkward and Jennifer helped ease the tension, just like she always did. When we released each other, I took a step back. I couldn't help it, but tears began to fill my eyes. I cared for Jennifer so much. I couldn't imagine her being sick. "Ozzie, are you crying?"

"No..." I said. "I'm sorry. It's just so good to see you."

"Now look what you've done. Now I'm going to cry," she wiped her forearm under her eyes quickly, and grabbed the wine and the flowers, and took them to the kitchen. "Rick! Tell Oz he can only join us if he promises not to cry anymore," she yelled as she got to the kitchen.

I felt embarrassed, but at the same time I didn't care. Rick met me in the hallway to their living room.

"You heard the lady, no more crying. There's been enough of that around here lately," he said as he walked over to greet me with a hand shake. "How are you, Oz? Good to see you're not walking with any limp anymore."

"I'm good, and the leg feels good."

Rick and I went into the living room and chatted, while Jennifer was in and out of the kitchen as she prepared things for dinner. Simply being around them made feel so much better.

We had a fabulous meal together, and we talked about the future. Considering everything, they were in good spirits, and I remember thinking that if they could overcome something like cancer, and be happy once again, then my leg injury was not so bad. They were so in love, and I found out they were meant to be together since day one.

"Oz, did I ever tell you how Jenn and I met?" Rick said as we sat in the living room after dinner.

"No, you haven't," I replied.

"I was just a kid back in Class-A ball. I was playing down in Savannah, Georgia for the Savannah Cardinals. One night after a game we went to a bar downtown, which, Oz, as you know, is a common occurrence down in the minors."

"That I do," I said with a laugh.

"Well, some of the guys dared me to go talk to a group of three girls that were standing together at the bar. I thought I was this big stud back then, so I thought, what the hell, I'll do it. As I got closer, I realized they were a lot more beautiful and intimidating than I first thought. As I was walking up, I remember focusing on Jenn. She was this beautiful, blonde, southern belle, and she laughed at something one of her friends said. She had one of the most beautiful laughs I ever heard, and the most beautiful smile. All of a sudden, I got nervous. I thought about turning around, or simply going to the bar and ordering a drink without saying a word. But the fear of getting harassed by the boys back at the table, was far worse than asking these girls if they wanted to have a drink with us. So I went for it. 'Hey!' I said trying to get their attention. 'My friends and I were wondering if you girls wanted to come have a drink with us.'

"All three of them turned and looked at me. 'Who's your friends' a tall brunette said. I looked and motioned to the table behind me. 'Sorry, but we can't' the brunette said. 'We are waiting for our boyfriends.'

" 'Okay,' I said, and I turned and walked away. I thought about pushing it, but when the other one was speaking, I looked right at Jenn, and got even more nervous. I couldn't say much else.

"When I got back to the table, the guys laughed at me for striking out. But it was more than they did, so they couldn't harass me too much.

"Later that evening, I walked up to the bar to get another round of drinks. Jenn was standing alone at the bar, also waiting to order a drink. I felt like an idiot standing there. I hoped she didn't notice me. Then she turned, and we made eye contact. 'Oh, shit' I thought. And we stood there awkwardly.

" 'Boyfriend's didn't show up?' I asked. 'What?' Jenn said confused, or she didn't hear me. 'Your boyfriends didn't show up?' I said again. This time adding, 'That's a shame. You deserve to be treated a lot better.' 'I don't have a boyfriend,' she said with that beautiful Jenn smile. 'I figured so,' I replied.

" 'Hey, can I buy you a drink...to, you know, make up for that lousy boyfriend standing you up tonight,' I said. 'I suppose so,' she said and smiled.

"We got to chatting, and we hit it off right away. Jenn was so sweet. She was unlike anyone I had ever met before. She noticed a big scrape on my elbow and asked what happened. I told her I got it sliding into home plate, and that's when she found out I was a ball player. She said she loved baseball. After awhile, she ended up going back to her friends, and I went back to my table. But about a minute later, Jenn and her friends came to our table and sat down. The boys were pumped, but I was in my own little world when Jenn sat beside me. We talked some more as the night went on, and at the end of the night something unexpected happened. She invited me back to her place. I remember thinking it was going to be my lucky night. I guess I was the stud I thought I was after all.

"When we got back to her place, Jenn made it clear that it was not going to be the random hookup that I thought it was going to be. 'We're not going to sleep together tonight' she said. 'But if you take me out on a proper date, we'll see what happens.' I didn't mind at all. I remember thinking how lucky I was to be there with her in the first place. She went to the bathroom and came back with a first aid kit. She cleaned my elbow and put a bandage on over top. Then she went to the kitchen and started to pull a bunch of stuff out of the cupboards. 'What are you doing?' I asked. 'I'm making you some breakfast. I can tell you can use it,' she answered. She ended up making me pancakes, eggs, and sausage. 'I can tell you need a nice healthy meal,' she added. 'Well, sausage isn't probably the most healthy' I said.

"After she finished cooking, she just sat there and watched me eat. 'Did you like the sausages?' she asked. 'I did,' I replied. 'Well they are healthy, they are actually turkey sausage. A good, lean protein,' she said, and smiled. From day one, all she wanted to do was take care of me.

"That night we didn't sleep together, but we went to her room, got into her bed, and just talked until we fell asleep. She told me that I needed someone in my life like her. She said that if I was planning on getting to the major leagues, I needed someone like her to take care of me outside of baseball. I figured she must have had too much to drink that night. But, as I would come to know, she was serious. In the morning she gave me her phone number and told me to call her. And I did the next night. There was so much chemistry between us, and like she said, I realized I needed her. We ended up falling in love quicker than I thought was possible. And all through the minors she was there for me. She supported me at every game, and she supported me off the field. There were times when things got tough, and I thought about quitting, but she wouldn't let me. She knew how important baseball was to me, and so it became important to her. We were a team. When I was with her, I improved so much, and I got to the majors far sooner than I thought I would. And it was all because of her."

When Rick was done speaking, I realized they were so much like my mother and father once were. "That's a beautiful story," I said. Just like when I was a kid, I wished I would have a story like that of my own someday. And maybe I could have with Elizabeth, or Lindsay, or Anne. Maybe I could have, but instead I never gave it a chance."Weren't you two ever worried what would happen if things didn't work out? I mean, Jenn, what would have happened if you stopped getting along, and you would be stuck in a town, or in some city who-knows-where, alone?" I asked.

Jennifer smiled. "Of course I didn't know if it would work out for sure. But Rick was so sweet, and was filled with so much passion. It didn't help that I thought he was cute as well," she said with a laugh. "It just felt right, you know? And sometimes you have to take a chance. Sometimes life is about finding out if things will work out or not. Put it this way, if you don't ever step into the batter's box, how are you ever going to score a run?"

She was right. When it came to the relationships I had in my life, I was scared to step into the batter's box, and the few times that I did, I was too scared of risking having things not work out, that I didn't even dare swing the bat.

At the end of the night, Jennifer asked if I would go with her to watch Rick and the Cardinals play the next night. She said she could use the company. It would be the first time I would be in the new Busch Stadium, but I wouldn't be on the field, I would be sitting in the stands. I knew it would be painful, but I told her I would love to.

The next day, before I met Jennifer, I walked and looked at

the statues of all the greatest Cardinals in history that were moved over from the old stadium. I found myself standing in front of Ozzie Smith once again. It felt terrible to know that the quest to have my statue out there someday was put on hold.

When I made my way to my seat, it felt strange to be sitting in the stands—I didn't think I would until I retired. I had to remind myself that I was there for Jennifer. We sat there silently as I took in the familiar smells and sounds of the game I loved. The game I had been away from for far too long.

"Ozzie, I thought about what you said last night...about not knowing if things would work out between Rick and I," Jennifer said as we looked towards the field. "Sure there were times I was scared, but when I was helping Rick, and supporting him while he followed his dream, it gave me a purpose. I felt like I was doing the right thing, and honestly, there was nothing that I would rather be doing. As long as we had each other, we were happy, and anything was possible."

"What about Rick. Did he ever feel bad about dragging you along everywhere he went?"

"You'd have to ask him. But I know that when things got hard in the minors, and we didn't have much money, we had to sacrifice a lot. And he did tell me that I could go back home. But I never wanted to. I'm sure he felt bad he wasn't giving me the life he thought I deserved at the time, but I knew he didn't actually want me to go home. Nobody wants to be alone, and even though it can be difficult sometimes, all we want is to be cared for and loved, no matter how hard things get. And that's what I did. That's what *we* did. And everything worked out."

"What if he didn't end up making it to the majors?"

"That wouldn't have mattered in the end. It would have been heartbreaking for both of us. But we would have gotten through it because we loved each other. I know this because Rick retiring at the end of the season tells me just that. We overcame cancer together. And he is willing to give up the best years of his career,

343

on a World Series championship caliber team, to be together. Because that's what matters to him. Baseball was never our life, it was only a part of it. A big part, yes, but we both knew it wouldn't last forever."

I was sitting there in a baseball stadium, probably learning the most important lesson about love. I realized that I could learn so much from Rick and Jennifer's relationship. I couldn't help but thinking their relationship was something that I could have had, if I was strong enough to let it happen. Instead of loving someone unconditionally like Rick and Jennifer loved each other, I decided to push people away.

As we sat there and watched the game, I told Jennifer about Elizabeth, and how the last time I watched the Cardinals from the stands was with her. I told Jennifer about Lindsay, and the short relationship we had. And I told her about Anne, and how I never let her get close.

I remember the Cardinals won the game that night, but I don't remember anything that happened. Jennifer and I talked the entire time, and I was caught up in all the mistakes I had made in my life.

When I got home, after all that Jennifer and I talked about, I thought about calling Anne. Then I thought, maybe I should call Elizabeth. Sadly, I was no better off than I was before. So I decided, I needed to focus on getting back to baseball, and maybe then, I would be willing to give it my all with love.

Chapter 76

In 2006, during my year off, the Cardinals were the World Series champions. As painful as it was to be sidelined that season, I was happy for Rick. He was able to finish his career on the highest note. Not only did he win a World Series ring, he was also the World Series MVP, and he led the league in nearly every hitting category all season. Rick retired early and left baseball, so he could spend time with the love of his life. On the other hand, I gave up the love of my life to play baseball. For it all to be worth it, I had to make my way back to the St. Louis Cardinals.

It was closing in on a year before I put my glove on and played catch for the first time since my accident. I didn't move around much, but I needed to build my arm back up. After that first time playing catch, I was amazed at how weak my arm was. I was so concerned about getting my leg back into shape, that I didn't even think about how my arm may have been impacted by all that time off. I didn't throw that much on the first time out, but that didn't stop me from being sore the next day. That was something I hadn't felt for a long time.

Slowly, I went out and threw more frequently as the days went on. I still hadn't taken any swings, and I was dying to get back in the cage. The first time I stepped into the makeshift batter's box in a tunnel, I was rusty, but it felt good being able to do the thing that I was meant to do. Hitting was like riding a bike. I was hitting the ball harder than I expected, and I didn't feel any discomfort in my leg. That was a great sign.

JESSE A. MURRAY

The ultimate test, however, would be taking ground balls and running the bases. As soon as I felt I was ready, I went out and took a few groundballs just to get the motions back. I could tell I lost a lot of jump that I had before. My leg was tight when I would bend down, and it was hard for me to get a good first few steps on the ball. I also struggled to plant my foot, and make a throw. I knew that I would not be making any spectacular plays anytime soon.

Although it felt great to be back playing the game I loved, I couldn't help but feel discouraged. It had been almost a year since my accident, and there was still not much hope that I would be playing the upcoming season. The doctors told the Cardinals that there was a good chance I would not be ready, and they insisted that I take as much time as I needed, so I would be able to come back healthy, and still have a prosperous career. They didn't want to put me in too soon and risk having me get injured all over again. Another injury would mean that there would be a good chance I would never be back to my old self.

Consequently, I did the only thing I could do. I worked even harder and pushed myself past the threshold, in order to get stronger and prove to them that I could play the upcoming season. I was determined to make a miracle happen. And I got the idea that a miracle may happen with a little help.

Being away from baseball was hard, and I desperately wanted to move my career forward. I decided I would do anything to help myself get back my spot on the Cardinals. That's where the idea of steroids came in. It was hard not to notice that many other players had done it, and at that point, I felt like steroids were my only hope. My understanding was that steroids wouldn't necessarily speed up the healing process, but it would allow me to get stronger in a shorter period of time. The one thing I did not know, was that once I went off of steroids, my body would not be able to handle the unnatural growth, therefore, I was prone to be injured again.

Regardless of the possible consequences, I stooped to the lowest of lows, disrespected the game, went against everything I had ever been taught, and started doing steroids. Maybe I didn't go against everything I was taught—I needed to do whatever it took to make it to the majors, so how was this any different?

I believe the way I was raised set me up for this moment—for this decision. A decision like many others, that I would also regret. I know it is not fair to always blame my childhood, but when you look at how I was raised, how could I not? I take full responsibility for the decisions I made, but I also feel like I never had a chance. It's hard not to think that it was all leading up to this moment.

I was shocking everyone with the gains I was making, and I was able to show the Cardinals that there was promise that I would be able to make it back sometime within the upcoming season. However, my goal was to be ready for spring training. With some unnatural help, I worked my ass off to achieve my goal.

In December, I was looking good defensively, my arm was strong, and I was hitting the ball a ton. There was some pain, discomfort, and tightness in my leg, but I didn't tell anyone. I was tough, and I was determined to play through it no matter the cost. I continued taking steroids up until a few weeks before spring training, and then I stopped. I felt I was ready to make my early comeback.

Chapter 77

In February of 2007, I reported to spring training. It was good to see my teammates again. Everyone was happy to have me back; except probably Adrian Albetrez, who was acquired from the Dodgers last year to play shortstop. He was the guy they replaced me with, and he played a role in helping the Cardinals win the World Series. He was a twelve-year vet in the game, and I was back trying to take his spot. I was not making things easy for the Cardinals.

Although it felt good to be playing again, I felt like I was back to being a newcomer. I was trying to make a team that had won the World Series without me. I didn't feel like I belonged anymore. Most of all, it was tough not to have Rick around. I knew him and Jennifer were travelling around Europe, and I was happy for them, but I also missed them.

From day one, I worked hard to show that I had recovered from my injury, and I had a good camp, but the real test was going to be the pre-season games. Jerry Atwell told me that the plan was to let me play a few innings, and to start off with a couple at bats, and then increase my playing time from there. He wanted me to take things slowly. If it was up to me, however, I would have played every game just to prove that I could play day in and day out.

In my first at bat against a young pitcher from the Toronto Blue Jays, I hit a long, deep fly ball to left field. I just missed it, and if I had made a little more solid contact, it would have been gone. It was good to know that I still had my power.

The next at bat I walked, and I made my way to first base. That was the first time I had been on base in a year and a half. Since I was always a stealing threat before my injury, I knew this would be the ultimate test for me. I got the sign from the third base coach, took my lead, and took off as soon as the pitcher made a move with his front foot. I beat the throw by a couple steps. I felt like I had done the impossible.

I continued to have a great spring training, and in the final week before Opening Day, I was given the honor on ESPN as the Grapefruit League's player of the week. I was hitting .650, with two home runs, 9 RBIs, and 5 Runs scored. I showed everyone that I was back to my old self. Yet, I was the only one that knew that I still wasn't one hundred percent. There was a tightness in my left leg that I would never be able to get rid of. Even so, I could still play the game.

A few days before the regular season began, I was told that the plan was that Adrian Albetrez and I would be competing for the starting shortstop position, but they made it clear that it would be more of a timeshare situation to start things off. In other words, whoever proved themselves would eventually beat the other guy out. It was nice to be back on the 40 Man roster without doing a stint in the minors, but I knew if anything happened, or if I were to reinjure myself, I would be sent back down. Either way, I was ready to continue my career.

In the second last game of spring training against the Pirates, I was starting at shortstop, and was hitting in the two hole, just like I did before my injury. In my first at bat in the 1st inning, I hit a deep, solo home run to left-center field. My next at bat came in the 3rd inning, and I hit a single up the middle. In the 5th inning, I was already up for the third time. We had a man at first and second, and on a 2-1 fastball that was left over the plate, I swung and the ball launched off of my bat, and sailed over the fence in left field. It was only the 5th inning, and I was already 3 for 3, with 2 home runs, and 4 RBIs.

I was having a great day, but the Pirates were hanging on, and we were only winning 7-5. It was still a close game.

My next at bat in the 8th, I hit a double down the line to left field. Donnie Wood struck out after me, and this brought The Crusher to the plate. On a 3-1 count, The Crusher hit a line drive off the wall in right-centre field. As soon as he hit it, I knew I had a chance to score. I made sure they couldn't make a play on the ball, and I took off. The third base coach waved me home, and I was running full steam.

The center fielder got a lucky bounce off the wall, and made a good toss to the cut-off man, and the cut-off man threw it on a line right to the catcher. When I saw the catcher set up to catch the ball, I slid feet first. At the same moment that I slid, the catcher put his knee down to block the plate, and my left foot jammed into his shin pad. The pain instantly shot into my knee and spread through my leg. I knew right away that it was bad.

The trainers ran out to my aid, while everybody gathered around to see what happened. No one ever wants to see another player hurt like that—especially in spring training. There was no way I could get up to walk on my own, and I was helped off the field, and I was taken straight to the clubhouse.

With my recent injury from the car accident, my trainers didn't waste time, and they took me to the hospital. There, it was confirmed that I had re-torn my ACL in my knee, and I would need surgery all over again. I was so determined to prove myself and make it back to the majors, that I put my entire career in jeopardy. I knew right then and there, that it would be extremely difficult to come back from a second injury to my leg; at least for a long time.

At first, that didn't stop me from being hopeful. Maybe this time I would start with the steroids a little earlier; I could work even harder; and in a year I could be back again. Part of me was optimistic, but at the same time I knew the odds were against me. Deep down, I knew I was done. Be that as it may, I still didn't want to give up baseball. I didn't want to give up my life.

I was back going through another round of surgery, recovery, and rehabilitation. It must be easier that I knew what to expect, right? The answer is no. It was so frustrating to be down and out after I worked so hard to make it back. The time frame for healing was a lot less than the injuries from my car accident, but I was still going to be out for the rest of the season. I had nothing to do to occupy my time.

This time around, I was even lonelier. I didn't have many visitors. My teammates were busy with their season, Rick and Jennifer were still traveling, and I was no longer seeing Anne. I continued with my interest in reading, yet, I also watched a lot of TV. I tried to follow the Cardinals, but I was not as into it anymore. It was painful to watch them from my living room, instead of from my starting spot at shortstop.

After a few weeks of letting my knee heal, I could feel the depression wipe over me. I was alone most of the time, and I spent my days doing nothing that I felt was productive. I continued with my rehabilitation program, and was starting to build back my range of motion and strength, but this time it took a lot longer. Or at least it felt like it did. I considered taking steroids again, but they had been in the news so much at that time, and the policies were a lot more difficult to get around. There was no guarantee they would help me anyway—the gains would likely make me feel like I was ready, before I actually was. I didn't want to make that mistake again.

I couldn't stand being on my own. I thought about contacting Anne, but why would she want to be with someone like me? Sure it made sense that she would want to be with a baseball superstar, but not with someone who would not make it back to the game in the foreseeable future. I didn't feel worthy enough to be with someone anymore.

There was not much for me in St. Louis, so I decided to head back to Columbia. Maybe Columbia is the place you end up, when all your dreams die?

Chapter 78

Everyone that has played baseball understands what it feels like to make an error. It's a part of the game. In baseball, the fewer errors you make, the greater you are. I believe this is also true in life. The people that are truly great, are the ones that learn from the errors that they make, and work hard to get out of bad habits, and better themselves.

There are many different kinds of errors in baseball. There are physical errors like dropping the ball, missing a ground ball, or throwing the ball away. There are also the mental errors, such as throwing to the wrong bag, forgetting how many outs there are, or making a mistake on the base paths. The bigger the game, and the more important the situation, the more the error hurts. Making an error in baseball is one of the worst feelings in the world. Part of it might be because everybody is watching. The other part is that you are letting your teammates down. These errors can eat a person up, and it can spiral down from there. The best advice is that you must forget an error as quickly as possible. That's one of the reasons why the game of baseball is so hard; it is often more mental than physical.

Why am I talking about errors, well, when I got injured, and found out it could be a career ending injury, I felt like I just let the ball go right through my legs to lose the World Series. The problem was that this feeling of humiliation did not go away. I couldn't come back next season and make up for it. I was done. I felt like I was going to be trapped living with this feeling for the rest of my life.

It's crazy to think about how much a game can impact your life. I mean, some people like my grandfather came back from war, and lived through all kinds of trauma, yet, he still managed to have some good things in his life. On the other hand, I was suffering from what happened in a game, and I was letting it ruin the rest of my life. But what I felt could be very similar to other kinds of trauma that someone else has felt or been through. It's sad when I think about it, and it makes me feel guilty in a sense, but either way, those feelings are real. What I learned, however, is that it's the way you cope with those feelings that makes all the difference.

My entire life, I coped with my life struggles by picking up a bat, and hitting baseballs. If I could no longer do that, how was I supposed to deal with my problems?

I figured out, with the help of my father, that when I drank, that feeling of humiliation would go away for awhile. As long as I kept drinking, there was a chance I wouldn't feel it all day long. I could temporarily erase the pain. But that pain always came back. Eventually, the more I drank, the worse I felt, so the more I drank. It was a vicious cycle. And it all started when I went back to Columbia.

Chapter 79

When I walked in the door with my bags, my father went to the fridge and grabbed a couple beers. He handed me one without saying a word. He looked older, and he was clearly drinking again. *Was this because of me?* I thought. But I knew the answer.

I sat on the couch, and my father sat in his chair. We cracked our beers, and we didn't say anything for a long time. We sat there watching TV. I can't even remember what was on. One thing I do know, is that it had nothing to do with baseball. I was positive there would be a game on, but I think it was too much to watch baseball at this point; not just for me, but for both of us. I played the same thoughts over and over in my head, and sat there in disbelief about how and why I was back at home. I think my father was just as upset as I was. I think his heart was completely broken.

I had no plan on what to do next. Neither did my father. My father told me the story of how I used to carry my bat and ball everywhere I went when I was a kid, and the story of the man in the grocery store. And then we sat there in silence for a long time. Every so often, my father would get up, head to the kitchen, and return with a couple more beers for us. After awhile, I finally broke the silence and asked my father, "What do we do now?"

"While you go unpack your stuff, I will go get us more beer," he replied.

I brought my bags to my old room, and it looked the same

as it did when I left. My Cardinals posters that I put up when I was kid were still on the wall, and it felt like time had stopped when I got drafted. On my dresser sat the ball from my first home run, and I picked it up, and thought of how I would probably never hit another one again. I also thought of the last time I saw Elizabeth, and the ball I was holding in her room. I wondered if she kept it. I put the ball down, sat on my bed, and finished the rest of my beer.

For the next few weeks, my father would go off to work, while I just sat at home and drank, until he joined me when he got home. There was nothing else for us to do. There was no more training, and I didn't even work at rehabilitating my knee. I had given up.

A variety of media outlets found out I was back in Columbia, and they tried contacting me for an interview, but my father got tired of all the phone calls, and he unplugged the phone. It's not like anyone important would call anyway.

Drinking with my father became a routine, and it was an easy routine to fall into. It was a lot easier to sit and drink and forget all of the thoughts I had—all of the "What-ifs" and the "What-am-I-going-to-do-nows." It was a lot easier to only worry about getting more beer once we ran out.

I bottled up everything inside me and became a quiet, lonely man just like my father; and my Grandfather Shaw for that matter. We were big, strong men that held all the hurt inside of us.

My life started going downhill from there. Looking back on it, everything happened so quickly. I started going by the school, and my old ball field at Rock Bridge, and I would watch the young ball players pursue their dreams. They were not that much younger than I was, but it seemed like a lifetime ago that I was in their shoes. Coach Gilmour was no longer there, but his replacement was my old assistant coach. He asked me a few times if I could speak to his players and give them tips and words of encouragement. I agreed, and I even went to help at a few practices. But eventually I started drinking more. It hurt to see these young ball players with nothing but potential for their lives, when I felt I didn't have any more potential. There was nothing that I could do with my life. I showed up a few times to these practices smelling like beer, and I was asked to leave. After a few more times, I was told to never come back. I was no longer allowed to go back to the place that was once like a home to me. Word had quickly spread that the great Ozzie Shaw was nothing but an alcoholic.

I stumbled home one day, and my father yelled at me. He had heard what happened at the school. He then offered me a job at Big O Tires—I still had money, but he said that he would not let me stay with him if I was just going to be a bum and drink all day. I refused his job offer. I was not ready for a job yet. I probably should have taken it; simply to keep myself out of trouble, and to save me from heading down the path I was about to head down. It all comes down to choices.

The following day I went back to the ball field at the school; I was drunk; I caused a scene; I urinated on the field; and the cops were called. That night I was arrested, and they made me sleep it off in a holding cell.

I found my way into the local newspaper once again, but not for my baseball talent. It was for drunk and disorderly, and urinating in a public place. My father came and picked me up in the morning. When we got back to the house, he lost it on me. He told me that he did not raise a failure, and that he wouldn't watch me ruin his reputation in town. We both had it out that day. We yelled and screamed at each other. I threw him up against the fridge, and heard the contents rattle within. I raised my fist, and was about to hit him. He screamed at me to do it. He said that I ruined his life when I born and I was ruining his life now, and I may as well end it, too.

Those words hit me deep in my core. He knocked the wind

out of me without putting a finger on me. I released him, and walked out of the house and slammed the door on my way out.

I didn't know where I was going, but I needed to get out of there. I still had my knee brace on, but I just kept walking. I went a few blocks, and without even thinking, I ended up at the Cooper household—just like I did several years before.

I knocked on the door, and Mr. Cooper answered, and he must have seen my distress. He asked if everything was alright, and he invited me in to sit down. Mrs. Cooper saw me walk in and was about to ask how I was doing, but stopped. She asked if she could get me a cup of tea or coffee. I didn't reply.

I sat down, and Mr. Cooper and Mrs. Cooper exchanged a concerned look. I looked around the room and watched Mrs. Cooper walk into the kitchen. I didn't know what I was doing there. I was confused and angry. I needed to get out. I got up and said under my breath, "I have to leave." All I heard was, "What was that, Ozzie?" but I made my way to the door, and left without saying anything else. I needed to get far away from there. Far away from everyone.

I walked directly back to my father's house. I went inside, and walked straight to my room without even acknowledging my father; who was sitting in his chair. I packed my things in the same bags that I came with. After I was all packed, I walked back out the door without saying a word—without even saying goodbye. At that moment I hated him so much. It hurts more than anything to think about this now, but that was the last time I saw my father.

Chapter 80

I hopped in my truck and made my way to the liquor store. It was such a stupid decision, but I bought my first bottle of hard alcohol. I didn't care what it was; as long as it would get me drunk. I bought a pint sized bottle of rum, so that I could easily conceal it while I drove. The only other time I had hard alcohol, was when a few teammates forced a few shots on me back in the minors.

I got back in my truck and took a couple large swigs out of the bottle. I didn't have a plan. I just knew that I never wanted to see my father again. I did ruin his life. I should not have been born. I had a lot of anger in my heart. I knew I had to get away. I couldn't think of anywhere to go, so I headed back to St. Louis. I finished the bottle along the way.

It's always easy to blame others for your own mistakes. But in reality we all have choices. Every day we have decisions to make. These decisions we make, we often use our past and the things we were taught to help us make these decisions. We all have a responsibility to try and make the best decision. I was entering into the lowest point in my life—which was caused by a series of bad decisions.

I would love to tell you that I went back to my condo in St. Louis, continued to rehabilitate my knee, continued to read, and finally started working my way back to the game I loved. But that's not what happened. That's not what I chose to do.

Weeks went by, and all I did was sit and drink in my condo.

The place was a mess. I was a mess. I would try to watch Cardinals games like I had done my whole life, but then the pain of not being there would fill with me with rage. It was not uncommon for me to wake up to things tossed around the room or broken.

One morning I woke up on the floor beside my bed. There was a baseball bat a few feet away from me, and shards of glass from a mirror near my closet. I must have took a swing at my own reflection and shattered it the night before. I hated myself. And the more I hated myself, the worse things became.

After awhile, I started to find myself on the other side of the river blowing money and drinking all night at Larry Flint's Hustler Club. I don't know why or how I ended up there. It was almost like I was doing things that I thought down and out people would do. Or I was getting bored with being alone. I was so far away from the person I was; from the person that I was supposed to be.

Eventually I got tired of St. Louis. I was still living too close to Busch Stadium, and it hurt to be that close—thinking I still hadn't played in the brand new stadium. I still had money in my bank account, so it wasn't hard for me to hop on a plane and head to a new city. I had been to a lot of cool places when I was traveling for baseball, but I wanted to go somewhere that didn't have a major league team. I ended up heading back to Nashville. I always liked it there.

In Nashville, I stayed at a nice hotel just off Broadway, and continued to drink. I think I enjoyed the ever changing nightlife that consisted of tourists flocking in and out. Maybe I was hoping to get lost in that world. Maybe I was trying to relive my climb to the majors. Maybe for some reason I was hoping to see Lindsay. Or maybe there was no reason at all.

One night, I was walking down lower Broadway, and I started at the top where I walked past Legends Corner—the place where I had met Lindsay a few years before. Then I headed all the way down the street, and turned left in front of the Hard Rock Cafe, and made way past bar after bar, until it started to get darker and less people were around.

I found my way to Printer's Alley, which I never knew existed. Printer's Alley had a few bars including a blues bar, and a gentleman's club called The Hidden Vault. A guy working the door at The Hidden Vault enticed me inside, but first, he said if I wanted to drink, I had to bring my own booze. He said that selling alcohol at a gentleman's club is illegal in Tennessee, but there was a little "hole in the wall" concession across the alley, where I could purchase alcohol. I bought myself two six packs of Budweiser, and went on in.

Not only did I have to pay a cover charge, I also had to pay a fee for the alcohol I brought in. All I wanted to do was drink, and I don't know why I chose that place. I went in and sat down at a table by myself. It was like being in an old basement. It is not the nicest place, but that is what it's appeal is. It's a part of the "dark and dingy" Printer's Alley that no longer has to be dark and dingy. They mostly do it for show, and that's part of the attraction, I guess.

I was sitting there on a Tuesday night watching these poor, naked souls strip for money. They would come around, sit beside me, and try to get me in the back room for a private dance. Some were old, some were young, some were girls you wouldn't want to look at with the lights turned on. They were weathered. They were not the type of girls that you could find at other establishments. They were girls that were meant for a place like this. I sat there drinking my beers, and talking with the girls that came around. I gave them tips for the sake of it. I had money, and honestly, I felt bad for them. The more money I gave, naturally, the more attention I received.

I remember one dancer I was talking to was a mother of two. I didn't know if this was part of her hustle to get people to give her cash, and if it was, it worked on me. I felt bad for these kids. Here there mother was trying to pay the bills by working at a place like this, and taking money from a person like me. Sadly, the way I was acting, and where my life was at, I was right there with them.

She kept on insisting that I go in the back with her, and eventually I did. I got in the back, sat down, and the first thing she did was take off all her lingerie. Just as quick as she took her clothes off, she put them back on. It was all so strange, so I asked her what that was all about. She said that in Tennessee, a dancer could not be fully nude within a certain distance from the customer. Therefore, they strip behind a certain line—which is actually painted on the ground—they put their lingerie back on, and then they proceed to give a private dance. I wasn't there for the nudity. I don't know why I was there. I was simply going with the flow and letting things happen to me. I told her I only wanted to talk, but I gave her more money, and we sat and chatted.

Eventually I went back to my table so I could keep drinking. I spent all night there. When things were even less busy, I had all of the dancers sitting at my table. We sat there, I kept drinking, and I kept handing out money. I was trying to be fair to all of them. I didn't want to be alone, so I wasn't. Most of the night we just talked. I told them my story, and I was getting sympathy from them. In a place like that, you can get sympathy from anyone if you have a pocket full of cash.

When the place closed for the night, I walked back up Broadway to my hotel. It was dark, quiet, and not many people were out. Those that were, were the ones that would be out all night. I saw a few musicians on the street, and I pulled out what I had left in my pocket and gave it to them. When I got back to the hotel, I was tired and drunk. It was ironic. I was stumbling, coming from a dark place, to entering one of the nicest hotels in Nashville. I walked across the beautiful lobby over to the elevators. I headed up to my room, sat on the bed, and felt alone again.

Go in any phone book and you can find the escort section, and you can have company up in your room within the hour at any time of day or night. Girls were only a phone call away. It was too easy.

I flipped through the pages, and tried calling a few girls, but they ended up being unavailable. At last, I gave up. That night in Nashville, I passed out alone. This wasn't my first time looking for escorts, however. Back in St. Louis, regretfully, that's where it began. I hated being alone, but after the escort left, I would end up wanting to be alone—until I didn't. I felt dirty and ashamed every time. How the hell did I get to this point?

And yet, it continued on. I was keeping company with people that were around for one reason: because I gave them money. The sad thing is, that was the way I wanted it. I could have just as easily been sober, went out to nice restaurants, nice bars, anywhere really, and met a nice girl. I could have even called Anne. But I was afraid to find someone who was nice. I was afraid to find someone that I would fall in love with. For this reason, I picked people that I would never fall in love with, and people that would never fall in love with me. I was afraid of getting too close to anyone. I was afraid of falling in love with someone and having them leave me; just like everyone did. I felt like I was destine to be alone. I was afraid of getting hurt. But because of all this, I was hurting. It was a brutal cycle that I was caught up in. I was traveling around the country and paying hired women, and spending time with them, so they would give me attention only for as long as I wanted. I was doing all of this while I was drinking, and I know for a fact, I would not have done these things if I was sober. Drinking made me do things that I would not normally do. Drinking was to blame for many things, but deep down I still knew, that I was the one that was choosing to drink in the first place.

Chapter 81

In other sports like hockey, football, or boxing, you almost want to be tense and on edge; you don't want to be too loose; and you want to be pumped up and ready to go. Baseball, on the other hand, no matter what position you play, you want to be loose. The more loose and comfortable you are, the better you will be. And, you have to have a clear mind. Your mind may be working to try and figure out the pitcher; what to do if you get the ball; how to pitch to this hitter, and so on, but you cannot be thinking about anything negative. You have to have short term memory loss for certain things. You have to play with no emotion, only instinct.

At this point in my life, having nothing outside of the game, I didn't have a clear mind. I had so many "what-ifs" and "why-mes" in my head, that I could barely function, and I was frozen thinking these things in a constant loop. If anything got hit my way, I wouldn't know what to do with it. I was completely unprepared.

When my life started to crumble, I was all over the headlines. I let all of my fans, my coaches, and most of all, my father down. And yes, I also let myself down. I saw and read interviews of former coaches, friends, and others that knew me, and they all had their opinion on my failures. Some felt sorry for me, and others criticized me. I tried not to let it get to me, but it was hard. And the hardest part was wondering what Elizabeth thought about it all.

Nonetheless, my issues and my failures did solidify my decision to let her go. It made it easier not to regret that decision. I did feel sorry for myself, but I convinced myself that she was better off without me—just like my mother was better off without my father and I. And I was right. The person I had become, was not good enough for anybody.

One of the biggest struggles I had was with my identity. Without baseball, I didn't know who I was. My sense of self was so unhealthy, and it caused a lot of damage to my well-being. I became obsessed with watching the internet and looking for what people were saying about me. It went from positive, to negative, to nothing at all. Searching for my identity on the internet was a dangerous thing for me to do, and in the end, I had no idea who I was, or who I was going to be. This was a terrifying time in my life.

It's ironic how the media portrayed my drinking. To them I turned into a young, party animal. It was almost accepted, because it was expected. What they didn't mention was the hurt behind it all. Sure I was drinking, but I wasn't doing it to have fun. Some young people do get caught up in the party scene—I saw it in the minors, and in my short time in the majors. If you give a young guy a huge paycheck and let him travel all over the country, chances are he is going to chase girls, party, and yes, he will probably end up in a strip club at some point.

If you think about it, it's the expected lifestyle and culture of a young person in general. For instance, look at what college life is like, or go to a club on the weekend. If you don't drink and party, you may be seen as lame or weird, and some people may think there is something wrong with you. Many people drink and party to fit in. Alcohol is a way to socialize. I even saw it back at those parties in high school. But, for some people, this could be a big problem. Some are able to grow out of it, and some cannot. And it's easier for some people to abuse drugs and alcohol—whether it's how they were raised, environment,

JESSE A. MURRAY

genetics, or whatever. It just happens. But I honestly think, as a society, we are a part of the problem. What we view as being normal, may not be the right thing.

Yet, as soon as you hit a certain age it becomes un-cool to puke or blackout after a night of drinking. But why was it cool in the first place? Why are so many high school and university kids reveling in a life of partying with drugs and alcohol? It is not glamorous, and it does not lead to happiness. That I can promise you. And, as in my case, when you're drinking alone, and you are using alcohol to cope, there is no good that can come from it.

During this foggy time in my life, I remember a time I woke up in a park, and I had pissed myself. My head was hurting, and there was dried up blood on my forehead. I was lucky that I hadn't been picked up by the police, or robbed. I walked miles back to my hotel. I must have been quite the sight walking in; I was dirty, drunk, and bloody. It looked like I had been mugged, but I only had myself to blame. I was depressed, and what I was doing was not enjoyable. I was definitely the young, party animal like some of the media said I was.

So why did I drink? I drank so I would forget. I drank to go on a vacation from my life. When I drank my brain would shut down and my responsibilities would no longer exist. I was on an alcohol fueled vacation for months, and there was no end in sight.

This probably won't make sense to many of you, but during this period of my life, I wasn't suicidal, but I didn't want to live either. There was no way I was going to consciously take my life, but at the same time I didn't care if I lived or died. I was so alone and hopeless that it was difficult to see anything positive about my life. If you ever felt this way, you'll understand the feeling of darkness that I felt, and the darkness I was living.

And things only got worse.

Chapter 82

After my second injury, I ruined my reputation, and I lost everything I ever worked for. I was completely lost and I had no idea who I was, and what I should do with my life. At the rate I was going, I was drinking myself to death. I was at an ultimate low—I didn't care about others, or myself. I was cut off from everybody I knew, and I was basically missing in action.

Rick had been trying to get a hold of me for several weeks, but I never answered my phone. One day the phone wouldn't stop ringing. I thought about turning it off, but just before I did, I decided to answer it. It was Rick on the other end, and he was distraught. He told me that Jennifer passed away the night before. He had tried to get a hold of me weeks ago —when they found out the cancer was back, and had spread to her lungs. Rick said that when they found out the cancer was back, the doctors said there was nothing they could do for her anymore, and she was going to die. He also said that Jennifer wanted to see me one last time, but they never could track me down.

I don't remember all the details from that phone call, because I had been drinking, but I remember the pain in Rick's voice. I was already so lost and in so much pain that I wondered how much I could possibly endure. Cancer is something you never wish on your worst enemy, and when it puts its mark on someone as beautiful and loving as Jennifer, it makes you wonder what the point of life is. I felt guilty that she wanted to see me, but I was nowhere to be found. I continued to drink in order to numb myself from the world around me.

I did manage to make it to her funeral in Savannah, but I barely remember being there. I was hung over and didn't feel well. I couldn't even be there for Rick—for the person that probably meant the most to me at that time in my life—a person who made my life so much better. Or at least tried to.

After the funeral, I went to Atlanta and I spiraled down into a deeper depression that consists of bits and pieces of hazy memories that seem like nightmares. I was battling with my own thoughts, and I drank with the hopes that I would not wake up.

I continued to fly around the country, and living in a state of numbness. In a way, I was already dead. In July 2008, I found myself in Las Vegas—a place I felt I could blend in, no one would recognize me, and no one would care if I was constantly drunk.

Around the same time that Rick called me and told me Jennifer passed away, I was also getting calls from my father, but I never answered. I still didn't want to talk to him. It wasn't until later, I realized that he must of been calling right after he had a minor heart attack at work.

My father probably needed me to be there for him, but I never answered. He was left completely alone. The bad news did not stop there. About a month after Jennifer's funeral, it was my uncle Frank that finally got a hold of me, and told me the news. My father passed away.

Uncle Frank told me the details about my father's first heart attack, and the weeks that followed. My father suffered a minor heart attack at work, and was in the hospital for a few days, but when he was released, he went back to work against the doctor's orders. The doctor told him to rest, cut down on his drinking, and start living a healthier life. But my father didn't change his lifestyle, he didn't stop drinking, and he had no one to look after him. It was just over a month later he ended up having a more severe, fatal heart attack at home, and no one was there to help him; just like his own father before him. When my father didn't show up for work—something that never happened since he started there—one of his coworkers went to his house to check on him. He saw my father's truck on the driveway, but no one answered. He checked the door and it was unlocked, and he went in and found my father on the floor in our living room. The TV was still on. I like to imagine that he died peacefully in his chair watching the game he loved more than anything in the world.

Uncle Frank told me I should make my way back to Columbia, because I was the one that would have to handle a lot of my father's affairs. My uncle Frank also said he would head to Columbia, and that I should meet him there, but I never did. I couldn't bring myself to do it. He called me over and over and left messages asking me where the hell I was. Eventually he made the funeral arrangements on his own. He told me the time and place, but I had no intention of going.

When I got into the major leagues my father quit drinking. But when I got injured, he drank more than he ever did. He drank because he had nothing left to do, and he had no reason not to drink. Part of him drinking himself to death was my fault. If I would have stayed in the majors, he would have been clean and sober. I let him down. I broke the rest of his heart he had left.

I would picture my father all alone in his house drinking, and this crushed me, because it was all my fault. It was my fault when I was born, and it was my fault when he died. I caused so much pain for those around me. I was now more alone than ever.

I didn't go to see him in the hospital the first time around, and I didn't go to his funeral. I was so hard on myself because I felt completely worthless. I didn't feel like anyone needed me around, so I kept to myself. I shut myself in at a series of cheap motel rooms, and drank away the days.

In a matter of months, I had lost two people that had a great influence on my life. All of these terrible things were happening around me, and I was off on my own path to destruction. I felt like I was nothing but a victim. I didn't even take the time to think of others that may have been hurting from these events. I was so self-centered and selfish that I didn't think of my mother, my uncle Frank, Rick, or Jennifer's friends and family.

Although I didn't care at the time, I think deep down I knew something had to change. There was so much going wrong around me that I needed something or someone in my life to step in and help me. What I failed to realize is that I needed to help myself. But sometimes we need something to wake us up and initiate a willingness to change.

A week or so after my father's funeral, I managed to get myself together enough to catch a plane to Columbia. Once I made it to Columbia, I was still hesitant to go back to my father's house, so I went and checked into a hotel. I was depressed and ashamed, but I knew I would have to go eventually.

When I walked into that house, it was eerie, and hard to believe that my father was no longer there. I walked into the living room, and I saw his chair, and his beer cans—everything was exactly how they always were—but he was no longer there. My uncle Frank walked from the kitchen and greeted me with, "Where the hell have you been?" He sounded just like my grandfather Shaw. But when he saw the look on my face, and the tears that were falling freely, he came and gave me a hug. I started to sob uncontrollably. I couldn't even remember the last time my father had hugged me. All the hate and anger drained out of me.

My uncle Frank and I talked for awhile, and he wondered what was going on with me. As I explained, he never scolded me; he just sat and listened. He told me I needed to talk to someone. He told me I needed help. He said that after he left the army, he was suffering from PTSD, and he sought help from a veterans support group. He said it changed his life. He told me that his own father bottled everything up inside, and so did my father, and he believed that talking and not suffering alone was the key to having a better life.

After we talked, we drank the remaining beer in my father's fridge as we started to clean up the house. It was all too familiar from the time they packed up my grandfather Shaw's house many years before—but this time it was my father. This time it was my childhood home.

A few hours later, I made my way to my old bedroom. Everything was left untouched—as it always was when I returned home—but there was one thing that was out of place. There, on my bed, was a crisp, white envelope with only two letters on it: "Oz."

I picked it up, left my room, walked outside to the back step, and sat down. *Who could it be from? Was it from Elizabeth? Or my mother? Or someone else?* My mind was racing, as I slowly opened the envelope. I pulled out the contents, and I was shocked to see that it was a letter from my father. I never saw him write anything in his life. I started to cry.

Dear son,

As you know, I have so many regrets in my life, but they are probably not what you think they are. The biggest regret I have, is not being the best father that I could have been. I'm sorry, Oz, for pushing you so hard, and making you push away the ones you loved. I'm sorry that I screwed things up with your mother. I always loved her. I just felt like she deserved better than the man I had become, so I pushed her away. I could have been a great man without baseball. I could have still went to school. I could have been a great father to you. Instead, I tried to make sure that you never made the same mistakes I made, and that right there was my biggest mistake. I could have made you the best player you could be, but I could have also taught you things about life and relationships. I could have told you to hold Elizabeth close and never let her go. What I never told you, is that you two were great together. You two reminded me of exactly how your mother and I were, and this scared me, considering how things turned out. But Oz, you were different. You were such a sweet kid. And I did things to knock that sweet part out of you. Remember when you broke up with Elizabeth, and all I said was 'You did the right thing, son.' I want you to know that I was wrong, and I am sorry.

I never told you, but after you got drafted, Elizabeth stopped by and returned the earrings you gave her. When I answered the door all she did was thrust out her hand, and said 'These belong to you,' and walked away. That was the last time I saw her, but I hope you two see each other again. You two were meant to be together. You two were something special. I'm sorry for not telling you this sooner.

There is so much I am sorry for but I want you to know that you were such a great kid. Watching you play the game, and seeing you work so hard made me proud. Every time I watched you play I thought to myself 'That's my son' and it brought a smile to my face. You are the best thing that has ever happened to me.

I'm sorry I wasn't there for you after your injury. I was hurting, but probably not as much as you were. I was completely selfish. I felt like a failure and I felt like I could be no help to anyone, even to my own son. I'm sorry how things ended between us. I hope you can forgive me for that.

I'm sorry I wasn't a better role model for you. The only thing I could hope for is that you learn from my mistakes, and do your best not to become like your father. If you happen to have kids someday, be there for them, and support them, and love them always. Be the best husband and father you can possibly be. Don't be a failure like I was.

You were a great kid, son, the best. And you still can be a wonderful man. It took me 46 years to learn that there is more to life than baseball. I want you to remember that. I know I didn't say it too often, but I am so proud of all the things you have accomplished, and I wish you nothing but the best in the future.

I love you son.

Your father,

Joseph Shaw

I sobbed as I sat on the back step with the letter from my father in my hands. He waited until the very end to tell me all the things that I wished he would have said years ago. My father learned that there was more to life than baseball, but it was too late for him. But it was not too late for me. This letter was everything that I needed to hear, so that I could move on, and be a better person.

I put the letter back in the envelope, and wiped away the tears from my eyes. I wished I would have spent more time with him in his last years. He was a changed man—a man I wish I would have known. My father was gone, but that letter saved my life. That letter was the motivation I needed to seek help.

The next few days consisted of staying at the hotel, and heading back to the house to pack up my father's things. It was a very emotional time. My father saved everything. There were boxes of stuff from his baseball days, my old clothes, and old photographs from when my family was all together. My father also collected newspaper articles about me and my baseball career and put them in our old china cabinet—from when I was a kid all the way up to my injury. I also found a copy of the picture of Jacob and I on our first day of high school. Jake's outfit still made me laugh. We were so young then—we loved baseball, the Cardinals, and we had the whole world in front of us. Finally, in my father's room I found the earrings that Elizabeth returned to my father.

Going through all that stuff made me realize that the

memories of the best years of my life were in that house. It made me sad to think of the friendships I had thrown away. It made me sad to think that I was so far away from the person I was, and the life that I once had. It wasn't my major league career that was the best time of my life; it was the time I spent with family and the friends I had growing up, and the memories I made with them. But that felt like a lifetime ago. I knew I could never go back to that time, but I had to do something. I had to stop drinking. I had to move on with my life.

Chapter 83

It was August 27th, 2008, and I was in a hotel room in Columbia, wondering what to do next. I should have been on a ball field somewhere. I should have been getting excited for the playoffs. But I was no longer a baseball player. I started to think about Jennifer, and my father, and when I had last seen them before they died. I started to get down on myself. I was about to fall into the same pattern—the same routine. I wanted to drown my thoughts with alcohol. But something was different this time. I had let go of a lot of the anger, and a part of me realized that this was no time to continue wallowing about the life I should have had. I didn't want to become like my father, and my father didn't want me to become like him. It was time to focus on what to do next. But I needed help.

I checked out of the hotel I was staying at, and immediately went to the bus station to buy a ticket back to St. Louis. I no longer had my condo there, so I had to check into another hotel. After putting things into motion, I wanted to have a drink. It was brutal. Once you realize you have a problem, and that you need to change, you will notice alcohol is everywhere. Luckily, I was able to hold off. But then I realized I needed alcohol to give me the courage to do some of the most basic things, and ironically, I needed alcohol to ask for help.

I knew he was busy with other players he represented, but I picked up the phone and called Vince Michael, my agent. This was not an easy phone call, but with the help of a bucket of

Budweisers, I had the courage to call. I asked Vince if he would be able to reach out to the Cardinals and get some help for me. He knew I was messing things up for myself, and he didn't have to help me. I let him down just as much as anyone. He would have made some good money off of me, but I was a bust. Business or not, I knew he was still a good person, and I knew that's why my father chose him. Vince came through, and the Cardinals organization did what they thought was best for me— they sent me to an inpatient rehab facility in St. Louis, and I was set to stay there for 30 days. I willingly went with the hopes that I could turn my life around.

Within a few hours, I realized I didn't want to be there. They asked me so many questions that I didn't want to answer. I hated talking about myself. I hated talking about my past. But most of all, I realized there were terrible people there, and I felt like I did not belong. I couldn't admit I was one of them. Sitting in group, I was hearing these horrible stories, and I realized that things could have been a lot worse. Regrettably, I never felt comfortable, and I refused to share my story. Even though we were all there seeking help for whatever reason, I felt I shouldn't be there. I ended up leaving after a few days. Since I wasn't on an active roster, my attendance there was voluntary. So there were no repercussions to me leaving—other than having to find a new way to get help.

When I left, I went out and drank. I had a problem. It is hard to believe now, that I thought it wasn't a big enough problem at the time. By leaving rehab, I knew I couldn't turn to the Cardinals organization again. If I still had a chance to get back in the game, they probably would have done more, but since my career was most likely over, they didn't have the same interest in me as they once did. That's how the game works. The game goes on with or without you. They did what they could for me, and I walked out, so now I was on my own.

I spent the next few days wondering what to do, and after

much deliberation, I made the toughest phone call of my life. I thought about calling my uncle Frank, but for some reason I was too ashamed, or too intimated, and I couldn't bring myself to do it. Instead, I called Mr. Cooper. When I was younger he was like a second father to me, and now that my father was gone, I felt Mr. Cooper was the only person I could turn to. I knew they had a good life and a stable life, and seeing how Jake was raised, I felt like they could help me—if they were willing to. I still remember the time I spent there as a kid. That was the only sense of normalcy that I experienced after my mother left. They were the type of people that my father told me to forget, because I wouldn't be bringing them to where I was headed in my baseball career. But, I ended up reaching out to them so they could bring me back to where I needed to be.

I called Mr. Cooper and made small talk. I asked how they were doing; I asked about Jake, and I was going to end it just like that. But finally, I worked up my courage—without the help of anything else—and said, "Mr. Cooper, I need help." Then I proceeded to tell him everything. From when my father and I fought, and everything that I had been doing the last few months. He stayed on the line and listened while I poured out my soul for almost two hours. He was patient through all the stories of my mistakes, the crying, the self-loathing, and the hopelessness that I felt.

To me it is a miracle that I called my childhood friend's father one night out of the blue, and he sat and listened. It's a miracle that he told me to come to their home as soon as possible and he would get me help. It's a miracle that he said he would get me on the right path. He didn't even consult with Mrs. Cooper. I had no idea what she thought of it all, but when I got there, she was always supportive. I know now, that they would have done anything to help me. That's the type of people they are. You can't find anyone more loving and caring than the Cooper's. I owe so much to them. They saved my life.

I bought a bus ticket back to Columbia, and made my way back home—the place that I thought had nothing left for me anymore. This ordeal that I had put myself through the last few months was on its way to being over.

When I got to their home, Mr. and Mrs. Cooper welcomed me with open arms. They never did judge me, or look down on me. They did everything they could to build me back up.

This is the point of my life that I spent a lot of time in self-reflection, and learning where I went wrong, and how I could make things better. But the first step was getting completely sober.

The Cooper's were a godsend. Mrs. Cooper fed me, and got me feeling healthy again. Mr. Cooper would read me passages from the Bible, and he told me stories of many people that had transformed, such as Moses, Job, and Saul of Tarsus. He told me stories of loss, redemption, and hope. Most of all, however, he listened. But, honestly, one of the most essential parts of my time with the Cooper's, was for the first time in forever, I was able to rest, and not feel guilty about it.

When I got my energy back up, Mr. Cooper decided it was best for me to start going to Alcoholics Anonymous (AA) meetings. Mr. Cooper felt it would be beneficial for me to hear stories of others who were in recovery. I was reluctant at first, because I didn't want to feel the way I did in the rehab facility, but Mr. Cooper offered to go with me. With Mr. Cooper by my side, I knew I could give it a fair shot. Ultimately, going to those meetings was the most important part of my sobriety, and my future.

The first meeting we went to happened to be at a church hall not far from Mr. Cooper's house. I felt strange going there, but I was grateful that Mr. Cooper was there with me. I probably would not have had the strength to go on my own.

Hearing the first few stories of the night was eye opening. People lost jobs, lost families, and some almost lost their lives because of their addiction. Some were years, even decades sober, and they still came to share their story to help others, and to keep themselves on track. I realized that no matter how long they had been sober, they still talked about the temptation that they faced. These were powerful stories to go with a powerful substance.

One of the last people to share that night was not much older than me, and what he said really struck a chord. "Hello, my name is Jeff, and I'm an alcoholic," he said to the group of fifteen or so sitting there. "I have been sober for just over two years now..." he stopped while everyone clapped. "In my recovery, I have learned a lot. I have seen and have caused so much hurt. I have tried to get sober, and I have failed. I failed because I could not be honest with myself, and because I was not willing to do the work. But one thing about recovery, is you have to educate yourself and have to work hard. You can't let someone do the recovery process for you. And most of all, you cannot make excuses. That will only lead to a relapse.

"You know, if everything went perfectly in my life, I don't think I would have had an alcohol problem. I used alcohol as an escape...as a way of coping with the hardships I faced. It was an unhealthy coping mechanism. If I chose anything else that was more positive, I believe my life would not have turned out so poorly. The major struggle I had was the inability to cope with issues in my life. If we were taught how to properly cope with life's problems, millions of lives would be saved. Instead, we often fall into addictions.

"Now, with alcoholism or any other drug addiction, I believe you are dealing with the devil. It's plain and simple, alcohol and drugs are fucking evil. They rob millions of people of their lives...physically, mentally, socially, and spiritually. You no longer own your own life. You are no longer responsible for the actions of the person you are when you're under the influence. Why? Because it isn't you. You make a choice when you drink, and the choice is this...you are giving away a part of yourself. A part of your brain. The very same part that controls your actions. It can be a deadly thing to do. We live in a society where we are afraid...afraid to be ourselves. We are afraid to feel. That is why we drink. And so, when it comes to recovery, we have to dig deep and find out who we are, and why we do what we do. We have to accept ourselves and our past, in order to move on with our lives.

"To be honest, truly honest with ourselves, and to love that person, is probably the hardest thing to do in the world. So many people suffer from not loving themselves. If you cannot love yourself, then you cannot love others, and you cannot live the way you are supposed to live. Many of us carry around hurt deep inside of us, and eventually it starts to seep through, and it becomes who we are. Know thyself, and you will come to know how to heal."

I sat and listened to this man talk and I was in awe. So much of what he was saying was true about my own life. I didn't love myself, so I couldn't love others. I carried around so much hurt inside of me most of life, and then, when things did not go my way, I turned to alcohol. I turned to alcohol to cope, and it only made things a million times worse.

That night I went back to the Cooper's and spent a long time reflecting on my life, and trying to understand why everything went wrong. It was a difficult task to undertake on my own. But in the next little while, the more I went to these meetings, the more valuable pieces of advice I picked up along the way.

Hearing other people share their stories opened my mind to what was going on inside of me. Just like many others, I felt shame, guilt, loneliness, and a sense of hopelessness. But there was one word that summed everything up: oblivion. One older man that shared his story said he drank so he could no longer feel the things he felt; he said he drank in order to go into a state of oblivion. I remember looking that word up in the dictionary when I got back to Mr. Cooper's house. Some definitions said it was the state of being completely forgotten or unknown. That is a major reason why I drank. I didn't want to die, but I just wanted to be forgotten, and I wanted to forget. I tried my entire life to become known and do things so others would always remember me, but when all that was gone, I no longer wanted to exist. It turns out that many others also felt this way. I wasn't the only one.

They say the first step of recovery is admitting you have a problem, and the first step is often the hardest. This time around, I never had trouble admitting I had a problem. I knew that I was doing the wrong thing. I didn't want to be an alcoholic. I saw how my father was, and when I became just like him, that's when I knew I had to change. I didn't have to lie to myself or others. I think that's why my recovery was easier for me. I didn't lie to my family, friends, and loved ones, because I wasn't close to anybody. There was no sneaking around or trying to be a functional alcoholic. I was completely dysfunctional, and it didn't last for years like it does for many people. Additionally, I didn't hurt as many people as others do. I was detached and alone, so it was all up to me to admit my problem and deal with it, for my own sake.

For the first few weeks I sat and listened at these meetings, but eventually I worked up the courage to tell my story piece by piece. It wasn't clear and recited like so many others, but it felt good to get it out. I knew the more I told the story, the better I would get at sharing it, and the better I would feel. And I found out right away that the more I shared, the more others were willing to help.

When I first shared my story, a few people came up to me and thanked me afterwards. They gave me their phone numbers and told me to call any time if I ever needed someone to talk to. One particular person, named Jared, came up to me and said he went to Battle High School and played against me when I was in my freshman year. He said he was a pitcher, and said that I actually hit one of the longest home runs he'd ever seen, off of him. Turns out he was able to use this story, and told it quite often, once I made it to the major leagues. He would tell people whenever he saw me play on TV that I had once hit a home run off of him. In a way, he was honored to have pitched against me. But what did he think of me now? I was embarrassed at first, but it surprised me that he was nothing but supportive, and he was there to help me get sober.

I learned in AA that alcoholics come in all shapes, sizes, ages, genders, religions, races, and social classes. Alcoholism does not discriminate. People with all different backgrounds had this one thing in common: they were all alcoholics. It didn't matter that I was young, and it didn't matter that I had been drinking for a shorter period of time than most. I was one of them. But I understood that I was lucky that I was able to seek help, and get help, before things got even worse.

The lessons that I learned in AA were truly invaluable. Not only did they remind me that a better life was possible, but they helped me understand that I was not alone. I started to go a few times per week, and then as I got comfortable, I went almost every day. I was back in Double-A, but there was no baseball this time around. Alcoholics Anonymous was as far from the minor leagues as you could get, but it was still a path I needed to take to move on with my life.

AA introduced me to a world that I didn't know existed. People did not have to suffer on their own. There was help out there. But there was one thing that was difficult for me to grasp. It was told to me that a Higher Power would be responsible for my recovery, and they said I had to give myself over to this Higher Power. This was hard for me because I was never particularly religious. My mother's side of the family was catholic and they went to church on Sundays, and I remember going a few times during some of the holidays when I was a kid, but that was it. Mr. Cooper also told me stories from the Bible, but I still didn't know much. The only thing that I knew that was remotely spiritual, was the idea of the baseball gods, and how you didn't want to anger them.

The good news was that many of those that were in AA, also didn't have a religious background. This gave me hope that I could be helped, and I could recover. But there was no denying that I would have to learn a lot about spirituality before I would be able to give myself over to God, or some other higher power.

Chapter 84

Unfortunately in AA, you see a lot of people come and go. But there was one person that was always there—his name was Dan— and he became my sponsor.

"Hey man, your testimonial really hit home with me tonight," he said to me as I walked outside past him. He was smoking a cigarette. I saw him speak a few times already. He used to be a marine, and he was somebody that had seen a lot of things, and had suffered a lot because of it.

"Hey," I replied, and stopped.

"You talked about not having a purpose anymore since you left baseball. Let me tell you something, you and I are not that different. I joined the army when I was eighteen and I was there for the glory, for the honor, and to make a difference in the world. The things I saw in battle were slowly ripping me apart, but I didn't know this until I came home. Everything is different off the battle field. You get to real life and it feels like you are nobody. You have no purpose. The brothers I had over there were either dead, or we lost touch because we were all spread out around the country when we got home. That was the ultimate feeling of loneliness. The ultimate feeling of unworthiness. I often wished I would have died over there. At least I would have an honorable death, instead of the dishonorable life I had back home. Isn't it sad how we have to go through hell in order to figure all this out?" he said.

"It really is. All of this could have been avoided if only we were told. My grandfather fought in the second world war, and when he came back he was a very quiet man. He didn't say much at all, and he ended up dying alone. I'm guessing he was probably hurting from a lack of purpose to a certain degree," I said, and then paused to gather my thoughts. "And here I am, I'm hurting because I no longer have a purpose...because I can't play *baseball* anymore. It sounds pathetic, doesn't it?"

"It's not pathetic at all. Sports and competitions have been around for a long time. Think about the Olympics in Greece, and the gladiators in Rome...it was entertainment, and it was a chance for many people to attain a sense of glory. These games were created in times of peace. But the military was where it all originated. Being a warrior was where a man would find his glory and it meant something. Others would look up to them and see that person as a leader, and as a hero. One could rise through the ranks to become someone. It was an opportunity. It is no different today. No matter what class, what race, or even where you live in the world, you can be somebody just by playing a sport or joining the military," he said. He dropped his cigarette on the ground, stepped on it with his right foot, and gave it a twist. "I think for a lot of people it's about hope as much as it is about the glory, and there is nothing wrong with that. The trouble is that no one tells you what to do when that opportunity and glory is gone."

"I guess you're right. And when it comes to sports, it's just a game, but yet, it is much more than a game," I said.

From that moment I knew that I needed to inform people of what I was learning. I needed to share my story, so that others would not make the same mistakes I did. I needed to educate others. Maybe that would become my purpose?

Dan was a huge help with my sobriety. He had been in recovery for awhile, and he had a lot of good advice, and he helped me with any doubts or concerns I had. The major concern I had, however, was figuring out how to believe in a higher power.

After one of the meetings, we went to a diner for coffee, and that was one of the key moments in my recovery.

"I've been learning about Jesus and have been reading the Bible, but what I am really struggling with is that I have never been religious," I said after we ordered our coffee. "I mean, I feel like a hypocrite because I never grew up with religion like so many others have."

"It doesn't matter if you grew up with religion or not. If you read the Bible, many people in there didn't find God until they were adults. That's what it's all about. It's about saving the ones that are lost, or the ones who are on the wrong path. And to be honest, it's not about the religion, it's about—" he broke off and hesitated. I could tell he was trying to find the right words.

"Let me put it to you this way," he continued. "It's not about religion or the church. It's not about Jesus, or Buddha, or whoever. And to be honest, it's not even about God. It's about letting go and giving yourself up to a higher power. This higher power is inside of you. It's a feeling, and it's a sense of peace. You get this sense of peace by letting go of all your loneliness, anxiety, fears, and ultimately, all of your worries and concerns. Once you do that, once you let go and have faith that everything will be okay, and that you will never be alone again...that's the most powerful thing you can do. That is what faith is all about. But God is only a name we give to this higher power, which is actually just a feeling of peace. Once you find that peace, it's like turning off the power switch to all the loneliness and worries that you have in your life. Once you give in, and that switch is turned off, you will notice that good things will start to happen in your life, and it will all seem like a miracle. Then you start to truly believe that there must be a higher power responsible for it all."

I sat there in silence for a few minutes and thought about it. Most of my life I felt alone. Without baseball, I felt worried and depressed. It was all about feelings. If what Dan was saying was true, I needed a higher power to let go of those feelings, and then my life would change. While I was deep in thought, Dan continued.

"It's all up to you, Oz. It's always up to the individual. You just have to let go and have faith. Have faith in knowing that you are not alone, and that you can find peace in your life if you really want to. Again, it's about accepting and knowing that everything will be okay...no matter what."

"You make it sound so easy," I said.

"The crazy thing is that it actually is easy. Here, think of it this way. Just imagine you're in a little boat...in the middle of the ocean. It's a calm, sunny, and beautiful day. There you are just floating along, soaking in the sun, and enjoying the peace and quiet. Then all of a sudden a life problem is tossed into the boat in the form of an iron weight. These life problems come in all different sizes and weights depending on what the problem is. Maybe you have a bad day for some reason, and that might be worth a little two pound weight. Maybe you lose your job, or get some bad news, and that may be a thousand pound weight. But every time you have one of these issues, it gets tossed in the boat. Normally, your ordinary problem won't really have an impact, it may be in the boat with you, but you can still float along without it causing any harm.

"But the more problems that enter your boat, the less room you will have, and if you have too many, there might not be enough room for you. So what do you do? You get out of the boat and you hang on to the edge for dear life. But things keep happening and the boat continues to fill up, and eventually it starts to sink. And while it's sinking underwater, you are still holding on to the edge. Problems keep filling the boat, and now it's sinking faster and faster, and deeper and deeper. You are running out of breath, and you are in a total state of panic. You do not know what to do. Yet, you're in such a state of panic, and you refuse to let go, even though all it is, is a boat full of problems. What you don't realize is all you have to do is let go, and let that boat full of problems sink to the bottom of the ocean. Once you do that, you will rise to the surface, find a new boat, and be back to floating along on a beautiful, sunny day," he said, and then took a puff of his cigarette that was near the butt. "And that's what God, or a higher power can give you. The power to let go of it all. Letting go gives you strength. That's how people are able to overcome such horrible circumstances in life. That's how people are able to survive and come out of hell, and they can even prosper. It's the ones that keep collecting and holding on to all their worries, all their mistakes, all the pain, all the loneliness, and grasp to these things with all their strength, that end up letting these things bring them down. It's like holding on to a boat full of problems with white knuckles, while we are drowning, when all we have to do is let go and rise to the surface."

Dan was right. It was all up to me. My attitude could completely change if only I would let go of all the anger, hate, loneliness, and shame I was holding on to. There is no wonder why people that suffer from so many of life's problems feel like they are drowning. It's because they are holding on to everything, and letting it all bring them down.

When I was feeling alone, I would hold on to that feeling and I would sink a little. If I had a bad game on the field, I would hold on to that feeling and sink some more. The only saving grace I had, was when I had a great game, it would lift me up and those worries and that loneliness would go away. But once I got injured, all the problems just kept piling on. I had nothing to bring me to the surface anymore. I kept grabbing on to these problems and holding on to them, and as a result, I was drowning.

And yet, I have been taught all this in baseball my entire life—whenever you make an error, or you have a bad at bat, or a bad game, the best thing you can do is to let it go, and move on. If you didn't, if you kept it in your mind, and held on to it, things would quickly spiral down, and get out of hand. Just like that, I realized baseball could have given me the answer I needed all along.

I walked out of that diner feeling lighter, and I felt like I was seeing clearly for the first time. From then on, everything in my life started to make sense.

Chapter 85

Were there days that I wanted to relapse? Of course. Some days were so hard that I wanted to drink and forget again. But I had to remind myself that I hated myself when I drank. I hated that guilt. I hated the pain of being a failure, and I did not want to go through it anymore. Every day of sobriety became a new triumph. It felt good to be batting a thousand when it came to my sobriety. The odds were no longer against me. I had a goal every single day that I would achieve, and I would feel good about achieving it. Days turned into weeks, and weeks into months. It wasn't until after a few months that I decided I could pursue a bigger purpose. I could start helping others and giving back.

During my recovery, I started to write again. Once I could no longer play baseball, it felt like I had nothing left. I felt like I had wasted my life on a game. But then I started to write down many lessons that can be learned from baseball. All of a sudden, I had a new purpose through writing. From there I started to write down memories from my life. And much of what I wrote during that time can be found in this book.

Finally, I was starting to realize that there is more to life than baseball. Why do I keep saying this over and over again? Honestly, it is a reminder. I have to keep reminding myself or else I may slip back into a depression. When I think about my past, it's still easy to get frustrated and disappointed. It's easy for me to get caught up in thoughts of: *If only, if only, if only.* I keep reminding myself that there are other things I need to focus on; that baseball wasn't going to make my life perfect, and that a person can do anything and be happy as long as they allow themselves to.

My life started to change when I got sober. The hardest part was over. I worked to build myself back up each day, so that I could be myself again—my best self. Through the transformation from being at my lowest, all sorts of hopes and dreams started to find their way back into my life. I knew that helping others would become my true calling.

I did know a lot about the game of baseball, but I think it was my work ethic far more than my talent that got me there. I believe anyone could be great at anything if they worked as hard as I did. But as I know now, working that hard on one thing is not always the best choice. It was time to start working at a new purpose—a purpose that would help others. I needed to give something back. I just needed a plan.

My father left everything he owned to me. This was a part of my second chance. I decided to go back to school at the University of Missouri right there in Columbia. I don't know why I stayed there, but I did. I wanted to go somewhere far away where no one knew who I was, but I didn't know where. Honestly, I think a part of me wanted to start over and live the way I should have the first time around. I wanted to do the work, stay focused, and see where it would lead me. I didn't have a specific goal, but I did know that I wanted to make positive choices. I felt that if I kept making positive choices, positive things would enter my life.

The summer before my first term at the University of Missouri in 2009, I decided to renovate my father's house. I was still staying at the Cooper's, but I knew I couldn't stay there forever. My father's house remained empty, and I couldn't bring myself to move back in. But Mr. Cooper suggested that I could renovate it, and it would become a new home—my home.

Mr. Cooper helped me out as we gutted the place. It was sad at first, but then it felt good to have a fresh start. We completely renovated the inside, and we even finished the basement. I left the backyard untouched, however. It was too important in my life, and there were too many memories that I didn't want to erase. And maybe if I had kids of my own someday, more memories could be created.

It felt good to be productive again, and at the end of the summer, everything was finished. I had a beautiful new home, but the office I created became special to me. The office had a window that overlooked the backyard, and a few feet from my desk, sat the old china cabinet that housed all of the memorabilia my father collected over the years. That room is a perfect mixture of my past, and a new beginning. In that office is where most of this book was written.

I once heard someone at an AA meeting say that everything ends right back where it began. This is true in life and this is true in baseball. If you are up at the plate, your goal is to make it back home. Some may get out; some may be left stranded somewhere along the way; and some may not even make it past home plate to begin with—until their next time up.

In life, I ended right back where I began. I was living in the house I grew up in, and going to school right there in Columbia. I was living the life I should have had when I graduated high school, but instead, I was already 27 years old.

Chapter 86

Going back to school was my second chance. It was a way to redeem myself, and to redeem my father. Although my father was gone, I was compelled to prove that his life was not a complete failure. If I could turn things around and be a better person, then maybe everything was meant to be, and, maybe then, my father was in fact a great father. I was doing this for me, for my father, Elizabeth, Lindsay, Anne, Jake, Aaron, Rick, Jennifer, Uncle Frank and his family, Mr. and Mrs. Cooper, and anyone who ever looked up to me or supported me. It was to show them that I could succeed in things other than baseball. I was determined to show them that I could succeed at life.

I took basic classes my first year of University. I took some History, English, Psychology, and Sociology classes. My first semester was a challenge. I was not your typical freshman, and I was older than the majority of the students in my classes. I looked around at these young faces, and couldn't help but thinking: *Here they are starting their lives...and here I am trying to get mine back.* I knew it was going to be a long road ahead.

In my first class, the one thing I dreaded happened: some students recognized me and the whispers began. I could only imagine what they were saying. I should have probably went to a different school, but I think with my recovery, this was the best place to be. It would be a challenge, and if I could overcome it, I knew things would turn out for the better. Either way, I found out that most people were supportive, and I simply ignored those that were not.

I became the student that I never was. I would go home and read my textbooks, complete my papers, and do everything as a good student should. When I was back in school, I thought of Elizabeth more than I ever had, and I imagined that I was making her proud. It was the thought of her that motivated me to do my best.

When I was having trouble, I even met with my professors and teacher assistants. Everyone was more than eager to help. This was a nice change. People were in my corner, and I didn't have anyone telling me that I was going to fail. There was no pressure—like there was when I was playing baseball.

My professors had so much passion for their subject. It was all about what they were teaching, and helping their students learn. I wish I had these teachers earlier in life. My high school teachers were more concerned about my talent, and my career in baseball, than helping me learn. Elizabeth tried to tell me the importance of learning back in high school, but I just didn't understand what she meant at the time.

Out of all my classes, I liked Psychology the most. What I was learning helped me understand the brain, and it was beneficial to my own recovery. Early on I had an interest in becoming a sports psychologist, or maybe even an addictions councilor. But I liked all of my classes. It felt good to be productive, and it felt good to gain some more "stats." But now my stats were grades on exams and papers, instead of batting Average, and on-base percentage. I started to feel like a normal human being. I felt like I could make my own choices, and I could be honest and true to the person that I was supposed to be.

During this time, I went and helped out with the Mizzou baseball team by maintaining the field. It wasn't much, but it was a way for me to get close, but not too close, to the game I loved. Just being out there, without any pressure, made me feel comfortable. It was therapeutic to me. I would cut the lawn, build the mound and batters' boxes back up, chalk the lines, water the field, and tarp it when it rained. I know some people made fun of me behind my back, but that didn't matter. Others came up to me and were supportive. Some even asked for my advice and I gave it.

For one of my projects in Psychology, with the help of one professor, he suggested that I should go and tell my story to local schools. I wasn't ready to go back to Rock Bridge, but I went to another high school in Columbia, and it was an enlightening experience. I was brought in to talk to a group of grade twelve students to share my story, and any insights from my experiences.

I remember I was nervous while I was being introduced—just like I was in my first game in the major leagues—but as soon as I walked up to the front of the room, and started to speak, that nervousness disappeared. I spoke from the heart, and I received a lot of positive feedback. Afterwards, the school I was at requested I speak to a larger group, and I did another talk a few weeks later. That was the beginning of a new way, and important way, that I could give back to people.

That year I was busy with school, grounds keeping, my sobriety, and doing talks at local schools. But it was a good busy. I was starting to feel happy. I was starting to live the life that my father should have had when he had me. He could have taken a different path, but he became bitter instead.

One day when I was walking on campus, I ran into Mr. Fielder. He was still a professor at the university. Over the years, he had won a number of awards for his breakthrough research, and he had gained tenure. It was ironic that all those years Elizabeth was worried she would have to pack up and leave, yet, it seemed like the Fielder's were in Columbia for good. We talked briefly, but he was running late for a meeting. He let me know that if I needed anything to stop by his office any time. He said he was proud of me. My own father never even said that to me in person.

But I often wonder when people say they are proud of someone, do they actually mean it? Is he really proud of me that I let his daughter go, failed as a major league baseball player, became an alcoholic, and started going to school almost a decade later than I should have? Or is he proud of me that I was finally making the right decision? That I will never know. I had a lot to make up for, but it was nice to see him. He was always nice to me, and I knew he was a smart man. He would be the ideal father-in-law, if I were to ever have one. Encounters like this were painful and could make me want to drink again, but I had the tools to focus on the positive, and cope with my own negative thoughts.

Not long into my first semester, the media found out I had been going to school, was working at the field, had done some talks at local high schools, and they wanted to do a story on me. They called me up for an interview, and asked me questions, such as: What courses was I taking? What are my plans for the future? How long have I been sober? And many others.

I didn't want people up in my business, but I thought it would help the people that used to look up to me, to see that I was doing better. I did the interview, and the article ran the next day. With that article, I received a lot more calls from schools, and from athletic programs that wanted me to come out and talk to their students and athletes.

I appreciated the kind words I had received from those that heard I was doing better, and said they were rooting for me. But I didn't want to bite off more than I could chew. So I kept a balanced schedule, and did what I felt I could do while completing my classes. This continued on for awhile, and in my second semester, I was starting to enjoy school even more.

I took more Psychology classes, and realized that I wanted to get a Psychology degree. The brain fascinated me in so many ways. I wanted to learn why we do what we do. I wanted to learn more about how things have an impact on our brains and our lives. The more I learned, the more I realized how much of an impact my father's teachings, and the environment he created had on the choices I made. The more I got into the science of it all, the more interested I became. I started to realize that everything has an impact on our lives: where we live, our parents, our relatives, our teachers, childhood memories and experiences, and all other life experiences—even the denials and delusions we tell ourselves because we believe we are protecting ourselves. They all have an impact on who we are, and the choices we make in life. The more I learned, the more I was able to improve the talks I gave, and consequently, the more I was able to help others.

One time when I was taking care of the field, I was cleaning out the dugouts, and I found a broken bat beside the garbage. It wasn't totally broken off, but it was split just above the handle. I picked it up, looked at it, and brought it up to my shoulder. It had been over two years since I had last picked up a bat. I walked out of the dugout, got in my regular stance, and took a few swings. It felt light in my hands. It felt great to swing the bat. I closed my eyes and thought of all those times when I hit home runs as a kid, then as a minor leaguer, and finally as a major league all-star. As much as I tried to destroy it, that part of my life was still there.

A few ball players coming on to the field snapped me out of it. "Hey, Ozzie, you want me to throw you a few? See if you still got it?" one of them asked.

I wished I could. I wanted to, but I was afraid of what the result may be. What if I didn't have it? What if I could no longer hit the ball? That was something I was not ready to find out.

"I wish I could, boys, but I have work to do...maybe another time," I said as I walked away carrying that old, broken bat.

That bat would no longer be used for baseball, but maybe I

could find another use for it? Ironically, that bat was a metaphor for my life.

Some people keep old souvenirs to show what they had once done, or had once experienced. I didn't want to be the same way. I didn't want to be a souvenir of what I once accomplished. I didn't want to be old, used, and broken. I wanted to continue to be useful, but in a different way. Like an old broken bat, I couldn't play baseball anymore, but I could be useful, and meaningful in other ways. I wasn't going to be just a memory. I was going to continue to live my life and become someone. Maybe not to millions of people, but to those that need me.

You could give an old broken bat to a kid, and you would see a smile on his face. He would cherish that old, broken bat. Maybe there will be others out there that will cherish an old, broken bat like me as well. That's one thing that is amazing and powerful about sports. One little thing can hold so much meaning—a foul ball caught at a game can be treasured by someone for a life time; an autograph can be a prized possession, and meeting your favorite player can be one of the best childhood memories.

To many people, professional athletes are heroes, and can truly make a difference in someone's life. I failed to be a hero on the field, but there were other ways I could still be a hero. I could go out and try to help others who were in need. I could give them hope and inspiration. It might not be with a bat and ball, but with words of wisdom, with my life's story, with my time, and with my ability to listen. I was willing to dedicate my life to making a difference.

I knew deep down that I still had a purpose. I just needed to find out what it was.

Chapter 87

In baseball, there are times when you will have to make a sacrifice bunt or a sacrifice fly. These acts are used to move the runners ahead to scoring position, or to score a run. You do these things for the team. You make a sacrifice for the greater good. Similarly, in life, sometimes you're going to have to make sacrifices to help others move forward on their path to success. Sometimes you have to put others before yourself. Sacrifices are understood in the game of baseball—players are respected when they make sacrifices—but this is not always the case in life. Unfortunately, when someone puts others before themselves, sometimes these sacrifices will go unnoticed. But too often we only think of ourselves. Now that I was getting my life together, I needed to start thinking of others. I needed to make a sacrifice. I needed to be like Rick Bellamy.

A few months into my recovery from alcohol, my old friend Rick Bellamy called me to catch up, and strangely enough, to apologize. Rick was still the same, caring person. He apologized that he wasn't there for me after my injury. I wanted him to know that it was okay. After all he had been through, he was still putting me before himself.

"I know it might hurt to hear this, all things considered, but I do want to say, that you were one of the best young ball players I have ever seen...the game was robbed that day you got injured," Rick said.

It meant a lot to me that a future hall-of-famer like Rick

would say something like that.

"Thanks, Bell."

"Oz, I also want you to know that Jennifer cared a lot about you. And I care a lot about you. I am glad you are doing better. Don't forget that I will always be here for you, Ozzie."

Having Rick back in my life was exactly what I needed. Besides Dan, and the Cooper's, I was still mostly alone.

In the next few weeks, Rick and I called each other quite often. We would spend a lot of time talking about what we went through in our careers, and in our lives. Rick spoke of Jennifer and his unconditional love for her, and the pain he felt after she died. I spoke of pushing everyone away, and not being able to cope with anything outside of baseball. After Jennifer passed away, Rick spent a lot of time and money supporting cancer research, and his passion to make a difference inspired me. I was sober and ready to help out as much as I possibly could.

Through our conversations together, Rick and I realized that even though the struggles we had experienced were different, they were also very much the same—in that we were both hurting, and felt alone. How many other players felt like us? How many others suffered off the field? How many others dealt with issues and still went out and played the game day in and day out, even when they were hurting? They did this because that was all they knew. That's the only thing they worked for. But what about those that were done with the game, and suffered like I did? What were their options?

Rick and I decided we needed to do something to help others that suffered like we did. We started to brainstorm a variety of ideas of how we could help. At first we wondered how many current and ex-players had suffered with mental illnesses like depression, anxiety, stress, and addictions? How many have suffered through having a family member being ill, or grief related to the loss of a loved one? How many players have suffered or are suffering? You hear rumors of stuff going around the league, and it spreads quickly, but it's still very hush-hush. What could we do to change that? But most importantly, what could we do to help?

The more we talked about it, the more we realized we could help people in so many different ways. We knew we were on to something important. After more discussions, and after doing some research, we thought about creating a charitable foundation. This would be a foundation that would give support to baseball players that were struggling in any area off the field. It would help those dealing with the realities of life during their career and after. This foundation would help baseball players develop an identity outside of the game. We thought we could even help coaches, managers, trainers, families, or anyone else related to the game of baseball.

Initially, we thought the best way to help others was through awareness. I had some experience going around to schools and giving talks to students. The positive impact that these talks had was inspiring. Consequently, I thought, what if other ball players that had suffered in their life, would share their story? They could share their story at schools, community events, conferences, and to individual teams in a variety of leagues all over the country, and even the world. Having players share their stories would show others that they are not alone. There would be a variety of topics that could be covered. Individual players could share their stories of loneliness, anxiety, stress, depression, grief, addiction, or any other issue that they have been through. It would help let everyone know that professional athletes are human. We go through the same struggles that others face; hardships do not discriminate. By helping each other, we would be able to make a huge difference. We could break a silence that was always present in professional sports. We believed that breaking the silence would help people everywhere.

Not only would these stories help those that were there to listen, but they would also help the player who was sharing the story; it would give them an opportunity to do something positive outside of the game. For ex-players, this could be the sense of identity, and sense of purpose that they may be struggling with once their careers are over.

It wouldn't be just about the stories, however, there would also be other ways that players could help out. They could donate money, organize charitable events, and create baseball camps that teach players of all ages. The foundation would give individuals the opportunity to help others in a number of ways. Ultimately, the foundation would be a community. A community of awareness, hope, and opportunity.

As we put things into motion, Rick and I became a team. We visualized how important this foundation could be. One night we sat in my backward in Columbia, and brainstormed a name for the foundation. We wanted it to be something to do with baseball, but not specific to it. Then it hit me.

"We want to advocate for people who go through stuff off the field, right?" I asked Rick.

"We do," Rick said looking towards the "Green Monster" in my backward.

"Well, what do you think about *Off the Field Foundation*," I asked.

Rick sat silently for a moment.

"It's perfect," he said.

And from there, we got the ball rolling.

Rick had a lot of connections, and through him we were able to get some people together to start the Off the Field Foundation. Surprisingly, I also had my own connections. Since this was going to be a charitable foundation, we needed to understand the ins and outs of how to run, fund, and sustain our foundation. I did a lot of research, and I reached out to some of my professors at the university, including Mr. Fielder, and they were more than willing to help. I also told Mr. Cooper about the foundation, and he thought it was a great idea. He in turn mentioned it to Jake, and Jake being a respectable lawyer in Kansas City, said he would be happy to help with the legal aspects of the foundation. Jake like always, was there to help me.

Rick and I reached out to some ball players and many were willing to help in a number of ways—whether it was sharing ideas, putting in the time, networking, and financial donations. The response and support we were getting was heartwarming. There were so many good people that wanted to contribute.

I ended up staying with Rick in St. Louis, and we leased some office space that became the home of the Off the Field Foundation. It didn't take us long to realize that the foundation was going to be bigger than Rick and I first intended. We needed to make sure it ran professionally, and would be able to run long after we were gone. After we set a board of directors and created bylaws, our foundation became official.

This became our passion project that meant more to me than baseball ever did. Eventually, I had to make a sacrifice, and after just one year of going to university, I had to put that on hold. I needed to focus on our work with the foundation—for the greater good.

Soon many good people supported our cause and donated their time and money towards it. We gave the chance for many to go around to tell their stories at schools, and ball fields across the country. We had athletes helping other athletes. We had players from the minor leagues get involved. Some players that never made the major leagues even came out to tell their shocking stories. We were able to help so many different people on and off the field. We were spreading awareness and giving people a chance to give back in a way that was easy and effective. We inspired people. We helped people. It was an amazing experience knowing what people could do if they are given the opportunity. We had all types of people that loved baseball willing to help out our cause. The Off the Field Foundation was there to help anyone and everyone that has been involved in the game. And by them helping out, we helped them. Together, we were making a difference.

Chapter 88

After about a year of hard work and dedication from all those involved, the Off the Field Foundation grew exponentially. It all started with a series of conversations between two friends, and it all started with having lost a part of our lives that seemed like our purpose. But we found a new purpose. We put all of our time and effort into creating something magnificent. It didn't happen overnight, but we created something that would help someone today, tomorrow, and beyond. We created something that genuinely made a difference. We did this through the experience of the game we loved. The game we did everything we could just to have the opportunity to play. But in the process, we brought meaning and made something positive out of our pain and suffering. We brought meaning to the ups and downs in life. But most of all, we brought hope—hope for those that feel like they will never be able to do anything meaningful outside of baseball.

Furthermore, it gave people a chance to give back. There was so much we could offer. The more people that got involved, the more diverse our foundation became. Some offered to give instruction to aspiring ball players—whether it be in hitting, pitching, or fielding. And for the younger kids they taught basic mechanics and rules of the game. Some were amazing with kids; others were amazing with minor league players. Eventually the Off the Field Baseball Camps were offered around the United States, and some ball players brought these camps to their home countries. They taught aspiring ball players around the world about the game, and about life.

As the foundation continued to grow, the better the programs we started to develop. We stressed the important of an education, and we created an academic branch of the foundation. Through scholarships, we set student athletes on a path to learning and living a life on and off the field.

The networks of support we developed spread in all different disciplines, and all different areas where we could help and make a difference. One of the most significant things we accomplished, with all the support we received, with all the stories that were shared, we got Major League Baseball to take a hard look at how players were treated in the minor leagues. The daily grind of the minors, thought to weed out players that wouldn't be able to cut it in the major leagues, was exposed for what it actually was: a vastly unfair, but unavoidable path to the major leagues. A path that is known to cause more harm than good.

I am proud to say, that Major League Baseball has taken on the responsibility to make the minor leagues a place where players can excel, and develop to their full potential, within fair conditions. Minor league player's have received a significant increase in pay, nutrition has increased, and in general, their way of life has improved. Players and families no longer have to suffer in order to follow their dreams. They no longer have to risk everything.

It didn't take long for everyone that loves baseball to realize that the level of talent in the major leagues has increased because of the changes made to the minor league system. In the end, America's greatest pastime is greater than it ever was in history.

It's still unbelievable to me to look back on what Rick and I, with the help of many others, have accomplished. At first we were the voice for anyone that had felt similar to the way we had. But quickly took off once we realized that there were more of us than we thought. We started to have such a huge impact, and eventually people were able to find their voice, and help others in the process. It was a domino effect, and today we are witnessing the significant difference we have made. The opportunities we create to help others is a remarkable experience. We are helping people and saving their lives. It is by far the most meaningful thing I have ever done in my life.

I was able to recover from all of my heartache and struggles in order to dedicate my life to help others. It's not just about being great on the field, it's about being great off the field. I was given a second chance and I was able to do things that make a positive impact on other people's lives. If my father was still around, I know he would be proud of me.

Chapter 89

Some of you are probably wondering if I ever relapsed while I was working with the Off the Field Foundation. Regretfully, the answer is yes. How could I do such a thing after being sober for over three years, and creating a charitable foundation that helped so many people? Why was I still making the same mistakes? The only answer is that every day is a struggle. Alcohol is everywhere. You probably do not notice it the way I do. When you are sober and trying to resist the temptation to drink, you realize you cannot hide from it. This makes it extremely difficult for people who are in recovery. Drinking is so engrained in our culture that it is normal to drink. Sometimes I just want that feeling of being normal. But I am not like everyone else. I am not "normal." I cannot have just one drink.

And for many people who relapse, their story is eerily similar to mine. It all started when I went to a restaurant for dinner. The waitress asked me if I wanted anything to drink, and I decided to have one beer. I knew it would be cold and refreshing, and I believed I could handle it just fine. But when the waitress came around again, she asked if I wanted another one. It was so easy to say yes.

When I finished eating, she asked if I wanted anything else, and I decided to have one more. After three beer, I was feeling good, and I decided to move to the lounge. Sure enough there was a game on, and at some point, I made the switch to hard alcohol.

I sat there and kept drinking, and watching the game by myself. To everyone else, everything was ordinary, but to me, I had just given up three years of sobriety. Before things got any worse, fate intervened in the form of a phone call from Rick. I answered it, and all I said was, "I screwed up." He could tell by the way I said it, what had happened. All he asked was where I was and I told him. He told me to stay there, and said that he was on his way. He came and picked me up. I was crying and I couldn't even pay my tab. The waitress must have wondered what the hell was wrong with me. Rick paid my tab and he helped me out to his truck. Between sobs, I kept repeating how sorry I was. Everything happened so fast. I was only trying to test myself to see if I could control myself. I struck out miserably.

Rick took me home and stayed with me all night. The next day I felt even worse mentally and physically. I had let so many people down. But Rick was there for me. He knew what was in my heart, and he knew that I would get better.

A few days later, I scheduled a board meeting at the foundation and told everyone what happened. Everyone was surprisingly supportive. Rick reassured everyone that nothing would change, and that we were still going forward. I learned in AA that everyone relapses. It's how you deal with those relapses that matter.

My relapse happened on October 3rd, 2012, and I am proud to say, that I have not touched a drop of alcohol since.

Chapter 90

When you dedicate your life to helping others, something strange happens: you develop a support system that you have never had before. When you are open with others, this creates a bond for life. It is a powerful experience. With the Off the Field Foundation, and all those involved, I felt like I was a part of a team again. I was held accountable for my mistakes and ready to make amends. I wanted to do it for them, and I wanted to do it for myself. I finally had a purpose, and I finally had people in my life that cared about me. They became my family.

All of sudden I had this sense of urgency that I wanted to get to know people. I wanted to make connections. One of the biggest regrets that I have is that I never paid attention to people. I never got to know them. I was a professional baseball player, but, I wouldn't even talk to anybody. Sure I would say my "thank yous'" when fans would congratulate me after a game, and I would sign autographs. But I never got to *know* anybody. All I was, was a number on the back of a jersey, or a scribble on a piece of memorabilia. I never let anyone get to know me, and worst of all, I never got to know anyone else. I had many opportunities to get to know people and make connections, but I never did.

Looking back, I wish I would have got to know my teammates, coaches, fans, bus drivers, waiters and waitresses, or even hotel guest agents that were there to serve me along the way. I wish I would have talked to people. Instead, I have all these empty memories of people and places that never had an impact on my life. They all blend together because I was focused only on doing what I could to play well, and get out of there as fast as possible. My life on the field was the only thing that mattered to me.

If I would have stayed in the game, I may have spent my entire career being known as an excellent baseball player, but other than that, I would have been lonely. That's not what life is about. As much as I wanted to be a ball player, I needed to have a life outside of the game. Sadly, it took a car accident, and a battle with alcohol to finally wake me up.

I remember when I came back from the minors in the offseason, and I had to leave Columbia because of the attention I was getting. People wanted to be my friend and get my autograph. I enjoyed the feeling of being admired, but I felt they were a distraction. When I came back after my injury, I didn't want people to see me because I was nothing anymore. Then I started drinking and people criticized me, and I received a lot of negative attention. It has been a strange journey. But things have changed. I have changed.

I have discovered that by helping others, and letting them know they are not alone, I no longer feel alone. Now, when I am back in Columbia, people stop me and say they are proud of me and the work I am doing. They don't want anything from me; they just want to say that what I am doing is a good thing. Some people say that I give them hope, and that I inspire them. It's a great feeling. I can hold my head up high because I know I am helping people, and that's all that matters. Showing people you love them and care for them is the most important thing you can do. It is the right thing to do. It's not about how many home runs you hit—it's about how many home runs people hit, because of you.

Rick and I have been through a lot, and we both lost the ones we loved the most. But as crazy as it seems, there is good that has come out of those hardships. He still thinks about Jennifer, and still loves her even though she is gone. I still think of my father, Jennifer, and Elizabeth, but the good we are doing, makes us feel a bit better.

But I had this urgency to get back the ones I had pushed away, while I still could. I finally reached out to try and reconnect with my mother. My father was gone, and I didn't have any family left. I knew it was important for me and my recovery. And I believed it was also important for my mother. Instead of pushing people away, I was going to do my best to pull them close. Through my work with the foundation, I had learned a lot. I took everything I learned from the good people in my life, and made it a part of myself. My goal was to help others like they helped me.

My mother and I spoke on the phone a few times, and finally I went down to see her at her home in Wichita, Kansas. She had a big, beautiful home. When she answered the door, seeing my mother with tears in her eyes, brought tears to mine. She looked so much the same. We hugged each other. I needed to. We needed to. I pulled her close.

I was introduced to my mother's husband, Glenn, and my half-sister, Michelle, and my half-brother, Nicholas. I don't know why, but as strange as it was, I was still excited to meet them, and they were excited to meet me. They were all very nice. Seeing those kids made me realize that good things can happen out of any situation. After some small talk, the rest of my mother's family left us alone to catch up.

My mother apologized and explained why she had to leave. She felt bad about holding my father back, and she felt we would be better without her. Then she told me something that surprised me. My father had written her a letter and sent it to her. She let me read it. It started off with the story of when he fell in love with her at first sight—the same story she had heard a hundred times before. And then he proceeded to apologize.

He said that he loved her from the first time he saw her, and even though he didn't show it, he has loved her every day since.

Although it was clear from our talk that my mother had a lot of pain in her past, she was happy. It was then that I realized, if you allow it to, life goes on no matter what. The lives of Rick, my mother, and myself are proof of that. No matter what happened in our lives, we can still have good things. We can still be happy. Could we have had a happier life? The answer is probably yes, but we must accept the things that happen in our lives. We must cherish the good memories, learn from the bad, and live the best way we can, every day.

It's ironic how we try and do so many things in our lives like pursue our dreams, be successful, make money, have nice things, but when it all comes down to it, it's about the people we have in our lives, and the ones we wish we still had. The thing we regret the most is not telling the ones we love, that we love them, and not spending more time with them. My father was a prime example of that. He wrote letters to my mother and I, telling us how much he loved us. This was something he couldn't say to us for many years. He never admitted he needed us. He never admitted he was hurting. Yet, when he was all alone, and when he was nearing the end, he realized what mattered most in life. It was family. It was love. If it all came down to it, and he had to choose love or baseball once again, he still would have chosen love. But this time, he would not have regretted that choice.

Family is what became important in my life. I visited my uncle Frank and his family, and I spent more time with my mother and her family. It wasn't long after we reconnected that my mother invited me over for another visit. When I got there, they had a few surprises for me. My aunt Amy and uncle James were there, and so was my grandma Minnie.

My auntie called me "Wizzy" and gave me a big hug, and I shook my uncles hand. It was strange to see them after all those years. And when I saw my grandma, she looked the same, just a little bit older, and appeared smaller. I was so happy to see her. Tears welled up in my eyes, and I gave her a hug. This time I was able to envelope her in my arms. And there was that smell. She smelt the same as she did when I was a kid. I felt like I was seven years old again in her arms. And with that smell, I was instantly transported back in time and everyone was there— including my father, and Grandpa Roy (he passed away a few years earlier).

My grandma still cooked the same and it's amazing how some things never change. She made the same donuts that I used to love as a kid. After dinner she brought them out and said she made them just for me. I couldn't believe she remembered.

My grandma lived in the same, old house in Mexico, but my auntie and uncle lived there too, so that she wouldn't be alone. That weekend we were all together once again.

I had my family back.

Chapter 91

What about love? What about Anne? I found out through Rick that Anne was seeing someone by the time I got my life back together. I was happy for her. I knew that a girl like that wouldn't stay single for long. And finally, I know this is the question all of you readers are waiting for: What about Elizabeth? I wish I could tell you about some beautiful story of how we reconnected and got back together—just like I always dreamed about—but I can't.

After I met with my mother and her family, and when things were going well with the foundation, I thought about reaching out to Elizabeth, but I couldn't do it. I didn't want to interfere with her life. I didn't want to interfere with her happiness. I could never bring myself to do that. Even though I think about her a lot and she means the world to me, I'm afraid I will never be able to connect with her again. She isn't the same person as she was in high school, and neither am I. We won't have the same connection that we did before. So I want to hold on to those memories and not create any new ones. I do not want to replace them.

Yet, why can't I move on? I can't move on because she will always be in my heart. I still love her. It was the thought of Elizabeth that helped me overcome the lowest point of my life. In a way, I am alive because of her. She was an inspiration and a motivation when I needed it the most. I know I can never be with her, but I still don't want to lose my love for her. In a way, all the good work I do now is because of her. I dedicate my life to help, because deep down, I believe she will be proud of me. It may sound sad to many of you, but at least I am doing something positive with my life. All I can say is that I am forever grateful to have known her. She is someone I will never forget.

I still wonder sometimes what would happen if I ran into her sometime in Columbia? What would we say to each other? What would happen? Would it lead to anything? I will never know until it happens—if it happens. It's something I hope for, but it is also something I dread. Regardless, I know she will read this book. She will find out how much she meant to me and how much she still means to me. It may make things awkward for her. It may be awkward for her husband and kids—if she has any. But she was someone that I could never leave out of my story. Elizabeth, if you're reading this, I am sorry if this causes you any discomfort. Just know you were too important to leave out.

As I look back on my entire life, I notice that my story was more about love, than it was about baseball. However, I only felt like I deserved love, if I played baseball. Without baseball, I felt like I was nothing. But when I go back, I remember every detail of my time with the ones I loved, whereas the majority of the baseball games that I have played all blur together. It is clear, that what matters the most, is love.

Sometimes I ask myself: Am I known for being that kid who stood out from everyone else on the field? Will I be known for being the Rookie of the Year in 2005? Will I be known for an injury that ended my career? Will I be known for my alcoholism? Or will I be known for starting the Off the Field foundation that has helped thousands of people all over the country, and possibly the world? I may be known for all of the above, and it all depends on who you ask. But if you ask me, I am known for turning my life around, and making a difference in this world. I am known for showing you that anything is possible.

Baseball, as in life, when you're up to bat, you might not get the pitches you want, but it's what you do with the pitches you do get, that matters.

For the last while, I have been spending my time between St. Louis and Columbia. But during the process of writing this book, I have been mostly in Columbia. Earlier today, I was sitting in my old backyard with a cup of coffee, thinking of all the memories I made back there. I thought about the times with my mother and father playing with me as kid. I thought about all those times with my best friend Jake. I thought about all those unforgettable times with Elizabeth. And finally, I thought about all those good and bad times with just my father.

I remembered when my father first brought Crow from the garage and pushed him into the ground with his big hands. I was just a little kid, and I was so curious about what he was doing. Then I remembered when my father said: *Just hit him in the chest, Son. If he doesn't catch it, that's his problem.*

Thinking back on that made me smile.

"I miss you, Pop," I said quietly.

I looked up above the Green Monster and into the blue sky. I felt at peace. Then I turned and made my way back into the house.

My life has been some kind of journey around those bases, but I finally made it back home.

Epilogue

My story, and the story of many others, goes to show that it is never too late for anybody. All you have to do is work hard and try and be the best person you can possibly be. If you do those two things, everything else will fall into place. I promise you will be able to overcome anything, and you will be able to catch whatever life throws your way.

I have been away from the game for some time, but I still love baseball. However, I do want to take this opportunity to give some advice to any young athletes out there. I think it is important for people to be cautious and to truly understand what being a professional athlete is like. For instance, many people don't realize the sacrifices that professional athletes make. They think they are living their dream and everything is perfect. A lot of times it is far from perfect. The minor leagues are a struggle, and like I said before, a lot of good players and good people don't make it for a variety of reasons. Once you make it to the majors, things are still not easy. You have to work hard and play when you are hurt and tired. The major league schedule is a battle. But you want to do whatever it takes to stay in the Show. Consequently, your family life might suffer and other areas of your life off the field.

Then you have to worry about what you will do after your career is finished. Often you don't hear about players outside of the game. All of a sudden you disappear from the spotlight. Many forget about you. They forget about the player. You are lost into oblivion.

Most of the time a fan has no idea what their favorite athlete's life is like outside of the game. Often they don't even care. They may see one of their favorite players a few years later on TV and think, "Wow, he sure looks old." And it's true— many players age quickly after the game. They are not training as much, not eating as healthy, and they do get older. You only see players in the prime of their athletic ability. After that, their physical ability is on a decline, and that's probably why they are no longer in the game.

Players come and go and that's the way it is. But leaving the game an athlete has worked so hard for can be a real shock. Every athlete has to ask, "What will I do next?" For some they may have a plan, but others are not so prepared. Many are left out in the dust and have to figure it out on their own. Losing the one thing they lived for and worked for all those years, can make them feel lost, hopeless, and depressed. It can be a real struggle.

The thing that no one tells you, is that it's what you do outside of the game that makes someone's life great. It's about family. It's about relationships. It's about love. Those are the things that are still around when you walk off that field for the last time. What they don't tell you is that the game is only a glimpse of your life. It's what you do after that will make or break someone. One of the biggest issues with sports is that they don't tell you this when you are starting out, because they don't want it to be a distraction. They want you to focus on one thing and forget everything else. That is exactly what I did, until there was nothing else to focus on. I had no plan for the future. I was at a complete loss.

When I got injured, I did not have a purpose. There was no real point to my life. As you know from my story already, from there everything just spiraled down. But in order to recover, I had to find a new purpose. My new purpose was to tell my story in order to help others in need. That was my new goal. For me to be able to help people, I had to be sober. I had to push myself. I had to take everything one step at a time. Every day that I was sober, was a day that I could help. I learned that you are only as good as what you are willing to do for someone else—especially someone in need.

I believe that when you are older and look back on your life, you are not going to think about how many games you won, or how many home runs you hit; you are going to think about the people you have spent your life with, and the people you have loved and lost along the way. That's why relationships are so important. They are the reason why life is worth living. When you are working towards something, it's important to enjoy the journey and the people you share it with.

I did give it my all every time I stepped on the field. It's disappointing to know that I didn't do that off the field as well. But I was lucky to have the opportunity to enjoy many years in baseball. If I could do it over, I would have enjoyed the little things. I would have enjoyed the process of getting ready for every game, every day. I would have enjoyed taking batting practice even more. I would have admired and noticed the name plate and number on my locker every time I saw it. I would have taken time to savor the moment of putting on my beautiful St. Louis Cardinals jersey each game. I would have enjoyed talking to other players and getting their advice. I would have enjoyed spending time with my teammates at all levels. Those are the things I would have changed during my career.

I did experience a lot and I accomplished things that others dream about. But we are on borrowed time. We can lose everything we have at any moment, so when you have something, hold it close, and enjoy it as much as you can. Enjoy every at bat, every run scored, and every time you have the opportunity to play the game you love. But more importantly, off the field, enjoy the people in your life, the cities you get to see, the ball parks you get to play in, your trainers, your coaches, the fans, and everybody that makes this game possible. It is a shame that most of my life, I never took the time to take it all in—I was only passing through.

Do I have regrets in my life? Yes I do. But everything lead to where I am at right now. It would be hard to not feel joy in what I have accomplished, and what others have accomplished with me. I know that everything in my life led to this moment. Even though it was hard, there is no denying that it was meant to be. I believe in the good that we are doing with our foundation. If I didn't go through what I went through, many people may have went without help. That is a terrifying thought to me. So I am thankful for every day of my life. I am thankful for having the chance to make a positive difference in so many other people's lives.

I want to remind you that if you are struggling in any way, I know it's hard to be vulnerable, but take comfort in knowing you are not alone. Take comfort in knowing that there are people out there that will do whatever they can to help. All you have to do is reach out and there will be a helping hand to pull you close, and not let you go.

Sitting here, reflecting on my life, and writing this book, has brought up a vast mixture of memories. I was forced to relive the good ones and the bad ones. I was forced to analyze the past that got me here today, and it was difficult to relive many things. There were so many times that when I was thinking back, I would find myself saying, "I should have done this, and I should have done that." It's always so much easier after the fact, isn't it?

For all of those reading this book right now, I want you all to realize the importance of taking time once and awhile to reflect on your life. Reflect on the decisions you have made; reflect on the good things, and reflect on the things you would change. You could even go as far as to do this on a daily basis. You could make this a habit. I promise you that with this habit, you will have less regrets in your life, and you will be constantly learning and growing every day. I believe with that one simple practice, my life would have been drastically different—for the better. It's still hard not to think that things would have been so much easier for myself, and those around me, if I had known what I know now, but instead when I reflect on my life, I must come to grips with the fact that for a lot of things, it is far too late for me. But I am blessed to be here today, and there is still a lot of hope for the future.

It is now 2015, I am 33 years old, and it has been eight years since I played my last game of baseball. The Off the Field Foundation continues to grow tremendously. The lives of so many players have greatly improved at all levels. The conditions in the minor leagues continue to get better, and major league teams continue to give more money to their minor league clubs. As it was mentioned earlier, the level of talent has notably increased in Major League Baseball. But I want it to be clear that it wasn't about making the athletic world a better place for entertainment purposes, it was to make the world a better place to live. And it has not gone unnoticed. Just the other day, at one of our board meetings, we discussed the possible expansion into helping other professional sports. We discussed the idea of the NBA creating the "Off the Court Foundation," the NHL starting the "Off the Ice Foundation," and the NFL starting the "Off the Field Foundation," and ultimately, the MLB branch would change its name to the "Off the Diamond Foundation." There has been a lot of interest, and now we are planning on how we will move things forward.

People tell me all the time that they are astonished by how much I have accomplished so far in my short life. To me, I feel like I have lived a few lifetimes already, and in a way, I have. There are so many things that I still want to accomplish, however. I hope to find a wife, and have children of my own someday. I want to be a great husband and a great father. Until then, I continue to make the most of every day. I continue to help others; I continue to pull people close, and I continue to be excited about what the future holds.

Every day I strive to learn, grow, and make a positive difference in the lives of others. What was once a path to follow one's dream, became a path to a better life, not only for a select few, but for them all. —Ozzie Shaw

Acknowledgements

First and foremost, I want to thank my beautiful fiancé, Kristen, for being with me and supporting me during the entire process of the creation of this book. She took on the laborious task of reading the first draft, and encouraged me not to give up during many points along the journey. In many ways, I could not have written this book without you.

I want to thank my good friend, Travis, for those writer's nights back in Nashville, and all the nights ever since—where we shared our dreams and pushed each other to follow our passions. Without you, I would have not had the motivation to put myself out there and go for it.

To my grandparents who read one story of mine back in high school, and ever since then always said I should be a writer—even while I was pursuing other things. It was your encouragement and belief in me that made this book possible.

To the person I dedicate my first book to, my uncle G, who was the very first person I showed my non-school related writings to, and ever since then, you always said, "Keep writing." I want to thank you for being a person that made me not afraid to share my dream of being a writer to, and for believing in me from the beginning.

Last but definitely not least, to everyone else who has supported me along the way. I appreciate it more than you can ever imagine.

—Jesse A. Murray

About the Author

Jesse A. Murray is a Canadian author and high school teacher. He has always had a passion for sports—most notably hockey and baseball. Ever since he first picked up a pen, writing has also been a passion of his. Jesse put his passions together as he wrote his first book: *Love or Baseball?* With his free time, he is currently working on three other manuscripts.

CPSIA information can be obtained
at www.ICGtesting.com
Printed in the USA
LVHW09s0315290918
591799LV00001BA/5/P